KAHN & ENGELMANN

Biblioasis International Translation Series

General Editor: Stephen Henighan

I Wrote Stone: The Selected Poems of Ryszard Kapuściński (Poland)
   Translated by Diana Kuprel and Marek Kusiba

Good Morning Comrades by Ondjaki (Angola)
   Translated by Stephen Henighan

Kahn & Engelmann by Hans Eichner (Austria-Canada)
   Translated by Jean M. Snook

KAHN & ENGELMANN

A NOVEL

Hans Eichner

Translated from the German

by Jean M. Snook

BIBLIOASIS

FIRST EDITION

Library and Archives Canada Cataloguing in Publication

Eichner, Hans
    Kahn & Engelmann : a novel / Hans Eichner ; translated from
the German by Jean M. Snook.

Original published Wien : Picus, 2000.
ISBN 13: 978-1-897231-54-8
ISBN 10: 1-897231-54-7

    I. Snook, Jean M., 1952- II. Title.

PS8559.1376K3413 2009   c833'.92   C2009-900928-5

Edited by Stephen Henighan
Cover photo "Still Life #72" by D.R. Cowles

Canada Council   Conseil des Arts
for the Arts   du Canada

Canadian   Patrimoine
Heritage   canadien

ONTARIO ARTS COUNCIL
CONSEIL DES ARTS DE L'ONTARIO

We gratefully acknowledge the support of the Canada Council for
the Arts, Canadian Heritage, and the Ontario Arts Council for our
publishing program.

PRINTED AND BOUND IN CANADA

*To my dearly beloved wife, Kari Grimstad, and
to Hermann Patsch, friend and much-admired scholar*

Contents

CHAPTER ONE

Sidonie 9

CHAPTER TWO

Gisa 53

CHAPTER THREE

Dezsö 83

CHAPTER FOUR

Elli 139

CHAPTER FIVE

Fraternal Feud 175

CHAPTER SIX

Kahn & Engelmann 205

CHAPTER SEVEN

Children 275

CHAPTER EIGHT

The Way to Haifa 301

Coda 321

Afterword 331

Glossary 333

Sidonie

1.

IN THE SUMMER OF 1938, a Jewish refugee is going for a walk on Carmel Beach. (Is he from Cologne? from Berlin? from Vienna? It doesn't matter.) Twenty metres out from shore, a man is fighting against the waves and yelling for help in Hebrew. The refugee stops to listen, takes his jacket off, folds it neatly (one should never act too hastily); and while taking off his tie and shoes as well, before jumping into the sea to help the yelling man, he exclaims indignantly: "What a fool! *Hebrew* he has learned. *Swimming* he should have learned!"

That's a travelling joke. It was told much the same way in 1789 in Mainz, when the first émigrés arrived there and went for walks along the Rhine in their elegant clothes. But precisely because it is a travelling joke, it is also a Jewish joke; for who has travelled (or, as is mostly the case, has fled) more often than the Jews? From Egypt, from Babylonia, from Canaan, from Spain, from Galicia, from the Third Reich. For me, though, this joke is situated once and for all at the foot of Mount Carmel, because I live a hundred metres above the beach and look out at the sea every morning with ever renewed delight, much as people in Weimar used to be able to look at the Ettersberg before the concentration camp was built there. (To be sure, there are inhabitants of Weimar again now who can look with delight at the Ettersberg; human memory is short.)

How did I get here, where I bathe poodles during the day so that I can walk along the beach in the evening? I will reconstruct it, although I am actually not very interested in myself. In one of Thomas Mann's early stories he writes that Schiller occasionally needed "only to look at his hand in order to be filled with an enthusiastic tenderness for himself." He could afford to do that. For the likes of us, interest in oneself, to say nothing of tenderness, is usually a sign of immaturity. At any rate, on my way to Haifa (Jews travel), there was one thing or another that may be worth mentioning as typical of the experiences of my generation; and because I am usually too tired in the evenings to undertake anything more sensible (I am getting old!), it may be worth my while to make the attempt.

I'll begin by rummaging through a shoebox full of old photographs that I inherited from my mother, along with a pile of yellowed letters and the princely sum of 15 pounds sterling. The oldest of these photographs – dating from about 1880, but technically quite good – shows a middle-aged woman and a girl of about seventeen years. The woman, with her straight hair combed back, her high forehead and dark eyes, reminds me of my grandmother; but of course she isn't my grandmother, but rather her mother, my great-grandmother. Like her mother, the girl herself – my grandmother – is wearing a heavy black cotton dress that fastens closely around her neck, is belted at the waist and falls below her ankles. On her feet she wears a pair of high-buttoned boots, to which I will return shortly. The only jewellery she is wearing is a cameo brooch, and if you take the difference in their ages into account, her face is astonishingly similar to her mother's.

But what was the story of those boots? In shoe stores when I was sixteen, you tried on the shoe – in my case an inexpensive mass-produced shoe – by putting your foot into an X-ray machine to see if it fit. After the Second World War, these machines were abolished because they might cause cancer; that wasn't a step backwards, because the X-rayed shoes usually didn't fit anyway. In my grandmother's day, there were still proper shoemakers. Such a shoemaker would sit in his store on a stool, the customer would sit down facing him, put his foot on a piece of brown paper, and the shoemaker would trace the outline, measure the height of the instep with a tape measure, ask about corns and similar troubles, determine the price depending on the design, the type of leather to be used and the ability of the customer to pay, and a week later the shoes were ready.

In Tapolca, a small city that was really hardly more than a large village a few kilometres north of Lake Balaton, there were four shoemakers, three of whom were Christians. The fourth was called József Kahn and even then (but it was, after all, the thirty-second year of Kaiser Franz-Joseph's reign) had the sideburns and shaved chin of the Kaiser. Since my grandmother (the seventeen-year-old in the photograph) needed boots in March 1880, that is, over a hundred years ago, she and her mother rode the few kilometres from her father's estate to Tapolca in a carriage and pair. Their coachman was called Moische, like the coachman of the famous rabbi of Tarnopol. While Moische waited outside with the horses, she entered József's store with her mother and sat down facing him. As József gently touched her ankle with his fingertips to place her foot on the non-carcinogenic paper, she was done for.

It is not known in which pogrom József Kahn's parents had been killed, and I also know little about the orphanage where, on bread and water, but a with a substantial meal on Friday evening, he received a very sketchy education. He was not a talkative man. However, it is known that he learned a trade there, shoemaking; because the Jews who could afford to do a mitzvah and support an orphanage liked to see their own children enter the family business, even if, as was usually the case, they had wanted to become doctors or lawyers; but they preferred to have the orphans learn a trade, because if too many Jews were businessmen, that provoked anti-Semitism. And since at that time there were three Christian shoemakers in Tapolca, but no Jewish one, József, after serving his

11

apprenticeship, opened a store there. My grandmother's parents, though, were estate owners, and so my grandmother was up against a brick wall.

One imagines – no: one used to imagine the Puszta as being inhabited solely by big estate owners and fiddling Gypsies. That is no longer the case today, because the Germans killed the Gypsies and the Russians killed the estate owners (work shared is work halved). Back then, though, people imagined that the Gypsies played their violins and the estate owners had immense estates where the corn grew that the people in Vienna ate with butter and salt for dessert, but where above all huge herds of cattle grazed – as Goethe put it, "spread out, carefully grouped / Horned cattle climbing up to the sheer edge." But in reality it wasn't like that even back then, not only because (in contrast to Goethe's Arcadia) there are no sheer edges in the Puszta, which is as flat as a table top, but also because small farmers lived there as well, and since neither the lord of the manor nor the horned cattle took care of themselves, farmhands and maids who neither fiddled nor owned cattle were also needed. Besides, back then there were also Jews on the Puszta, and they were usually neither maids nor farmhands, neither estate owners nor small farmers, because for hundreds of years they had been forbidden to own land, and when that changed after the "Compromise" of 1867, it had become a maxim for most of them that the use of a spade was *goyim naches* ("something the locals do"). So why was my grandmother's father an estate owner? Probably the family tradition I have to rely on for my reconstruction had turned a cattle trader who also owned land into an estate owner who also traded a few cattle as a pastime. In any case, he was prosperous, and that was a problem. My grandmother, you see, the seventeen-year-old, "rash and foolish, typical female! Seized by the moment, acting on a whim," as Goethe wrote, had hardly felt the shoemaker's fingertips on her ankle when she was done for.

When the boots were ready a week later, however, Sidonie Róth – that was my grandmother's name – didn't get to see József;

Moische picked up the boots from the city. But Sidonie declared that they did not fit, and so she drove to Tapolca again, this time without her mother, and went into the shoemaker's workshop while Moische waited with the horses and fell asleep with boredom. A good hour passed, and when Sidonie came home again with the boots, which mysteriously did fit now, she announced to her parents that she would marry József or no one.

At first they took it for a bad joke. József? The shoemaker? Sidonie stood her ground. Her mother wailed and her father roared. "You want to marry József? That *nebbish*, who hasn't learned anything proper and doesn't know where the bread for his breakfast will come from? That nobody who's even too stupid to scrounge? Is that why I gave you an education? Like hell you'll marry József, you'll marry a decent person who amounts to something, that's what you will do!"

Siddi said nothing, and Dezsö Róth roared until his voice cracked. "You want to marry József? Is that why I've been slaving away like *meshuga*? Is that why" (and since my great-grandfather, both because of his poor education and for chronological reasons, couldn't quote Kafka's father, then Kafka's father must have quoted my great grandfather) "I've marched through the snow in bare feet and worked my fingers to the bone, for you to marry József? I'll lock you up until you come to your senses, you stupid goose!"

Since his roaring was fruitless, Sidonie was placed under house arrest, and her mother tried persuasion. "You'll worry your father to death, Sidi, and if you are really stupid enough to marry József, he won't give you a penny, I know my husband. What will you live on with József? He sells three pairs of shoes a month, two of them to you and the third on credit. You're used to expensive clothes, good food and good manners, how are you going to live with a scrounger?"

"Don't be cross with me, Mama, but József's manners are just as good as Papa's, and you don't need to worry about what we'll eat, I'll take care of that."

"But why would you want to marry Jószef? In Budapest you can have whomever you want, you're pretty, you'll get a good dowry, your Papa knows the best families, and then you can live in the sort of luxury you're accustomed to, you're a good catch, so why do you want József? Put that idea out of your mind, I forbid you to marry him!"

"I know that you forbid it, Papa has also forbidden it, but I'll still marry him."

Sidonie was as stubborn as her mother, the conversation went in circles and the house arrest continued. It was supposed to give the girl the opportunity to think matters over and arrive at a better conclusion.

She did think it over, but arrived at a different conclusion from what her parents had hoped. After three weeks of careful consideration, she crawled out the window at first light one morning, landed on a hotbed that soiled her dress but broke the fall (when my mother jumped out the window, she fell on hard cobblestones) and set out for Tapolca. She arrived as the sun was rising, slept for two hours under a hedge (there was no point in fussing about her dress anymore), washed herself at a well and walked into József's store at eight-thirty to – what other business could she possibly have there? – order herself a second pair of boots. Quite apart from the fact that there was no carriage waiting outside, József needed only to cast a glance at the girl's clothes to realize that something was not right. But he was not the kind of person who asks questions. So he got out a piece of brown paper and drew the outline of her foot (although he of course had the outline he had taken previously; a good shoemaker doesn't throw that sort of thing away). She stayed for two hours, bought herself a roll and a glass of milk for breakfast, walked all the way home and sneaked back into her room again unnoticed; because except for Moische, who was supposed to be standing guard outside her door, but was once again sleeping like a log, everyone else was in the fields. Three months later, my great-grandmother (she had barely stopped crying and now had to start again) discovered that her daughter was pregnant.

The bad news (or rather the good news; because my grandmother will have known very well what she was doing) could not be concealed from her father, who roared so much that he got laryngitis and had to go to the doctor. (As a cattle trader, he had more confidence in the veterinarian, but it wouldn't do for an estate owner to have his throat painted by a veterinarian; it was bad enough to have a pregnant daughter in the house.) After he had his throat painted, he continued roaring until he lost his voice completely. But since Sidonie's only answer was: "I will marry József anyway," and as her father could no longer roar, he boxed her ears. That was a mistake, as it didn't have the desired effect, and how was he to go about finding a well-to-do husband in Budapest for a pregnant girl who also had a swollen cheek? Besides, he had put himself in the wrong by doing so, and now her mother was *against* him.

So things took their course. Róth spent a number of sleepless nights, and when his voice had recovered, he started roaring again and displayed a considerable vocabulary. "You're pregnant by József, you goose? By that clumsy oaf, that *ganef*, that silly ass, that fool, that *nebbish*, that *shlemiel*, that swindler, that nobody, that complete idiot? May a dog's tail grow between your legs!" (Hungarian curses are in a class of their own; when it comes right down to it, every second Hungarian janitor is a King Lear). Finally, he recognized that it was all to no avail – there was no wall harder than my grandmother's head – and he resigned himself, albeit grudgingly, to the inevitable. He had a long talk with the rabbi in Tapolca, who happened to be a relative ("Why not," he said, " she will have pretty children, I'm already looking forward to their bar mitzvahs"), and then in a great rush, as if to outstrip the three months, the wedding date was set.

The wedding was quite an event. From all the regional Jewish communities, everyone had been invited who had any standing or reputation – or who didn't: Sidonie had made sure

15

behind her father's back that all the Kahns would be present as well (József had three older brothers who were all as poor as he was).

It will come as no surprise that Róth didn't pass up the opportunity to display his wealth, but it also goes without saying that the ceremony followed the old rite that had hardly changed in hundreds of years. The wedding took place on a Tuesday, because on a Tuesday and only on that day, the Lord had said twice while creating the world that it was good. While the guests partook of the cold buffet prepared by a cook and two assistants Mother Róth had brought in from Budapest, József and Sidonie, who, as was customary, were fasting, admired the golden illuminations on the *ketubah*, the marriage contract, which, to be sure, stated only what was self-evident. Róth had had the document written by a calligrapher in Brno. After the *ketubah* had been signed by two witnesses, József pulled the veil Sidonie was wearing down over her face, because Rebecca had been wearing a veil when she saw Isaac for the first time, and the rabbi blessed Sidonie as the sons of Bethuel had blessed Rebecca: "You, our sister, grow to many thousand times a thousand."

In front of the *baldachin* that was standing outside, decorated with two beautiful old *talleisim*, József put on the white coat that he normally only wore on Yom Kippur, and Sidonie, who looked so delightful in her wedding dress with the long train that Mother Róth burst into tears, walked solemnly around him seven times, because it says seven times in the Torah: "and when a man takes a wife." The rabbi spoke the blessing over the bride and groom, they sipped wine from a silver cup, József put the ring on Sidonie's finger and repeated the old wording after the rabbi: "*Harei at m'kudäschät*" (with this ring, be sacred to me according to the law of Moses and Israel). Then the rabbi read the text of the *ketubah*, and the seven guests of honour said the *sheva berachos*, the seven blessings spoken over a bride and groom. Finally – that was the end of the ceremony – the cantor placed a glass wrapped in a napkin on the floor under the *baldachin*, and

József crushed it underfoot; because just as he now crushed the glass, so the temple had been destroyed, and the time of exile had begun. . . .

Then, notwithstanding the buffet, a banquet was served, for which the Budapest cook had prepared seven courses. Father Róth proposed a toast, and no sooner was he finished than the director of the orphanage, who was there at Sidonie's instigation, got up and to her dismay made a speech in which, although he of course spoke Hungarian, he quoted Schiller's "Song of the Bell" in the original German. "Take up your wanderer's staff with joy," he exclaimed, although it wasn't clear who was supposed to wander where, and he went pale with pride when he also managed to work the "herds of well-fed, broad-browed cattle" into his address, with reference to the land Róth owned. Fortunately, he didn't quote the lines about the "bridal bouquet" and the "church bells" in the poem. (When I was sixteen and quoted Schiller in the presence of my Uncle Jenö, who was an educated man and could speak good High German when he wanted to, he would say: "Don't quote that crazy stuff, that is *goyim naches*.") Champagne, Bordeaux and Tokay flowed in abundance, and when the guests at last went home, no one had dared to ask why the invitations had only been sent out at the last minute.

But the wedding was the last thing Dezsö Róth did for his daughter, and so my great-grandmother, when she wanted to dissuade Sidonie from marrying the shoemaker, had been partly right with her warnings. To be sure, her husband didn't go to his grave for sorrow, but he also really never helped his daughter with a single cent. Even when he died, she got nothing: he had a son as well, and the inheritance went to him undivided (it wasn't very much, since Róth with advancing age had made some bad business decisions). Incidentally, I don't have much to tell about the son. I only know that he had the misfortune of growing old, so that, when the Germans occupied Hungary, he was still alive and died an agonizing death.

2.

"A *shlemiel* lets everything fall, a *nebbish* picks everything up," is the proverbial definition. Dezsö Róth had done his future son-in-law an injustice – but it really is time that I call him my grandfather! My grandfather was neither a *shlemiel* nor a *nebbish*, but a simple, serious, decent man who knew he played only a modest role in the world, but didn't lose face. I remember him as an elderly gentleman whose hair had got a little thin, but whose Kaiser Franz-Joseph sideburns were just as blond in 1938 as they had been in 1880, when my grandmother found them (the beard and the entire József) so irresistible. In the evenings, the old man liked to drink a glass of caraway brandy while smoking his cigars, and since for some obscure reason he had got the idea that someone was stealing his brandy, he would make a thick pencil line on the label after he had filled his schnapps glass, so that he could check the next day to see if any was missing. But since he sometimes forgot to make the line (after all, he was over eighty), the brandy the next evening would be half a finger's width below the line, and so he had the proof in his hand. He never did discover that while I didn't steal his brandy, I now and then stole a cigar to bribe my friend Giddi May to play Beethoven instead of Scarlatti on our piano. When he died, he left a large supply of cigars in pretty wooden boxes. He had the good luck of dying peacefully in his bed two weeks before the Germans, to the cheers of the people, marched into Vienna.

That was almost sixty years later. In 1880, he could afford neither brandy nor cigars, and when my grandmother threw herself at him (to put it as it was), he fully understood that Dezsö Róth did not want a shoemaker for his son-in-law, and that there would be an argument – quite aside from the fact that there are serious punishments in the Talmud for what had happened in the small room behind the store during her two-hour visit. But very few men could refuse a seventeen-year-old as pretty as my grandmother then was, and when my grandmother wanted something, it was a good idea to obey her. By the way, he bit with bliss into the sweet apple, although he did ask himself what they were supposed to live on. Mother Róth had made it clear to him that his father-in-law would not help out, and his shoemaking barely brought in enough for a bachelor. He did have a kitchen and two rooms behind the store, one with his bed and the other with his leather supplies; but the kitchen was small and the rooms were tiny. However, when the rabbi had said the final blessing and Sidonie moved in with József, his worries proved to have been unnecessary. She had left her fine clothes at her parents' house, sewed curtains from material that her mother had had lying in some drawer for years, and for lunch, instead of baked carp, she and József ate potatoes with butter and milk that tasted better to her than any carp ever had. In spite of the crazy stuff I was not allowed to quote in Uncle Jenö's presence, "sensual pleasure and spiritual peace" got along together splendidly in József's house.

Since there was no room for a cradle in the tiny bedroom, and there was no money, let alone extra space, Sidonie halved my grandfather's store with an imaginary line and confiscated one half. There she set up the cradle in a corner, had József build her a table of cheap wood that could stand outside in front of the store in good weather and began selling vegetables. At first she knew nothing at all about such a business, but she learned very quickly to buy from the local farmers at low prices, and on the table she constructed real works of art out of tomatoes, green peppers, corn, potatoes and cauliflower. When winter came (it was high time: Sidonie was in the ninth month), her vegetable sales had already brought in enough for the young couple to rent two rooms on the top floor; that wasn't expensive then in Tapolca.

The baby was a girl, and behind her husband's back, Mother Róth smuggled diapers and little shirts into the city. Sidonie – she did ask my grandfather, but he knew to say yes when his wife asked him something – called her Gisa. Even as a baby she is said to have been unusually pretty, like the Róths, with black eyes and curly black hair. Then came two boys. The first was Jenö, in whose presence I was later not allowed to quote Schiller, and my grandmother called their second son Dezsö after her father, although it was not customary among Jews to call a child after a living ancestor. Old Róth, who must have been an uncommonly stupid and stubborn person, promptly got it into his head that she had given his grandson this name deliberately to make fun of him. He also took it amiss that she – the daughter of the estate owner Dezsö Róth – sold vegetables, and when he drove to Tapolca, Moische had to go a long way around so they wouldn't pass the store. That was all the more absurd since the other Róths – there was an entire army of brothers and sisters, brothers-in-law and sisters-in-law, who knew very well that they themselves had been the children of poor people – had nothing against the Kaiser Franz-Joseph sideburns and thought the vegetable store was very nice. They went a long way around in order to admire the little towers of corn and tomatoes, and without these customers Sidonie wouldn't have been able to rent the two top floor rooms so soon. But no one could talk to Róth about his daughter, and his siblings eventually found that his constantly wounded feelings bordered on persecution mania. Fifty years later, family members would still occasionally remark, when someone complained loud and long: "He's yammering like Dezsö," although old Róth was long since dead and his grandson, my Uncle Dezsö, was full of enthusiasm for life, seldom yammered and liked to laugh loud and long. It was my Uncle Jenö who inherited the tendency toward persecution mania.

3.

Even more clearly than any memory of the real Jenö, I remember a postcard-sized photograph in the brown shades that, in the thirties, were unfortunately fashionable not only in photography. There he sits on a camel, the pyramids in the background, and in spite of the desert heat he's wearing a business suit with a white shirt and tie. (Incidentally, in the photographs in the shoebox I inherited from my mother, Jenö can always be recognized by his strange eyes that always look as if they were opened wide by some unnatural means; his eyes make people afraid.) But so as to be able to travel from Vienna by train, ship and camel to the pyramids, my Uncle Jenö first had to walk from Tapolca to Vienna (just as the rabbi of Tarnopol had to walk from Warsaw to his home town). Like everything in the world, there's a story behind that. (The only thing that doesn't have a story behind it is the word of God: "Let there be light." God then created the heaven and the earth and everything below it, in it and above it in six days, and sometimes I think he shouldn't have been in such a hurry.) But instead of telling the story behind *that*, I first would like to tell a story that is only indirectly related to Jenö's walk to Vienna.

When I was ten, I had finished public school and went to the trade school in the second district of Vienna, on Kleine Sperlgasse. There were two stationery stores nearby, the Christian store owned by the widowed Frau Zwirnknopf, and the Jewish store owned by the Epsteins. Frau Zwirnknopf was a tall, high-bosomed, friendly woman who, with a single exception – the Epsteins – seemed to show endless goodwill to the entire world. In her neat, attractive store, there was a pleasant smell of paper, cleansers and the new wood of the shelves. I occasionally bought some little thing there, perhaps a pencil, and curiously sniffed the smell. But you had to pay for the order and cleanliness, and when I needed more than a pencil I went to the Epsteins. There, the goods were not neatly labelled on new shelves, but were piled in big, disorderly heaps, and since someone had always forgotten to close a door or a window, and a gentle wind wafted through the disarray, there wasn't a smell of anything, or at most of cholent from the neighbouring cholent baker's; but the prices were lower there, and Frau Zwirnknopf knew that and felt threatened, all the more so because the Epsteins had resorted to the dirty trick of closing their store, not on Sunday like all proper people, but on Saturday. So in the end, in March of 1938, without comprehending that along with the competition she would also lose most of her customers, she was

21

among the thousands at the Heldenplatz, the huge square in front of the Royal Palace, who cheered the Nazis as they marched in. That illustrates a bit of social history, and it may be worthwhile to go a little further back.

Joseph II's Tolerance Edict of March 31, 1783, admitted the Hungarian Jews to all professions, allowed them to lease land and abolished the Jewish identification badge. Soon, though, many restrictions were revived. The Jews were not allowed to buy real estate, to lease land from the aristocracy, to study any subject other than medicine, and so on. They only obtained full equality after the Compromise of 1867, and with that a short golden age began for the Jews in the Hapsburg countries, especially in Hungary, where they could fill a gap, since there was hardly a middle class yet. They founded factories, studied law, suddenly there were Jewish academics, engineers, violinists, world-class composers in Hungary. It's touching to read how the Jews back then in the Hapsburg Empire assessed their situation. "We believe," wrote Gerson Wolf, for example, in his 1883 history of the Jews of Austria, "that the entire period of time under discussion can be divided into two parts. The first, earlier time, reaches from the period when the Jews immigrated to Austria until the last expulsion from Prague in 1744; it is the time of tribulation and suffering. It was followed by the second period, the period of struggle and victory, of the principle of equal rights."

The fact that Wolf in 1883 was so confident of success when looking to the future shows that he did not understand what was going on. When I spent a few days in Vienna in 1950, I looked at the display in a bookstore window and noticed a coloured print, for use in schools, of Christ among the disciples. It showed a demonstratively Aryan, blond, blue-eyed Jesus in the centre of the picture and eleven disciples who hardly differed from those in Leonardo da Vinci's Last Supper. The twelfth, Judas, had black hair, a long nose and was repulsively ugly – a caricature from the *Stürmer*, the Nazi propaganda sheet. That was the old clerical anti-Semitism, dating back to the church fathers: the Jews are the murderers of

Christ, and does it not say in the Bible that his blood shall be upon them for all eternity? At the same time, however, the coloured print shows the new, racial anti-Semitism that became epidemic when the Jews were able to move more freely for the first time in two thousand years.

While Gerson Wolf abandoned himself to his dreams, the word "anti-Semitism" had been around for exactly ten years – Wilhelm Marr had coined it in 1873. But there were also the writings of Gobineau and Chamberlain; Dühring's book had recently appeared, which stated that the "Jewish question" was to be solved "by exterminating them," and in Vienna the followers of Georg von Schönerer were singing the pretty little verse: "It matters not whom the Jews are trusting, the fact remains that their race is disgusting." Then the politicians in Austria and in Hungary discovered that anti-Semitism brought votes, and they helped the clergy incite the farmers and the petit bourgeois. . . . It wasn't difficult, because now there were more and more Epsteins, not to mention Jewish cattle traders, industrialists, lawyers and doctors, and every Epstein generated his own Frau Zwirnknopf. With the equal rights and the "victory" that Gerson Wolf had so naively celebrated had come envy, and with envy, hatred.

The extent to which you felt the hatred depended on who you were and where you lived. My grandmother had grown up in a well-to-do household, surrounded by maids and servants, spoiled by her mother and their Bohemian cook, protected when she went for rides by the coachman Moische. She had not felt the pressure that weighed so heavily, for example, on a Jewish peddler. In Tapolca, of course, she heard a swearword now and then. She knew that *zsidó* meant not only "Jewish," but also "miserly," and what the farmers said when someone haggled persistently: "He haggles like a Gypsy for a horse, and a Jew for cotton." But she was so in love with her József, so happy in her small family, so proud, too, of her own enterprise – in the summer months her vegetables soon brought in more than József's workshop – that it didn't bother her what people said behind her back, and when a bad word was spoken in her presence, she had a sharp tongue and could stand up for herself. But then it happened – it was in April, 1883, Gisa was just two years old – that a stone flew through the window of the room where the little girl was sleeping. There's a story behind the stone, too.

On Saturday, the first of April, 1882, in Tiszaeszlár, in the county of Szabolcs, the fourteen-year-old Christian, Esther Solymosi, was sent by her employer, a Jewess by the name of Huri, to the next village to do some shopping and she didn't return. Incidentally, the small Jewish community in Tiszaeszlár needed a new kosher butcher at that time, but one who could also function as their cantor, so they were looking for someone who could not only butcher, but also sing. Nevertheless, there were three candidates. (As the Yiddish saying goes, "The Lord is just. He gives food to the rich and appetite to the poor." The German saying, "Hunger is the best cook" is not as witty; but apparently hunger is also the best singing teacher.) So after the evening meal they had a meeting to audition the three candidates, which meant that the light was on unusually late in the synagogue. When there was still no sign of Esther in the next few days, it occurred to her mother to link her disappearance with the light that had been on so late, and soon the rumour made the rounds that the girl had met a terrible end in the Jewish temple: it was almost *Pesach*, the Jewish Feast of the Passover, and didn't everyone know that Jews need the blood of a Christian child for Passover?

A month later, the rumour arose that the four-year-old son of József Scharf, the Temple sexton, who had recently been seen playing with Christian children, had said he was present when his father, his older brother Móric and the butcher (that is, the one who had in the meantime got the job) had killed Esther. Two weeks later, the district court ordered a preliminary investigation.

The examining magistrate, János Bary, was no less certain than Esther's mother that the Jews needed Christian blood for their Passover, and so in his eyes the accused were unquestionably guilty. He therefore saw it as his task not to investigate, but rather to prove this unquestionable guilt. He found villagers who testified that they had heard "screams of distress" from the synagogue. That wasn't surprising, because hunger is perhaps not the best singing teacher after all, and it's no miracle that it sounds like a scream of distress when a butcher has to sing. Bary interrogated, among others, the thirteen-year-old Móric Scharf; and since he, as was reported the next morning in the Budapest Catholic daily newspaper *Magyar Allam*, "resorted to denying everything," Bary took him "into protective custody." At that time, protective custody wasn't a death sentence, as it was later under the Nazis, but it was enough for Móric. He was put up in the house of a policeman by the name of Györgi Vay, in whose loving care adults had confessed to things that hadn't happened, and he soon signed a statement: he, Móric Scharf, had looked through the keyhole of the synagogue door and seen the butcher, assisted by his father, cut Esther's throat and collect her blood in a pot. From that point on, some of the Hungarian newspapers reported on the "ritual murder in Tiszaeszlár" as if it were a proven fact, and the rabble broke the Jews' windows in the villages and looted their houses.

The trial soon became a sensation in Europe, with not only the Hungarian, but also the Paris and London newspapers reporting on it. There was a certain element of cruel comedy inherent in the rest of the trial, just as there had been at the beginning. Since Bary feared that Móric might go back on his coerced statement in court, he made sure the boy was subjected to a thorough brainwashing, and the preliminary investigation dragged on. In the middle of June, raftsmen pulled a corpse from the river to which Tiszaeszlár owes its name. The corpse was wearing Esther's clothes, but there was no sign of a cut on the body. Bary was an imaginative man and explained away this problem by saying that the raftsmen, among whom there were Jews, must indeed have pulled Esther's corpse out of the Tisza, but then have put Esther's clothes on another corpse that they substituted for hers. The proceedings went on for months, but the question was never asked how the raftsmen had managed to procure a second corpse so quickly, even though it was rather pertinent to the investigation. Admittedly, there are junk shops where you can buy almost anything, but there presumably wasn't a shop in the county of Szabolcs with a supply of six-week-old corpses. The raftsmen were arrested, and the policeman Györgi Vay, with whom we are already acquainted, made sure that two of them confirmed Bary's theory. The young Móric also did what he was told and recited to the court exactly what he had been taught.

But now two new problems came to light; first, it turned out that the prayer room in which the "slaughter" was supposed to have taken place could not have been seen through the keyhole of the temple door; and second – this sounds like something from a fairy tale, but is documented – the corpse, after it had been buried and exhumed three times, was positively identified as the corpse of Esther Solymosi by a scar on the big toe of her right foot. Meanwhile, the number of accused had risen to thirteen, and in the courtroom, in addition to the journalists who had hurried there from the whole of Europe and who were driven to despair by Hungarian spelling, there were sometimes as many as 250 spectators who clapped, whistled, howled and placed bets on the outcome of the trial. Györgi Vay challenged one of the defence lawyers to a duel, and although the latter had never had a rapier in his hand, he felt he couldn't bow out with the world press looking on, took some fencing classes on the weekend and inflicted a wound on the policeman's upper arm; so Christian blood really did flow in Tiszaeszlár. By the time the reporter for the *Times* had finally learned to spell the name of the village with two sz's and an accent over the second a – in August 1883 – the trial was over, and the three judges read out an exceedingly muddled document, in whose thirty pages the verdict "not guilty" was not to be found, but rather only the finding that "József Scharf and his co-defendants were accused of murder. The fact that this cannot be proven prevents the assumption that a murder was kept secret." The thirteen defendants were released from jail, and the Jews who had fled from

Tiszaeszlár returned to their looted homes. In the Hungarian parliament, Gyösö Istóczy, who by the way had already pleaded in 1878 for the founding of a Jewish state in Palestine to get rid of them, announced that Christian parents could never be sure "that their child who has suddenly disappeared, will not become a victim a few days later of the fanatical Jews who surpass even the cannibals in their ritualistic madness," for in spite of the acquittal "everyone was convinced in his innermost heart that the unfortunate Esther Solymosi had met her tragic end in the synagogue of Tiszaeszlár." The right-wing press complained that "the justice system was controlled by Jews," and the mob was howling.

Small causes, large effects. If Frau Huri had kept the fourth commandment, according to which you should do no work on the Sabbath, nor your son nor your daughter, nor your man servant nor your maid servant, then she wouldn't have sent Esther Solymosi to Tiszaeszlár to do shopping, the girl wouldn't have drowned in the Tisza, the reporter for the *Times* wouldn't have had to learn the orthography of Hungarian place names, no stone would have flown through the window of my grandmother's room, Uncle Jenö wouldn't have been photographed on a camel, and I wouldn't have been born in Vienna – perhaps not at all – and wouldn't be bathing poodles today in Haifa. But Frau Huri didn't keep the commandment, and the stone flew. There was the sound of breaking glass, the child screamed, and my grandmother, who had jumped out of bed in alarm, saw that the girl's forehead was bleeding.

The damage wasn't great. My grandmother swept up the broken glass, my grandfather made sure the stone disappeared from the house, and a workman put new glass in the window. The small wound on the girl's forehead healed without leaving a scar. In my grandmother's mind, though, there was a wound left that didn't heal. The atmosphere in and around Tapolca had changed. When my grandmother bought cabbage or radishes from the farmers and a dog growled, they had previously said "down" or whatever you say in Hungarian. Now they let the dog growl, because hadn't they read in the newspaper that Christian children weren't safe as long as there were Jews around? Sidonie had become hypersensitive, she felt their mistrust, she saw the veiled threat in the farmers' eyes, and when she had read a particularly bad inflammatory article in the *Magyar Allam*, she feared for Gisa. She didn't like it anymore in Tapolca. Of course, when she spoke about it with József, he said phlegmatically: "Don't worry, Sidi, it was never any different, it's the same everywhere," and since she loved the kind, handsome man she had won for herself in the battle with her father, she dropped the topic. She also didn't have the time to be moody, because in addition to running the vegetable business, she soon had four children to care for: she gave birth to Jenö in 1884, Dezsö in 1885 and her second daughter, Klara, in 1886. But it tormented her to think of her children growing up surrounded by the hatred she saw in the farmers' eyes, and she was worried about the future. What would become of the boys in Tapolca? (She wasn't worried about the girls, they would get married.) What could they learn in this one-horse town? Should they be apprenticed to their father, or to the Jewish glazier? That wasn't good enough. Sometimes now, in the narrow bed that she shared with József, she would lie awake until the early morning hours, thinking of the stone that had come flying through the window, and thinking of the future. But she was happy with her husband and the children, and so years passed before she reached a decision.

4.

If you need advice, you go to a rabbi. Since the rabbi of Tarnopol wasn't available to my grandmother, she went to the Kálmans.

"Sidi!" exclaimed Malke Kálman, who had opened the door. "How nice that you have come to visit us again! Come in and sit by the stove, you look frozen through. Gyula and Sara are here too."

Like my great-grandmother in the photograph, Malke was wearing a black cotton dress that reached down to her ankles. If you had an eye for that sort of thing, you could see that she was observing the rule and was wearing a wig. As Sidonie entered the parlour, the rabbi, who was her second cousin and the successor of the rabbi who had blessed her marriage, got up from his chair to greet her. His appearance reflected the division in the Hungarian Jewish community. He sympathized with the Orthodox Jews and wore a caftan, but he tried to steer a middle course: his full beard was carefully trimmed. Gyula, his brother, a school teacher by profession, was a Reform Jew. He wore an ordinary business suit and was clean shaven.

"Welcome," said Miklós Kálman with a certain degree of ceremony. "You bring blessing to our house." Then the women began to talk, about Gisa, who was getting prettier and prettier, about Malke's Ruben, who was already reading the Talmud, about the younger children, until Miklós interrupted them: "How's business?"

"The same as ever," said Sidonie. "József makes shoes, and the goyim don't pay."

"The goyim pay no worse than the Jews," said Gyula, who was a good Hungarian patriot.

"That's true, but God knows they also don't pay any better," said Sidonie.

"Tell us what's on your mind, Sidonie," said Miklós. "There is something you want to talk about, you didn't come through the snow to tell us your Jenö is eating rock candy."

"You're right, as always, but I don't know how to begin. I'm no longer happy in Tapolca. I'm worried about the children, I don't want them to grow up in a one-horse town where people break my windows."

"That happened a long time ago," said Gyula.

"But I can't forget it," said my grandmother. "When I go to the farmers, they're glad to see me, who else buys their eggs, but I see the hatred in their eyes, and my boys fight with the neighbours' children."

"There is hatred everywhere," said Gyula. "That is our fate. But we live in an enlightened country, the day will come. . . ."

"Maybe," said my grandmother, "but when? You know how the newspapers incite hatred. I don't want my children to grow up with hatred. And what should become of them here? Should the boys be apprenticed to my husband and mend boots all their lives? I don't want them to be peddlers."

"You're exaggerating," said Gyula. "Your father grew up in a village and became a rich man."

"I don't want the children to turn out like my father," said Sidonie, "but they should learn to understand the way of the world, I don't want them to become country bumpkins in this one-horse town."

"Am I a country bumpkin?" said Gyula. "I've been living in Tapolca for twenty years. And Miklós? He is known everywhere as a learned man."

"Jenö is a bright child," said Miklós, "if you were good Jews, you and József, I could prepare him for the yeshiva like my Ruben."

"That's not so easy," said Gyula. "If the boy is to have the right education, he has to attend the yeshiva in Pressburg, and where would the money come from for that? Róth doesn't help, and shoemaking doesn't bring in enough."

"Miklós didn't study in Pressburg either, but he has still become a famous man," said Malke proudly. "He just recently published another article in A Magyar Szinagóga."

"Your Ruben has his nose in the Talmud all day long," said my grandmother, "but Jenö doesn't. And this isn't just about Jenö."

"So what are you thinking about?"

"I don't know," said my grandmother, a little disingenuously. "I wanted to ask you for advice."

"If you really don't like it here anymore," said Miklós, "go to Vienna."

Then none of them said anything for a little while, and the complete silence of a winter evening prevailed, the sort of winter evening they had back then, when there was no sound of a motor on the roads and no humming of a refrigerator in the house. "Go to Vienna!" That was what Sidonie had wanted to hear, and yet that wasn't it. Of course the children had to grow up in Vienna, that would be best for them. But couldn't it be Budapest? People spoke Hungarian there, they had relatives and acquaintances there, she had gone there every few months with her parents to shop – but Vienna? Vienna was foreign to her. Suddenly she saw an endless labyrinth of streets and squares in front of her whose bumpy cobbled pavement she had to cross in high-heeled shoes while countless cab drivers kept yelling at her in an incomprehensible dialect.

"My German is so poor," she said at last. "I don't know a soul there. What should we live on?"

"God will help you," said Gyula.

"I know the rabbi of the Schiff Schul in Vienna, Chaim Ledermann," said Miklós, who was an expert, so he knew that you have to help God a little if you want Him to help. "He's a *tzaddick*, one of the few still around. If you want, I can write to him."

"You people are *meshuga*," said Sara. "You have enough to eat and a fire in the stove, and you go dancing on ice."

"Have you spoken with József?" asked Miklós.

"No."

"He won't want to go," said Gyula.

"He will understand that it's best for the children," said my grandmother. "But you may have to help me a little."

5.

The rabbi of Tarnopol – at some point I do have to tell this story, so why not now? – from time to time, the famous rabbi of Tarnopol went to visit his colleague, the hardly less famous rabbi of Warsaw, to discuss contentious theological issues with him. When he once again travelled to the Polish capital city for this purpose in the spring of the year 1782, his coachman Moische, as we already know, drove him in a carriage and pair. (Malicious gossip has it that the reason for his trip was to clarify the question of whether the lighting of the recently invented matches was considered work and was therefore forbidden on the Sabbath. Of course that's not true, because at that time it had already long since been determined that every way of making fire counts as work. When I'm visiting good Jews on Friday evening, I'm not allowed to smoke, not because I wouldn't be allowed to smoke a cigarette if it were already lit, but because I'm not allowed to light it. Incidentally, I know from reliable sources – "from the most reliable sources," my Uncle Jenö used to say – that it was a very important question that led the rabbi to Warsaw.) After the contentious passage in the Talmud had been interpreted in a way satisfactory to both learned men, with the help of a commentary by Moses Maimonides which in its turn needed its own commentary, the rabbi had travelled half the way back home again when he stopped at an inn located on the country road and ate a meal, while the coachman Moische sat outside on the box seat and kept an eye on the horses.

After a while, the rabbi looked out the door, which was standing open because of the early onset of summer weather, and noticed that Moische was asleep.

"Moische, are you asleep?" called the rabbi.

"I'm not asleep, I'm speculating."

"Moische, what are you speculating?" asked the rabbi.

"I'm speculating, if you drive a stake into the earth, where does the earth go?"

"Moische, don't sleep, so the horses won't be stolen."

A while later, when the rabbi had just finished eating his borsht, he looked out the door again and saw that the coachman was dozing.

"Moische, are you asleep?"

"I'm not asleep, I'm speculating."

"Moische, what are you speculating?"

"I'm speculating, if you drive a stake into the earth, where does the earth go?"

"Moische, don't sleep, so the horses won't be stolen."

When the rabbi was finishing up his meal with his coffee, the coachman had already shut his eyes again.

"Moische, are you asleep?"

"I'm not asleep, I'm speculating."

"Moische, what are you speculating?"

"Rabbi, I'm speculating how we can get to Tarnopol without a horse." The story doesn't say if the rabbi of Tarnopol continued on foot, but I have to assume he did. If that was the case, then he was following an old tradition of his people. In the course of the Jews' long history, a good many things have been forbidden them, many by themselves (for example the lighting of a match on the Sabbath), many by others. In Hungary, for example, at the beginning of the nineteenth century the Jews were still forbidden to own property outside of the *Judengasse*, the Jewish street, to acquire the master craftsman's diploma and to stay in the Hungarian mountain cities. As thanks for these favours they were allowed to pay *Leibmaut* or tolerance tax, which, after its abolition in 1782 and its reinstatement in 1792 was called "customs duties." ("From tolerance tax to customs duties," my Uncle Jenö could have said, "that's progress.") But one thing was never forbidden them: to travel, in fact, in the course of their history travelling just about became the compulsory national sport: from Egypt to Canaan, from Canaan to Babylon and back again to Canaan, to Greece and Italy, over the Alps down the Rhine valley, then from there, when the crusaders practised killing people there as a preliminary exercise to freeing the holy grave, to Poland and Galicia, where they brought their Middle High German, from which Yiddish developed. . . . Even in China there were Jewish settlements whose inhabitants had once travelled there from the Mediterranean along the Silk Road by way of Baghdad, Samarkand and Kashgar, and by the time of Chiang Kai-shek they looked like Chinese, but still strictly observed their ancient ritual.

So my grandmother, when she walked from her father's estate to Tapolca, had followed a long tradition; but that was just the beginning. Now she had the task of convincing my grandfather of the necessity of going to Vienna. But you need only to take a look at the two people to know that she succeeded. Among the photographs I inherited from my mother, there is a studio portrait of my grandparents from the early twenties. My grandfather had dressed up for the picture. He is wearing a dark suit and a vest with a watch chain hanging from its middle buttonhole, a white shirt with a starched collar and a wide tie. Sidonie is wearing, as always, a simple black dress, this time with a silver locket. Her hairstyle shows that she could now afford a good hairdresser. Both of them look very serious: the time had not yet come when photographers asked their customers to smile. But while my grandfather's face is a kind and attractive average face, my grandmother's makes you think – it expresses (and that was not the case with the picture of the seventeen-year-old with which this account began) – it expresses, with its firm chin and with the slightly downturned corners of its mouth, a degree of strength and determination that could intimidate a police officer. Even if you didn't know that József had been a poor orphan and Sidonie the daughter of a wealthy man, you could tell at first glance who held the reins in this marriage. The conversation in which Sidonie communicated her decision to her husband began at nine o'clock in the evening. When she turned out the light two hours later, he had consented.

József had, however, won the concession that their move would not take place in the depths of winter, but at the earliest in mid-April. That gave them time to plan and make preparations, and as my grandparents discussed what to take with them and what to sell and compiled the bills they had to pay, it turned out that what they had earned for themselves in ten years of hard work was less than nothing. Since the vegetable store didn't bring in much in the winter, and it was getting more and more difficult for József to compete with the mass-produced shoes pouring in from Bohemia, while there were four children to feed, there was barely enough money in the house to pay the rent. No help could be expected from Sidonie's father, and so their move would perhaps not have taken place at all if Mother Róth hadn't diverted fifty florins from the housekeeping money behind his back. So they could pay their bills, and they would have been able to find the money somehow for the train tickets; but when my grandparents made inquiries about the cost of moving their furniture, kitchen utensils, clothes and leather supplies, that was a sum that a Baron Pálffy paid out when he wanted to have a nice day in Budapest, an amount, therefore, that surpassed József's wildest imagination. . . . Sidonie was too proud to borrow the money, for example from the Kálmans, so once again she had to have a bright idea.

She would, she thought, as she lay awake in their narrow bed beside the blissfully slumbering József, need a cart in Vienna on which she could display her vegetables until they could afford a store: it was clear to her that she would have to contribute to the family's keep in Vienna too. So wouldn't the obvious thing be to build the cart here, load the furniture and little Klara on it, harness yourself to it and *walk* to Vienna? Hardly had this idea occurred to her than it became her decision, just as ten years previously she had had the sudden conviction in the shoemaker's store that she would marry József, or no one.

This time she had everyone against her. József was in despair. In the sixty years my grandparents spent together, they only had two arguments – when Sidonie decided to go to Vienna, and when she decided to return to Tapolca. Each time there was a violent argument. The children hid, József roared almost as much as Dezsö Róth had; he had a fit of violent temper in which he almost hit his wife and instead, since he changed his mind at the last moment, threw a plate at the wall, but my grandmother looked him in the face with the corners of her mouth turned down and said: "Don't you want the best for your children?" Three days passed before he capitulated and consulted a cart builder, who shook his head like Malke and muttered "*meshuga*," but then, because he also had four children to feed and the customer is always right, was willing to help. Boards and cart wheels were bought, the cart builder did the carpentry and József helped. In the evening hours he made comfortable walking shoes for the family, everything that could be sold was got rid of, and by the beginning of May they were ready: the cart was waiting outside their door.

The loading of the cart, accompanied by the hooting and yelling of a dozen street urchins, took them hours: beds and chairs, sole leather and upper leather, tools and toys, clothes, plates and pots. There was a towering load on the cart. "The cart is going to tip on you, guaranteed," said Gyula, who was looking on, shaking his head. In the end, they had to unload everything again and sift through it, most of the furniture had to stay behind. Then they loaded the cart a second time, and when that was done it started to rain. József spread a tarpaulin over the tower they had built, tied it down and looked at his watch: it was late in the afternoon. So the Kahns ate their evening meal at Gyula's and spent the night on makeshift beds. The next morning the sun was shining, Dezsö made the dangerous climb up onto the tarpaulin, Klara was lifted up, and now they found out what József had long since suspected: the cart was too heavy. He could pull as hard as he wanted, with Sidonie pushing, and then Gisa and Jenö pushing too, with the street urchins hooting, but the cart didn't budge. After a few minutes they gave up, because if the cart couldn't be moved on level ground, it was pointless to try to pull it over hill and vale to Vienna. So Dezsö climbed down again, the street urchins, who had got bored, went away, my grandparents stood in the empty street not knowing what to do, and then – hadn't Gyula predicted that God would help? – a miracle happened: up the street came the well-known Róth carriage, Moische was sitting on the coach box, Mother Róth, who had said her goodbyes the previous day in tears sat beside him, and on a long rope behind the carriage trotted a third horse. Mother Róth – what doesn't one do for four grandchildren and a daughter? – had stolen it from the stall with the help of the coachman.

6.

József hadn't been happy to take to the road, but I like to imagine how he went up the hill behind Tapolca with his family. He was leading the horse by the halter, and Sidonie was walking beside him in a white blouse and a black skirt that reached down to her ankles. The two "big ones," Gisa and Jenö, couldn't be stopped from running ahead and running back again: for them the journey was a wonderful adventure. There were so many things packed on the cart that it was higher than it was long or broad, and the two little ones were sitting on top, which was a foolish place for them to be, because if they had fallen down they would have broken their necks. From the top of the hill they had a good view of the lake and of the small town with its two little churches and the attractive town hall; my grandmother looked back without regret.

As they went down into the valley, József pulled the brake as the cart builder had told him to do, but the cart still went quite fast. Then the road got worse, and soon they discovered that the gauge of the cart wheels was too narrow: the wheels didn't fit in the ruts left in the stony sand by the large wagons drawn by heavy workhorses, and the cart swayed. At the bottom of the valley lay Sümeg – Sidonie knew the village because she had sometimes bought turnips and cabbage there for her stand – and the road ran past the railway that would have brought them to Vienna in a few hours. Then the road rose again as they entered the edges of the Bakony forest, and now it became evident that Mother Róth would have done better to steal an ox instead of the pretty little horse (it was a bay with a white star on its chest). The horse had a hard time of it, and József made a stop when they reached the first larger clearing, unhitched the animal and gave it a few tufts of grass.

"It will be hard going all the way to Vienna, Sidi!"

"Don't worry, József, we'll get there."

They took the little ones down from the cart, sat in the grass and had milk and buttered bread.

In the late afternoon the Kahns came to the estate of a cattle dealer with whom Sidonie had been previously acquainted, but since he knew her as the spoiled daughter of Dezsö Róth, she was ashamed to call on him. So they went on and slept in the forest an hour's journey past Janóshaza.

The next day was the beginning of their misery. The Kahns may have had wanderlust in their blood, but they didn't have it in their legs. The children's feet were sore, and the farther they went into the forest, the more eerie it got. Twice they saw deer, to the children's delight. At a fork in the road, a wolf stood and stared at them. József stared back. The people they encountered seemed more of a threat. The Kahns didn't look as if they ate pork every day at their noon meal. When they came to a clearing where there was a poor cottage, the dogs growled, and Sidonie thought she could see hatred in the farmers' eyes: if a Jew was a peddler, he was a thief, if he was a cattle dealer, he was a cutthroat – and perhaps not just figuratively. Hadn't it said in the newspaper that Christian children weren't safe when there were Jews around? If the farmers couldn't read, the priest read it to them. When the road went uphill, the horse wasn't strong enough, they had to push and pull. When it went downhill, the brake squealed, the cart threatened to tip over, so that they had to take the children down from the tarpaulin and carry them. Jenö could hardly lift his feet anymore and started to cry. So they had to stop, and stop again, and they heard wolves howling. They did not dare to sleep in the open again. The third farmer they asked allowed them to sleep in his hay overnight for a small fee.

The next morning Sidonie's feet were sore too, but she tried not to limp and didn't mention it; that would have been an insult to József, who had made the shoes. Gisa went ahead with dogged determination (she was her mother's daughter), but when her father spoke to her, her answers were brusque and monosyllabic. Jenö had to be carried half the way.

"Was this really necessary, Sidi? We weren't badly off in Tapolca!"

"Be good, József. Where there's a will, there's a way – and don't we want to do what's best for our children?"

By late morning the forest began to thin out, now and then there was a large, ploughed field, the road got better and sloped down gently to the Ödenburg plane. After their midday stop to rest and eat – there was still some bread, cheese and smoked meat in the large basket Mother Róth had brought them – a forest warden with his dog and shotgun joined them and told them about the *Sch'wa Kehilot*, the Seven Communities in which his prince's Jews lived. They reached Ödenburg in the afternoon, admired the municipal theatre and the tall tower and turned into the Jewish quarter. . . .

Narrow little streets, so narrow that it proved to be an advantage that their cart had such a narrow gauge; houses and huts built so close together and on top of each other that you could hardly tell where one ended and the other began; now and then on the doorsteps they would see an old man in a caftan with a broad-brimmed hat, *peyes* and an untrimmed beard, now and then a small store. József asked for the rabbi. He was very young, had a goatee, so he was reformed, and proved to be friendly and open-minded. You're travelling to Vienna? A beautiful city, a magnificent city. The Burgtheater, the new opera house, the new university – Paris and London couldn't be any more beautiful. And the newest building, the synagogue on the Schmalzhof, neo-Gothic, perhaps too much in the style of a church, why does one build a temple *goyim naches*, but splendid, there was no other word for it! "Is there a shoemaker there?" József asked. He had never heard of neo-Gothic before and, since the rabbi was speaking German, understood only about half of what he said. "Three, so two too many," said the rabbi, who didn't know József's trade. My grandmother asked humbly in Hungarian for a place to spend the night.

In the Jewish quarter of Ödenburg, as in most comparable Jewish communities, behind the synagogue, somewhere between the Schul and the *mikve*, there was a small, shabby room meant to

39

accommodate people passing through, but Sidonie had a personality that made it impossible for the rabbi to put her and her husband and their four children in such a dump. So he wrote something on a piece of paper and called for the *shammes*, a short, crippled man whose shoulders were constantly twitching. When he returned a quarter of an hour later, he led the Kahns to the outskirts of the city where there was a spacious factory in which the enamelled roofing tiles were baked that were so popular in Vienna back then. Not far away was the house of the owner, one of the rich Jews of Ödenburg who could afford to pay for the special permit to live outside the ghetto. He received the Kahns in his paved courtyard with the intention of putting them up for the night in a barn somewhere, but he had reached the stage in his life where his children were big louts, while his grandchildren weren't yet born, and he liked Klara and Dezsö, who stared at him with big eyes. So he invited them into his house, and the Kahns spent three days in the style in which Sidonie had lived before she had married József: feather beds, a linen cloth and silver candlesticks on the large table, roast duck and poppy-seed cake – and they could finally wash themselves again properly!

The Kahns were refreshed and rested when they continued on their way. They spent the night a short distance past Ebreichsdorf, once again in a farmer's straw. From there, it was hardly more than a five-hour walk to Vienna for a vigorous traveller, but the children's feet had only partially healed during the days of rest and were soon sore again, and after they had walked for hours in the Bakony forest without seeing another vehicle, they now had to share the road with an ever increasing number of carts drawn by large draught horses bringing firewood, lumber, crates of eggs and milk cans to Vienna. József was pushed to the edge of the road, their cart was constantly about to tip over, the little ones had to be carried. So they progressed with difficulty over the Petersbach, uphill to Rotneusiedl and with squealing brakes down to Liesing, where the flood waters were so high that they hardly dared to cross the rickety bridge. When they were halfway up the Wienerberg, their horse's flanks started trembling. It stood still, and József tugged the reins in vain. "The poor animal can't pull anymore today," he said at last, "we'll have to stay here somewhere." Sidonie crossed the road and appealed to the farmers who were coming from Vienna with empty carts. Finally, she found a carter who, after quickly negotiating the price, harnessed one of his work-horses to their cart. Half an hour later they were at the top of the last hill, and before them lay their goal. . . .

Vienna! It was resplendent in the afternoon sunlight, with St. Stephen's Cathedral in the centre, with the Ringstrasse and its magnificent buildings that the rabbi in Ödenburg had described so enthusiastically, with the palace of the Kaiser who, József thought, held his hand protectively over the Jews; land of the Phaeacians with its operettas, waltzes and knackwurst. . . .

Vienna at the turn of the century! It has long since become legend, although or just because people have written so badly about it: the Germans don't understand it, and the Austrians have too much to suppress. Who still knows to what extent back then it was a Jewish city, with Sigmund Freud and Theodor Herzl, with Mahler and Sonnenthal, with Schnitzler and Beer-Hoffmann, with Victor Adler and Karl Kraus? Who knows, for example, that Johann Strauss the Elder, that most genuine of all Viennese, was born in the Leopoldstadt, that is, in the *Mazzesinsel* where most of the Jews lived, because his Jewish grandfather had immigrated from Budapest? But it goes without saying that this legendary Vienna will hardly ever be mentioned in this account, and that the Kahns didn't take much notice of it. . . .

Even so, my grandparents knew enough about Vienna to head for the Leopoldstadt when they had the Wienerberg behind them. It was evening when they arrived, and József asked, in the little German he knew, where they could stay cheaply. At last a bearded old man in a caftan directed them to a wide, three-storey house in the Kleine Sperlgasse, whose façade, decorated with pil-lars and lions, did not reveal that those parts accessible only through the courtyard were slums. A doorman sent them, in a

Viennese dialect that for József and Sidonie was almost unintelligible, to a side staircase in the narrow courtyard. While the children waited with the cart, they climbed up three flights of worn stone steps, and at the end of a long corridor they knocked on a door with the inscription "Miriam Perelbaum." A shabby, tin-plate *mezuzah* was nailed to the doorpost.

The three nights my grandparents spent in Frau Perelbaum's "hostel" were the low point of their lives. (So they were fortunate people.) The "hostel" had previously been a spacious apartment, with dining room, study, bedrooms and a large kitchen. Now it had mattresses on the floor, strewn with clothes, boxes, suitcases, boots and all sorts of utensils, between which a few old men and women and a dozen neglected children lay, squatted and sat. Frau Perelbaum allocated József a corner that had three dirty mattresses lying in it. It smelled of boiled cabbage.

Sidonie sat down and divided the remaining food among the children – dry bread and a small piece of cheese – while József went down the three flights of stairs again and after long negotiations arranged to have the horse and cart brought into the narrow courtyard. When he returned, the "hostel" had begun to fill up. An old man was praying, the family beside the Kahns was eating something out of a pot, a young woman was scolding her husband in Yiddish, two children were scrapping about something, an infant was crying, a blind beggar was cowering on the bare floor in a corner, in another three men were playing cards by the light of a kerosene lamp. The air was so stuffy they could hardly breathe. Sidonie washed the children at a tap in the corridor. When they came back in, they were all so exhausted that they were able to sleep in the midst of the noise and the crowd.

The next morning they started looking for an apartment. József asked Frau Perelbaum, they asked passers-by, they ran upstairs and downstairs. At noon, on the advice of Frau Perelbaum, they went to the Leopoldstadt Temple's canteen; there was stew and watery coffee. Then Sidonie and the children went to Augarten Park, and József continued looking on his own. The thing was, that although every year hundreds of families were emigrating to America from Vienna, as from all parts of the monarchy and the shtetls in the east, there was also a steady influx of people, so that for every apartment that became free, a promise had been obtained weeks in advance, a pre-payment had been made, a deposit for the key paid. By evening, they had found nothing. During their evening meal at the canteen (here too there was the poor-people-smell of boiled cabbage), Sidonie said: "You know, József, Miklós gave us an address, we'll go to the rabbi of the Schiff Schul."

7.

The next morning, Sidonie and Josef – soon after their move he no longer wrote his first name with ʒs and the accent – walked the five minutes to the Schiff Schul, having entrusted the children with a heavy heart to the care of Frau Perelbaum, because Josef thought it would be inappropriate to take the whole family along when they went to see a rabbi. A bearded young man ushered them into a waiting room with a big window, where a mixed group of people were sitting on simple chairs and benches: old men in caftans, a man in an elegant dark suit who had likely come to arrange a bar mitzvah, a rabbi from out of town whom the young man informed in Yiddish that he was invited to the midday meal, a cripple, a mother carrying a sick child. My grandparents waited a long time. When they were finally called into the consulting room and the man behind the desk stood up to greet them, they were almost frightened. It was a giant who offered them his hand, a good head taller than Josef, under a broad-brimmed hat a shaggy mane of black hair, a black beard with silver streaks, a large stomach, but the shoulders of a wrestler: Chaim Ledermann.

Until the Kristallnacht, you could see a considerable amount of Vienna's Jewish history in the façades of its synagogues. When the temple in Seitenstettengasse was built in 1824, it was still considered advisable to conceal it behind a modest façade, which had the advantage of, among other things, saving it from arson in 1938, because it and the adjacent houses were part of the same building. So my dear fellow citizens had to content themselves with vandalizing it with hammers and crowbars. The Leopoldstadt Temple, completed in 1858 (burnt to the ground on the Kristall-nacht), was free-standing and looked very impressive with its Roman arches and Moorish décor: the time had come that good old Gerson Wolf had described as the time of victory and triumph. For Vienna's Orthodox Galician and Hungarian Jews, though, the Reformed worship service in this synagogue was a thorn in their flesh. So they had their own synagogues and eventually built themselves the Schiff Schul in the Grosse Schiffgasse, a by no means impressive, but attractive building, consecrated in the month of Elul 5624 (September 1864), burnt to the ground on the Kristall-nacht. When their rabbi died in 1870, they got Chaim Ledermann from Brno. Since he didn't write books, the historians don't know anything about him, but that's nothing to praise them for: the Mannheimers and Jellineks and the rest of them were scholars, but Ledermann was, as Miklós had said, a righteous and just man – in fact one of those thirty-six *tzaddikim* who according to the legend must still exist in the world so that it will not come to an end.

The *baal-shem-tov*, Rabbi Israel ben Eliezer, the founder of Hasidism, is said to have prophesied that his soul would return to the earth after forty years. When forty years later Rabbi Friedmann in Sadragora became very famous, people said of him that the soul of the "Besht" had entered his body, and there were effusive admirers of Ledermann who maintained the same of him. But I would consider this assertion incorrect even if I did believe in the transmigration of souls, because Ledermann was not a Hasid. In his own special way, though, he was a mystic, and when he was so overcome by the power of prayer that he began to dance, which in view of his corpulence must have been a grotesque sight, he expe-rienced the *Shekinah*, the living presence of God. But he also had a practical side, and that was a blessing for my grandparents as for many others: he looked after the *cheder*, the *mikve*, and the entire conglomeration of kosher butchers, smoked meat producers and bakeries that belonged to the Schiff Schul complex, and after his death an entire organization, the Adass Jisroel, had to be founded to take over these tasks. If there was really a secret connection between Ledermann and one of the great legendary rabbis of the east, then I'd be more likely to guess it was with his namesake, Rabbi Chaim Ben-Gurion, of whom it is said that God gave him the gift of speaking with every petitioner in his own language. In any case, after Josef had introduced himself in broken German, Ledermann answered him in fluent Hungarian. He knew that there were still many petitioners in the waiting-room, but he took his time. How was Rabbi Kálman, from whom Josef brought greetings? Was little Ruben still so hard-working? Did Sidonie run a kosher household? "She does her best," said Josef, and my grandmother blushed. But the rabbi liked the pretty young woman who had come to Vienna because she wanted "the best for the children." So they needed a place to stay for themselves and the four children? They were to come back again in two days and bring the children with them.

When they called on the rabbi two days later, he seated the two boys on his desk and asked them if they knew the evening prayer. Jenö rattled it off: "*Eli melach hoaulom . . .*" Then Ledermann clumsily wrote an address in the Roman alphabet, from which it was evident that he preferred to write in Hebrew. He had found an apartment for the Kahns in the home of Ruthenian Jews who lived on a small street, Malzgasse, not far from Untere Augartenstrasse, where for the past six years the horse-drawn streetcar had gone from the bridge over the Danube Canal to Augarten Park.

They lived in close quarters on Malzgasse, almost as close as in those days in Tapolca before the Kahns had rented the upper storey. But the Ruthenians – their name was Horowitz, and they had a small business that sold wood, coal and coke – were friendly and helpful and took care of selling the horse. The cart could be

45

converted without much effort into a vegetable stand, and Sidonie found a place at the Naschmarkt, the large open-air market not far from the centre of the city. With the help of Baruch Horowitz, who knew people everywhere in the neighbourhood because of his coke business, Josef soon found a small store in the vicinity of the Schiff Schul whose rent he could afford. The next step proved to be more difficult: the trading licences had to be obtained. So while their children played with the Ruthenians' children in the backyard, my grandparents went up Untere Augartenstrasse and over the bridge to the police station in Rossauer Lände, which at that time was still called Elisabeth Promenade. "You know enough German to deal with this," Sidonie said to her husband unsuspectingly.

At the police station they were questioned at length, had to show their identification, and were then permitted to buy big forms for a few kreuzers. After Baruch had helped them fill out the forms, they took them to the Licence Office on Babenberger-strasse. In glorious spring weather, they went along the Ring, mar-velled at the university, the city hall and the two museums, and finally arrived, full of hope and cheerful, at the high double door that had been described to them in the police station. In front of the door stood a man in multi-coloured livery whom Eichendorff would have described as "as broad and magnificent as a puffed-up turkey." Josef explained the purpose of their visit to him, mention-ing only the shoemaker's workshop, since he was afraid to mention *two* trading licences. The turkey squinted at him with a friendli-ness as bright as the spring weather and said: "What d'ya want? Ya wanna licence? Come on, ya won't be gettin' a licence fer a shoe-maker's workshop now in all of Vienna."

However, the turkey was no cannibal (turkeys usually aren't), took pity on them and told the Kahns the way to the "appropri-ate" room. There they waited for a while, were once again ques-tioned at length, had to show their identification, were finally permitted to present the filled-out forms – and they were missing one document. On the way back, my grandparents, who didn't want to go back the same way, got lost in the Inner City, but finally did manage to arrive at the office in Rossauer Lände before closing time. After they once again had to wait, the police officer to whom they told their troubles clicked his tongue for some unknown reason, and expressed his regret that he could not issue the document, his colleague on Babenbergerstrasse was the person to see for that. Therefore, my grandparents went through the Inner City again the next morning, marvelled at the St. Stephen's Cathedral and received a friendly greeting from the liveried turkey standing before the double door. The Licence Office, though, he then said, was closed to the public on Tuesdays and Thursdays.

The next morning, for variety, my grandparents went along the Ring again (thank God it wasn't as far as from Tapolca to Vienna), but on Babenbergerstrasse it turned out that the officer on duty there was responsible for filling out the missing printed form, but the form itself could only be obtained in Rossauer Lände. There, the friendly police officer, in whose waiting-room they had to wait as long as in Ledermann's, clicked his tongue and sent them to the nearest tobacco shop, to one of those stores in Austria where, since the selling of tobacco is a state monopoly, you can also buy postage stamps, excise stamps and forms, and whose owners usually regret nothing so much as not having a waiting-room where they could let their customers wait. In addition to the form, Josef bought a cheap cigar that the tobacconist cut for him with a palm-sized guillotine that was screwed to the counter. When my grandparents, on the second morning after that – because on Thursdays it was not open to the public – after an unusually long waiting time were allowed into the office on Babenbergerstrasse, it was the wrong form, and then it was Whitsun holiday and all offices were closed for a week. They were in a real predicament; because since my grandparents had left Tapolca, they hadn't had any income, and the small amount of money they had got for the horse was as good as gone. What should they do?

"Before the law stands a doorkeeper. To this doorkeeper comes a man from the country and requests admittance to the law," it says in Franz Kafka's famous parable. Kafka was six years old when my grandparents arrived in Vienna, and they wouldn't have read him even if he had been one of the Viennese celebrities, as his friend Max Brod later was. But my grandparents would have understood the "man from the country" as a literal translation of the Hebrew "am-haaretz," which is also used in Yiddish and refers to a provincial, a man who doesn't know his way around, and in this man they would immediately have recognized a picture of themselves. I can't imagine, though, that my grandmother would have hauled a stool to Babenbergerstrasse and waited patiently outside the double door until the end of her days, as the man does in Kafka's parable. In order to do at least something, she went back to the tobacco shop where, as the tobacconist told her, the wrong form could not be taken back because it was "already written off" in the inventory; and since a Viennese tobacconist is half public servant and acts as if he were a full one, there is little point in arguing with him. (My Uncle Jenö, who was a specialist in this area, used to say "It takes two for a real quarrel: one who doesn't give in, and another who also doesn't give in.") Since the form had only cost five kreuzers, they could put up with the loss, but two weeks after Whitsun my grandparents had three wrong forms and no licence.

"We must bribe somebody," said Josef uneasily.

"I think so too," said Sidonie, "but how do you do that?"

"You put a banknote in between the forms," said my grandfather, who had procured a trading licence in Tapolca.

"How much?"

"I don't know, maybe we should ask Horowitz."

So they went to the Ruthenian and gave him a detailed account of the whole story, although he was already familiar with some of it.

"Did the policeman really click his tongue?" asked Horowitz.

"He certainly did," said my grandmother.

"Five kronen may be the right amount. I don't know, though, to whom you would have to give them, to the goy in Rossauer Lände or the goy in Babenbergerstrasse."

"I hope not to both," said my grandmother, for whom five kronen was a huge sum of money.

"We can't know that," said Horowitz. "Maybe they both take bribes, then everything's fine, but if you're unlucky, they'll both be honest. . . . That can turn into a nasty business, it's strictly forbidden to bribe officials, you must not try it with the wrong one. Maybe you should get a lawyer."

My grandmother must have told the story to her children, and my Uncle Dezsö loved to retell it on *erev Shabbos*, when the family sat at the big table that was extended to its full length. He showed us how the police officer had clicked his tongue, and when he quoted Horowitz's remark, "if you're unlucky, they'll both be honest," he shook with laughter. But that was thirty years later. In 1889 it was no laughing matter for my grandparents, because where should they get the money for a lawyer? They didn't even have enough money to rent the workshop where Josef wasn't allowed to work. They discussed it for a long time, and finally Horowitz said: "Rabbi Ledermann found living quarters for you, maybe he can help you now too."

Even the best rabbi is not all-powerful. It is said of the *baal-shem-tov* that through the power of his prayer he was able to ensure that the Jews murdered in the Chisinau pogrom would only have to spend an hour in hell. (They later said that when compared to the agonies of hell, their suffering during the pogrom was as light as a garlic skin.) The rabbi could not ensure by his prayer that the Jews of Chisinau were not murdered. But although rabbis are not all-powerful, they are powerful.

(The *bochers* of the great Polish rabbis from the time of the Hasidic revivalist movement met now and then in Warsaw or Lodz to have learned conversations, but spent a fair amount of time boasting about the miracles performed by their masters and arguing about which of the latter was the most powerful. Says the *bocher* of the rabbi of Warsaw: "My rabbi is the greatest of all. I will tell you a story. I was travelling with my rabbi in an open carriage from Lodz to Warsaw, and suddenly I see it starting to rain. Rabbi, say I, what should we do? We're ten versts from Warsaw, we'll get soaked to the skin. Says the rabbi, don't worry, and he said a *broche*, and there was rain to the right and rain to the left, but where we were, there was no rain at all." Says the *bocher* of the rabbi of Lodz: "That's nothing, I will tell you a story. I was travelling with my rabbi from Lodz to Warsaw, it was a Friday, and suddenly I see the first star in the sky. Rabbi, say I, what should we do? We're ten versts from Warsaw, and now the *Shabbos* has begun, we must not travel anymore, we will have to spend the night on the open road. Says the rabbi, don't worry, and he said a *broche*, and it was *Shabbos* to the right and *Shabbos* to the left, but where we were it was no *Shabbos* at all. . . ." Chaim Ledermann couldn't turn a Saturday into a Friday, but he was powerful.)

My grandparents had to wait a long time. (My Uncle Jenö would have said, our ancestors had to wait forty years for entry into Canaan, and that in a desert. So why not two hours in a comfortable room for admittance to Ledermann?) When they were finally admitted and told the rabbi their tale of woe, he listened patiently and asked a few questions. "I don't really know," he said at last, and then added: "Go home, children, something will occur to me."

Three days later a well-dressed young man appeared in Horowitz's store and asked for Josef Kahn. He was from the chamber of commerce, he explained to Josef, Rabbi Ledermann had sent him, he had already made enquiries. With his uncovered head and his clean-shaven face, the young man didn't look as if he belonged to Ledermann's congregation, but he seemed to know what he was doing. He went with Josef and Sidonie to the Rossauer Lände, from there to the tobacco shop, back to the police, where the new forms they had bought at the tobacconist's were stamped so many times that it seemed as if they were founding the United Nations, and to the Licence Office in Babenbergerstrasse. Since they had to wait everywhere, it took the whole day, but when they arrived in the late afternoon at the building guarded by the turkey, a miracle happened: they were admitted to the mysterious man whom the officials called the "Chef" (to Josef's amazement, because he had always thought a chef was a cook in a big hotel). He cast a fleeting glance at the papers – there was a small mountain of them now – signed one of them, and then everything went like clockwork. From the "Chef's" room they went to the tobacco store (not to the one in Rossauer Lände, where Josef had bought the wrong forms, but to another one in the vicinity of Babenbergerstrasse), from there back to the Licence Office where the turkey was just locking the entrance but did let them in and to a minor official on the top floor where, strangely enough, the three of them (Sidonie and Josef hadn't opened their mouths all day) were admitted immediately. Then excise stamps were stuck on, and a messenger, accompanied by my grandparents and the young man, who apparently were no longer allowed to touch these sacred objects, carried the mountain of paper back to the "Chef." He signed his name again and gave the forms to another official to stamp, for in a well-organized office in Austria the man who is allowed to sign doesn't stamp, and the man who is allowed to stamp doesn't sign. Then the "Chef" said: "Well, you will receive the trading licences by registered mail."

When the three had left the building, my grandmother was overjoyed, but asked a little apprehensively: "What did that cost?"

"Why?" asked the young man.

"I mean," said my grandmother, who wanted the best for her children and had therefore decided to learn as quickly as possible how to deal with Austrian officials, "whom did you bribe?"

"What are you thinking of?" said the young man with the justified pride of a man who has climbed Mount Everest. "You just have to know how to talk to these people. And now with all these wrong forms you can paper your living room – if you have one."

CHAPTER TWO

Gisa

1.

"MAY I JOIN YOU for a minute, Miss? I'm Emanuel Ginsberg."

The young "Miss" was sitting at one of the small marble tables next to the big windows in Café Ginsberg that looked out on the south side of the Karmelitermarkt, the large open-air market north of the city centre. She was seventeen, approximately the same age her mother had been when she had fallen in love with Josef, and she took after her mother: she had the same high forehead and energetic mouth, combined with the finely chiselled nose of her father. With her dark eyes and wavy black hair she was what the English used to call an "Israelite beauty."

"Certainly," she answered self-confidently and neutrally, neither declining nor inviting his advance.

Emanuel Ginsberg was in his mid-fifties, with greying hair and a small, trimmed beard. In addition to the café that bore his name, he also owned Café Schubert on the Opernplatz, which brought in much more money, but he had bought that exclusive café just recently and didn't feel as comfortable there as at the Karmelitermarkt. Café Ginsberg had a regular clientele of Jews and Christians, merchants and workmen, the people shopping at the Karmelitermarkt and the shopkeepers themselves, on whose account the café opened at six a.m. Ginsberg knew most of them by name.

"The view is not the best," said Ginsberg, after he had sat down with the young lady, "but a good café, like a studio, must have a northern exposure so that the guests have good light for reading newspapers without the sun shining in their faces."

Gisa looked across the wide, unevenly paved street at the market; at the stall across the street a young man, his big hands chapped red from the cold, took a fish from the ice and began to fillet it. "I have nothing against the view, there's always something going on outside," she said.

"Fish and vegetables and second-hand clothing," said Ginsberg. "Have you ever been in a studio? Young Klimt sometimes drinks his coffee here."

Gisa didn't know who Klimt was, whose secession from the Association of Austrian Artists in the spring had caused a sensation among the initiated, so she said nothing.

"You sew for Löwy, Miss?"

"Sometimes I do, Mr. Ginsberg. But how do you know that?"

"A good host takes an interest in his guests. But isn't that work too hard for such delicate hands?"

An attentive listener would have noticed a few discrepancies in his remarks. Ginsberg wasn't just a "host" but the owner of the café, and a cafétier who "takes an interest in his guests" is usually not competent, but rather a comic figure. Sewing is not hard work, and Gisa's hands weren't delicate, they were the broad, powerful hands of her mother, who could take hold of something and not easily let go again, once she had grasped it. As well, he hadn't actually answered her question, and the "minute" he had asked for had long since passed.

"You must excuse me, Mr. Ginsberg," said Gisa. "I have to go home. Otherwise my parents will start to worry about me."

"The coffee is on the house, with your permission, Miss Kahn," said Ginsberg, so he also knew her name. "Do bring your esteemed parents with you the next time, so they can see for themselves that you're in good hands at Café Ginsberg!"

As it seemed to my grandparents in retrospect, their first nine years in Vienna had gone very quickly. Chaim Ledermann had sent Josef some business, and although his little workshop did no better than in Tapolca, it did no worse. He still had his sole leather sent to him from Isak Lövy in Pest. Things had been more difficult for Sidonie. In Tapolca, the farmers had usually brought her the fruit and vegetables, and when she went to them as a buyer, it was up to her when she went. In Vienna, she had to be at the farmers' market at six a.m.; and although she now had two carts, the big one with its permanent place at the *Naschmarkt* and a little one for transporting her wares, she would not have been able to manage if Josef hadn't helped her before he began to hammer and sew. Fortunately, she didn't get pregnant during their first three years in Vienna, and then Mother Horowitz took care of the children while my grandmother served her customers at the market. When my mother was born in 1893 – with the typical patriotism of the Hapsburg Jews, they named her after the Empress Elisabeth – the vegetable cart had stood empty for a few months and some of the customers had gone elsewhere.

They were poor and not poor: there was enough to eat, it was always warm in their apartment, even in the most bitterly cold winters (Horowitz gave them a discount on the wood and coal), but my grandparents could still barely pay their bills. "We might just as well have stayed in Tapolca," said Josef sometimes, but Sidonie disagreed. When she went through the better parts of the city after the day's work, she would often stand in front of a particularly elegant store and say to herself, Jenö will have a store like this, or, Dezsö will buy that store some day. The world was there to be conquered by her children. In the meantime, they had a happy childhood. . . .

In the literature on Kafka, which has been focusing recently on Kafka as a Jew, you can sometimes read that the Jews of the Hapsburg Monarchy in Kafka's time (that is, when there still were Jews in the Monarchy) led a "pariah existence." That is, at the least, inaccurate. I really do know someone who grew up on

Landstrasse, in the third district of Vienna, where because he was a Jew, he was maltreated by the teachers and beaten up by kids at school. But it was different in Leopoldstadt. Of course, there was always an anti-Semitic demonstration somewhere. There were inflammatory speeches in parliament and during election campaigns, there were fights at the university; but that didn't affect the children, and the parents who read about it in the newspapers shrugged their shoulders: it had been worse in Hungary. My grandmother had become a close friend of Mother Horowitz and was happy on Malzgasse. The fact that the Ruthenians were devout Jews who observed the rituals made them all the more appealing, and the yearly sequence of religious holidays, whose rites my grandparents now followed more closely under the influence of their landlords than they had in Tapolca, brought variety and gave the year a pleasant rhythm, especially since Miriam Horowitz taught her friend how to prepare the traditional dishes for the feast days.

The religious year began on the first day of the month of Tishri, in September, with the New Year's celebration, Rosh Hashanah, which we called "Rascheschone" (as I still to this day pronounce the name, to the dismay of my son, who loves to correct my Hebrew). For the main course, there was *tsimmes*, made of brisket of beef, carrots and other ingredients, sweetened with honey, and for dessert there was honey cake. Nine days later came Yom Kippur, the Day of Atonement, and both families fasted; Baruch and Josef spent the whole day at the Schiff Schul. Still in September or in the first days of October came Sukkot or Sukkos, as it is called in Yiddish, the series of holidays that commemorates the Hebrews' journey from Egypt to the Promised Land. In the few days between Yom Kippur and Sukkos, Baruch and Josef erected a tabernacle in the backyard, in which, after we had thanked God for freeing the Jews from slavery, we took our meals, and since Sukkos was also simultaneously a festival celebrating the fall harvest, Sidonie brought the *esroigim* from her stand, the traditional fruits with which to decorate the tabernacle. (If someone did something too late, so that it was of no use anymore, that was called the "*esroigim* after Sukkos.") In December we celebrated the revolt of the Maccabees, the menorah, the big candelabrum with seven branches, stood on the table and the children were allowed to light the festive candles with a small candle called the *shammes* or servant – one on the first day, two on the second, until finally on the last day of Chanukah all seven candles were lit. . . .

March brought Purim, the Feast of Lots, when we read the Book of Esther. The two families exchanged gifts, the women baked Haman-doughnuts filled with poppy seeds and honey, and the children wore fancy clothes. Finally, in April, the Exodus from Egypt was celebrated for the second time, more extensively; that was Passover, the most beautiful celebration for the children. Since the people of Israel had no time on their flight to bake proper bread, nothing leavened was allowed in the house, and all dishes that had ever come into contact with anything leavened had to be removed from the house. The women packed them in a large crate that Baruch hid somewhere, and Miriam and Sidonie brought the Passover pots and Passover porcelain up from the cellar. The festivities began with a large feast, the Seder, at which we prayed for a very long time, but there was also variety in the ritual. In memory of the bitter time of slavery in Egypt, we ate bitter herbs, our glasses were filled four times with red wine, and in front of Baruch, who conducted the Seder, there was an extra glass of wine for the prophet Elijah, and the door was left open in continual expectation of his showing up. The youngest of the boys, Dezsö, recited the "manishtaneh": "How does this night differ from all other nights? Every other night we eat leavened and unleavened food, on this night we eat only unleavened food. . . ." The children hunted for a hidden piece of matzo, and the child that found it got a present.

Baruch's sons went not only to the public school, but also to the *cheder* in the Schiff Schul, so that they could read Hebrew fluently; but Jenö and Dezsö had learned little more than the rudiments of the language, and the girls barely knew the alphabet, so they were terribly bored during the long prayers. After public school came vocational school – the school for workmen's children and the lower middle-class, after which, at age fourteen, you could be an apprentice, a handyman, or an errand-girl. No one thought of the academic high school, not even Sidonie. Jenö was brilliant, but spent a fair amount of his time inventing derisive nicknames for the teachers and his fellow students, and only worked hard when something interested him. Gisa, who was no less intelligent, helped with the housekeeping and had little time for school. When she was fourteen, Horowitz found a position for her as an unskilled worker in a blouse factory, where according to the new factory law put through by the Social Democrats, young people under the age of sixteen were to work "only" ten hours a day, or sixty hours a week. Gisa got up at five o'clock in the morning, took a basket in which her mother had packed her a lunch, and walked the long way to Brigittenau – the tramway didn't go there – and only got home again around five in the afternoon, exhausted and, when the weather was bad, soaked to the skin and freezing cold. My grandmother observed the child's misery for a while and then intervened: she had not come on foot from Tapolca to let the girl be ruined. So Gisa quit, but what was she to do then? In Leopoldstadt and in the first district of Vienna, she went from store to store, and wherever she suspected the owner might be Jewish, she asked for work. In nine stores out of ten, she was sent away by the sales ladies, and when she did get to see the manager, he didn't need a "young thing who knows nothing about the business." Hermann Löwy, who sold custom-made blouses and blouses from the rack on Nestroyplatz, actually didn't need a young thing either, but he felt sorry for the pretty girl who was visibly dejected after three weeks of looking for work, and since she had learned to use needle and thread and a sewing machine at the factory, he decided to take her on. What he paid her was just enough for her to buy herself a hot lunch every day in an inexpensive restaurant, but it didn't stay that way for long. Gisa wasn't just clever, she knew how to fit in, her pretty face helped, and three years later, although she still occasionally sewed a ribbon onto a blouse or let a hem out if no one else was available to do it, the seventeen-year-old was already Löwy's top sales lady, to the annoyance of her colleagues. On her way home across the Karmelitermarkt she could afford to buy herself a cup of coffee and on special occasions even a piece of cake. . . .

"How nice that you have come here again," said Ginsberg when he next saw her at her little table by one of the big windows. "You won't get better coffee and cake anywhere else!"

Gisa, who had sold two expensive silk blouses, was feeling generous. "Sit with me if you wish, Mr. Ginsberg."

He did so, and the waiter brought him a glass of sherry.

"You're from Hungary, aren't you, Miss Kahn? How long has your family been in Vienna?"

Since the evening sunlight was shining so beautifully on the Karmelitermarkt, and she wasn't in a hurry, she told him how they had come on foot from Tapolca. "But that's a long way for such delicate feet!" said Ginsberg, shaking his head. "Tell me about Tapolca, I'm familiar with Lake Balaton, but only the other side of it."

A good host takes an interest in his guests. Ginsberg spied on her, that is, he questioned the head waiter and the cashier, and when Gisa was sitting at her little table again a few days later, he asked about her family. While they were chatting, a young man wearing a dark blue velvet jacket and a beret à la Richard Wagner sat down at the next table. "But that's Klimt!" exclaimed Ginsberg. "I must introduce you."

Klimt cast a glance at Gisa, was taken with her and turned on the charm. For weeks, he had been looking for the right idea for the central figure in a painting he was working on, Miss Kahn was a gift from God, she would look lovely in a kimono with her hair pinned up and an amber-coloured comb in it, wouldn't she sit for him, the painting would cause a sensation. Ginsberg was delighted that Klimt shared his taste, but didn't trust the painter and quickly turned the conversation to other things.

In early summer, Mother Róth came to visit. In order to make the trip to Vienna possible, she had enlisted the help of their family doctor and invented a chest disease that had to be treated by a specialist in Vienna. (Back then there still were physicians who would really come to your home. Since there were no antibiotics, they couldn't do much to cure most illnesses, but one good family doctor was worth two psychiatrists.) Mother Róth brought life into their house: specialists are expensive, and she had money in her purse. The family rode up the Kahlenberg and then the Leopoldsberg, to Grinzing and Mödling, ate Sachertorte at Sacher's, the most expensive restaurant in Vienna, ate chocolate cake with rum topped with plenty of whipped cream at the Cobenzl, and cream slices at Demel's, the most prestigious confectionery. Gisa's visits at the café at the Karmelitermarkt ended, and when Mother Róth travelled home cured after two months and Gisa returned to her former routine, Ginsberg had made a desperate decision.

"How lovely to see you here again, Miss Kahn! Your esteemed grandmother has probably returned to Hungary?"

"Yes, unfortunately," said Gisa, leaving the impression that she hadn't much missed the visits in Café Ginsberg. But Ginsberg didn't let himself be bothered by that consideration.

"You have come at just the right moment. You won't believe what came in the mail this morning. Richard Heuberger sent me two tickets to the Opera Ball!"

That wasn't true. Ginsberg was acquainted with Heuberger, who frequented the Café Schubert, but the composer, who had finally had his breakthrough with his new operetta after four operas had quickly disappeared from the programme, was fully enjoying his new-found fame and had better things to do than send Ginsberg complementary tickets.

"That was nice of him!"

"Yes it was," said Ginsberg, "but I don't like to go to the opera alone, and what should I do with two tickets? You would do me a great favour if you came with me, Miss Kahn!"

Gisa still didn't exactly know who Klimt was, but she'd seen posters with big lettering everywhere for the Opera Ball. Anyway, she had got used to going out and didn't want to spend every evening at home again.

"I don't have an evening gown," she said, after thinking it over briefly.

"You look like a princess in every dress," said Ginsberg beaming.

In order to go to the Opera Ball with Ginsberg, Gisa had to get her parents' permission. "Ginsberg?" said my grandmother, who sometimes bought fish or meat at the Karmelitermarkt. "But Gisa, he's old enough to be your father!"

"He could be your grandfather," said Josef, backing up his wife.

"I'd like to go to the opera sometime with my grandfather," said Gisa. "By the way, he's nice and modest and doesn't want anything from me."

"That remains to be seen," said Sidonie. "In any case, you can't go alone with him. Take Jenö along, he should see something new too now and then."

It goes without saying that Ginsberg received this information with mixed feelings; because he had been looking forward to spending an evening alone with Gisa; also, he was sure the boy didn't have a decent suit, so it was questionable whether he would be allowed in; but third, Ginsberg didn't have any tickets, the operetta was sold out, and now he was supposed to get three seats right away! But a good cafétier is very resourceful. He spoke with the head waiter in Café Schubert, and back then, head waiters were almost as powerful as rabbis. The waiter arranged for the cafétier to have Count Festetic's box, since the Count was away at his estate in Hungary. After lengthy deliberations, Ginsberg decided not to wear tails, but rather his most fashionable dinner jacket, and hoped for the best. Jenö came, as expected, in short trousers, but since people took him and Gisa for Ginsberg's children and Ginsberg gave the usher twice the usual amount for a tip, no one made a fuss.

In the intermission, Ginsberg and his guests walked around the foyer looking at the other people's evening gowns (not entirely without envy on Gisa's part); Jenö liked the long dresses but thought that the men in tails looked like waiters. Ginsberg had to explain the plot of the operetta to him, which wasn't easy, because the explanation was full of words like "domino" and "chambre séparée" that the boy had never heard before.

In the second intermission, Ginsberg and Gisa drank champagne and ate little salmon sandwiches; Jenö got a big piece of cake and was allowed to sip from Gisa's glass.

While Ginsberg brought his guests home in a coach, he had a brilliant idea. The next morning he bought a suit with long trousers for Jenö and had a porter deliver it to Malzgasse. Of course the suit didn't fit and had to be exchanged, but it wasn't without effect on my grandmother: as long as Jenö was included, she made no further protest when Gisa wanted to go out with Ginsberg, and thus began weeks of undreamt-of pleasures for Jenö. He ate roast veal at Ross's (perhaps, Ginsberg thought, their mother might prefer him to take her children to a kosher restaurant), and when the Orpheum Society made a guest appearance in Vienna, the three of them saw a Yiddish play that had many members in the audience in tears in the third act before it all ended well. When they went to the Krone Circus, Ginsberg took Dezsö along with them too. Then came the day – they were in the Prater, the large public park in Vienna's second district, and on the main avenue the chestnuts were already falling from the trees – when Ginsberg took heart, while he was waiting with Gisa for Jenö, who was on the merry-go-round. "You know that I love you," he said suddenly.

"Yes," said Gisa and registered silently that that was the first time someone had declared his love to her; she thought it was high time.

"I'm old enough to be your father," said Ginsberg, "but you know that I'll cherish you." And since Gisa didn't say anything, and nothing better occurred to him, he added: "We can afford to have a villa in Pressbaum."

"Yes," said Gisa, who didn't know where Pressbaum was.

"May I talk with your parents?"

"I don't know."

If a diplomat says yes, he means maybe; if he says maybe, he means no; if he says no, he's not a diplomat. If a lady says no, she means maybe; if she says maybe, she means yes; if she says yes, she's not a lady. But Gisa really didn't know what she should say. The merry-go-round's organ was playing the overture to *Freischütz*.

The conversation with my grandparents was not easy to arrange, because Ginsberg didn't want Gisa to be present; that sort of thing was much more difficult before there were telephones. When the day came, he proceeded as if he were taking out a loan. A childless widower, Café Ginsberg and Café Schubert, two rental properties in the third district, he would (we've heard this already) cherish Gisa. My grandfather said nothing, my grandmother didn't say much, and when Ginsberg had run out of clichés and left, nothing was decided.

"Do you know that Ginsberg was here?" asked my grandmother when Gisa came home.

"No, Mama."

"But you can imagine what he wanted?"

"I can imagine it," said Gisa and looked out of the only window in the room into the dismal inner courtyard.

"You're not going to tell me that you love him," said my grandmother.

"He's old enough to be your grandfather," said Josef.

"You're exaggerating, Papa. By the way, he's nice and modest, and I don't want to spend the rest of my life sewing blouses."

"You don't sew blouses, you sell them. I won't allow it, we aren't that badly off. Just yesterday Baron Pollak ordered a pair of patent leather shoes from me."

The Baron's father had bought his title in 1863 and had gone bankrupt ten years later when the stock market crashed, which didn't prevent the son from living high on the hog. On principle, he wore only shirts that had a small crown embroidered on them.

"Pollak likes to wear patent leather shoes," said Sidonie, "but he doesn't pay his bills. Gisa should make up her own mind."

In early November, after consulting with Klimt and a jeweller, Ginsberg had an engagement ring made that consisted of a large solitaire diamond in an art nouveau setting that looked as if it could, in an emergency, be used as a screwdriver. At the end of the month, they celebrated their engagement in the banquet hall of Café Schubert. Mother Róth came and brought presents, her husband stayed home and nursed his grudge. A real estate agent who had properties in Pressbaum sent orchids. At the insistence of my grandmother, the wedding was not to take place until early summer – her own wedding had gone ahead hastily enough – and Gisa kept on working at Löwy's, despite Ginsberg's objection. But on her way home, she regularly drank her coffee with her fiancé in the café at the Karmelitermarkt, and she let him take her to the opera and the suburban theatres, with Jenö often continuing to come along. In early March, with the help of a small sum that Mother Róth had diverted from the housekeeping money, she went to Tapolca for two weeks and stayed with Gyula Kálman. A month after her return, when Ginsberg once again came out of his office in the late afternoon to have coffee with Gisa, as he did now almost daily, she was sitting as usual at the little table with the northern exposure from where you could look out over the cobblestones at the south side of the Karmelitermarkt, but sitting beside her was a young man whose strikingly big hands were chapped red.

2.

The Rabbi of Tarnopol – not the famous one who travelled with the carriage and pair, but a relatively unimportant one, a later one – once took the train from Tarnopol to Warsaw and found himself alone in the coupé with a priest. The two men of God got to talking, and finally the priest asked: "Tell me, Colleague, have you ever eaten pork?"

"To tell the truth, yes," said the rabbi.

"Good, isn't it?" said the priest.

"Tell me, colleague," asked the rabbi, "have you ever slept with a girl?"

"To tell the truth, yes," said the priest.

"Better than pork, isn't it?" said the rabbi.

In my childhood years in Vienna I was richly blessed with uncles and aunts. There was Uncle Jenö and Uncle Dezsö, Aunt Gisa and Aunt Klara, their respective wives and husbands, my father's two sisters and my stepfather's two sisters, my cousin Martin, whom I called Uncle because he was so much older than I was, and finally the "Hungarian clan," the Róths, the Kálmans, my grandfather's nephews and nieces – in short, an entire Honvéd regiment that I've always had the greatest difficulty keeping straight in my head; because the second uncle of a second cousin was, of course, considered to be my uncle. Among those relatives I found less interesting back then was my Uncle Jakob Pinsker, a taciturn man who, in contrast to my other uncles and aunts, did not work for a living. In 1938, his younger daughter brought him to Holland. After the German occupation, he went underground disguised as a farmer and never said a word on his evening walks through the village, so he wouldn't be recognized as a foreigner and a Jew, and in this way he survived the war. When he was eighteen, he wasn't unusually taciturn, and when something was important to him, he could even display a primitive, but not entirely ineffective persuasiveness.

Pinsker observed the kosher food laws back then, but there was another law he didn't take too seriously: he had a thing with girls. The Pentateuch has a drastic punishment for that. If it were taken seriously, there wouldn't be enough stones in the entire world. But I am (and not just because I'm sitting in a glass house) opposed to judging young men like Pinsker harshly. For some of them, it's like an illness. I can understand that Sophocles, when he

65

became impotent in his late seventies, gave thanks to the gods that he was finally rid of that demon.

Pinsker was by no means a Sophocles, but sometimes all he needed was to cast a glance at a girl strolling across the Karmelitermarkt and he'd go out of his mind. Then it could happen that he would cut his finger while filleting a carp (he sold fish at the market), or when someone bought two fish, he couldn't add up the kreuzers. (When I was twenty, to my delight and torment, short skirts were in style. Pinsker could consider himself lucky that that wasn't yet the fashion in 1899, or he would have landed in an insane asylum.) It's not surprising that Gisa caught his eye when she passed his fish stand on her way to the Café, and not even the stupidest person would have failed to notice that she was something special (ten years later she had the reputation of being one of the most beautiful women in Vienna). In this regard, Pinsker wasn't stupid, quite the opposite: he was, if you'll pardon the metaphor, in this regard both a gourmand and a gourmet, and he kept an eye on Café Ginsberg. When she left the Café and Pinsker could manage to get away from his stand (he was merely an employee there, so it was of no consequence to him if he sold one less carp because he'd been away for a short while), he ambled along after her.

Ambling along after a girl was a popular pastime back then in Vienna. Naturally, the girl noticed it (as she was supposed to), and if she wanted to be spoken to, she stopped in front of a store window. If she didn't want to be spoken to and went past an attractive store window, then there was an emotional conflict. Gisa was spared the conflict; because she didn't want to be spoken to, but also there weren't any attractive store windows between the Karmelitermarkt and the Malzgasse. She didn't stop, and Pinsker didn't speak to her.

When the winter began and Gisa was already wearing a coat instead of her woollen jacket, Pinsker had reached the point where he could think of nothing else but the girl in bed (or behind a bush in the Prater, although the weather wasn't conducive to that anymore). He tossed and turned all night long, unable to sleep, and neglected his girlfriends. When Gisa suddenly disappeared (those were the fourteen days she spent at Gyula Kálman's in Tapolca), he prowled around Löwy's store whenever he could leave the stand for a quarter of an hour and searched every side street between the market and Malzgasse. When she returned, he made up his mind to act. When she crossed the Karmelitermarkt again, heading for Café Ginsberg, he blocked her path, stretched out his hand and said: "Haven't you lost a button, Miss Kahn?" On his chapped red hand lay the large, blue button from a ladies' coat.

It didn't take a genius to think that up. The trick existed long before there were buttons. Maybe even Hermann the Cheruscan accosted pretty girls with a little silver bracelet in his hand when he was young.

"Don't be silly," said Gisa, and wondered how he knew her name.

"But it is possible that you've lost a button!"

"I sew my buttons on securely."

"I'll gladly believe that, it's your job."

"How do you know that?" asked Gisa, without noticing that she was quoting herself.

"I made inquiries."

"That's outrageous!"

"I just wanted to know," said Pinsker. "But are you sure it's not your button?"

"You're really talking nonsense!"

"I'm sorry, but if you come for a little walk with me, I'm sure I'll think of something smarter."

Gisa stood still and didn't say anything, and Pinsker, who was standing firmly with his legs apart between her and the entrance through which she could escape into the café, felt encouraged. He gently but possessively put his hand around her shoulder and led her the few steps back to his stand.

"If that's really not your button, then I have something better for you, Miss Kahn." He took a carp from the ice, wrapped it with a quick twist in newspaper and pressed it into her hands.

Gisa was momentarily at a loss as to what to do: she couldn't go into the Café with a fish in her hands! But she was more amused than annoyed, and Pinsker, who was grinning from ear to ear, looked as harmless as a lamb with his uncombed long hair. "You know what," she said at last, "put the fish on ice for me, I'll pick it up later."

"At your service," said Pinsker gallantly and gazed triumphantly after her as she now at last crossed the Marktgasse and disappeared into Café Ginsberg.

He'd made a start. To be sure, Gisa did not pick up the fish, although, God knows, the Kahns could not afford a carp every Friday evening. She even made a little detour on the way from Nestroyplatz to Café Ginsberg, so that she didn't have to pass the fish stand. But Pinsker could keep an eye on the Café even while he was serving customers, and before a week had passed he was once again standing beside her on the cobblestones of the Karmelitergasse. "You didn't keep your word, Miss Kahn," he said simply.

"What do you mean?"

"The carp!" he said. "The carp that I kept fresh for you in a mountain of ice. What did I say, a mountain? A Mount Everest!"

Gisa laughed, although it made her shudder to think that a week had passed since then.

"Then what did you do with the fish?"

"A business secret. But you have to make it up to me. How about a walk in the Prater?"

Gisa thought of the conversation by the merry-go-round, and it occurred to her that she had been bored with Ginsberg in the Prater. He hadn't wanted to go to the shooting gallery, that wasn't refined enough for a man who associated with Klimt and Heuberger, and only Jenö had ridden the merry-go-round. "I have a date in Café Ginsberg," she said at last.

"Ordered fish must be picked up, and dates must be kept," said Pinsker sternly. "But you have Sunday free, don't you?"

"I'm engaged," said Gisa and blushed. She discovered to her consternation that she would be embarrassed to admit she was engaged to a man who was old enough to be her father.

"Being engaged doesn't hurt," said Pinsker. "You can still go to the Prater when you're engaged. We'll go to the Punch and Judy show and ride on the merry-go-round. If I get good tips, there'll be enough money for the Ferris wheel, and if we're lucky, there'll be fireworks. I'll wait for you by my stand on Sunday at two, like an ordered fish."

There was enough money. Admittedly, they didn't ride on the merry-go-round, but they did go to the shooting gallery, and even though Gisa missed the mark "by a mile," as Pinsker said, she nevertheless won a Teddy Bear. Their car on the giant ferris wheel, which was still gleaming new, rose slowly to the height of the tree tops, stopped there a little while and climbed higher. St. Stephen's Cathedral rose up over the sea of houses, the Danube streamed through the bed that had been dug for it twenty years before, the Vienna Woods glistened in the sun peeking out from between the clouds, and when they looked straight down, they felt slightly dizzy: the people on the square below looked as small as dolls. Gisa, of course, had the window seat, and when Pinsker leaned forward to see better, he put his hand on her knee. Then they walked along to the Third Coffee House, where they could hardly find a place to sit, and they sat there for a while pressed closely together over a stein of beer. On their way back along the main avenue to the Praterstern, where there were already electric streetcars, they walked silently side by side because nothing else occurred to Pinsker, and Gisa was worried. All that really wasn't proper for a bride, she had had to tell her mother a lie, and now she would have to invent new lies.

Before falling asleep, she tried to think of the villa in Pressburg that Ginsberg wanted to build, and felt Pinsker's broad hand on her knee.

The next Sunday – once again, Gisa hadn't been able to say no to him – in the late afternoon, for ten kreuzers each, they took

the bus that two draught horses pulled along Lainzerstrasse. They
went to Schwenders' "Neue Welt," a popular outdoor restaurant
with a famous view, and in the twilight of the big guest garden,
with red, green and yellow lanterns shining everywhere between
the trees, he suddenly took her into his arms.

Her first love! Gisa actually hadn't experienced love before,
in the exact sense of the word. She liked Ginsberg, who touched
her gently with his fingertips as if she were a fragile ornament. She
knew he was in love with her. She trusted him, and with good reason. She was too clever to let herself be very impressed by his fine
talk of Klimt and Heuberger, the Secession and the scandals in
the Opera, but she knew that in his own way he was a man of the
world who had done well and would take care of her. She could
contentedly envision how she would run the household for him
and how she, as a rich woman, would help her parents and would
make it easier for her brothers to get ahead in the world. But did
she really like Pinsker? In fact, she didn't like him. On the contrary: everything she possessed in the way of pride, self-respect
and hope for the future resisted this uncouth fellow whose aspira-
tions didn't go beyond the fish stand at the Karmelitermarkt. But
she was attracted to him. When she went out with him and had to
lie to Ginsberg and her parents, it seemed to her as if she were
treading on thin ice over dark water where (to quote Rilke, whose
name she'd never heard in her entire life) horrible things were
grinning at her.

Since I spend my life with dogs and read a lot about dog
breeding, I know to what extent all of us come programmed into
the world. A Labrador retriever retrieves things with passion; you
don't have to teach him how to do it, it's his purpose in life. A
young sheepdog with a good pedigree can manage a whole herd of
cattle and can learn in a few days how to drive a herd of sheep
into the fold, whereas a retriever just yaps and doesn't get the
sheep into line. Gisa was her mother's daughter. But my grandmother had been lucky – the young man with the blond Franz-
Joseph beard was a good and reliable person – she both loved and

liked him with his steadfast simplicity. With Pinsker it was different. Gisa didn't like him, and what she felt for him wasn't love (she didn't have the vocabulary to be able to put it in words), but rather sexual dependence; it was as if she had been infected with the addiction from which he suffered. She wasn't looking into a promising future, as her mother had back then in Tapolca. She was of two minds and was afraid, because while she didn't understand *how* he was slowly and pleasurably bending her into shape, she knew that he had power over her. When he wasn't around, she saw him as the lout that he was; when he touched her, she couldn't say no. One day he would go too far (she both feared and desired it), and then she would be entirely at his mercy. . . . Just how helpless she was became evident when he insisted one day on going into Café Ginsberg with her "for a little snack." (We already know that Ginsberg saw the two of them there; he withdrew discreetly, and the head waiter made sure they had to wait a long time for lukewarm coffee and stale pastry.) Ultimately, she (like Pinsker) couldn't get to sleep anymore at night, lost her appetite, was next to useless in Löwy's store, and when she came down with the flu and a high temperature kept her in bed, it was a relief for her. By the time her temperature was back to normal, my grandmother had decided that something had to be done.

3.

"It's time we had a talk, Gisa. What is wrong with you?"

"I had the flu, Mama. What else should be wrong with me?"

"Don't try to fool me, Gisa. You're going out with Pinsker?"

"I went for a walk with him in the Prater."

"And you lied to me. You don't get sick from going for a walk. Does he know that you're engaged?"

"I told him."

"And you weren't ashamed? Before him? Before Ginsberg? Before yourself?"

Gisa was crying.

"Bawling won't help," said my grandmother. "Did he make you pregnant?"

"I told you, I just went for a walk with him!"

"Then it's a very simple matter, you don't need to make such a fuss. You're simply not going for any more walks with him, you'll break it off, that's all. What do you want with that good-for-nothing who has his fingers in the till?"

Gisa was sobbing so much she could hardly speak. "I can't help it, Mama. I've tried to break it off, but I can't."

"Then I'll talk to him and tell him to leave you alone."

"That won't work, Mama. He won't listen to you."

"Then you'll have to go away for a while. I'll arrange for you to get away."

This was in keeping with the doctor's recommendation, who had suggested two weeks in the country to recover from the flu. They didn't have enough money for her to stay in a guest house at a holiday resort, but my grandfather had a brother who lived in a village near Keszthely. Gisa spent three weeks there, it rained, she sat in the old farmhouse, did some knitting and was bored. When she came back, nothing had changed, and when the walks with Pinsker began again, my grandmother was seized by a sort of panic, and the necessity of putting an end to the relationship became an *idée fixe* for her.

What followed now is difficult to reconstruct, at least for me. I had a long talk with my mother about it in London. She, of course, only knew everything from hearsay, but she understood it better than I did. "You didn't really know your grandmother," she said, "you were only eleven or twelve when she died. She was a clever woman, but when she had made up her mind to do something, there was no point in trying to talk her out of it. Later on, she *did* accept Jakob, but at first she couldn't stand him, she thought he was a good-for-nothing. Not that Gisa would have had to marry Ginsberg, that wasn't it, but she couldn't be allowed to marry Jakob, that seemed to my mother to be a horrible disaster, to be averted at any cost."

Sidonie had moved to Vienna because she wanted the best for the children, because she wanted them to work their way up in the world – and now Pinsker! She fought with Gisa, just as her mother had fought with her in Tapolca, but to no avail; the girl just got increasingly defiant and desperate. She lost weight, couldn't sleep, had a second bout of the flu, the family doctor shook his head and prescribed bed rest and camomile tea, but if they took their eyes off her for moment, she was out of the house. So there was only one solution, to get away from the Karmelitermarkt, away from Vienna. . . .

"Things can't go on like this with Gisa, Josef, we have to save the child, we're going back to Tapolca."

My grandfather, who was only partially in the know, thought he hadn't heard her properly. "You mean, we should visit my relatives? Now, when the weather is still so uncertain?" And when she explained to him what she had meant, it was as if she had hit him over the head. So they were supposed to give everything up again? Was it really such a disaster if Gisa went to the Prater with Pinsker? Shouldn't she amuse herself a little, wouldn't she still marry Ginsberg? She wasn't that stupid!

Josef put up a fierce fight, as never before in his life. He hadn't wanted to come to Vienna in the first place, this madness had been her idea, and now they were supposed to go back, just because that goose went for a walk in the Prater with a lout? He roared, he banged his fist down on the table, he swore as is only possible in Hungarian, he threw the boots he was working on at his wife's feet. He almost behaved as badly as Father Róth had, in bygone days. By midnight their argument had got so loud that Baruch Horowitz came into the room in his dressing gown and asked what the devil had got into them. A few minutes later, Miriam arrived as well, and then all three of them tried to dissuade my mother, which didn't make things any better. She was outvoted, and at one o'clock in the morning she made a concession: she would talk with the rabbi.

Josef and the Horowitz couple went to bed reassured, because it seemed obvious to them that Ledermann would talk her out of this nonsense. However, when my grandparents went to the rabbi the next morning, it turned out differently. My grandmother did the talking, while my grandfather remained stubbornly silent, as if to indicate that he had nothing to do with this crazy matter. Ledermann listened patiently, asked a few questions, and then looked at my mother for a long time. "What you intend to do," he said at last, "is completely unreasonable, but if you don't do it, you'll reproach yourself for the rest of your life. So go and do it!" (which proves that he really was a *tzaddick*: not only a just man, but also a wise man). Then he got up, kissed my grandmother on both cheeks and said to Josef: "You have a good and brave wife; be patient with her, and God will protect you."

Josef walked out of the Schiff Schul as if he had trouble waking up from a nightmare; he couldn't understand that the rabbi would support the "nonsense," although he had recognized it as such. Sidonie took him by the hand and led him like a child back to Malzgasse, but then went to work with frantic energy. She gave up her stand at the market and gave notice that they would move out of their apartment. She tried to collect what Josef's customers owed him, but that wasn't much. Finally it turned out that they were in the same situation they had been in before: they could have afforded the money for the train tickets, but the cost of moving their belongings was prohibitive. My grandmother acted as if that were a bagatelle: they had come to Vienna on foot and they could now walk to Tapolca – this time they even had the cart already! By now, Josef had completely capitulated, submitted to everything silently and did what Sidonie asked him to do. Horowitz got a horse for them, his wife packed baskets with bread, butter and cheese and put herrings from a large barrel into preserving jars. They left Josef's leather supplies and most of the furniture behind, to be sent for later, if they could ever afford to do so, but in the end, the cart was so overloaded again that you felt sorry for the horse.

It was not as it had been ten years before, and in many ways it was easier. The boys were big enough to help by now, and Klara could go on foot. The horse that Horowitz had got for them wasn't as pretty as the mare Mother Róth had stolen, but it was stronger. The weather was good for travelling, neither too cold nor too hot. . . . But back then my grandparents had been full of hope, convinced that a better future lay ahead of them, and now they were fleeing back to the grey little town they had come from. For Jenö and Dezsö it was still an adventure, and little Elisabeth, whom they always called Elli, squealed with delight when she was lifted up onto the tarpaulin; but Josef was angry with his wife and with Gisa, who traipsed behind, her eyes puffy from crying and feeling terribly guilty, and Sidonie regretted her decision before the sad little procession had even reached the suburbs.

At least they knew the way this time. It went up the Wienerberg, from the top of which they had seen the city for the first time, downhill to Liesing and then steeply uphill again to Rotneusiedl, and although they now had a stronger horse, they had to push and pull at two bends in the road. With squealing brakes, the cart then went down the hill to Petersbach, and a short distance past Ebreichsdorf they again spent a night in the hay. When they reached Ödenburg, the rabbi – it was the same one, but he didn't recognize them – again found lodging for them, but this time it was very modest. A few hours past Ödenburg, the forest began, the road got worse and the cart threatened to tip over; my grandfather carried Elli on his shoulders, Klara complained about sore feet. When they asked a farmer for a place to stay for the night, they were turned away: a Jew was a peddler and therefore a thief or a cattle dealer and therefore a cutthroat. When the children couldn't go any farther, Josef turned into a clearing and used the tarpaulin and the mattresses they had with them to make a place for them to sleep. In the early morning, they were awakened by the frost, and for breakfast they ate the last of their provisions. The children complained of being hungry and thirsty, and dogs growled at them as they passed the farmers' humble cottages; but late in the afternoon, an hour's distance before Janoshása, my grandmother swallowed her pride for the children's sake and showed Josef the way to the cattle dealer's who had done business with her father.

They stood for a long time in the paved courtyard that was teeming with chickens and geese before the old man came out and, shaking his head, learned that the young woman in the dusty, crumpled dress was Dezsö Róth's daughter. A servant unhitched the horse, and in the large oak-panelled living room, where a fire was burning in the hearth, Körmendi asked my grandmother what brought her here. Not wanting to expose Gisa, she made something up, and Körmendi, noticing her embarrassment, didn't insist on details. An hour later they were all washed and refreshed and sitting at the big table with its Moravian tablecloth, enjoying a bowl of diced carp in aspic. They stayed for two days, and finally Körmendi offered to have his coachman bring them to Tapolca in a hay wagon. Sidonie didn't let Josef answer and declined the offer. She hoped to be able to get to Tapolca from Janoshása in a day, but she had forgotten how bad the road was. The children had blisters on their feet, Elli and Klara were crying, my grandfather walked along silently and stubbornly beside the horse, leading it by the halter; they couldn't buy milk anywhere. In the early afternoon one of the wheels came loose, and Josef had to repair it by the roadside as best he could with his shoemaker's tools. They spent the night in Sümeg, all seven of them in a tiny room in the only inn. From there it wasn't much farther. Three hours later they were at the top of the last rise, then they walked between ploughed fields, the road took an abrupt turn to the left, and below them in the distance were the church spires of Tapolca. . . .

It was not the Promised Land they were returning to, but it was a familiar place where there were helpful relatives, where Mother Róth could visit them, where they hadn't lived so badly before. . . . Josef pulled the brake on gently as the road began to slope downward, the horse was almost trotting, an hour later there were houses on either side. They crossed the market square, turned into the Jewish quarter and went around the corner to Miklós Kálman's house. My grandfather was leading the horse by the reins, my grandmother was walking beside him and suddenly stopped dead in her tracks. Standing patiently in front of the house, his legs apart, wearing a dark suit and tie, was a young man with chapped red hands. He had taken the train.

4.

To the Rabbi of Tarnopol comes Jossel Bernstein. "You know, Rabbi, that I have only one room and seven children, a wife and a mother-in-law. The children scream and fight with each other, my wife sweeps up, my mother-in-law bakes braided loaves and screams at the children, and I'm supposed to read the Talmud in the same room. It's unbearable!"

"You have six hens in the yard," says the rabbi. "Take the hens into the room!"

Bernstein does so, and after a week he's back again. "It's unbearable," he says. "The children scream and fight with each other, my wife sweeps up, my mother-in-law screams at the children, I want to study the Talmud, and when I scratch my head, a hen alights on my hand."

"You have a goat in the yard," says the rabbi, "take it into the room."

A week later, Bernstein is back again. "I think I'm going *meshuga*," he says. "The children scream, my wife sweeps up, my mother-in-law screams at the children, when I scratch my head, a hen alights on my hand, the goat bleats and shits on the floor, and I'm supposed to study the Talmud!"

"You know something?" says the rabbi. "Throw the hens and the goat back out again, and you'll see how much room you have."

My grandparents and the children got cleaned up at the well behind Kálman's house and when they were rid of the dust from the journey, they went into the parlour for dinner. There was *Fogosh*, the famous Lake Balaton perch that was considered a special treat in Vienna, but didn't cost much in Tapolca back then. But my grandmother had no appetite for the fish: diagonally across from her sat Pinsker. In Miklós's house there were now, in addition to his own family, the seven Kahns and Pinsker, and when Gyula Kálman and his family came to visit after dinner, it was as crowded as in Jossel Bernstein's room. But Miklós wasn't bothered by it and didn't bring a goat into the room; he did what a rabbi is there to do: to mediate not only between God and man, but also between man and man. He spoke for a long time with Gisa and Josef – he had already spoken with Pinsker – and then took my grandmother into his study and told her the story of Isak Meier, who had an IOU from Major Pforzheim. Since the Major was insolvent, as always, he put a pistol to Isak Meier's chest when he was drunk and forced him to swallow the IOU. Meier chewed and chewed, and when he had swallowed the paper, he said: "Put the pistol away, Major. And the next time you write me an IOU, please write it on a sandwich."

Since my grandmother didn't see what the story had to do with her, he explained it to her.

"You should avoid what is avoidable, Sidi, and resign yourself to what is inevitable. Since Gisa has made up her mind to have Pinsker, let her. You married Josef although your father fought against it tooth and nail. Gisa is your daughter. And while we're talking about you – Josef was no prince either, and for all I can see, you're not sorry you married him. Look at your five children, may God protect you – and I really mean, all five."

"There's no comparison," said my grandmother. "There is no better man than my husband. Pinsker is a good-for-nothing, he has his fingers in the till, and if you think he's going to amount to anything, you can wait until *Jurigelt*."

"How do you know he has his fingers in the till? And what are you fussing about, he sells fish, you sell vegetables, what's the difference? Gisa's a clever child, she'll straighten him out. You mustn't think only of Gisa, you went to Vienna so that the boys would amount to something, have you forgotten that?"

My grandmother paced up and down the room, and Miklós gave her time. Finally, after a few minutes had passed, he continued.

"No one likes to give in, Sidi, you least of all, but think about Isak Meier. Should he have let himself be shot? You, too, will do what you have to – but make up your mind quickly. If you don't return immediately, Josef will lose his workshop, and you your stand. Or better yet: Josef can take the train back in the morning and take care of everything, and you and the children can stay and celebrate Passover with me, so that you won't have come to Tapolca for nothing. I've already looked at the schedule, a train leaves tomorrow morning at eight o'clock."

My grandmother had a silent battle with herself. Then she drew a deep breath and swallowed, although it was no sandwich. The next morning, Josef returned to Vienna, and the day after that, Mother Róth came to visit. With money she had diverted from the housekeeping funds, she bought train tickets for my grandmother and the children. Pinsker was assigned the task of taking the horse and cart back to Vienna. A journey on foot from Tapolca to Vienna didn't seem too high a price to him to be allowed to marry Gisa, and he managed it easily in four days.

5.

"How nice that you are back," said Ginsberg. "I've missed you. But you look tired, and you're getting more and more delicate. That suits you, but I worry about you."

Gisa was sitting in the Café at the Karmelitermarkt, at her usual little table by the window. She had let three days pass, because she was afraid of the conversation with Ginsberg that now had to take place, and in which she would have to hurt his feelings.

"You've been sickly for weeks," Ginsberg continued. "May I take you to my doctor?"

"A doctor can't help me, Emanuel." She looked down at the tabletop so she wouldn't have to see his worried face. "It's not working out with us, Emanuel. It's terrible for me to have to tell you this, but it doesn't work."

Ginsberg saw tears running down her cheeks. "Is it because of Jakob?" He had kept his eyes open since he'd seen Gisa sitting with Pinsker at the table, and he was aware that he was in his mid-fifties and she was eighteen.

"Not just because of him."

"I think you don't know what you're doing, Gisa. I can provide for you and your family too. You won't have much joy with Jakob."

"I know. A disaster has struck both of us, you and me, but we'll have to live with it. I don't like to hurt you, Emanuel, but there's no other way."

She took off the ring Klimt had designed and put it on the marble table between her coffee and his liqueur. "I have to give the ring back to you, Emanuel."

I should have a serious talk with her, thought Ginsberg, but he couldn't bring himself to reproach her or to boast about his money. The week before, he had already had the train tickets to Tapolca in his pocket, but then didn't go after all, because he couldn't bear the thought of forcing himself on her. He looked her in the face – she had raised her head and with moist eyes was looking at some undetermined spot in the distance – and a wave of tenderness flowed over him. She was just a child! And then he made the calculation: when she's thirty, I'll be almost seventy.

"What should I do with the ring, Gisa? Don't act too hastily, I'll give you time." But since she was shaking her head, he took a small silk handkerchief out of his vest, wrapped the ring in it, put it in her purse that was lying on the table and snapped it shut. "Come to me if you ever need help. I'll always be there for you."

Then he stood up and walked as quickly as he could back to his office.

A week later, Gisa went to Dorotheergasse and entered the famous pawn shop. The young man who served her took a long look at the ring, a long look at Gisa, and then placed the ring in a small box lined with black velvet. "I am sorry, but you'll have to wait a while. It isn't easy with such large gemstones. Please make yourself comfortable!"

Gisa sat down on the chair he had shown her before he disappeared through the double door at the back of the room. At first she waited patiently, then, since she hadn't been given a receipt for the ring, uneasily. Finally, an elderly gentleman in a well-tailored suit appeared behind the counter and beckoned to Gisa with a little bow. "The setting," he said, "is unfortunately only worth as much as the gold in it, but the stone is genuine. I can't weigh it without taking it out of the setting, but if you need that much money, we can lend you 5000 kronen for it."

That was more than Gisa's father earned in his shoemaker's workshop in five years.

To the best of my knowledge, the ring was redeemed again in the year 1905. Today, it's in Beverly Hills, California. Gisa's daughter, my Aunt Olga, who is much older than I am, but actually my cousin, showed it to me when I visited her in 1972. With those 5000 kronen, Gisa, who actually was my aunt, founded the firm Gisela Kahn; the founding of the firm took place before she married Pinsker. At first, it had half a dozen sewing machines and was located in a cellar in Brigittenau, where the rents were cheap – I only know that from hearsay. But I remember exactly her later, large, elegant store on the upper floor of a building on the Tuchlauben; it wasn't a drawback that there was no store window, because Gisa, and later her daughter and son-in-law, sold blouses that were manufactured somewhere in the suburbs wholesale. At that time, the firm was called Gisela Kahn & Co., but the "Company" had already left.

CHAPTER THREE

Dezsö

1.

Owê war sint verswunden alliu mîniu jâr! "Alas, where did the years all go!" Writing around 1200, Walther von der Vogelweide spoke for all who feel themselves getting older. More than three years have passed since I began to write this account. The reason for my slow progress is that I only occupy myself with these old stories when I feel like it. Of late, something entirely different has filled my evenings: my son bought me a chess program. If I set the level of difficulty only at 4, it still plays very quickly, and I still have to concentrate if I want to beat it. When I was at my best, I could play a short game of chess blindfolded; now I get confused if I'm in a complicated position and have to think five or six moves ahead. I'm getting old, old, old. . . .

My power of concentration is not what it used to be, I have arthritic pains in my right knee, but there is also a phenomenon which, for lack of a better term, I call "vanishing time." The last three years seem to me as if they had been three weeks. Apparently there are now neurological explanations for this symptom of senescence; but as far as I'm concerned, there's no need to search for somatic causes. The vanishing time is a natural result of the fact that there's not much going on in my life anymore – unless I consider it a noteworthy event when I save a sick cat's life by giving it a needle or operating on it. But what doesn't happen in three years when you're young! You learn Latin (blissful times when you started to learn Latin in the second year of secondary school!) and are filled with enthusiasm because the Romans were able to say "I would have been forgotten" with a single word. (I, in any case, found that quite splendid.) You learn how to ski – with difficulty, I was too fat. You discover a wonderful book in a bookstore, Mieses-Dufresne's *Textbook of Chess* (published by Reclam, but in hard cover), and thanks to the money that Aunt Mitzi tucked in your pocket just an hour before, you can even buy it. You write your first poem. Your table tennis score reaches 20-18 when you're playing against Moritz Fischer, who is ten years older than you are (but you still lose). You almost get Liesl Blaubart into bed with you – almost, because at the critical moment the doorbell rings, I'm stupid enough to answer it, and it's Giddi May wanting to play Scarlatti on our grand piano. Three weeks later I'm finally successful with Sylvia. . . .

When I was younger – in the years when I could play chess blind – before going to sleep, I'd sometimes count all the girls I'd slept with, and when the number got up to two dozen, I was proud of it, instead of being ashamed. Since my prostatectomy, I don't take very much delight in these memories, and I have really only now admitted to myself how often the physical relationship, on my part, was without a closer human relationship. Indeed I'm shocked, when I look back, how few really close human relationships there have been in my life. My former girlfriend Celia, who probably won't be mentioned anywhere else in this account, but who likely knew me better than anyone else did, once said I had "difficulty making friends." That may be true, but it was much worse before I came to Israel than it has been since. "So now you know," says Bendemann senior to his son Georg in Kafka's "The Judgment," "what exists apart from you, until now you've known only about yourself!" Kafka's interpreters, as far as I know, have hardly paid any attention to this sentence, but it is the decisive sentence in the story, and Bendemann senior says expressly that

that is why he condemns his son to death. I know what Kafka meant, because until I was over forty, I myself was (if I may quote Kafka again) "actually" an innocent child, but "even more actually" a devilish person who, if you take the word "know" seriously, really didn't know that there was anything other than himself.

Still, there were exceptions, Korry, for example, I'll get around to telling about her at some point, or little Arpád. In the mid-fifties, I took a three-week holiday in the Tyrol, where I stayed at a small guest house, and when I stepped outside one morning, everything around me was in a dense fog. Then, suddenly, there was a break in the fog, and through that break I saw, about a thousand metres above me, an alpine pasture in full sunshine – a small hut, a green meadow, a tall, light-green larch tree. It was as if I were suddenly looking into paradise. That's how the hours I spent with Arpád break through the mist of my memories (strangely unclouded despite the terrible end he met).

Have I already mentioned that I spent the summer of 1933 with my mother and my brother in a village on Lake Balaton in the vicinity of Tapolca? (My parents had called my brother Hans after Uncle Jenö, which is Johann in German; why my parents called me Peter, which is not a Jewish name, I do not know.) The village is called Abrahamhegy, and the Kálmans – of course not the ones my grandmother had consulted with fifty years earlier about moving to Vienna, but their children – had a country house there. They were astonishingly like their parents. Ruben not only became a rabbi like his father, but was also his successor in Tapolca, while Gyula's younger son Aaron had become a school teacher. (The older son was a prominent lawyer in Budapest, and I never met him.) The house was just big enough for the Kálmans – Ruben and his young wife, his brother and his sister-in-law and the three boys (the seven-year-old Arpád and the school teacher's two children who were approximately the same age as Hans and I). So we stayed at a guest house.

I can't for the life of me remember what I did last Tuesday, but I remember the quiet hour that my brother and I had to spend in our room after lunch as if it were yesterday. The wooden shutters were closed on the big single window, and specks of dust danced in the sunlight that streamed through the heart-shaped opening carved in the shutter. I can also see the bathing beach in my mind's eye as if I were there yesterday. A resourceful man had bought up a piece of sandy shore, removed the reeds that made the lake almost inaccessible for long stretches, and built cubicles on three sides of his property. The fourth side was the small beach. I spent many hours on the flat roof of the cubicles, playing chess with a school teacher from Budapest who couldn't find a better partner. I lost every game, but was always full of hope again the next morning. . . .

I also remember the Friday evenings that we spent at the Kálmans'. When we arrived around seven o'clock, the table was already set, with the candelabra standing in the middle of the table. The celebration began when Rachel Kálman, the rabbi's wife, lit the candles in the prescribed manner. The match could not be blown out, and my Aunt, as I called Rachel, laid it on a little plate that had been put there for that purpose, where it went out on its own. Then she covered her eyes with her hands, blessed the Sabbath, said the short prayer about the reconstruction of the temple, and then came the dramatic pause while we waited for the entrance of the "bride," the Sabbath itself, which we welcomed with an old song from the sixteenth century, the "Lecha Dodi." . . . For me, the long prayers that followed were less dramatic. Since there was no synagogue in Abrahamhegy, they were read in the house. Ruben led and read them aloud in a whisper while the two bigger Kálman boys, their prayer books in their hands, whispered with him at a rapid tempo. (I didn't understand a word.) Then Ruben said a more ceremonious blessing over the challot, the two loaves of wheat bread baked from braided dough. (There had to be two loaves, because during the forty years that the Hebrews had spent in the desert on their way to the Promised Land, twice as much manna fell from the sky each Friday as on the other weekdays, so that the People of Israel didn't have to collect it on the Sabbath, which would have meant breaking the law that they should rest on the Sabbath.) It was Aaron, the school teacher, who always provided the main course for the festive meal – the big fish that he got up every Friday morning at three o'clock to catch. (Sometimes I kept him company on the narrow dock that led through the reeds to the lake, not because I was interested in fishing, but because the sunrise over the lake was so magnificent.) At the end of the meal we sang again, a song that I can't identify, but whose pretty melody I can still hum; and while we were singing, we all walked around the room, and everyone kissed everyone else. I did the calculation, it was ninety kisses each time.

The older Kálman boys were preoccupied with their Talmud studies and didn't take me seriously, because I could hardly understand the simplest Hebrew prayer, so we didn't become friends. But I was nuts about Arpád – to use the slang expression. The little boy had already started to learn German in school, so we could communicate with each other, and he taught me Hungarian words – *cukorka, játszma, sütemény, levelezölap*. I called him Béka, which means "frog," and he didn't take the pet name amiss. We went for walks together, caught butterflies carefully with a green net, so that we could release them unhurt after we had admired them, I supervised his first attempts at swimming, and I even played marbles with him, although that was actually far beneath me. Once, in a field outside the village, we saw a bull with its horns lowered charging at a dog, and Arpád explained to me that the reason the bull was so angry was because the dog had stuck its tongue out at it. ("Tongue, red," he said, and then repeated the words in Hungarian.) Sometimes, when he couldn't make up his mind after breakfast how he wanted to start his day, I'd skip the chess game on the roof of the cubicles to be with him instead, and that was no small sacrifice on my part. I can't remember, though, that it saddened me to say goodbye to him, and I never tried to renew our friendship; so in the end, my "difficulty making friends" manifested itself here too.

The following year, the civil war broke out in Austria. I was busy learning Latin, reading Karl May and studying chess games described in Mieses-Dufresne, so at first I took little notice of the political events. But when the armed forces sent by the government took aim from the Kahlenberg and shot at the council houses where the working-class rebels had taken cover, that prompted me to write a poem in the rhythm of a ballad I had read in which I celebrated the heroic workers as if I had confused them with the Nibelungs in Hebbel's pompous trilogy. That was my first poem, and it had unpleasant consequences for me and my family. A few days later, my brother (who was more than two years older than I, so fourteen) went for a walk after dinner with a friend, and had a copy of my poem in his pocket. In the vicinity of the War Office, a policeman stopped him and searched him, and after the policeman had read my poem under a streetlight, he took my brother and his friend to the nearest police station, where they spent the night in a cell.

The man in the raincoat who came to our apartment the next morning looked like one of the Gestapo spies who undermined people's sense of security in Vienna after the *Anschluss*, but identified himself simply as a "police officer." My mother had hardly slept a wink all night. After he told her rather brusquely that she didn't need to worry about her son, who was "well taken care of," he took the confiscated page out of his pocket and asked who had written it. When I revealed myself to be the author, not at all fearfully, but rather full of pride, he was nonplussed, looked at the fat twelve-year-old boy in lederhosen and said: "So you're the revolutionary who's up to this nonsense?" Then I was interrogated. Did we talk about politics at home? Did we criticize the government? Were my parents Social Democrats? After I had answered no to everything and explained that I had only written the poem in the same vein as what I read in the papers, the man muttered something about "Jewish journalism" and left. An hour later my brother came home, very pleased at how he had got through the adventure, and told us that he had even had a proper breakfast with coffee and a roll in the cell. But when I applied for a passport three years later, planning to go on a holiday trip, my application was denied, and so I have never had an Austrian passport. Later on, I had more than enough other passports – a "Jewish passport" in 1938, i.e. a German passport with a big J stamped on the first page, then a stateless person's passport, a British and a Canadian passport, and now I have a Jewish passport again, an Israeli passport in which I am identified as "Dr. Dr. Peter Engelmann," which is somewhat of a nuisance.

The poem was the first of many that I wrote in a number of lined school notebooks. After the *Anschluss* I tore it out of the notebook and destroyed it, just to be safe. What follows after the torn-out page in that notebook isn't more poems, but rather aphorisms from a later time when I was reading Oscar Wilde, but had also picked up a little Nietzsche. "The simpler and more stupid a person is," I pronounced precociously, "the happier he is. But I fear the stupid people say the opposite." – "People who are above average try to avoid the mob or to suppress it. They do so because they can't merge with it." – "When the devil discovered that people had been made happy by doing evil things, he gave them a conscience." – "Faust's apostrophe to a beautiful moment, his 'Stay awhile,' is a cheap trick. Once you start to think about being happy, the moment is no longer beautiful. Another example of the detrimental effect of thinking!" In a second notebook there are poems that are typical of a fifteen-year-old, second-hand love poems with a lot of Weltschmerz, between them some "Wise Sayings" disastrously adapted from Goethe, but then, toward the end of the third notebook, there's a noticeably new tone: I had discovered Rilke's *Book of Images*, and now there were poems with countless alliterations, internal rhymes, assonances, and the subjective tropes suggested by rhyme and rhythm that don't require too much thought:

> I'll place my hands upon my face
> and stand a while behind closed eyes,
> until all things that gently pace
> with my pulse shyly synchronize.

Actually, now that I read it again, I'm surprised at how bad it all is, and how greatly I overestimated it; because there was really no shortage of good examples!

For the past twenty years or so, the Vienna of the turn of the century has been a fashionable topic for intellectuals, and it really was a fascinating time. But there was an exceptionally active intellectual life in Vienna right up until the *Anschluss*, particularly among the Jews. In my circle of acquaintances there was hardly an apartment that didn't have a grand piano or at least an upright, and there were books everywhere. We made music, talked about the latest books by Werfel or Stefan Zweig, read Wildgans, Nietzsche and contemporary trash, and I read Schopenhauer and Kant's "Prolegomena." In the Jewish Sports Club, the Hakoah, where Hans and I took swimming lessons, we trained obsessively because we wanted to show the goyim that we weren't just "hucksters," but could also do the high jump and throw the hammer, and when it came to water polo, the Hakoahs played with fanatical determination (because they were always playing against an anti-Semitic Club). However, you "were someone" in the Hakoah not only if you won in the backstroke or in hurdles, but also if you wrote books or played the violin well, and the Hakoah may have been the only sports club in the world where being well-read counted for almost as much as a victory in high diving. There's no better way for me to illustrate the atmosphere there than with an episode from my own life. When my brother's friends were going into raptures about Rostand's *Cyrano de Bergerac* and told me that it was senseless to read the play in German translation, I took a French course in the Bellaria, the government-run language school, to keep up with them.

My brother could perhaps have done very well in sports, but had no ambition to do so. Since it could be foreseen that there would never be enough money in our family to pay for him to study at the university, he'd been attending a trade school since 1934 to train as an electrical engineer. What he was interested in above all, though, was music, and he played the piano for two to three hours a day. We knew two girls who had good voices, Gretl, who is now a fat old lady in Brooklyn, and Ilse, who was rounded up by the Nazis in 1940 and disappeared without a trace. Ilse took voice lessons and sang like an aspiring opera singer, Gretl sang quietly and humbly, and my brother and I preferred her style. So with Hans or Fredl Schwarz at the piano, there was a lot of singing in our home on Augartenstrasse, above all Schubert, Schumann and Brahms, and now and then a song that Hans had composed himself. I still like his songs today, but Hans had no illusions about his talent, and if anyone had suggested it, would readily have admitted that his little creations were imitative.

But what about me? You don't see yourself, unless it's in the mirror, but then you only see the face you put on for the purpose of looking in the mirror; and whereas in my mind's eye I can very clearly see Uncle Dezsö drinking the dressing out of the salad bowl, for example, I have to piece together a picture of myself by looking at old notebooks – with difficulty, because the Peter Engelmann of 1935 or 1938, or even of 1945 is a complete stranger to me, and not one I find particularly likeable. It's not that he was really unattractive. On the contrary, after the fat boy suddenly got much taller when he was 15 or 16, it was not uncommon that a girl would have a crush on him. He was clever and quite good looking with the curly black hair he had inherited from his father, and was popular enough in school to be chosen year after year as the class spokesman. But anyone who became fond of him got very little in return, it didn't affect him, at best he would seem to enjoy it and was quickly finished with everyone, and if he didn't "beat on closed gates with bloody fingers" like the fool in Hofmannsthal's drama, it was only because he knew very little of himself. Also like Hofmannsthal's fool, he learned about life by reading, and as was fashionable in his circle of friends, he thoroughly despised everything practical, useful, concrete, and was convinced that really cultured people shouldn't concern themselves with anything other than music and poetry, or if need be with something completely divorced from reality, such as chess or number theory.

I doubt that the extent to which this Peter Engelmann was concerned with himself and shut off from the world is rare enough to be deemed abnormal; but he probably did have one small psychological defect that may have had something to do with his father's death and was exacerbated by his anger over his mother's remarriage. For example, on an early afternoon he might walk over to visit his (actually his brother's) friend Fredl Schwarz in Landstrasse, the third district, not very far from the centre of the city, chat with him and his sister for a while, play a little on their Bösendorfer grand, which we all liked because it had lighter action than the piano on Augartenstrasse, and then he'd get lost on the way home. That was absurd, because he'd gone that way dozens of times; but suddenly he'd find himself on a completely unfamiliar little street, wouldn't know what direction he was going when he entered it, would make a couple of turns, come out on a main street, but then go in the wrong direction and get hopelessly lost. Then he panicked, urgently needed to use the toilet, and could count himself lucky when with a desperate effort he somehow got oriented again and, bathed in sweat, made it home in the nick of time. . . .

It occurs to me only now that I never got lost on the way to a friend's, but only on the way home – a fact that even the most inattentive psychologist would probably find significant. What I cannot understand as easily is that the same sort of thing is still happening to me now. For example, if I'm going home from visiting someone and am not really concentrating on where I'm driving, but rather thinking about, say, a report I've just read about a new type of cat food, and I suddenly notice that I'm not on the way home, but in a completely unfamiliar suburb of Haifa . . . then I still have a panic attack, but I'm no child anymore, I park at the curb, light a cigarette and am soon in control of the situation again. What I find more unpleasant are the recurring nightmares I have every few weeks, all with the same pattern. For example, I'm in Paris or Brussels and leave my hotel to buy cigarettes, but I don't have anything on except my pyjamas. Then I can't find my way back because the street the hotel is on has changed entirely, I can't remember the name of the hotel and am half-naked and without money or identification, completely helpless. . . .

I never got lost when I went to Hütteldorf to visit Korry or on the way home from there. She was the only person with whom I had real contact. I no longer know where I met her. It certainly wasn't in the Hakoah, because I can't imagine her as a swimmer or a track and field athlete, she was simply too elegant for that. I can see her in my mind's eye, though, with a tennis racket in her hand, and even that wasn't in real life, but in a play by Schnitzler, because she was an aspiring actor, and in the winter of 1937-38 she even read one of the secondary roles now and then in a radio play for Radio Austria. It was on her account that I went to the Rothschild Hospital Clinic, which was supposed to treat patients with serious speech impediments, to learn how to pronounce a rolled r, because if you read the beginning of Rilke's "Cornet," "Riding, riding, riding, through the day, through the night, through the day," with a guttural r, it didn't sound good.

I took the streetcar to Hütteldorf and then had a ten-minute walk to the attractive old house where she lived. It was crammed full of antique furniture that her father collected. (On the veranda at the back of the house, I accidentally knocked a chair over and its back broke. "That was a Louis Quatorze," her father said emotionally, and I was filled with remorse.) By the way, she was half a year older than I, and in 1937 she was still a little taller and treated me like a younger brother, while I so greatly admired her that I hardly dared to put my arm in hers when we went for walks. But when she had time for me, I told her about a novel I wanted to write, and read my poetry to her (with the newly learned rolled "r"). . . . In the autumn of 1938 she crossed the border illegally into France, I occasionally got a letter from her from Marseilles while I was still in Vienna and even when I was in England in early 1940, and then nothing more. After the war, I succeeded in locating her sister, who had also never heard from

Korry again since that time. The reason for her silence is not hard to guess.

With that, I see I've arrived at the year 1938, and since the chronology of this account is in any case completely confused, I'm going to leave telling about my childhood years for another time, and continue now with how it really was in 1938. The *Anschluss* and its consequences didn't leave a trace in my poetry notebooks. I was more interested in Rilke than in the real world; the circumstances forced me, though, to take note of what was happening. At that time in Austria there were the usual skiing holidays in the second week of February, and most of my fellow students went to the Tauernpass, a popular skiing area, under the supervision of one of the teachers. I didn't have the money for the train fare, and when I happened to meet Uncle Martin walking on Kärntnerstrasse and had to explain to him why I wasn't in school on a weekday, he took a few bills out of his wallet. So I travelled after the group, and the train ride wasn't uninteresting. Wherever the train stopped the platform was full of people, some in uniform, the younger ones in short pants and white knee socks; they were shouting "Heil Hitler" and singing the viciously anti-Semitic Horst-Wessel-Lied, even though the German Nazi Party had been outlawed by the Austrian government. They knew that their time had come, and that they no longer needed to conceal anything. Since the train was delayed by the demonstrations, I missed the bus to the top of the pass and had to walk the last ten kilometres. I met up with an old farmer's wife who told me there were political rallies almost every day in the surrounding mountains, both by the Christian Socialists and by the Nazis. When I asked which party drew more people, she said: "The Nazis, of course, they have free beer."

Then came the 12th of March, and I was curious enough to go to the Ringstrasse, where my dear Viennese were cheering the Germans as they came marching in. Since I wasn't cheering, and with my curly hair didn't look very Aryan, a young hooligan suddenly started hitting out at me, but it wasn't difficult for me to disappear in the crowd. Historians estimate that half a million people crowded into Vienna's first district; I can still hear their yelling.

The street scene in Vienna changed overnight, above all in the Jewish districts. The Orthodox Jews in their caftans, with their full beards, peyes and broad-brimmed hats, now lived in constant fear of being attacked and hardly ventured into the street any-more, and the passers-by, if they weren't Jews, all had the swastika in their buttonholes, so that you had to wonder where the hundreds of thousands of badges suddenly came from; but that had all been well prepared, and there were not a few who, like Poldi Priminger, Aunt Mitzi's younger half-brother, already had their SA uniforms hanging in the closet. Soon you could see men and women in their respectable middle-class clothing being forced by men brandishing rubber clubs to kneel down on the cobblestones: "patriotic" election slogans had been painted on the sidewalks, and they had to try to scrub them off with brushes or their bare hands. Among the scrubbers was our family physician, Dr. Grübel, who was stopped on his way to assist with a birth. When he was released an hour later, he continued on his way, helped deliver the child, went back to his office, took care of his patients as if nothing had happened, and when the waiting room was finally empty in the late afternoon, he took Veronal. The cleaning lady found him the next morning.

At first, for most people, daily life still continued at the usual pace in spite of everything. Gellert, the German novelist and poet I was reading at the time, tells the story of a man who, in his haste to flee from an enraged camel, falls into an old well shaft. Halfway down, he just barely manages to find a hold in the crumbling stones and notices a few strawberries growing there. With the snorting camel above him and the deadly depths below, he takes pleasure in eating the strawberries. That's the way people are, and it's a good thing. I, for example, not only continued going to school as long as I was allowed to – the trade school for Industrial Chemistry on Rosensteingasse – but also

95

continued spending long afternoons reading poetry and playing Chopin or Debussy on the piano to the best of my ability, and the grown-ups around me continued, as long as they were allowed to, going about their business and engaging in their usual pastimes. I think about that, because people have so often reproached the Jews for having stayed in Austria and in Germany until it was too late – a completely nonsensical reproach. Was it really just due to recklessness or ignorance that so many Jews, like my Uncle Paul, for example, simply could not believe that the epidemic of megalomania and brutality that was inundating the country – the land of Goethe and Beethoven – could be anything more than a passing plague? Couldn't their optimism be seen as touching? And even if you had no such illusions – what could you do? Admittedly, it was still possible on the 12th or 13th of March, if you had the presence of mind and the determination to do it, to drop everything, leave everything behind and go to Czechoslovakia, for example, from where you would ultimately still have been deported and murdered. A few days later, however, all the borders were closed, and if you had a "J" in your passport, you were sitting in the trap. When about three dozen countries sent delegates to Evian to the International Conference for Solving the Refugee Question, only one country declared itself willing to accept refugees, the Dominican Republic; and not much came of that either.

Still, if you had money or contacts, there were means and ways. If you had a foreign bank account, you could get a visa to Argentina or Brazil, and a passage to Shanghai was affordable. If you applied yourself early enough and had a sponsor who would sign an affidavit for you, there was still a small window of opportunity for you to be allowed into the United States, but the quota for Austria was soon reached. My friend Sylvia made her way to Romania, got on one of those leaky, run-down boats that the English prevented from landing on the coast of Palestine, and she drowned. A friend of my brother's, Paul Ellbogen, who had won the Austrian Junior Championship in the breast stroke in 1937, crossed the border by swimming across the Danube on a dark night, and in a long, round-about route reached Israel.

As for me, I went to the American Embassy in May of 1938, stood in the line-up for two hours, got the forms to fill out, and if I had had an affidavit my turn would have come in 1944; nevertheless – strawberries! Gellert would have said – while I was standing in line, I managed to strike up a friendship with an attractive brunette who was also standing in line, and with whom I spent a few pleasant evenings. . . .

Hans and I owe our survival to an English White Paper. The English government let itself be persuaded by the Jews in England to permit the immigration of a considerable number of young people who would be somehow selected by the Jewish Relief Committee in London. Hans and I owe our being among the "chosen" to our Uncle Martin, from whom we had not heard in a long time. Although he was fighting hard for his own existence, it occurred to him in April of 1938 that he should do something for the children of his deceased friend Sándor. So he did two things. First, since we were running around in terribly shabby pants, he had two custom-made suits made for each of us, and those were the only custom-made suits I have ever possessed. Second, he instructed his representative in London, a man by the name of Zwillinger, to get English visas for us with the help of the White Paper. How Zwillinger managed that, I do not know, although I worked for the Relief Committee for three months in the spring of 1939. I only know that the Committee had been assigned a completely impossible task, because many dozens of petitions and applications came in every day, and the ladies who worked there, usually without pay, had to decide in some sort of mysterious manner to process case A, but to file case B, which, while it was part of a rescue operation, was also in effect, although the ladies who donated their time to the committee could only guess this, a death sentence. The mood in the offices was one of desperate, hysterical gaiety, since it was essential for the ladies to focus at all times on the rescue operations and to suppress their knowledge of the death sentences. But the place was in complete chaos, because there weren't enough work-ers, and the files were piled high on their desks, just as in Kafka's *The Castle.*

My file must have been at the bottom of one of these piles, because for a long time nothing happened. So I kept on going to the Chemistry School until, at the end of May, as the result of a vote arranged by the Ministry of Education, Jews were denied the right to attend school with the "Aryan" students. To my amaze-ment, I nevertheless received my diploma four weeks later; the school principal must have been a brave man.

In the summer, the Hakoah still held its track and field events in the Prater: it had obviously not occurred to anyone to "Aryanize" that section of the park, as had been done with the *Dianabad* – the swimming pool used by the Hakoah's water sports section – or its summer location, the *Stadionbad.* ("Aryanization" was a kind of government-sponsored robbery: the Nazi authorities confiscated a shop or office or house and sold it for a song to a well-connected party-member.) When the mosquitos became un-bearable in the late afternoons, our trainer, Sedlacek, would light a small fire and we would sit in its smoke. Sedlacek, who by the way was not a Jew, had a limp; before the World War (the First one, of course), he had been a famous sprinter, but in 1915 on the West-ern Front a bullet had shattered his knee. Now he stared morosely into the fire: the little kingdom he had built up for himself was dis-integrating. . . . Then came the autumn and Kristallnacht, and now life in Vienna had really become uncomfortable. On the after-noon of the 9th of November, Giddi May had been leafing through the newspapers in his regular café in the second district when a bunch of rowdies in uniform and in civilian clothes started chant-ing "Croak, Jews!" in the doorway, pushed their way into the café and began to beat the customers with steel rods. Giddi fled into the washroom, waited until the noise had died down somewhat, tore the door open, pushed his way through the crowd with his head lowered and got out. The three thugs who pursued him couldn't catch him, even though he had a cut on his forehead and the blood was streaming down his face: a good high jumper has to know how to run.

We found out about his adventure when he came to our place the next morning with a big bandage on his head to – strawberries! strawberries! – play Scarlatti. Through the open window came the smell of burning buildings. Incidentally, Giddi May's piano playing saved his life. He found a singer who was stupid and unmusical but had a nice soprano voice, and he got a visa to Turkey as her vocal coach.

Even more depressing than Giddi's head wound was the fact that my brother's closest friend had been taken from his apartment by the SA. Just as he had no idea why he had been arrested and transported to Dachau, he also had no idea why he was released again three weeks later – that was indeed a rare case of good luck. He didn't say anything about the three weeks, they had threatened to pick him up again immediately if he so much as said a word about it, but he did pull up his shirt at our place on Augartenstrasse and show us the welts on his back. I ran to the bathroom and threw up, but there was worse to come.

As a child I had a lot of trouble with my teeth. Our dentist, Hermann Walfisch, a strikingly tall, big-boned man, had his apartment and dentist's office on the mezzanine floor of the building. He liked children and showed that, among other ways, by always giving us candies: "Ildefonso candies," that I was very fond of, as well as a sticky white stuff that tasted of peppermint that I can't remember the name of, but that may have contributed considerably to my cavities; not that much was known back then about dental hygiene. His "technician," who helped make crowns, bridges and dentures, was a red-headed Polish Jew with freckles, whom Walfisch always just called the "red dog." But Walfisch was a good-natured, cheerful fellow who liked to sing Yiddish songs. It is part of Jewish mythology that Jews are not drinkers, but a song about a rabbi he particularly liked to sing had the refrain: "Oy yoy yoy, tipsy as a goy."

In 1935, when Hans and I, God knows, no longer needed a

nanny, and my parents were also no longer in a position to pay for one, Walfisch married our Annie, who had to convert before the wedding – a rite performed in the Schiff Schul in the traditional manner, that is, with complete immersion. Shortly after Kristallnacht (someone – a jealous competitor? – must have denounced him), his apartment and dentist's office were searched by the Gestapo with the Nazis' usual brutality; the contents of all the drawers in the apartment and the cupboard with the instruments in the office were simply dumped on the floor. The result was the obvious, because since Walfisch made gold crowns, he naturally had a small supply of gold on hand, and Jews were not permitted to own gold. So he was taken away, and in mid-December Annie got a package in the mail with his clothes and the infamous news, "Shot while trying to escape."

In the meantime, the air had gotten thin around us too. Of the *mishpoche*, the wider family, we were the only ones still there; most of our friends, despite the "J" in their passports, had somehow managed to get out of the country, and the camel was snorting so forcefully now that the few strawberries still around no longer tasted good to me. The English passport I was longing for still hadn't arrived, and we hadn't heard anything from Zwillinger in a long time. Then, shortly before Christmas, a friend from the trade school told me that after Kristallnacht the Belgians and Dutch had called off their border patrol. Such rumours were circulating constantly; what we of course couldn't know was that this one had reached us long after the fact. We had our family consultation, although such outings were dangerous, in Ginsberg's sad-looking café at the Karmelitermarkt. Of the large windows that let in the northerly light Ginsberg so valued, two had been smashed; the remaining two were smeared with swastikas and slogans. On one of them, in white oil paint, it said "Croak, Jews!" and on the other "Don't buy from Jews." Of the large crystal chandelier that had shed sparkling light when the north light wasn't strong enough, only a few shards of glass remained. There was no head waiter anymore, and a withered little old man we had never seen before served us poor coffee. We didn't take long to make up our minds.

My mother, depressed and frightened, said with astonishing apathy: "Do what you think is right, you're no longer a child," and my stepfather explained to me that they unfortunately didn't have any money in the house. It took a fit of rage on the part of my brother to induce him to borrow the money for my ticket and ten marks "pocket money" from Uncle Paul, his brother-in-law, so that I could get on the train for Cologne the next morning with Heinz Polatschek. Since my cousin Edith lived in Amsterdam, we had decided to go over the border into Holland.

The train was full of soldiers, giving the impression that the war Hitler had been preparing for since he seized power was now imminent. In our compartment, a young lad in uniform asked where I was going, and when I said "to Holland," he looked me in the face for a moment and answered: "I can understand that." At the main train station in Cologne we studied the schedules for the local trains, and then went for a walk for an hour because we didn't want to reach the border before nightfall. In comparison to Vienna, it was very peaceful in Cologne. Whereas in Vienna almost everyone who was not a Jew was wearing a swastika in his button-hole, so that we might as well have already been wearing the yellow patch, in Cologne it was about every third person. We took a leisurely stroll to the Cathedral and through the old part of town, and felt safer than we had in months. Finally, each of us bought a meat sandwich (neither of us had much money), got on the local train we had chosen – and this is where my memory goes blank.

I don't understand why I've almost completely forgotten most of the "Dutch" adventure I'm about to describe; but try as I may, I can only report a few disconnected fragments of the next ten or twelve hours. We had got out in a village near the border and walked north – from Egypt to Canaan, from Turkey to China, why not from the Third Reich to Holland? – until we were stopped by a small group of German soldiers. The Dutch, they said, had complained in Berlin about the number of refugees coming across the border night after night, and now that was over, and we would have to return to Cologne. Then (and this I can see again clearly and distinctly in my mind's eye), we stood in the dark for a long time – probably for several hours – outside a small house the soldiers had gone into somewhere in the vicinity of the nearest train station. "Do you think," Polatschek said at last, "that they've left us standing here unguarded so that we can have a chance to escape?" "Maybe, but I have no desire to get myself shot while trying to escape," was my response, although of course I knew that Hermann Walfisch had not been shot while trying to escape, but had been murdered or beaten to death. We were dressed for a stroll in a city, since we thought, stupidly, that we would attract less attention that way – so our luggage consisted of a briefcase each with the barest essentials – which meant that we got chilled to the bone (the winter of 1938 was unusually cold) and walked back and forth in front of the house, stamping our feet to try to get a bit of warmth into our toes. Finally, in the grey light of dawn, a sergeant and two soldiers came out of the house and took us to the train. "Don't try it again," said the officer as we boarded the train. "If we catch you again, you'll go to Dachau."

In the main train station in Cologne, each of us ate a meat sandwich again and talked things over. Maybe the Belgian border was still open? There was a vending machine where we could buy a hiker's map of the Eifel for 20 pfennigs. We sought out a place five or six kilometres from the border, studied the timetables again, and then had to put in time for an entire day, which wasn't pleasant in the cold. In normal times, we would have visited an art gallery, but we didn't know if Jews were allowed in the museums in Cologne and were afraid to ask. Before our departure, we bought hot sausages, even though we didn't have very much money left.

We got off the train in Berg, which I remember as a wretched little town. There was snow on the ground outside the train station. We looked at the little pocket compass I had bought before leaving Vienna and found a country road that went approximately in the direction of the border. After an hour, it had gotten dark, and there were woods on either side of the road. Polatschek stopped and got a flashlight out of his briefcase, I handed him the compass, and then we took as direct a route as possible between the trunks of the tall trees toward the northwest. It was hard going: there was thick underbrush, we climbed over cattle pens and barbed wire, sometimes we had to scramble up steep inclines, and our street shoes and raincoats were ill-suited for such a hike. "We were really stupid," said Polatschek grumpily. "We didn't want to draw attention to ourselves, but who goes on such a hike in a dress shirt and tie?" Two hours later, we saw lights between the tree trunks and didn't dare turn on our flashlight anymore. Without it, of course, the compass was useless.

Around six in the morning, after walking twelve hours without seeing anything that looked like a border – we imagined a no man's land with warning signs and barbed wire – we came to a poor dirt road with a small house on the right hand side. "I don't think we can continue on much longer," said Polatschek, "it's simply too cold. Also, I haven't known for a long time what direction we should take, I don't have a clue where we are, maybe we went in a circle!" We knocked at the house, and after a while a gaunt, unshaven man in knee breeches and a dirty white shirt opened the door and said: "Yes?"

"We've lost our way. May we come in for a while to get warm?"

The man looked us over, and we must have looked really miserable; my teeth were chattering with the cold. "You don't have to tell me any stories," he said at last, "I know what you want. Come in, you're freezing."

The room was warm. On one wall there was a large colour print of Hitler, and on the opposite wall a print just as large showing Christ on the cross, who seemed to be staring sadly at the man across from him. "Sit down," said the man, and after a while an old woman brought us large cups of weak black coffee with plenty of sugar, and went away again. The man obviously had no desire to get into a conversation with us, but after we had finished our coffee, he said: "Now you need a good sleep." The old woman showed us into a small room whose only piece of furniture was a shaky old double bed. We lay down without getting undressed, covered ourselves as best we could with our raincoats, and fell asleep right away.

In the early afternoon, the man woke us up and gestured toward the room with the two colour prints: "Time to eat." The woman served up thick pea soup from a big pot, and I have seldom in my life had soup that tasted so good. That was our last meal for a long time. When our plates were empty, there was black coffee again, and then the man said suddenly: "Without help, you can't get out, you'll lose your way again or someone will catch you. In Wallerscheid there's a border station, that's where you have to go, you can be smuggled across." Then he told us the way, we thanked him and went.

Later, after the end of the war, I would have liked to thank the man and send him a food parcel, but I didn't know his name. The house to which he directed us wasn't far and wasn't difficult to find. We opened the door, which wasn't locked, and got quite a shock.

In Joseph Conrad's *Lord Jim*, there's an incredibly vivid description of the pilgrims on Jim's ship. It's about three pages long – I wish I could write like that. What we saw in the big room (of course I didn't analyze what I saw at the time) was a sort of cross-section of the German Jews: perhaps sixty or seventy people who were standing around on the dirty wooden floorboards or sitting on the scattered chairs in the room. There were elderly full-bearded East European Jews in caftans; men in custom-made suits, white shirts and ties; women in fur coats; a few adolescents in short trousers; an old man with snow-white hair and a cold pipe in his mouth; a young, freckled lad with a conspicuous amount of gold in his teeth, who told me later that he came from Berlin and was a waiter; twenty-year-olds in shabby jackets and unironed pants; a young woman with an infant in her arms. . . . As we soon found out, there was a thriving business going on there. Some enterprising SA men were bringing the Jews for 400 marks each – that wasn't chicken feed back then! – in private cars from Cologne to Wallerscheid, where the border patrol, who got their cut, passed them on to a Belgian smuggler who charged his own fees.

We didn't see anyone from the border patrol, but in the late afternoon a young man who looked like a farmboy or a woodcutter led us half an hour's distance into the woods, stopped in a clearing, and to my surprise (this was not how I had imagined human smuggling!) lit a large wood fire: it was bitterly cold. We stood around and waited (next to travelling, waiting had also become a Jewish national sport). By the time the fire died down, night had fallen, and finally the young man stood up on a fallen log and said in a dialect I could barely understand that the Belgian probably wouldn't be coming, so we should go back to the house we came from. Since he went ahead of us with long strides, we soon lost contact with him. The seventy frightened people who were all talking at once made slow progress. When Heinz and I reached the country road that, we hoped, would lead back to the house on the border, the young woman with the infant joined us. A half moon in the sky shed a little light, but the way seemed to have gotten longer, and the woman was getting worried: "We must be going in the wrong direction, we'll all freeze to death." I knew there was no relying on my sense of orientation, but I turned around and lied: "No, no, we're on the right track. We passed the big pine tree there on our way out."

It really was the right track, and we spent the night in the overcrowded room. Most people lay down on the dirty wooden floor; I got hold of three chairs, lay across them and fell asleep immediately, as I had the day before – happy times, when you can sleep under any circumstances! Then we were standing and sitting around again, and I began to suffer serious hunger pangs. In the late afternoon, a man in a grey-green uniform entered through the back door and made a short speech. The arrangements didn't work anymore, the Belgians didn't want any more refugees, the smuggler had got scared, and we had to get ourselves out of there as quickly as possible: the Gestapo were likely to pay a visit. If we wanted, we could just take off without a guide. . . .

Quite honestly, I can't be angry with the Belgian government. As I later found out in Brussels, after Kristallnacht ten or twenty refugees a day arrived in Brussels; by the end of November it was fifty or sixty, by mid December over a hundred, and the Belgians had their own problems: the Belgian Nazis were getting louder and louder. . . . But be that as it may: we had to get across without a guide, for what else could we do? The young man we knew from the day before brought us back to the clearing, stood on the fallen log again, gave us directions in his unintelligible dialect, wished us luck and headed back to the house on the border. Then the entire group set itself in motion, the bearded men in caftans, the ladies in fur coats, the young woman with the child in her arms. In the direction the man had pointed us there was a narrow path that soon disappeared in the underbrush. Now there were discussions about which direction we should take, children were crying, the entire column forced its way through the bushes like a herd of elephants. Heinz, who was walking beside me, got nervous. "We can't do it like that, Peter," he said. "A group of seventy people can't cross the border illegally, we can be heard for kilometres around." So we broke off from the group, turned left and made our way through the bushes as quickly as possible. Later I felt badly that we hadn't taken the woman with the baby with us, but a young man joined us who was seven or eight years older than we were.

After a few minutes, we dared to have a whispered conversation. The man was called Franz Meixner and spoke a dreadful suburban Viennese dialect. He was – until then I didn't know there was such a thing – a Jewish prole who had got by in Hernals carrying bricks and shovelling snow. The woodcutter who had described the way to us in the clearing had been as unintelligible to him as to us, and this time we didn't have a map. We knew, though, that Belgium must lie approximately north of us, so with the help of the compass we went in that direction, and once again, as on our attempt at the Dutch border, we had to crawl over fences and barbed wire and gradually gained altitude. Finally we reached a field with a high shooting stand in the middle of it. I climbed up and saw nothing but wilderness as far as the eye could see. So Heinz and I continued on quite discouraged, while Franz followed a few steps behind us like a loyal German shepherd. After a while the plateau came to an end, there was a steep decline, and as the moon began to set we reached a road. Trusting to luck – we had no idea where we were – we turned left, and half an hour later we came to a big house. It was four o'clock in the morning, so hardly the right time to knock on someone's door, but we were exhausted and my feet were unbearably sore.

We knocked for a long time before the door was opened by a woman in a dressing gown with rollers in her hair; behind her a tall, broad-shouldered man, both in their thirties. Heinz explained again that we had got lost in the woods, and asked if they could put us up, whereupon the woman, to our surprise, excused herself in quite understandable German for having let us wait so long. "There's no other house here far and wide," she said, "and drunks always knock here on their way home from the pub."

We went through a small hallway into a room with a large calendar hanging on the opposite wall. I instinctively went over to take a look. Under the date – it was the 24th of December, and I celebrated the fiftieth anniversary of that date with champagne – there was a place name that meant nothing to me, and under that, "District of Malmédy." We'd made it.

The woman went back to bed, the man lit the wood stove and put a pot of water on to boil. While we drank the coffee he poured for us – it was weak, and there was neither milk nor sugar – I explained to him briefly who we were, which didn't seem to surprise him. "Here at the border we know what's going on," he said. "You're not safe here, so you have to get to Brussels as quickly as possible, but we'll talk about that later." When we had finished our coffee he showed us into a large, unheated room whose only furnishings were two large sacks of straw lying on the beautiful parquet floor. "You can lie on the one," he said, "and cover yourselves with the other. If you have to relieve yourselves, you'll have to go outside, the toilet is frozen."

Heinz was clever enough to lie in the middle. Franz and I pulled on opposite sides of the upper sack, which wasn't wide enough for three sleepers. After a while I was awakened by the cold, but Franz was awake too and he stood up and urinated in a corner of the room on the parquet floor. When the woman called us for breakfast, the urine had frozen solid, Franz opened a window, carefully picked up the thin, yellowy sheet of ice from the floor and threw it out. There was weak black coffee again and heavy dark rye bread, and we really devoured the three slices that the man put on each of our plates. In addition to us and the married couple, there were five children around the table, an eight-year-old boy and four little ones. We hadn't finished eating when the man got up and left the house. "My husband is a truck driver," said the woman, "but he doesn't work in the winter. If he works, we don't get any unemployment benefits or child welfare payments, so it's better if he does nothing, then he at least has time to cut wood." Then she explained to us that the Belgian police here and everywhere in the border zone were arresting refugees (she said "Jews") and sending them back to Germany. "When my husband is back, we'll decide what you should do."

I made friends with the boy, who was called Jacques and reminded me of Béka. Heinz still had a few cigarettes – for some reason we smoked Asta with a red tip – and since my lighter didn't work, the boy fetched a can of gas, to my horror poured gas in his mouth and spit it into the lighter. When I said to him, appalled: "Don't do that, gas is poisonous," he said indifferently: "I spit it out again right away" and rinsed his mouth. The lighter worked.

When the man returned, he explained the situation to us again: "You have to get to Brussels. If you make it to Brussels, you won't be sent back to Germany."

"But how are we to do that?" asked Heinz.

"I can take you there in the truck. You lie down in the back, and I cover you with straw. But I don't have enough gas and not enough money to buy any."

"We don't have Belgian francs," said Heinz.

"German marks will do."

The marks we still had left would hardly have bought five litres of gas. From a slit in the lining of his coat, Heinz took out a five-dollar bill that he had hidden there for an emergency.

"I'll have to ride to Trois-Pont to change that," said the man (we already knew that he had a good German name, Dieter Brauer, as is not uncommon in the border zone). "I can go there by train."

When it was time for dinner, he still wasn't back. There was a large pot of potatoes in a thin broth with a few pieces of meat floating in it. Outside the window it started to snow. The woman put the four little children to bed and then she and the boy sat with us. She was in a bad mood and didn't say much. "Men are such a problem," she said. "You can't rely on any of them." Outside, the falling snow was as thick as a curtain.

Brauer didn't get back until after ten o'clock. He was so drunk that he was staggering, and the boy burst into tears. "Let's go to sleep," said the woman. "Things will be better tomorrow."

I was convinced that Brauer had gotten drunk on our five dollars, and I spent a restless night. When we got up it was still snowing, and the snow was so deep we could hardly see where the street began. For breakfast there was coffee and rye bread again. Brauer had apparently already had his breakfast, but he came and sat with us after a while. "It's not going to work with the truck," he said. "I can't get it out of the courtyard, and if I shovel it out, I'll get stuck on the street. You'll have to take the train." Then he took his wallet out of his coat, gave Heinz a piece of paper showing the exchange rate, and counted out the bills on the table: 235 Belgian francs. "I'll send Jacques to the train station to see if the coast is clear. He's inconspicuous. He can also buy your tickets."

"We'll disguise ourselves as English tourists," said Heinz. "We'll have to speak English really loudly."

"I can't speak English," said Franz.

"Then don't open your mouth," said Heinz. "Not a word!"

Brauer knew when the train to Trois-Pont would be coming through, and sent the boy on his way. Ten minutes later, we followed Brauer, who was looking around suspiciously. It was difficult wading through the deep snow, but after a while we reached a little village, and Jacques came toward us, waving happily. "It's all right," he called, "there's nobody at the station."

"It's still too early," said the man. "You'll have to wait until we hear the train. Jacques will go along with you and stay with you until you board, I'll wait for him at the Post Office." We thanked Bauer for all his help and shook his hand, then we heard the train approach, and Jacques ran ahead. When we arrived on the platform, the train was already there. Heinz gave the boy fifty francs, and we got on.

In Trois-Pont, where we had to change trains, Heinz and I went into the waiting room, while Franz trotted along behind us. We bought an English newspaper and a pack of Lucky Strike. (We didn't know they weren't English, but American, cigarettes.) After we looked up the number of the platform where the train to Brussels would stop, we sat on a bench and read the newspaper that we had divided in half. Franz sat a few metres away with a sour expression. His feelings were hurt because we weren't talking to him and were acting as if we didn't know him. There was hardly anyone on the platform, but after a while we heard a child's voice speaking German. Peering cautiously over the edge of my newspaper, I saw a couple in city clothes with a little boy walking along the track. Suddenly, two men in uniform emerged from the waiting room, had a short conversation with the family – I couldn't hear what they said from where I was sitting – and led them out of the station. Then our train came, and by late afternoon we were in Brussels.

2.

Of course all this has nothing to do with my Uncle Dezsö, and so it shouldn't be included in a chapter that bears his name; but that can't be changed now. The title is problematic anyway, because the chapter is more about Dezsö's older brother than about him, and it's only called "Dezsö" because I won't grant Jenö a chapter of his own.

The immortal Leo Rosten tells the story of Samuel Brodski, who emigrated from his shtetl to England and worked in his brother-in-law's laundry in Whitechapel. When he got his first week's pay, he decided to treat himself and went to a kosher restaurant that his brother-in-law had recommended. The waiter was Chinese, but explained the menu to him in fluent Yiddish. When Brodski was paying the bill after finishing his meal, he asked the cashier: "Are you the owner?" "Who else?" said the cashier. "That was excellent chicken," said Brodski, "but tell me, why does the Chinese who served me speak fluent Yiddish?" "Hush," said the cashier. "Don't speak so loudly. He thinks he's learning English."

My Uncle Jenö learned both Yiddish and English in England. How that came about will be shown later in this chapter, although the family stories about Jenö's years in England are both sketchy and unreliable. We have only his own versions, and they can't be trusted.

It goes without saying that Jenö and Dezsö had proper bar mitzvahs, naturally in the Schiff Schul. (Mine was in the Seitenstetten Temple because my stepfather wanted to impress his acquaintances. There was never a penny in the house, he had to borrow money to pay the electricity bill, but the bar mitzvah had to take place in the most exclusive temple in Vienna.) When Jenö was called upon to recite the required chapter from the Torah, Chaim Ledermann still conducted the service but had left Jenö's preparation to a younger man. Jenö was brilliant.

Although he was of slight build, he already had the skills of an orator when he was thirteen, and when he stood on the *almenor* and recited the prophet Habakkuk, you could have thought you were listening to an experienced prayer leader, if it hadn't been for his unchanged voice. That was in the morning of the *Shabbos*, and in the evening there was a celebration at Horowitz's, to which Ledermann came too. He had developed a soft spot for my grandmother.

Dezsö didn't have Jenö's skill as an orator, but he was diligent and attentive and had prepared himself so well that he hardly needed to look at the book during his recitation. The old men in the congregation patted him benevolently on the shoulder when the service was over. This time, too, there was a celebration at Horowitz's, but Chaim Ledermann wasn't present: he had had a stroke and died. A few weeks later, Jenö left school and found a job as an apprentice in the office of an English export firm that had a branch in the fourth district. He didn't learn much there, though, except how to make fun of his boss's English accent. Then one day he didn't appear for the evening meal and wasn't there for breakfast either. When Josef went to the police in Rossauer Lände, the policeman on duty took the matter lightly and said that's just the way it was, boys of that age ran away now and then, he'd come back again of his own accord, he probably hadn't made off with the pencils belonging to the firm Fowler & Co. But the agitation at home only subsided when a few days later a postcard with an English stamp arrived. It showed the Tower Bridge, and on the back in beautiful handwriting in the Roman alphabet: *Fond greetings from the capital city of the world! Your devoted Jenö.*

Meanwhile – in the summer of Gisa's wedding – the time had also come for Dezsö to leave school and seek his fortune, but without having to cross the English Channel for that purpose. The first step wasn't difficult. Among my grandfather's customers was the owner of a ladies' clothing store on Rotenturmstrasse who liked the clever lad who pushed the brown paper under his feet in the shoemaker's workshop. He chatted with him in Hungarian;

although his name was Bamberger, he was Hungarian by birth. Which section of the Torah had Dezsö recited at his bar mitzvah? Was he good at arithmetic? Was he interested in women's fashions? The idea that you could be interested in women's fashions had never occurred to the fourteen-year-old, who was interested in the Renz Circus and in football, but he was no fool. "I'm interested in everything," he said.

"Everything is a bit much, but better than nothing at all," said Bamberger and offered him a job as errand boy.

The next years of Uncle Dezsö's life can be described quickly. At that time, he was a handsome, sturdy lad with wavy black hair and dark eyes. (The three older siblings, Gisa, Jenö and Dezsö, were all like the Róths, with black hair and a dark complexion, while Klara and Elli were more like their father, as blonde and blue-eyed as Hitler's experts would have expected of pure-blooded Aryans.) Dezsö now got up at six o'clock, had coffee and a roll with his parents, and strolled along Rotenturmstrasse to open the store. Then he swept up, dusted shelves, unpacked shipments, brought coffee from the nearest café, fetched his manager's second breakfast from Priminger's Delicatessen on the Graben, and learned to address the wife of Counsellor Melzer, when she entered the store, as "Frau Baroness," and to address Mrs. Müller as "Frau Counsellor," wildly inflating the customers' titles, as was customary in the better shops in Vienna. But he not only listened attentively, he kept his eyes open, learned what sort of clothes were shown to the "Frau Baroness," and which to "Frau Counsellor," learned to match the shop window displays to the seasons and even to the weather, and soon began to take a genuine interest in ladies' fashions. In the evenings, he went for walks in the Prater, and now and then one of the salesladies took him out to Kriegler's (back then at 22 Rotenturmstrasse), the confectionary that wasn't as famous as Demel's, but whose Linzer cake was just as good. He had no worries about the future. Didn't Gisa already have almost half a dozen seamstresses working for her? What she had done, he could do too, when the time came. . . .

One year after her wedding, Gisa's business already brought in enough for her and her husband to live comfortably. Jacob quit work at the Karmelitermarkt, and since Gisa didn't want him in the store and he could do nothing other than sell fish, he now spent his time reading the paper or going for walks in a tailored suit that Gisa had bought for him. Three years after Gisa's wedding, my grandmother sold her vegetable stand, and in 1905 the weekly allowance she got from Gisa was already substantial enough for the Kahns to move into a bigger apartment. Actually, both my grandmother and Miriam Horowitz regretted that; it had become a pleasant habit for them to run the two households together. But Horowitz's wood and coal business also had done well, he no longer needed a tenant, and the new apartment on Untere Augartenstrasse – the apartment where I was born – was barely two minutes away from Malzgasse.

There were long intervals between postcards from Jenö, and then suddenly he was back again. The Kahn family – that is, my grandparents, Dezsö, Klara and Elli – had just sat down for the evening meal when he walked into the room, wearing a checkered, English-style suit, and said in English, "How do you do?" My grandparents and the children jumped up from their chairs, they embraced, and Jenö sniffed the air. "What's for dinner? Chicken? It's a good thing we aren't peasants. If a Jewish peasant gets chicken to eat, either he is sick, or the chicken is."

In the meantime, a porter had arrived and Jenö tipped and dismissed him.

"You've grown a head taller," said my grandmother. "But do sit down, dinner is waiting."

"I will," said Jenö, "but first I have to unpack a few things." He opened the larger of the two suitcases and produced a box of cigarettes for his father, a brooch for his mother that is now in the possession of my sister-in-law, gold necklaces with Star of David pendants for the girls and a pipe for Dezsö, although Dezsö didn't smoke. Then they could eat and talk, first of all about those who had stayed in Vienna. Did Mother still have to work so hard at her stand? No. Did Baron Pollak still have his patent-leather shoes made by Father and still not pay for them? Unfortunately, yes. Was Dezsö learning something respectable? Did Pinsker still smell of fish? Had the girls been good? Of course. Then Jenö began to show off, telling what it had been like on the boat, where everyone had been seasick except for him and the captain, how he had arrived in London without two pennies to rub together and had gone hungry for three days, how London was a breathtaking city compared to which Vienna was a village, how he had learned in Whitechapel, the Jewish East End, to eat kippers for breakfast, how the English didn't have coffee and cake at a confectionary in the late after-noon, but "high tea" instead. . . . Mainly, though, he talked about his great friend, Sammy Löwenzahn, about his competence, his beautiful apartment in Whitechapel, his willingness to help, and how he, Jenö, had learned not only English from his great friend, but also Yiddish. . . . (When I met Löwenzahn in 1939, he no lon-ger had an apartment in Whitechapel, but a house in Golders Green, where the rich Jews lived, he no longer spoke Yiddish and was no longer called Sammy Löwenzahn, but Sidney Lionel. Jenö was no longer alive, and long before he was buried in the Viennese Jewish Cemetery, he had ceased calling Löwenzahn his "great friend," but with his particular gift for finding the unforgiveable, deadly accurate expression, he called him the "perfumed Polack" – a term of contempt that the Austrian-born bourgeois Jews sometimes bestowed on their lower-class immigrant fellow Jews; it was at least correct insofar as the Löwenzahns really did come from Poland.)

I'm not sure how Jenö had made the acquaintance of his great friend: on a walk in Hyde Park, in the kosher restaurant in Whitechapel where the Chinese waiter spoke fluent Yiddish, on the train to Liverpool? The story was different every time he told it. (On the train to Liverpool, the joke goes, sits a young man who wants to make his fortune on the stock market. Across from him sits a well-dressed man reading the *Financial Times*. That, thinks the young man, is my first contact. "Excuse me," he says, "can you tell me the time?" The other man keeps on reading as if he hasn't heard anything. After a while, the young man tries again – if you want to have success on the stock market, you can't afford to be shy – and says somewhat more loudly: "Excuse me, but can you tell me the time?" The man he has addressed keeps on reading without batting an eyelid. The young man takes a deep breath and says: "*Excuse me, but can you tell me the time?*" The distinguished gentleman puts down the *Financial Times*, looks the young man in the face and says: "Come off it, I know what you really want, you don't want to know what time it is, you want to make my acquaintance, but what would be the point of it? Let's assume I tell you what time it is. That's a beginning, we start talking with each other, you are a clever young man, we arrive in Liverpool, and I invite you to my home. I introduce you to my son, a charming person, you become friends. You go to cricket matches with him, he invites you to his place and introduces you to my daughter, a charming girl! Three months later you come to me and ask for her hand in marriage. But what's the point? You want to marry my daughter, and you don't even have a watch!")

It doesn't matter how Jenö met his great friend Sammy Löwenzahn alias Sidney Lionel; in any case, as Jenö told us, Löwenzahn took him to a restaurant in Whitechapel where the waiter, an Ashkenazy from Galicia, spoke fluent Yiddish, ordered roast goose for them and got him a job in a candle factory, where he threaded wicks through metal moulds, which he then filled with melted wax from a big metal can – a boring and poorly paid job. But when Jenö's knowledge of English was adequate, he found him a job in the headquarters of "Perolin." Perolin was a pine needle extract that you squirted out of a tin can with a nozzle – "Two squirts," said the advertisement, "and your apartment smells like a pine forest." (Jenö maintained that he had met a man in London called Pine who smelled like Perolin.) The Perolin Company also sold the oiled sand that used to be sprinkled on floors to keep the dust down when they were swept.

Jenö began to work his way up at Perolin. At first, he had no more significant tasks than sweeping up (of course with sand that smelled like a pine forest), bringing the clerks their sand-wiches and delivering their tea twice a day, making sure to put the milk in the cup first and then the tea, as is the English cus-tom. As in a novel by Dickens, the clerks on their high chairs huddled over their work in dark rooms that were inadequately heated in cold weather. But Jenö was good at arithmetic, and he could talk – not only in German, but also in English and Yiddish; and because he had the gift of believing everything he happened to be saying, he spoke with such conviction that others believed him too. After a few months he had persuaded the sales manager to let him work as a representative in the East End for two hours a day, and then, after a probationary period, full days. And so, for a tiny commission, he went to all the junk shops in White-chapel to talk the shopkeepers into putting Perolin Spray in their shop windows. Initially, that was hardly better than pouring can-dles. Jenö went from store to store in sunshine and in rain, in fair weather and in the close, sooty London fog that takes your breath away; he talked in Yiddish and English, demonstrated the sprays, was sent away and came back persistently after three weeks. His feet were as sore as they had been on the walk from Tapolca to Vienna, and after the accounts were balanced on the weekend, he got such a small sum of money that he could barely afford to eat bread and herring six times a week – on Fridays he went with Löwenzahn to a restaurant. That he did not give up can be ascribed to Löwenzahn, who hadn't read a line of Marx but understood capitalism from direct experience. "You should-n't work for wages," he lectured. "Look at the poor devils who slave away in the factories until they spit blood, and the boss has the profit. Have you ever seen a worker who can eat until he's full? Or do you think the clerks at Perolin can afford more than pickled herring for lunch? You have to work on your own account. If you work for a wage, you are a *shlemiel* and will remain a *nebbish* to the end of your days."

"But when I sell Perolin Spray, am I not still doing the work, and the firm has the profit?"

117

"That's right," said Löwenzahn, "but it's up to you how much you earn, and when you have saved enough money, you can make yourself independent."

Jenö listened as if Isaiah were preaching, but he wasn't one to save money. If he was invited somewhere, he had to arrive by cab, even if it meant going hungry for two days. Three months after he had started selling Perolin, he ordered his first tailor-made suit and paid for it in instalments. When he went to dinner with Löwenzahn on *erev Shabbos*, his tip was too generous. But when he had once sold a store the sprays, he could deliver the refills; he showed the salespeople how they should demonstrate the pine scent, and after two years his manager turned the business for the entire East End over to him. In 1907 the firm sent him back to Vienna as its general representative for the Monarchy. He had just turned twenty, but since the firm had not previously sold any Perolin to the Austro-Hungarian Monarchy, the risk was small.

3.

"Fifty years is a long time," said Horowitz after he had tapped on his glass and risen from his chair. "Josef Kahn has been a real *mensch* for fifty years – a good father, a good husband, a good friend. May he live another fifty years in good health and happiness in the bosom of his family. I remember how he arrived in Vienna with his Sidi and the little children, and had nothing and was hungry – "

"God is just," said Jenö, "he gives food to the rich and appetite to the poor."

"We didn't go hungry," said my grandfather.

"Be quiet and let him talk," said my grandmother.

"I remember how he arrived and was hungry," Horowitz continued, "and how he now sits in the new apartment like a king with the sceptre in his hand, *kanehore*, and looks at his wife and their five children, and he deserves his happiness. May God grant him health and contentedness and a long life, amen."

"I want . . ." said Josef, but since the whole family got up from their chairs, crowded around him, embraced and kissed him, he couldn't continue talking. When the tumult had subsided and Horowitz had tapped on his glass again, my grandmother got a little box from the sideboard and placed it on the table in front of my grandfather. "This is from me and the children," she said and watched as Josef took off the lid and from the tissue paper in the box brought out a solid gold pocket watch with a small chain. Then she disappeared into the kitchen and came back with a steaming soup tureen.

The table in the new apartment was extended as far as possible, but people were still sitting very close together: at the head of the table Josef and Sidonie, who only sat on the edge of her chair because she got up every minute to check on things in the kitchen or to bring bread that Josef then sliced, on the sides Papa and Mama Horowitz, Gisa and Jakob Pinsker, Mother Róth, who had again come down with a "chest illness" so that she could come to celebrate her son-in-law's birthday, Miklós Kálman, Dezsö, Jenö and Klara, beside her Ferenc Kahn (a second generation nephew of Josef's), at the foot of the table Elli and beside her Gisa's daughter, the five-year-old Olgerl. (In order for me to imagine how the woman who is now well into her eighties looked as a child, I have to study photographs, in which she can be easily recognized: back then she always wore a large bow in her hair, as did her sister Edith later.) Everyone was talking loudly at once while eating the soup – a nourishing chicken soup with noodles and giblets. "You lead a good life now," said Mother Róth to my grandmother, "I'm glad that you don't have to go to the market anymore."

"It is my good fortune to have good children, *kanehore*," said my grandmother, whose vocabulary had expanded considerably through her friendship with Miriam Horowitz. "Gisa didn't want me standing at the market anymore, with her so well off, and she gives me money every week, she can afford to, and Jenö does too. He is living on credit, but doesn't want to fall behind his sister."

"I am not living on credit," said Jenö, "my commission is paid to me monthly, and when we do the year-end calculations, there will be a lot more there than I was paid, if they don't cheat me out of it in London."

"The English don't cheat," said Horowitz.

"All people cheat," said Jenö, "there has never been anyone who didn't cheat. My friend Löwenzahn once said to me, some cheat because they want to, and some cheat because they have to, that's the only difference."

"Don't believe it," Dezsö called diagonally across the table and smacked his tongue. "If you're lucky, they can be bribed, but if you're unlucky, they'll all be honest."

"How are you, Mama?" asked Sidonie. "You haven't had a chance to say anything."

"Not bad, not bad," said Mother Róth, "but I worry about your father. He doesn't talk to anyone and complains about everyone, and he speculates – he speculates in property and grain, he buys and sells, and no good comes of it, it's not like it was earlier, when he succeeded in everything. If he buys land, the prices fall, if he buys wheat in the field, the crop fails. How should things go well with him, when he doesn't talk to anyone? Now he wants to dismiss Moische, because he is not so young anymore and has rheumatism, but I won't allow that, he should enjoy a peaceful old age with us."

Meanwhile, Klara and Elli had cleared away the soup plates, my grandmother got up from the edge of her chair and ran into the kitchen to bring out the main course: a huge tureen with a cold carp surrounded by a sea of jelly with onions and carrots. (I have never again eaten such jelly as my grandmother made, and I've searched all of Haifa in vain for a recipe for it.) A second, even larger tureen that Gisa brought from the kitchen held steaming potatoes. "You haven't said grace," said Miklós. He waited until the voices had subsided, and quietly said the prayer that of course should have been said before the soup. Then Josef poured more wine for them, wine that Jenö had brought, and my grandmother served the carp.

"Did you come to Vienna just because of my father, Uncle Miklós?" asked Jenö.

"It was a fortunate coincidence," answered the rabbi. "I'm participating in a conference here on combatting anti-Semitism, I'm supposed to write a report on it for A Magyar Szinagóga."

"The anti-Semitism isn't that bad," said Horowitz. "We have equal rights in the eyes of the law, and people don't bother us, what more do you want? There are Jews in Parliament, Victor Adler, the founder of the Austrian Social Democratic Party, is a Jew, we do not need to live in fear anymore."

"Maybe here," said Kálman, "but you know what's going on in Russia. In Chisinau there were over a hundred dead, and no one knows when the next pogrom will be."

"There is enough hate-mongering here too," said Jenö. "Look at the newspapers, what they print. This person is a Jew and that person is a Jew, there are too many Jewish lawyers, there are even Jewish officers, where will it lead to, they should throw us all out. At the university there was another riot, the German Nationals beat up Jewish students."

"Herzl is right," exclaimed Ferenc, "we will never be treated with respect until we have our own country. Have you read the The Jewish State, Jenö?"

"Don't talk to me about Herzl, Ferenc," said Horowitz. "He wanted to take us to the Blacks in Uganda. It is good that they disagreed with him in Basel two years ago. Or is anything about Uganda written in the Talmud?"

"It is also not written in the Talmud that Herzl will lead us to Israel," said Kálman. "It is written that the Messiah will lead us to Israel."

"If you wait for him, you can wait until Jurigelt," said Jenö.

But Kálman didn't let that bother him. "We must also allow the Lord to take His time," he said and took a second helping of jellied carp.

Before the cake was served – it was an almond cake that could not have been made any better, even by Sacher – my grandfather stood up and cleared his throat until there was quiet. "I am fifty," he began, "and fifty years are a long time, as Baruch has said. I have spent them well with my beloved wife and children – "

"Even if you had to do a lot of walking," Jenö interjected.

"In well-fitting shoes," said my grandfather and waited until the laughter had subsided. "I am grateful to you for the presents," (there had been other presents besides the watch) "and I am grateful to you for your love and loyalty. But today, we are celebrating something else besides my birthday. As you know, my Klara has got engaged to my dear nephew Ferenc – it makes a father happy when his daughter remains in the *mishpoche*. I wish you good fortune, and may your children be as good as mine are."

"*Kanehore*," said Ferenc in a deep, resonant voice. (His main job later was to sit by the cash register in Gisa's store and at the given moment, with his powerful voice, say "nem," which means "no" in Hungarian; but more about that later.)

"Tell me about yourself, Dezsö," said Kálman, who was sitting beside him. "What do you do? How are things going for you in your job?"

"I have now started doing the shop windows. You know that I work for Bamberger on Rotenturmstrasse. Until last month I always helped the decorator, but now I do everything myself."

"But you are colour-blind, aren't you?"

"Yes, but nobody knows that outside the family. I trained the errand boy to tell me the colours, and I tip him to keep his mouth shut. I had electric lighting and little floodlights installed, like they have in the best stores on Kärntnerstrasse, and I bought new mannequins from a firm in Mödling. Bamberger thought I spent too much money, but now he sees that it was worth it."

"You will amount to something," said Kálman. "But how about Klara and Ferenc?"

"Ferdi isn't the brightest," whispered Dezsö, "but Gisa will find a job for him, he has just now come to Vienna from that one-horse town in Hungary. You know that Klara is working for Löwy, where Gisa started. So actually, with the exception of Jenö, we are all in the garment business."

In the afternoon, Kálman had listened to a lecture on the plight of the Russian Jews, and Dezsö's remark reminded him of it. There is no way out for us, he thought. "If a Jew opens a store, he is called a wheeler-dealer or a rip-off Jew. If we study, there are too many Jewish doctors and lawyers – God knows, in Buda-pest now, every second lawyer really is a Jew. Karl Kraus com-plains that the press is controlled by the Jews, he should keep quiet, he himself is a Jew. In the shtetls they are starving, and when things improve and they can move around a little, the Cossacks come. In Lodz and in Krakow, the Jews are social dem-ocrats and read Karl Marx, and then they are accused of inciting the masses to revolt. Maybe Herzl was right after all, not about Uganda, that's nonsense, but about Palestine. But then where should the Arabs go?"

The cake had been made in the largest cake pan my grandmother owned, but it was soon eaten to the last crumb, and then came a bowl of pastries, among them the poppy-seed crois-sants that I so loved as a child. I still buy myself some now and then in the Hungarian Bakery near the ship museum in Derech Allenby. Fresh coffee had to be brewed to go along with the past-ries, and Gisa followed her mother into the kitchen, where she put on an apron over her evening gown, which was actually too elegant for a dinner in the family circle. "You've heard, have you, that Ginsberg has got over it?" she said, while she took the coffee grinder between her thighs and began to grind the beans.

"How so?" asked my grandmother.

"He has married a young widow, he invited me to the wed-ding, but not Jakob."

"And is he now building her a villa in Pressbaum?"

"He is now moving in very high society and building on the

123

ring. I'm glad for him, he was good to me, and I hope he will
⌐appy with his young wife."

"And how are things going for you and your husband,
Gisa? He looks good in the new suit, with his waxed moustache."

"Be careful with the hot water," said Gisa, who was handling the coffee. She had hoped her mother wouldn't ask, but then
she was glad to have the opportunity to talk about him after all.
"Maybe I should have let him stay at the market, although it really
hadn't looked good. I was embarrassed to have Ginsberg and the
seamstresses know that he was standing there all day long for a few
pennies, and now he doesn't know what he should do to kill the
time."

"Can't you use him in the store, Gisa?"

"God forbid," she said. "I don't want that, Mama, he does-
n't understand anything about it, and I don't like it when someone
interferes in my business. The personnel have to know who is the
boss. That's why the firm is still called Gisela Kahn, although that
isn't my name anymore."

"Maybe Jenö can use him at Perolin. Should I talk with Jenö?"

"Jakob won't want to. He'd rather sit in a café and be
bored."

"Well, if it's just that, you shouldn't complain," said my
grandmother, "if he is otherwise a good husband to you. Can't he
at least help pack things in the store, now that you are also supplying Gerngross?" She already had the can of fresh coffee in her
hand, but hesitated in the kitchen doorway because she sensed
that Gisa had something else on her mind.

"I would rather that he didn't come into the store at all.
He takes money from the till, as if I weren't already giving him
enough, and the way he walks around and watches everything
makes the girls who work for me nervous." But with that she had
said more than she had actually wanted to say. "Come, Mama,
Papa is waiting for his coffee."

When they entered the dining room again, Jenö was shooting his face off. "You have to do business with England," he said.

"If you come from Tapolca, Vienna is a big city, but you have to have seen London!"

"Vienna is big enough for me," said my grandmother, "I've lost my way here enough times."

"You can lose your way everywhere, Mama, but everything here is really provincial! In London you have all of India and all of Africa at your feet, you export everywhere, woollen materials and calico and machines!"

"If London is so magnificent, why didn't you stay there?" asked Dezsö spitefully.

"Because I longed for carp the way Mama cooks it," said Jenö laughing. "That is the only thing that can't be found there. But of course you can also import from England, which is what I'm doing now with Perolin, that's just the beginning, I'm going to found an import firm!"

"Perhaps Papa can join you in working for Perolin," said Klara. "He slaves away so at the shoes."

"I don't slave away," said my grandfather, "I like being in the shop."

"But it doesn't bring in much," said Klara, who was feeling very grown-up since she had become engaged to Ferenc.

"That's because Papa makes such old-fashioned shoes," said Dezsö. "The fashion changes every few weeks, you have to keep up with that. Now shoes are pointed at the front, not as wide as Papa makes them."

"You don't understand that, Dezsö," said my grandfather. "I don't make old-fashioned shoes, I make comfortable shoes that fit my customers – are they supposed to get corns from my shoes?"

"You are right, Papa, don't let the children interfere with the way you do things," said my grandmother, although she knew that Dezsö was right. If fewer customers came and Josef no longer had to hammer and sew ten hours a day, that wasn't a disaster; the children would take care of them. . . .

4.

My grandfather turning fifty and his daughter Klara getting
engaged to her cousin Ferenc weren't the only events of those
years. Rilke published his first two major volumes of poetry, the
Book of Hours, and the second, expanded edition of *Book of Images*,
and so became responsible for the fact that I arrived at my present
job of bathing poodles by way of studying German literature. (At
my Uncle Paul's, who was my stepfather's brother-in-law, I held
the first edition of the *Book of Images* in my hands. It was stupid of
me not to think of asking him to give it to me as a present – I'm
sure he would gladly have given it to me, because although he collected first editions with a passion, he didn't think much of Rilke,
calling his poetry Puerilke Lyrics, a pun he borrowed from Karl
Kraus. Five years later, when he turned his face to the wall and
starved to death in the Theresienstadt concentration camp, his
collection was down to just a single book, a first edition of Raabe's
Hungerpastor.) Sudermann's play *Stein unter Steinen* (*Stone among
Stones*) premièred in Berlin's Lessing Theatre, which led him to
Gerhart Hauptmann, and Einstein formulated the theory of rela-
tivity. My grandparents took little notice of all that. After fifteen,
after twenty years, they were still living like foreigners in Vienna,
though admittedly without being aware of it. They spoke mainly
Hungarian with each other and had hardly any friends, except for
Baruch and Miriam Horowitz, but they did have a steadily increasing flock of cousins, nephews, nieces and their children in Hungary or as visitors in Vienna who were called Róth, Kahn or
Kálman, and with whom they now spent a few weeks every summer. Following Gisa and Jenö, Dezsö had also moved out of the
apartment on Untere Augartenstrasse, but it had become an
established tradition for the whole family to gather there on *erev
Shabbos*. Slowly but surely, though, my grandmother began to find
the family too small. Why was there still only one grandchild? She
gave any number of hints. "Don't bother me with that," Jenö
would say then. "When I get married, it has to be someone

special." Klara and Ferenc should have gotten around to getting married by then, but he simply wasn't advancing in the world, he worked as a cutter, the job was so poorly paid that he couldn't afford an apartment, and so their marriage was postponed again and again. Why Gisa sixteen years after she had Olgerl still did not have a second child was a mystery that Dr. Grübel, the family physician, couldn't solve; Jakob performed his marital duty thoroughly and conscientiously, and the fact that he, if we can put it this way, also performed extramarital duties could not have stood in the way of Gisa having children. . . . ("People are funny," said Ginsberg, who as we know took an interest in his guests. "Jakob Pinsker has the most beautiful wife in Vienna, and he plays around." "But Mr. Ginsberg," said his head waiter, "*you* have the most beautiful wife in Vienna.")

But even if there was only one grandchild for the time being, my grandparents took great delight in their children, and they lived comfortably. To be sure, the time had come in the shoe business where mass-produced shoes were starting to replace hand-made shoes, and anyone who still had shoes made to measure was not going to a little workshop on Malzgasse. So Josef's store brought in less and less, and according to family tradition he was soon left with only those customers who, like Baron Pollak, didn't pay; but that was no disaster. "Let them buy the cheap mass-produced shoes," he would say, when yet another regular customer had deserted him. "They'll get corns, real doozers of corns." And he wasn't so far off the mark with that comment, at least as far as women were concerned: as the number of shoemakers declined, the number of corn surgeons increased. One of my childhood memories is of such a man. He would come once a week to our apartment, put on a green apron and occupy himself with my mother's feet. (If he only came once a month after her second marriage, and then not at all, it wasn't because she didn't get corns anymore, but because she couldn't afford to pay him.) By 1909 things had got to the point where my grandfather let Jenö persuade him to close his shop, and since he didn't want to sit idly at home, he started selling sand for Perolin. Working as a door-to-door salesman he thought was better for his health than spending his days in the damp shop bent over his stool, and he enjoyed walking through the suburbs with his case of sand samples. The shoes whose soles he wore out were made, as previously, by himself.

In contrast to my grandfather, who was still going door to door thirty years later, Jenö soon tired of the sand and the Perolin sprays, and not a moment too soon because the men in the Head Office in London had also tired of him. . . . The trouble was, he had rented a luxurious office for himself on the Graben that corresponded to his self-image and to the great future he foresaw for himself, but vastly exceeded the needs of a Perolin branch for the Hapsburg Monarchy. Since he knew that, and was generally of the opinion that the entire Monarchy was "provincial," he had decided to expand the business and travelled with considerable success to the Middle East. The first postcard in my collection that shows my Uncle Jenö on a camel with the pyramids in the background is dated 1910 (there is another one from 1938!). But the gentlemen in London didn't see why Cairo should be supplied through Vienna, it wasn't in the contract, which also didn't state that London had any obligation to pay the rent for the office on the Graben. . . .

To tell the truth, no English export firm ever had a more ingenious representative than my Uncle Jenö. ("If he holds his nose shut," said Dezsö admiringly, "he can sell cowpies to a cake shop.") The exclusive hotels in Cairo all began to smell like pine forests, and the number of crates delivered to the Nordbahnhof for Jenö doubled from year to year. But in the end, it was still just sand and Perolin, and there are limits to what you can earn from selling spray cans. There were no limits, though, to the expenses. As a matter of principle, Jenö travelled only first-class, and since travelling in the heat of the Egyptian summer was exhausting, he made up for it by taking a few days' holiday in Italy on his way there and his way back. There was nothing in the contract that stated that the Head Office in London had to pay for these holidays, but did he not have every right, indeed, was it not his duty to fortify himself for the stressful battle with the obstinate people who didn't understand that only by using oiled sand could they avoid the whirling up of dust and bacteria that was detrimental to their health? And finally, there weren't just contracts, there were moral obligations whose fulfillment should be expected at least of the English, who were famous throughout the world for their fair play! Before he, Jenö, had first set foot on desert sand, no one in Egypt had ever heard of Perolin. Now the name was as well-known as the English royal family, and all Cairo smelled like a pine forest. . . . But what, for example, about the six bottles of champagne that were emptied in one evening in the most expensive hotel in Alexandria? Of course a representative has to entertain his customers – but Muslims don't drink alcohol! One day, a man from London appeared unannounced in Jenö's office to examine his books. Jenö had the porter throw him out, and three months later a lawsuit began simultaneously in Vienna and London.

Meanwhile, Jenö had changed his line of business: he now imported furniture from a London firm in which his "great friend" Löwenzahn had a share. The commission on a sideboard amounted to thirty kronen, and in the autumn of 1911 Jenö bought himself a villa on the hill above Pressbaum, a large, dark wooden house, with some land and a barn. In the autumn of 1912, he thought he had discovered that the furniture firm had pulled a fast one on him with the invoices, so he travelled to London and promptly got mixed up in a second lawsuit that, while he lost the first one, ended with a settlement. The next opportunity for Jenö to enter into a business was presented by his younger brother.

What did Jenö look like back then? I have never gone to the trouble of putting the many photographs in my shoebox in chronological order, which wouldn't be easy at all, because the only ones with dates on them are the portraits taken in professional photographers' studios. If I had gone to the trouble, there would have been a big gap. There are several very old photographs, including the one of my great-grandmother and my grandmother when she was seventeen, because old Róth had been able to afford to go to a court photographer in Budapest. Then there is nothing for a long time, in particular, there are no photographs of my mother and her siblings, because my grandfather of course did not have a camera, and it would never have occurred to him to pay a lot of money to a photographer to perpetuate a sight that he could see daily free of charge. The gap doesn't close until Gisa's blouse factory brought money into the family. Then came the time when cameras were no longer so expensive, but taking pictures with a tripod and black cloth took more effort than it does today, and people went to considerable trouble arranging their subjects before taking a picture. That's why there are so many group photographs in my collection, with four or six, ten or twenty family members, and acquaintances who can no longer be identified. . . .

In these group photos, Jenö stands out, he is different from the others. For a long time I though I was just imagining that because I know too much about him, but I've tried it out on acquaintances to whom I showed the photographs, and they were bored until they noticed Jenö and they asked me: "Who is that?" Depending on which photograph they were looking at, the man who got their attention is between twenty-five and fifty, clean-shaven, his hands behind his back, usually wearing one of his checkered, English-style suits, his straight hair parted, his mouth a thin line, looking directly at the camera and, therefore, at the person looking at the picture – and it's that look of his that stands out. His eyes are too big, they look as if they were open as far as possible, and they express some sort of challenge or threat that can't be more closely defined. . . . But what am I supposed to answer? If I said: "This is my father's murderer," that wouldn't be true. So I just say: "That is my Uncle Jenö, a strange fellow. . . ."

My Uncle Dezsö tends to make the opposite impression in the group photos: his slightly rounded face, the neat little moustache, the wavy hair, above all the happiness that is evident even when he isn't smiling – all that invites your confidence, you sense that he is a person at peace with himself who knows how to enjoy eating his cucumber salad, so to speak. No one in the family could laugh as heartily as he did. Since he was tall and had a powerful build, it didn't detract from his appearance that he was already inclined to be corpulent in his mid-twenties; he only became really corpulent after 1938 in Buenos Aires. In contrast to Jenö, who was always in a hurry (he who hurries too much gets on the wrong train), Dezsö let things come to him. At first, he was satisfied serving customers at Bamberger's on Rotenturmstrasse, and creating shop window displays that gradually became quite famous. When it was still fashionable to be a little on the plump side, he had long-legged, thin mannequins made for his new models and placed them in poses that related to each other. He experimented with small floodlights that cast dark shadows, and occasionally, although Bamberger did not sell men's suits, put a man in tails or something eye-catching like a chimney sweep in among the long-legged ladies, and soon people expected something strikingly unusual from him. That was lucky for him. In 1910, with new models that he had ordered especially for that purpose, he had a shop window display entirely in blue, with a chair in the centre, over which he draped a snow-white pair of men's trousers. Lying diagonally across the trousers was supposed to be a wide, dark red tie that he had the errand boy bring him. White and red – those were the colours of the Babenbergs, who had ruled Austria from 976 to 1248, and the colours of the Austrian flag. When Bamberger entered the store in the early afternoon, he said: "That was a stunning idea of yours, Dezsö, with the bright green tie amidst all the blue dresses! Nobody is going to go past without stopping to look!"

"Pardon me, Mr. Bamberger?" said Dezsö, taken aback.

"I mean," repeated his boss, "I find it striking, that you put the green tie in the middle of the blue display."

Dezsö went pale, but got control of himself and said: "Well, Mr. Bamberger, I have to get a bright idea every now and then. . . ." The errand boy – whether he had misunderstood Dezsö or did it to annoy him remains unclear – got his ears boxed, but kept Dezsö's colour-blindness a secret.

131

The fact that Bamberger only showed up at his store on Rotenturmstrasse in the early afternoon was nothing out of the ordinary. Why should he go to a lot of trouble when Dezsö was taking care of everything anyway? Gradually, without their talking about it, Dezsö took on the responsibilities of a manager. He saw to the collection, set the prices and supervised the personnel. Soon it was he who showed the salesladies how they should present the dresses. They sold twice as many dresses as before, but people are strange: the more the business prospered, the less Bamberger was interested in it. You can't say that he felt pushed aside by Dezsö; Dezsö didn't push, and after all, Bamberger owned the store; but he felt unneeded when he made his visits, he just stood around, and from month-to-month he grew increasingly fond of "loafing about," or doing nothing. By the autumn of 1912, things had reached the point where one afternoon he walked into the little office that had previously been his, but where Dezsö usually worked now, to talk to him about the future.

"I'm not interested in the store anymore, Dezsö," he said. "I've worked hard long enough, I would like to sell the store and retire."

"You're not serious, Mr. Bamberger!"

"The city air is bad for me," said Bamberger, who had suddenly realized that he was sitting in the visitor's chair, and the young lad behind the desk was sitting in *his* chair. "I just had the opportunity to buy a lakeside plot with a house in Zell. You know I have the rental property in Landstrasse, that brings in enough money, but for the house in Zell I need cash. But I don't want the store to go to a stranger. You have been like a son to me all these years, maybe you can take it over. I need 200,000 kronen in cash, you can borrow it from a bank and pay off the rest later."

That was an opportunity not to be passed up – but 200,000 kronen? Dezsö was the son of a shoemaker, it wasn't so long ago that his mother turned over every kreuzer before she spent it, and now 200,000 kronen? To be able to put 200,000 kronen on the table in cash, you had to be a Rothschild.

"May I think it over, Mr. Bamberger?"

"Think it over, Dezsö. But if I were you, I'd grab it."

"If I were you, I'd grab it," said my grandmother as well, when Dezsö asked her advice. "When the store belongs to you, you'll make a fortune. Maybe Gisa can help you a bit."

The next morning she went to Gisa's store on Tuchlauben. Gisa was working on the spring collection, showed her mother new models and a large assortment of lace that had just arrived from Belgium, and Sidonie didn't get a word in edgewise for a long time. When she finally explained what had brought her there, Gisa angrily threw the lace back into the carton. "I can help a bit," she said, "but not as much as I would like. The store easily pays for the cook and the nanny and whatever else I need. Jenö's friend, you know, Löwenzahn, has also provided me with contacts in London, although he and Jenö have gone separate ways. With what Jakob spends, though, I could buy a house."

"What does he spend it on?" asked my grandmother, and, when Gisa didn't answer, "Why do you give it to him?"

"I give him what he needs. But what should I do when he comes into the office and empties the till? I can't argue with him in front of the personnel."

My grandmother calculated that over ten years had passed since Olgerl's birth. Moreover, she had seen Jakob in Café Schubert with an extra from the Burgtheater who was done up like an expensive whore, and she knew other things from hearsay. "I don't know," she said at last, "there's a limit to everything, maybe you should separate, you have reason enough."

"Unfortunately, I love my husband," said Gisa in a resigned way. "God forgive me, I love him."

While this conversation was taking place, Dezsö was consulting with his brother in a café on the Opernring that was now his favourite hangout. Since Jenö's falling out with the furniture company, he had no regular job, speculated in shares and spent many hours a day there reading the financial columns in the newspapers that he had piled up in front of him. "You have to understand, Jenö," said Dezsö as he spooned whipped cream onto his coffee, "what Bamberger is offering me is a once-in-a-lifetime opportunity, this sort of offer isn't going to come along again, but 200,000 kronen? Just the interest on that adds up to 7,000 kronen a year, if a bank will lend me the money!"

"You're talking as if 200,000 kronen were a fortune," said Jenö, "but for that you couldn't even buy a house in Hietzing. A house on the Graben now costs half a million."

"So I should do it?"

"*We* should do it. Why are we brothers, the two of us will do it. I still have 20,000 kronen from the settlement with the furniture company, I'll take out a mortgage on my villa in Pressbaum, and the bank will lend us the rest."

"But you already have a large mortgage on your villa," said Dezsö, and taking a pencil out of his pocket, he started writing numbers on the edge of one of the newspapers that lay on the chair beside him.

"That's no disaster," said Jenö. "The prices in Pressbaum are rising, everybody wants to build on the hills above Vienna, I can easily take out a mortgage for another 40,000. And we can bargain with Bamberger."

My grandmother was opposed to the idea of their being business partners. "Gisa will lend you 20,000 and vouch for you for 40,000 at the Kreditbank," she said, when Dezsö told her of Jenö's suggestion. "That's not a bad beginning. Don't you want to be your own boss on Rotenturmstrasse? Jenö is clever, but he knows nothing about fashions."

"He doesn't need to," said Dezsö. "I will run the whole show, I have done that for a long time, and the way he can talk with people, no one else can do that. . . ."

"He can talk," said my grandmother, "but he can also spend money. With the profit you'll make from the store, you can pay off the mortgage in a few years and be a rich man. If you go into partnership with Jenö, with his villa in Pressbaum and his eternal restlessness, you'll never be out of debt. But you are no child anymore, Dezsö, sleep on it and do what you think is right."

Jenö could talk. He talked with Dezsö, he talked – which Dezsö didn't like very much – with Bamberger and got the cash payment down to 180,000, he took out the second mortgage on the villa and dealt with the Kreditbank, and when he visited Dezsö three days later on Rotenturmstrasse, he triumphantly placed a piece of paper on the desk, on which, scrawled in indelible pencil (there's no writing implement I hate as much as indelible pencils), he could read:

60,000	– Jenö
20,000	– Gisa (at 3%)
<u>100,000</u>	– Kreditbank (at 3.5%)
180,000	

The lawyer who had lost Jenö's case with Perolin but had won a considerable settlement from the furniture company drew up the bill of sale with Bamberger, and soon, above Dezsö's famous shop window displays, there was a business plaque with the inscription

```
KAHN BROTHERS
FORMERLY LEONHARD BAMBERGER
```

The fact that the firm now had two managers, one of whom knew nothing about the business, didn't seem to have any drawbacks. Dezsö was always there and made sure that the customers felt comfortable on Rotenturmstrasse. The sales ladies continued to say "Baroness" and "Counsellor" and still smiled politely as they showed the twentieth outfit to the butcher's wife, whom they addressed as "*Kommerzienrätin.*" Now, however, they modelled dresses in a way Dezsö had come up with, they took mincing steps and walked in a semi-circle, causing the long ball gowns to flare out attractively. Business was flourishing. It annoyed Dezsö that sometimes, when he returned from lunch, he would find Jenö in one of his English suits sitting in his (Dezsö's) office studying the stock market reports, so that Dezsö had to sit somewhere else with the bank book and the bills; and it annoyed him that his partner, after a few weeks, was convinced that he was now such an expert about ladies' fashions that he could lecture his younger brother on the proper way to run the store. For example, because the villa in Pressbaum was not exactly cheap to maintain, with its two mort-gages, roof repairs, gardener and the parties he gave there from time-to-time, he wanted to get as much money as possible as quickly as possible out of the business, and so came up with the bright idea of raising all the prices by thirty percent: he called that "bringing them into line with Kärntnerstrasse" and informed Dezsö in a brilliant torrent of words that it was easier to sell an expensive dress than a cheap one. So Dezsö had to take an hour to explain to Jenö that their clientele on Rotenturmstrasse was respectably middle-class and that *Kommerzienrätin* X or *Regierungsrat* Y bought the ball gowns for their daughters at Kahn Brothers precisely because they were cheaper there than on Kärntnerstrasse. Jenö said yes, no, and yes again, but he went to Paris and came back with green-and-white-striped blouses that Dezsö resolutely refused to display, which led to two long arguments: the first because Jenö, who was now also an expert in shop window displays, absolutely wanted to have a display in which everything was green and white, and the second because he stubbornly insisted, when the blouses still were not sold after three months and finally had to be marked down below cost, that they would have been a sensation and that the ladies would have scrambled to buy them if they had been properly displayed – an assertion Dezsö could not disprove. "You are simply not of an enterprising nature, Dezsö," said Jenö, "with-out me, you'd still be a minor employee." However, as mentioned, business was flourishing, and Dezsö could put up with a few annoy-ances. He had a talent for enjoying life, went with friends to the taverns in the outskirts of Vienna where the new wine was sold, flirted with saleswomen from other stores – not the ones on Rotenturmstrasse, he had stopped doing that when the firm was still called Leonhard Bamberger because it undermined his authority – and went to balls several times a year. But he lived in a modest bachelor apartment in the first district, ate most of his meals at his parents', spent much less than his share of the store's profit, gradually paid off his part of the mortgage and soon had a small amount of capital with which he began to speculate in real estate, showing a caution and a healthy instinct that the much more brilliant Jenö lacked. Then came 1914, and with it many changes: Dezsö's active duty at the front that just about cost him his life, his marriage that Jenö disapproved of, and their big argument that brought the first rift into the family – but in the meantime other things had happened that I'll have to reconstruct.

CHAPTER FOUR

Elli

1.

IF I BELIEVED in an almighty and benevolent God, as Chaim Ledermann did, I would not be able to make much sense of my family's history; because there would have to be justice in this best of all possible worlds that this God has created, and to take a random example, but one that immediately springs to my mind, it would not be easy to understand why my mother, of all people, such a delicate, simple and kind person, suffered such great misfortune – just as it, per contrarium, makes no sense to me, *si c'est écrit là-haut*, why the Kahns were able to save themselves when the gas chambers in Auschwitz and Belsen, Majdanek and Sobibor were running full tilt, so that we are now able to enjoy our beautiful walks along the Pacific or the Mediterranean beaches. . . . "We give thanks to Hitler," we joke thoughtlessly, "if he had not existed, we would at best be living in Pressbaum today." But such thoughtlessness is horrible and not the way I really think, because for me, my own survival is sometimes a problem; I don't know what I have done to deserve this mercy, and I find it hard to believe that the world really needs a Viennese Jew who bathes poodles in Haifa. But as far as my mother is concerned, if I had Ledermann's mythopoetic mind, I would imagine a dialogue something like this:

The Lord is sitting in his office in heaven – it resembles the office Dezsö used to have on Rotenturmstrasse but is somewhat larger, and the desk is made of Karelian marble – and the archangel Gabriel is standing in front of him with a yarmulke on his head.

"Tell me, O Lord of Hosts," says the archangel, "why you gave Dezsö the gift of turning everything he touches into gold, and you threw Elli, the lamb, to the wolves?"

"It is the fate of the sheep to be torn to shreds by the wolves," says the Lord.

But Gabriel has been studying the Talmud for thousands of years and cannot be fooled. "That's well and good, O Lord of hosts," he says. "But wasn't it you who decided that it would be Elli's lot to be a lamb?"

"There always have to be lambs," says the Almighty. "You don't want the wolves to starve, do you?"

"In a well planned world," says Gabriel, who has studied not only the Talmud, but also Leibniz and Marx, "the wolves would be vegetarians."

"Not all animals can be vegetarians," says the Lord. "What would that lead to?"

So they debate for a while, until the Lord loses patience. "Were you there, you little ratfink, when I made the leviathan?"

"Don't be silly," says Gabriel, "you could intimidate Job that way, but you can't do that with me. You know very well that I was there, I made the ribs according to your instructions."

"I wish I had your chutzpah," says the Lord, "then the world would be a different place."

Perhaps the length of this introduction is indicative of my reluctance to tell my mother's story, but that is an inhibition that I share with her. On the long winter evenings in London, she liked to talk about the past and told me with pleasure, for example, about Dezsö's *joie de vivre*, how he liked to laugh, and with what delight he drank the dressing out of his bowl when they had had cucumber salad on *erev Shabbos* on Augartenstrasse (Goethe is said to have done that too, but that's the only similarity there is between Goethe and my uncle). She even liked to tell me about Jenö, although she should actually have hated him, because she wasn't remembering him as her husband's enemy, or as the alcoholic he later became, but rather as her beloved, admired older brother of 1905 or 1910, as if everything that came later hadn't happened. All of us retouch the past; what we remember is always a mixture of fiction and truth, *Dichtung und Wahrheit*, and it is quite right that people have so seldom taken it amiss that Goethe glosses over some things in his autobiography with that title. However, my mother did not like to talk about herself, and I had to rely on other sources of information, above all on my Aunt Olga, as I call her, Gisa's daughter, who is much older than I am, but is actually my cousin. Since the death of her husband, she lives only in the past and remembers everything – sometimes just the facts, because she doesn't always appreciate the psychology behind the actions. In that regard, Uncle Martin would have been a better source, but he sometimes suddenly stopped talking, because this distinguished and decent man lived by the motto *de mortuis nil nisi bene* and preferred to remain silent about everything that was unpleasant. When I visited him in his apartment in Beverly Hills, where in spite of his roundabout route there via Buenos Aires he still had some of his beautiful Viennese furniture, and asked him about my father and his suicide, he told me how this so cheerful man had slowly gone out of his mind during the last year of his life, and said: "Your mother did not support him." But when I wanted to know more about that, he was already sorry to have made a disparaging remark about my mother and abruptly changed the topic. He was no longer alive the next time I visited California, but in the meantime I had already given his remark enough thought and no longer needed an explanation.

It must have had a formative influence on Elli's character that she was by several years the youngest of five siblings. When the pioneers in the Canadian north walked in single file, the first person had to wade with difficulty through the deep snow, but the last person was already walking on a smooth track. It was in this sense that Elli was the last. That means not only that she did not have to walk from Vienna to Tapolca in 1899 because she was sitting comfortably on the tarpaulin, but also that by the time she reached the age where that sort of thing mattered, there was enough money for pretty clothes (quite apart from the fact that they were in the business). She was spoiled by her parents and her siblings as the baby of the family, and although she wasn't beautiful like Gisa, who turned the heads of all the men on the street, she was pretty in a conspicuous, immediately appealing way. I have already mentioned that the three older ones resembled the Róths with their black hair, dark eyes and complexion that can tolerate a lot of sunshine, and which I like so much about the girls I see walking along Carmel Beach. The two younger ones exaggerated, as it were, the paternal line, they were blonde and blue-eyed with complexions as white as milk, and when they (they were inseparable as children, as later on again in old age) went for a walk through the Augarten Park or the Stadtpark in colourful dresses and summer hats, people turned around to look at them too. At that time, they looked stunningly alike, and even in the photographs from the 1920s, it's easy to see that they were sisters. They had the same wavy hair, the small straight nose and moist eyes, they were both half a head shorter than the older ones, and they were noticeably high-bosomed, which was considered chic at the time. (That's probably why they were so fond of wearing high-waisted dresses with a belt, which further emphasized their high bosoms.) Klara, however, had already started to put on weight, and when I had a dog in Canada in 1953 – she was called Hedda, and may be part of the reason why I became a veterinarian – I sometimes called her Aunt Klara because of her wide forehead and wide jaw.

In school, Elli learned what there was to learn there – reading, writing and arithmetic, as well as some geography and history, the last two subjects taught primarily with a view to creating loyalty to the Kaiser and Austro-Hungarian patriotism, in Elli's case with great success: like so many Austro-Hungarian Jews, she retained a touching devotion to Kaiser Franz-Joseph until the end of her life, and when she was very old she was still adamant that there would not have been a Hitler and the Second World War would not have happened if only the Hapsburgs had remained in power after 1918. It was Jenö who caused her first sorrow, as he would later cause her the great sorrow that destroyed her life. She loved her parents, she loved all her siblings, but she clung to Jenö with passionate admiration, and when the lad suddenly disappeared from Vienna, the seven-year-old was inconsolable for weeks and burst into tears every time his name was mentioned. It was good that her parents could arrange for a diversion. In Hungary – in Tapolca, in Vasvár, in Szombathely – they had any number of uncles and aunts and cousins called Róth, Kahn or Kálman. (My second cousin Walter, who grew up in Vienna but spoke good Hungarian, tried to count them all and came up with over seventy, of whom, though, barely a third survived the Holocaust.) Elli and Klara spent the summer after Jenö's departure in a village near Vasvár, where hens and geese walked around on the street and there was a carp pool, like the one on Dezsö Róth's property, where the children could go wading. My mother often told me how they all used to run barefoot through the mown fields to dry off. The village children were used to that, while my mother got sore feet right away, but that wasn't so bad. There was always a cousin called Róth, Kahn or Kálman to give her a piggyback ride home if she started to cry.

Then all of a sudden her admired, beloved brother was back again, to whose countless other distinctions and superior features was now added an aura of distant lands, of the "big world." . . . Now he liked to take his little sister out to a café, where he ordered their slices of cake in English, which went well with his checkered suit. It was great fun when, although he was speaking German with Elli, he did so with the English accent he had learned as an apprentice. Elli would try not to laugh, go red in the face and then burst out laughing, scandalizing the waitress, who found it impolite of the little girl to laugh at the gentleman who was taking her out for coffee; for an Englishman he spoke such good German!

While Klara went to work as an errand girl at Löwy's, Gisa had already rented a part of the upper storey on Tuchladen and took my mother to work in her store as soon as she could leave school at the age of fourteen. Elli did whatever needed doing; she sorted the mail, learned how to use a sewing machine and helped pack things. (When she helped me pack my things forty years later in London, I could take my shirts and suits uncreased out of the suitcase in Paris or Amsterdam.) What she didn't learn was independence. There was always someone there to make the decisions for her and to keep an eye on her, whether she was strolling through the Wurstelprater fairgrounds with Klara and Ferenc, or whether Dezsö took her to a wine locale. In the store she was "almost the owner's daughter," at home she was everybody's pet, and when she needed a hat or gloves, she was immediately advised by her mother, Jenö, Dezsö or the three of them together. She didn't dislike that, but she didn't reach the point where the apron strings are cut and a young person finds herself. So at sixteen she was physically already a young woman, but psychologically still a child, and that created a tension that had to be released somehow.

When she was crossing the Ringstrasse with Jenö one afternoon in May of 1910 to get to the entrance of the Stadtpark – the lilacs were already in full bloom – her leg twitched, it went off on its own, so to speak, and she made a little leap. Jenö stopped short, but that was the time when his first lawsuit was about to be decided, he was telling his sister how brilliant his lawyer was, and he kept on talking. When they reached the big beds of roses in the park, the same thing happened again. "What's that you're doing, Elli?" he asked impatiently – the brilliance of his lawyer, who "had never yet lost a case," was important to him and he wanted Elli to listen.

"I don't know," she said, "I have a sort of tingling in my leg."

A week later, the leg went off on its own again. Elli had been suddenly overcome with tiredness on Tuchlauben in the early afternoon and had gone home. Now she was alone in the apartment, and when she went across the dining room, her leg twitched. She stood still for a moment, and then started walking back and forth on the large Persian carpet (it's unbelievable how inexpensive those carpets were back then!). Every third or fourth time, she made a little leap. After a few minutes she gave up this fruitless activity, got her Diabolo out of a drawer that was stuffed full of old things – she hadn't had it in her hands for a long time, so she had to search for it – and went into Augarten Park.

Do people still know what this toy is? Elli was much too old for it. It consists of two sticks that are tied together with a string about fifty centimetres long and a notched little wooden wheel that you set on the string and make it turn rapidly by moving the sticks a certain way. Then you flick the little wheel into the air and catch it again on the string, which is devilishly difficult. (Is that why the toy is called Diabolo?) Elli was out of practice and at first did not succeed in balancing the wheel on the string, but then she got the knack of it again, the little wheel flew into the air and landed on the string. As long as she played with great concentration – you had to flick the wheel up as high as possible and still catch it again – everything went well. When her concentration let up, her leg twitched, and the wheel fell to the ground. A few boys had stopped on the gravel walkway to watch her, and they laughed. Elli tried again: the little wheel flew up toward the blue sky, but then her leg twitched, Elli almost lost her balance, caught the wheel with her hand and went home. In the evening, she spoke to her mother about it, and the next morning the family doctor came, Dr. Grübel, a bearded man in his thirties, who later looked after me as well.

The examination took place in the children's room, where Klara and Elli, and later my brother and I and our nanny slept. Elli was not running a temperature, and when Dr. Grübel pulled down her left eyelid with his thumb, his trained eye could determine that she was not anaemic. He examined Elli with the help of a big black stethoscope, knocked on various places on her chest and back to find out where it sounded muffled and where it sounded hollow, and found that her lungs were healthy. Then he asked her to sit on the edge of the bed with her legs crossed and knocked on her knee with a rubber hammer he took out of his breast pocket. The reflex was normal, but as Elli stood up, her leg twitched.

"The child . . ." (damn it, she was no longer a child!) "the child is perfectly healthy," said Dr. Grübel at last, as he put his instruments back into the black leather bag that was the sign of his profession. "A symptom of puberty, nothing more. A little more bed rest and a lot of fresh air will do her good." Then, because a doctor has to prescribe something, he prescribed an iron supplement, and my grandparents accompanied him from the room. In the hallway, he said in a low voice: "I just told you a half truth, Mr. Kahn. That may be a transient symptom of puberty, or maybe not." And, turning to her mother: "Keep an eye on the girl, it's fine for her to keep working in the store, and she should eat well and go for walks, and beyond that we'll just have to wait and see if it goes away."

So Elli drank the iron supplement, worked in the store and went for walks, but it was horrible. It wasn't so bad in the store, where there were always bolts of material or sewing machines she could hide behind. On the street, she was exposed to everyone's view, and her leg was temperamental: if there was no one to be seen far and wide, then it did what it was told, and she strolled along in a leisurely fashion like any other seventeen-year-old who is just going for a walk to kill time. But if someone approached her, then she suddenly felt the tension (Rilke had just at that time described the phenomenon in his novel *The Notebooks of Malte Laurids Brigge*), gathered all her strength, and then, no matter how hard she fought against it, the little leap came. Since people turned around to look at her – she was, as mentioned, pretty enough to make people turn around after her – it was almost as bad as a nightmare in which you have to cross the street naked, and since Dr. Grübel, who she went to see three times at two week intervals, could not help, he sent her to a famous specialist.

Two days later, Elli spent half an hour with her mother in the specialist's waiting room, and things didn't look good there. There was a little boy with a crooked shoulder, a teenager whose mouth was jerking in the most frightful manner, a monstrously fat fourteen-year-old girl who sat beside her tiny, withered mother and stared motionlessly ahead; then an old man was led into the room by an attendant, and a woman came in with a quietly whimpering baby. When Elli's turn came at last, she noticed that the specialist shook her mother's hand, but not hers. Then he asked a few indifferent questions, performed the usual examination with the pulled down eyelid and the surreptitious knock on her knee, and finally, while the doctor sat with his elbows on his desk, Elli had to walk back and forth in the examination room. After ten or twelve steps, her leg twitched, and the doctor said "Aha." When she took a second leap he said "Aha" again, and when it happened a third time, he sat up triumphantly and said: "Aha! That is St. Vitus's dance." Then Elli had to sit with the patients in the waiting room again while the doctor spoke with her mother, and a quarter of an hour later she was home again in the apartment.

Although it was a weekday, Elli stayed home the next morning, and soon she was alone. Klara was of course long since at Löwy's (she was conscientious and clever, but no replacement for Gisa); my grandfather was going door to door where he didn't sell much sand (it didn't matter, because his wife gave him pocket money out of the brown envelopes, and he had hardly any expenses anymore, since Jenö bought him his cigars directly from Cuba, thereby circumventing the monarchy's tobacco monopoly); my grandmother had made an exception to her normal routine and gone to the Tuchlauben store to help pack a shipment of blouses for a customer in Liverpool who was getting impatient. It was quiet in the apartment and on the street, with only the sound of the streetcar at ten minute intervals. Elli sat lost in thought. She had never read Rilke's *Malte Laurids Brigge*, but she knew what St. Vitus's dance was. So all her dreams and hopes had come to an

147

end, she would never have a boyfriend, never have a husband, never have children. Instead, she would spend her life as a useless, ridiculous cripple whom people pointed at. . . . After a while, she started letting out a hem on a dress that had got too short for her, but then she put it aside again, because there was no purpose anymore in such an activity. If she had St. Vitus's dance, it didn't matter if the dress was five or ten centimetres too long or too short, it would still just hang in the cupboard. She thought of going to Augarten Park – Dr. Grübel had prescribed plenty of fresh air – but she didn't dare to leave the house. Finally, she went to one of the two windows and opened it. (It has been years since I've seen a double window like that: the outer window opens outward, the inner inward; between the two windows lies a window cushion that is supposed to keep out draughts when the window is shut, and if the sun is too bright, there are hemp ropes to let down a blind.) Elli leaned against the cushion, looked out and watched the streetcar drive past. At that time, on the entire Untere Augartenstrasse, from the bridge to the park, the streetcar ran on a single track. In front of the house there was a switching place. The streetcar coming from the park stopped, the driver got out, switched the track over and stopped the streetcar on the siding until the streetcar coming from the bridge had gone past. After Elli had watched that always identically repeated manoeuvre for the third time, she took the cushion off the window ledge, put it on the dining room table, waited until the street was completely empty and jumped out the window.

From the third storey it was a six-metre drop to the cobblestones of the pavement, but she fell in a lucky way, and at that age people are resilient. She broke her thighbone, was taken to the hospital by ambulance and recovered in a few weeks. When she could walk again, her right leg was slightly shorter, which could be compensated for by an insole in her shoe, and her foot no longer twitched.

Of course Elli was now even more lovingly cared for. Her parents and her siblings competed with each other in spoiling her, but a new epoch in her life began. She took dancing lessons and discovered that the insole did not impede her. She occasionally accompanied Jenö and Dezsö to a ball and discovered the dream world of the Viennese operetta. The Kahns liked to go to the operetta *en famille*, especially since Jenö usually arranged for them to have a box. If he went to the opera, he took only Elli along, and it had to be a light opera; Wagner was out of the question, that was, like Schiller's poetry, "*meshuga.*" After March of 1912, though, there was sometimes a third person with them. "Today, Elli, I would like to introduce you to a friend of mine," Jenö said. "We sometimes meet for a little snack in Café Schubert." (That was not only one of the two cafés that had almost – by a fish's breadth, one might say – come into Gisa's co-ownership, but also the one where Jenö now studied the stock market reports every morning in all available newspapers.) In fact, the siblings had hardly taken their seats than a black-haired young man walked up to their table and more indicated than took a little bow. "Hello Jenö; may I kiss the young lady's hand?"

"May I introduce you: my sister Elli – Sándor Engelmann," said Jenö, of course pronouncing the S correctly, like sh, because Hungarian was, strictly speaking, Engelmann's mother tongue.

"So you are Miss Elli, about whom I have heard so much," said Sándor before sitting down.

Elli looked at him attentively and observed that Jenö and his friend were very different. Her brother wore a yellow tie with his checkered suit, he looked enterprising and stood out, whereas his friend in his dark suit seemed almost too respectable. And while Jenö with his wide-open eyes looked threateningly at the world, his friend, although he was obviously in the best of moods, was a little shy. . . . But Jenö hadn't yet finished his introduction. "Sándor manages a men's fashion store in Linz," he said. "He comes to Vienna every few weeks to educate himself."

"You're teasing me," said Sándor Engelmann. "You know that I travel to Vienna every few weeks because I have to look at the shop window displays."

Shop windows? Displays again? A representative from Lodz goes through a shtetl –

There aren't any shtetls anymore, where the Jews were crammed into a maze of tiny streets, studied the Talmud, had children and lived on thin air. Burnt to the ground, torn down, expropriated, the owners having died of thirst in cattle cars, or been murdered in Auschwitz, in Belsen, in Chelmno, in Majdanek, in Sobibor, in Treblinka – is it still permissible to tell a Jewish joke that was originally in German? Maybe so.

A salesman from Lodz goes through a shtetl, notices that his watch has stopped, and finds a store with the window display full of clocks – pocket watches, pendulum clocks, cuckoo clocks, an old ship's chronometer. Admittedly, they all show the wrong time, but the salesman nevertheless enters the store and asks the man behind the counter to repair his watch. "You want *me* to repair your watch?" asks the man. "I do circumcisions."

"But if you do circumcisions," asked the representative, "why do you have nothing but clocks in your window?"

"Well now," said the man, "if you did circumcisions, what would you put in your shop window?"

2.

Sándor Engelmann – my father, to get this matter straight right away – really did travel to Vienna every few weeks to look at the shop windows in the Inner City, not those of a watchmaker and not those of a circumciser, but the shop windows of the elegant ladies' and men's fashion stores; because what people wore in Vienna, they wore six weeks later in Linz, and so it was one of his regular tasks to take a look around in Vienna. It was a task he enjoyed, even before a trip to Vienna meant seeing Elli again. Although Linz did have a municipal theatre and guest performances, it could not be compared with the music scene in Vienna; and Jenö was in Vienna, the friend he so admired, who had seen the world, understood the mysteries of the stock exchange, quoted Heine and Goethe, could explain exactly why *Carmen* was a better opera than *La Bohème*, and whom the waiters, although he had left school when he was fourteen, addressed as "Herr Doktor." . . . In order to fully understand this admiration, though, you have to know something of my father's background. "You have to understand," my Aunt (cousin, really) Olga once said to me in Beverly Hills, "your father came from the country, he felt unsure of himself."

Among the photographs my mother brought to England, there are many from the war years. They are usually group photos of soldiers in uniform and show, besides young men I cannot identify, Sándor Engelmann, his brother Matthias, sons of my grandfather's brothers, Dezsö, Jenö and relatives from the Róth side of the family – all of them were in the trenches. There are also very pretty pictures of Elli and Sándor from the post-war period, but above all a late studio portrait of my father that I love very much. It hangs now in a special place in my study and shows a serious man with a little "English" moustache that was fashionable then, and with black, almost curly hair over a high forehead. Although the photographer chose the three-quarters profile, you can see if you look very closely that his nose was not exactly straight – a trait my brother inherited, but I didn't. Under bushy black eyebrows, dark and sad eyes look out at you. . . . When Sándor met Elli, he must have looked at the world very differently.

What I can call to mind about my father is minimal; I was only five years old when he died, and I don't have many childhood memories anyway. I do remember, though, that he had a hollow about the size of a teacup in the small of his back, where, as he explained to me, splinters of a grenade had had to be surgically removed. I also have a clear memory of my father lying on his back on the double bed in my parents' bedroom – which my mother later shared with my stepfather, to my helpless rage – singing arias and snatches of tunes from popular operas in his good tenor voice, such as "Santuzza, don't tempt me" or "Your tiny hand is frozen," but also ballads by Löwe; he had records of what he liked to sing, the old hard rubber records with a dog on the label ("His Master's Voice"), that I played when I was ten or twelve on one of those old-fashioned gramophones that you had to wind up for each new side of a record. My father had been dead for some time then, but since hardly anyone else in our house bought records, the little music collection still reflected his taste unadulterated in the 1930s. One of his favourite songs was Karl Löwe's "Song of the Clock," which I would still sing today (because of the record), if I could sing at all – that sentimental tract against suicide that starts with a metaphor:

> Wherever I go, I always
> carry a clock with me,

– and that ends with the singer, whose metaphorical clock has finally stopped, emotionally assuring the great clockmaker that it wasn't his fault, because

> O Lord, I caused no damage,
> it stopped of its own accord.

The fact that my father like to sing this, of all songs, and then still damaged his metaphorical clock, would be a psychological puzzle if it weren't the case that most people more or less ignore the words when they sing a song. But although I remember so little about my father, I am quite well informed, thanks to the stories my mother told me in England and my Aunt told me in Beverly Hills. In my mother's notebook in which she entered dates and place names for me when she was in England, she wrote in her best handwriting: "Alexander (Sándor) Engelmann, born June 13, 1889 in Oszidék, Yugoslavia." (The name of my stepfather is not to be found in the notebook, which means that, twenty years before his death, my mother had deleted him from her list of the living and the dead.)

After my father's death, I spent a few weeks with his relatives in Oszidék. The village on the Drava belonged to Hungary until 1918 and consisted, when my father was born, of hardly more than six dozen farms, in front of which, with the one exception about to be mentioned, there were huge piles of manure. It was a friendly place, with a lot of trees and a wide, unpaved main street, but it had changed markedly in the years between my father's birth and his death. In front of the Engelmanns' house in 1889 and still in 1927 there was only a very small manure pile, because they had only one cow and a few goats, but a good dozen turkeys in the courtyard that were fed corn. You put the dried-out corncobs in a funnel, turned a crank, the corn kernels fell into a tin can, and when you then shook the kernels out onto the ground, the big birds fell on them as if they hadn't had anything to eat in weeks. To get to the next city with a horse and wagon, took two hours in the summer, and three or four hours in the winter. If the wagon got stuck in the mud, most of the farmers whipped their horses, but Bär Engelmann, my father's father, climbed down from the box, waded into the mire up to the rim of his boots, and pushed.

The beating of horses played a considerable role in Dostoyevsky's life and in Nietzsche's life, but Bär Engelmann didn't know that. He was a simple man who led a simple life. His pride and joy were the quince he grew in a small field on the side of the Drava opposite the village. Every autumn, his wife made huge quantities of quince cheese, incredibly long rolls, almost as wide as a child's head, that you could cut into apricot-coloured, semi-transparent slices of jelly-like consistency that tasted sweet-and-sour. (Every autumn during my childhood in Vienna, the postman brought us big packages wrapped in brown paper that contained this delicacy, and now in Haifa, I buy quince cheese whenever it is available: the taste of quince reminds me of my childhood, albeit without awakening such a world of memories as Proust's *madeleine*.)

So Bär Engelmann grew quince that his wife made into quince cheese. But growing quince is – if I may steal from Thomas

153

Mann again – "not an adequate purpose in life," and Bär Engelmann did not have another one. He was an umbrella-maker and had a little workshop in the back of his house, but the farmers in and around Oszidék didn't buy umbrellas, there wasn't much to do in the workshop, and that grieved Engelmann. It also grieved him that there was no Jewish community in Oszidék. They had to travel many kilometres to the nearest synagogue, and there wasn't even the minyan, the minimum number of ten men without which no proper Jewish prayer service could be held. In 1893 he leased the small property to his brother, and since he had heard of the Sh'va Kehiloth, the Seven Communities, he moved to Mattersdorf.

I have spent a fair amount of time studying the history of the Sh'va Kehiloth and would like to write down everything I know about them. But if I gave in to such temptations, I would, like a second Tristram Shandy, never get to the end of this account, and so I'll limit myself to the essentials. The history of the Sh'va Kehiloth begins in 1496, when the expulsion of the Jews from the new part of Vienna, the Neustadt, ushered in a long period of travelling for them. Many of them moved to the vicinity of Ödenburg, about two dozen settled in Mattersdorf, the present-day Mattersburg, but their existence there was unsafe. They were expelled in 1544, but in 1546 they were allowed to return again because the man who owned that stretch of land, Hans von Weisspriach, suffered from a shortage of money that had become acute when he was no longer receiving the taxes and honoraria from "his" Jews. When Weisspriach died, they were expelled again; but in 1572 there were once again nine Jewish families in Mattersdorf. In 1622 Kaiser Ferdinand II leased the dominions of Forchtenstein and Eisenstadt to Count Esterházy, and since the Count likewise needed money and was an enterprising man, the time for the Sh'va Kehiloth had come: in return for payment in gold, he permitted the founding of eight Jewish communities: Eisenstadt, Deutschkreutz, Lackenbach, Kobersdorf, Frauenkirchen, Kittsee, Neufeld and Mattersdorf. (By the way, the history of the Sh'va Kehiloth demonstrates, as do so many others, that travelling has remained the involuntary national sport of the Jews. Jews from Eisenstadt survived the Holocaust in London, Manchester, New York, Silver Spring, Ramat Gan, Tel Aviv, Haifa, Budapest, Buenos Aires and Shanghai, as well as in undocumented places in Switzerland, France and Chile. Jews from Eisenstadt were deported to Buchenwald, Riga, Modliborczyze, Ungvár, Litzmannstadt, Miskolc, Kielce, Minsk, Nisko, Izbica, Opole and other places, but only a few of those survived.)

For each of the eight communities there were detailed letters of protection, signed by the Count and later by the princes who were his descendants, that laid down the rights and duties of the Jews, but these agreements could be revoked at any time by the patrons; the eighth Kehila, Kehila Neufeld, was dissolved in 1739 by a despotic act against which no objection could be filed. So the Jews of the Seven Communities (in the reports known to me they are always just called the Seven, never the Eight Communities) tried hard to be in the good books of the prince and his entourage, and showed this, among other ways, with gifts at New Year's, Martinmas and Easter. The Eisenstadt gift list from New Year's of 1739 has been preserved, and although it is too long to copy here in its entirety, it is too amusing to pass over in silence. The reigning prince received 25 Kremnitz ducats, 24 oranges, 24 lemons, two pieces of rock candy, two sugarloaves and two geese, the reigning prince's valet received two florins, the bishop six oranges and a goose, among other things, but the schoolmaster only received 51 kreuzers (so nothing has changed in that regard). In all, they gave gifts to over 50 people, but even that didn't always help: the Imperial Expulsion Edict of 1671, for example, also applied to the Jews under the protection of the Esterházys, and since they had to leave immediately, they had to sell everything they couldn't carry with them at a loss; and when they were allowed back four months later, because the prince didn't want to do without the taxes and gifts of his Jews any more than had Hans von Weisspriach in his day, and had therefore gone to the Hofburg himself to plead his case, they had no possessions anymore in the ghetto, and the

Mattersdorf Jews, for example, had to start from scratch again on a forested piece of land that the prince rented to them. . . .

It was on this piece of land, where all the trees had been felled, that the "new" ghetto was located when Bär Engelmann arrived in Mattersdorf in 1893, but the times had changed. The Esterházys' privileges had come to an end, for almost a century now the Jews had been permitted also to settle outside the ghetto, and since 1867 they had equal rights according to the letter of the law. However, the Mattersdorf Jews were conservative, they (at least the orthodox among them, who still lived on the previously forested piece of land) observed the old customs so strictly that in 1938 the exit from the "new" ghetto was still closed with a chain every Friday evening. . . . In 1893 they of course also had a charitable organization that helped Bär Engelmann find a small house at the edge of the ghetto where the streets were no longer so narrow. There was a workshop attached to the house, rather like a summer kitchen, and its potential was not left unexploited for long: the people in Mattersdorf needed umbrellas, trade relations soon developed with the other *Kehiloths*, and after a few months Engelmann was able to open a small store where, in addition to umbrellas, people could buy belts and phylacteries, *mezuzahs* and oil lamps, ribbons, buttons and calico. The new way of life pleased Engelmann for a while, and above all he enjoyed the daily visits to the synagogue. When he went through the door and down the three prescribed steps into the vestibule, he saw the large chair for the *mohel* and a gigantic cupboard reaching right up to the ceiling that contained all the necessary equipment for the service; when he pushed aside the green curtain, he saw the many high desks and the few rows of benches to the *almenor* standing in the centre, over which arabesques of thin iron supported the brass lamp; he enjoyed it every day to the full, as much as someone who has been shipwrecked and thirsty for days enjoys a drink of water.

It goes without saying that he took the two boys, Matthias and Sándor, to the temple with him. Of course they had to attend the normal Hungarian school whose curriculum was determined in

156

Budapest – and that was a good thing! – but they also attended the *cheder* where they learned Hebrew. In the little free time remaining to the boys, they played with the other children in the narrow streets of the ghetto, and it wasn't hard for them to make themselves understood in the babel of languages: there were Hungarian Jews, "water Croats," that is, the descendants of Croats from Bosnia, whose forebears had fled from the Turks and who still spoke Croatian as well as German, Galician Jews who were mostly Hasidic and whose mother tongue was Yiddish, as well as Bohemian and Moravian Jews whose great-grandparents had moved to the District of Eisenstadt on account of the marriage laws. The Bohemians and Moravians were for the most part "enlightened," that is, impious, and moved out of the ghetto into the city or suburb as soon as they could afford to. They felt superior because they took part in the German culture which, as they could not know back then, a few decades later, after Lessing, Goethe and Heine, was to reach a second, unforeseeable high point with Hitler, Eichmann and Mengele. The Galician Jews felt superior because the Bohemians and Moravians couldn't read a sentence of Hebrew without getting stuck, and the "water Croats" felt superior because neither the Moravians nor the Galicians were capable of growing as much as a turnip, but the children understood each other in four languages and played in harmony. All of them (even the Bohemians and Moravians) took part in the Jewish festivals, and little Sándor now got to know the Jewish religious year properly for the first time, partly with pleasure, partly, because they prayed for many hours, with boredom: the celebration of the Sabbath, Purim, Pesach, Shavuos, Rosh Hashanah, Yom Kippur, Sukkos, Chanukah. He became accustomed to wearing the yarmulke, but he also – and that was the other end of the spectrum of experiences accorded the little boy in Mattersdorf – occasionally listened to good music: there was a long musical tradition in the *Sh'va Kehiloth* (Carl Goldmark had spent ten years in Deutschkreutz, and Ruwen Hirschler in Lackenbach had paid for the young Franz Liszt's piano lessons), and the Bohemians and Moravians revered

not only Lessing, Goethe and Heine, but also Mozart and Beethoven. In Mattersdorf, the provincial small town, they got a touch of
what the wonderful world outside had to offer.

So it was not a bad life that the Engelmanns led in Mattersdorf – and yet they did not stay. Helga Engelmann had not wanted
to leave Oszidék from the start, and she could not adapt to the
new environment. Although the quince cheese, now made by her
sister-in-law who had moved into the house with her family, came
every autumn by mail in huge packages, it didn't taste the same as
it did "at home," and she missed everything else – the goats, the
turkeys, the big enamelled kitchen stove, the cool drinking water
from their own well, the fresh corn in the summer (of course not
the sort of corn they fed the turkeys). And what was a delight for
Bär, the many hours in the Temple, meant very little to her: girls
didn't go to the *cheder*, so they didn't know enough Hebrew to follow the worship service, which meant that Helga either stayed
home or sat on the hard bench on the balcony without participating and had trouble staying awake. But her husband also found out
that nothing in life is perfect: he missed the fresh air and the work
outdoors, he longed for his orchard, and it turned out that making
umbrellas in Mattersdorf provided him with no better purpose in
life than the quinces in Oszidék. Of course he couldn't admit that,
because he had insisted on moving to Mattersdorf, despite his
wife's opposition. So when she complained and felt sorry for herself, he chewed grumpily on his pipe and said: "We are among
Jews, business is going well, what else do you want?" When he let
his guard down, though, he was soon saying: "If only we had at
least an apple tree!" and in the end it turned out that the new lifestyle, all the sitting in the workshop, in the Temple and in the
small apartment wasn't good for him. He couldn't sleep at night,
he lost his appetite, and he began to have stomach aches that
became unbearable. The Eisenstadt physician he went to was, in
contrast to Elli's specialist, an intelligent man, and after he had
performed a minimal physical examination, but had listened to
Engelmann attentively for a long time, he said succinctly:

"Mattersdorf isn't good for you, go back to the country." So, in the spring of 1897, just at the time when the quince trees bloomed in Oszidék, when Helga once again burst into tears because she was so lonely for the goats and turkeys, her husband said, to her amazement: "Well now, if you absolutely want to, I'll do you the favour and we'll go back."

Since my father only spent a total of four years in Mattersdorf, I have gone into far too much detail about the *Kehiloth*. But this is *my* account, and if I had written fifty pages about Mattersdorf (for example, there were tabernacles there with brick walls and removable roofs, and other curious things), it would have been my right to do so. Also, Mattersdorf was a significant period in Sándor's life: a bright boy can learn a lot in four years.

In Oszidék they added three rooms to the house, so that there was enough space for two families. The trade relations Bär Engelmann had established in Mattersdorf didn't break off, so he continued to supply the stores in the *Kehiloth* with umbrellas, and his stomach aches disappeared as soon as he could devote himself to his quinces again. For the boys, though, it wasn't easy to get used to the rural environment again, especially not for Sándor, who for a long time after their return to Oszidék clung to the tradition of wearing the yarmulke, and so the village boys laughed at him, until one day he forgot to take the yarmulke off while bathing in the Drava and it floated away; he couldn't rescue it, because he couldn't swim. To be sure, once the boys had their bar mitzvahs behind them, for which they had had to travel to the nearest city, the Engelmanns were faced with the same problem that my maternal grandmother had foreseen early on and had solved with a long journey on foot: the village had nothing to offer the boys for their future. But when Matthias was old enough, his father was able to apprentice him to a Mattersdorf tailor, and an older sister took care of Sándor (there was no reason for me to mention her earlier); she had married a travelling salesman who by accident had wound up spending a few days in Oszidék, an unimportant man who would later play a small role in the history of the firm Kahn &

Engelmann. Now she was called Paula Herzog, lived in Linz and took in Sándor at Bär Engelmann's request. (That was the difference between the old Engelmann and the farmers in Oszidék, that he, like my grandmother for her children, had ambitions for his boys and wanted to give Sándor the chance to amount to something.)

In Linz, Heinrich Herzog found the boy a job in a men's fashion store where, like Dezsö a few years earlier on Rotenturmstrasse, he swept the floor, fetched the manager's coffee, and learned what there was to learn. It would be boring, though, to report in detail on his business career: it contained no garish green ties or long-legged mannequins, as in Dezsö's case, but just diligence, good will and a quick intelligence. Since he lived at his sister's and had almost no expenses (Paula was a dressmaker in her spare time and soon earned more than her husband), he could soon afford to travel to Vienna now and then for a short visit. Later, as we already know, he had to do that so that he could study the shop windows. But for the time being, when Helga had tucked the money for a standing place at the opera in his pocket, he merely indulged himself in the delights of *La Bohème* and *Tosca*, after which he had to return to Linz on the night train. It was still a while before he could afford a hotel room.

While my father learned the mysteries of men's fashion and the basics of Italian opera techniques, he also forgot some things. In Mattersdorf, he had had an intimate relationship with his god, who was as real for the little boy as the chair he sat on, but in Oszidék there was no religious community in which his belief could have matured, and in Linz, like his brother-in-law and his sister, he soon went to the temple only on the high holidays. So it was no problem for him that the store where he worked – it was called Adolf Pressburger & Sons, was Aryanized in 1938 and went bankrupt in 1939 – was also open on Saturdays. By the way, Adolf Pressburger was no longer alive, the older son had a wine business, and the younger son, who managed the store, quickly discovered that, to use his own expression, he had had *mazel* when he hired

Sándor as an errand boy. Eight years after he had begun as an errand boy, Sándor, at the unusually early age of twenty-two, had full signing powers in the firm, and when he went to Vienna now, he travelled at the cost of the firm. In the autumn of 1911, in the foyer of the Court Opera during the second intermission of *Rigoletto*, a man in a checkered suit asked him for a light, and they got to talking.

Jenö! He could be charming when he wanted to, and he almost always wanted to, not for the sake of gaining any advantage, but just because he liked to talk and took pleasure in witty or sardonic turns of phrase. . . . So Jenö and Sándor had a chat – more precisely: Jenö chatted and Sándor listened – about Verdi, about the baritone who had also sung the court jester at La Scala, about the lawsuit with the furniture company, about the most recent scandal at the Burgtheater, and when the bell rang for the beginning of the third act, Jenö had made a conquest. After Rigoletto had collapsed in grief over his daughter's corpse, Sándor looked around for the checkered suit, and the evening ended with a long talk in Café Schubert.

Sándor admired Jenö, he admired the man who was five years older than he was almost as boundlessly as Elli admired him, and it almost goes without saying that he fell in love with the sister of the man he so admired. As for Elli, she found Sándor intelligent and nice, and it was to his credit that he was Jenö's friend, but that's as far as it went for the time being; because at that time there was someone else in her life, of whom I know (from Olga, because my mother didn't mention this episode) little more than that he was a medical student. She had apparently met the lad at some dance, and she went for walks with him behind her parents' back in the Stadtpark or met him in a small café in Alsergrund where both of them could be certain they wouldn't be recognized. It wasn't a "great love" for either of them and might have done well in a comedy by Kotzebue or Iffland because the student came from a well-to-do Catholic family, and if he had had the courage to tell his parents about a relationship with a little Jewess with a small dowry, they would have threatened to throw him out and disinherit him. But a little love was enough to block my mother emotionally for the time being as far as Sándor was concerned. Sándor, though, was the friend of her beloved brother and a smart young man with a zest for life, and what eighteen-year-old girl does not enjoy having two admirers? Moreover, in addition to the fundamental and incomparable distinction of being Jenö's friend, Sándor had the advantage that as Jenö's friend, their parents made him welcome, and so he was able without secrecy to take Elli out not only to a small café in Alsergrund, but also to Demel's, or, with or without Jenö, to the latest operetta or wine bar or (usually then with Klara and Ferenc) ball. This made up for the fact that after such evenings Sándor had to travel back to Linz on the early morning train and then go directly to the store from the train station. Between visits he wrote to Elli, sometimes in Hungarian, more often in German, letters on which he spent long evening hours: he didn't trust his spelling in either of the two languages. Those letters were still in one of my mother's shoe boxes in 1945. After her death, my brother searched for them in vain. What he found was less pleasant – the correspondence between my father and Jenö.

3.

The Hebrew words *ayen-hore* mean "the evil eye." In Yiddish you fend off this evil by murmuring *"kanehore"*; but you also use this expression, as we have already heard Horowitz do, in the sense of "knock on wood!" or also "thank goodness." In his book *The Joys of Yiddish*, the incomparable Leo Rosten illustrates the use of this expression by telling the following joke.

   An old man – you imagine him wearing a caftan – is called to testify as a witness in a trial. "How old are you?" asks the judge.

   "I am eighty-one, *kanehore*," says the man.

   "Pardon me?" asks the judge.

   "I am eighty-one, *kanehore*," says the man.

"Answer my questions without embellishments," says the judge. "How old are you?"

"Eighty-one, *kanehore*."

"If you don't answer my questions without embellishments, I'll have you locked up!" roars the judge.

"Allow me to put the question," says the defence lawyer. "How old are you, *kanehore*?"

"Eighty-one," says the man.

In the years before the First World War, the Kahns had good reason to say *kanehore*, and my grandparents, who had learned the saying from Horowitz, said it often. They were fortunate and were thankful. When the grandparents accompanied their children to a ball and admired their daughters' ball gowns, Sidonie might say to Josef: "Could you have imagined this when we were still in Tapolca?" And Josef would sip the champagne Jenö had bought for them (he actually preferred drinking caraway brandy or just simply some fizzy pop) and say: "Your vegetables would not have brought in that much, let alone my workshop. I am glad I no longer have it, Humanic and Bata are ruining the shoemakers, they do nothing more now than mend shoes. But you see Dezsö always complaining that the patent-leather shoes pinch his feet; if I had made them for him, they would fit. The girl that he has brought along doesn't appeal to me at all, he shouldn't marry her!"

"Don't worry," said my grandmother, "he won't, he has too much *gewure* for that."

No less than they enjoyed such gala evenings, Josef and Sidonie enjoyed Friday evening, when the family was together. My grandmother insisted that all their children come, and if Jenö brought his friend Sándor and Gisa her little Olga, then there were eleven of them, including Ferenc, who was considered a member of the family although the wedding still had to be postponed. It was no longer a proper *erev* Shabbos that they celebrated, only the smallest remnant of that remained, the blessing my grandfather said over the meal, which was quite a feast. The first course was usually chicken soup with noodles, complete with the giblets, stomach, liver and neck that you fished out with a spoon, but then held in your fingers and nibbled. (For a long time after 1938, I didn't get a taste of such a proper chicken soup; but you can get an excellent one at Dvoretzki's in the Derech-Hayam.) If the main course was a goose or baked chicken, then nestled against the big plates were little crescent moon-shaped plates for the bones, on which was written in ornamental lettering *For the Dog*. When my grandmother took the cover off the bowl of potatoes, a little cloud of steam rose up. If there was wine, then Jenö had brought it, although he was almost always in debt. To help with the serving, there was the Bohemian maid my grandmother could now afford thanks to the brown envelopes, but my grandmother still sat on the edge of her chair and leapt up continually to check on things in the kitchen. At the right time of year, there was corn on the cob that we buttered with a fork. (As a child, I always enjoyed watching how the butter that I spread over the hot corn with my fork melted and flowed golden-yellow between the tines onto the light yellow kernels, and one of my most distinct memories of my grandfather is of how, in the last years of his life, when he no longer had any teeth, he used to take the kernels off the cob with his fork.) But there was also cake, and to go with the coffee there were poppy-seed croissants on which Elli, who liked to help in the kitchen, had strewn liberal amounts of powdered sugar. . . .

They ate relatively late, because Gisa, Dezsö and Klara usually only got away from the store after six; and since it was customary not to have a big meal on Fridays at noon, they had a good appetite by dinner time. The meal took a long time, partly because of all the talking and laughter. Dezsö loved to tell jokes, which were sometimes quite primitive. For example, he told how a family of nine had cutlets for dinner, and when there was only one cutlet left in the bowl, suddenly the lights went out. Then there was a scream of pain, because in the bowl there was one hand with eight forks stuck in it. Or he told how a guest at Baron P.'s could not swallow the tough braised beef, and in a moment when no eyes were on him he threw the piece of meat to the dog in the corner; but when he looked more closely, it was a porcelain dog. What Jenö told was less primitive, particularly the Hasidic jokes with their characteristic deceptive punchlines that make you think the joke is over when it is actually just beginning.

"You all know," he began, for example (and he told this joke, if that is really the right term for it, to me as well, twenty-five years later) "that *ani lo jodea* means 'I don't know.' Keep that in mind, otherwise you won't understand the joke." (It was good that he began that way, because the women didn't know Hebrew.) "Once upon a time there was a shtetl in Russia where the Jews lived well, and one day the governor came and said: 'The Tsar has decreed that all of you have to leave.' But since the governor was a learned man who also knew a lot about Jewish things and was proud of this knowledge, the rabbi was able to persuade him to let it depend on the outcome of a competition: the governor and a representative of the shtetl would ask each other questions. The first one who couldn't answer a question would have his head cut off. If it was the Jew, then the Jews had to leave; if it was the governor, he got his head cut off, and the Jews could stay. Fair enough – but who was supposed to risk his life by going up against the learned man? 'Not I,' said the rabbi, 'if I slip up, what should become of you in foreign lands without spiritual support?' 'Not I,' said the rich man, 'if I slip up, how are you going to live in foreign lands without my business sense?' And so each of them had his own excuse, and only the *shammes* said he was willing to try. . . . The *shammes*? There was great consternation among the Jews. That halfwit who could do nothing but sweep the temple was supposed to match his skills against those of the learned man?

"On the agreed-upon day, the governor came to the market square in his fine clothes, followed by the executioner, naked to his belt, the shiny sword in his hand. When the governor saw that his opponent was the *shammes*, he laughed and said: 'In that case, you may ask the first question.' 'Governor,' said the *shammes*, 'what

165

does *ani lo jodea* mean?' 'I don't know,' said the governor, and the executioner cut his head off."

There were howls of laughter around the long table. Jenö took a sip of wine and continued:

"There was great rejoicing among the Jews. They crowded around the *shammes*, patted him on the back, and finally one of them asked: 'Moische, you are only the *shammes*, how did you think of the only question that could help us?' 'That's easy,' said the *shammes*. 'When I was still a small child, I went with my father to the Rabbi of Lodz, and my father asked him, Rabbi, what does *ani lo jodea* mean? Then the rabbi said: 'I don't know.' Well now, if the great Rabbi of Lodz didn't know, then the stupid goy wouldn't know either!'"

When the laughter had died down, my father said: "That's not really a joke, it is a legend."

"May the Lord always hold His hand so protectively over us," said my grandmother.

"*Kanehore*," said my grandfather.

"It was terrible for the Jews under the Tsar," said Ferenc.

"Why *was*?" said Dezsö. "Is it any better today?"

"It is better here," said my grandmother. "Here we don't need to be afraid."

"There's enough hatred incited against us here as well," said my Aunt Gisa. "If you read the newspapers, they can make you feel sick."

"If we worried about what the goyim say, we'd all hang ourselves," said Jenö.

"The Kaiser will protect us," said my grandmother.

"*Kanehore*," said my grandfather.

It was like that, or something like that, when there were still ten or eleven of them sitting around the extended table. Then came 1914, and the table no longer needed to be extended; Josef still said the blessing over the meal, but otherwise only the women were still there.

There are many books about the enthusiasm that the declaration of war aroused in the Austrian populace, but there was little of it to be felt in my family, especially since Jenö expatiated on how England had never yet lost a war and would win this one too. But no one tried to get out of active service, surprisingly not even Jenö. Gisa tried to keep Dezsö out of the war. She had landed a contract for officers' shirts and offered to have him declared "indispensable," but Dezsö didn't want that; he would feel ashamed in front of the girls who worked in the store. Jakob, Jenö, Dezsö, Ferenc and my father were all drafted the first winter of the war. They served on the western front, but there are countless war novels that describe what went on there. I will only record a few things here that happened before they reported for duty.

It's understandable that Elli's medical student was one of those swept away by the general excitement. He volunteered immediately, but in a long conversation he had with Elli in the café in Alsergrund before he was called up, he didn't cut a very good figure. While giving himself airs as a hero who was joyously prepared to put his life at risk for God, Kaiser, and Fatherland, he proved to be a moral coward: while he was not afraid of Russian or English rifles, he was afraid of his own father. He didn't know, he said, when he would come back, maybe he wouldn't come back at all, but if he did, then the main thing he would have to do was make up for lost time, get his medical degree and obey his parents' wishes, who would never approve of a union with a non-Catholic, and so on. So it was time to say goodbye, goodbye not only for the duration of the war . . . Elli burst into tears, but then refused to have him walk her home, where she feigned a sprained ankle to explain her teary face. . . .

A month later, my mother had another conversation with Sándor. In this conversation there was no talk of God or the Kaiser or the Fatherland, and it didn't take place in a small café either, but in Hotel Sacher. It was certain that he would soon be drafted, Sándor said simply, so a parting was inevitable, a very painful parting for him. Elli had long known that it was his one and only wish to be able to spend the rest of his life with her. He was not a rich man, he was only an employee, and it was uncertain if he would get his job back after the war; but he understood enough of the business that he would be able to take care of her. He would (and since it occurred to him in the middle of this sentence that he was talking about reporting for military duty the way he would talk about a business trip, he got tangled up and had to start the sentence again), he would do his duty with a lighter heart if he knew that she would wait for him. . . .

"You're springing this on me," said my mother, which wasn't entirely true; because it hadn't been difficult to guess why Sándor had invited her to Sacher's.

"That was not my intent," said Sándor, "I don't think I have said anything to you that you haven't known for a long time. I also don't want to press you, but we are pressed for time. You don't have to answer right away if you can't, but please don't forget that I won't be here much longer."

Elli watched as Sándor lit a cigarette and let the coffee get cold. I doubt that she would have been able to express her thoughts clearly, but it isn't difficult to do that for her. She was on the rebound, and she was making comparisons. She loved blond Franz, but he was a stupid boy, he had chattered about God, Kaiser and Fatherland and had left her in the lurch. Sándor was a man, and it could not be denied that she liked him. . . . It had always been nice going to the opera with him, or for a walk, or to the new wine festival, and he was Jenö's friend. . . . "Give me a little time," she said at last, "there are still a few days before you have to go away." And when they sat in Hotel Sacher again two days later, she didn't have the heart to say no to him.

4.

There wasn't another engagement in the family until 1917, when Dezsö got engaged to my later Aunt Mitzi. There are gaps in what my mother has told me about it, so I prefer to stick to what Olga

told me in 1982 in Beverly Hills. I had flown to Los Angeles to par-
ticipate in a conference on signs of aging in dogs, gave a paper on
deformations of the hip bone (the usual 30 minutes, with slides),
and listened to a dozen or more other papers because I wanted to
find out more about new methods of treating canine arthritis. Of
course I also spent a few hours with Aunt Olga, who was almost
eighty. I found her astonishingly healthy and lively – she had had
her knees operated on in the previous year and could now walk
quite well again. She liked it when people stopped for a snack at
her place, but I persuaded her to come with me to the Beverly Hills
Café, because for one thing the short walk would do her good, and
also because of the excellent strawberry cake with whipped cream
that is served there. As expected, she immediately began to remi-
nisce, she lived entirely in the past, and this time she got to talking
about how Mitzi travelled around Europe like a restless spirit in the
last years of her life, so overdressed that people turned around in
the street to look at her.

"She always had red hair," I said.

"No, Peterl, you're wrong about that. She was originally
just reddish blonde, but in 1930 the chauffeur convinced her that
Dezsö was having an affair with an actress, and then she had her
hair dyed fiery red."

The logic of this decision escaped me, but instead of asking
Olga to explain it, I asked her how my uncle had met Mitzi.

"You know how fat Dezsö got in Buenos Aires," said Olga,
who just drank coffee while I ate strawberry cake. "He was a little
corpulent before the war (she meant the first one) – you were that
fat too as a child – and because of that, he didn't want to eat a lot
for lunch. Sometimes he had a roll with sliced meat brought to the
office from Primingers, sometimes he went there himself, it was
good for him to stretch his legs – but do you even know who the
Primingers were?"

"You mean the delicatessen on the Graben?"

"Yes," she said, "it's not there anymore, now there's a bookstore there, but back then it wasn't just any delicatessen, it was the

169

finest, Primingers were the first to bring in specialties from Pressburg, and behind the store there was a huge smokehouse, Mitzi
showed it to me once, that was when your father was still alive, a
handsome man, and always so cheerful, until the last year. . . ."

"And that's where Dezsö met Mitzi?"

"Even when she was a little girl she helped in the smokehouse, a terrible job, with the smoke and the boiling water, can you
imagine how hot it must have been in the summer! By the way, I
don't know how she got into the family, her surname was Mehl – "

"Why Mehl," I asked, "she was a Priminger, wasn't she?"

"Look, Peterl, I was only ten or twelve back then, I only
know all this from hearsay, but I can swear to you that on Mitzi's
certificate of baptism it said Maria Mehl. Later on, she served
behind the counter – "

"Not so fast, Olga," I interrupted. "Why Mehl, when she
was a Priminger?"

"You can't imagine what a crowd the Primingers were," said
my cousin. "There were two brothers and a sister whose husband
also worked in the smokehouse, and there was also a butcher and I
don't know who else, and with the heat from the big vats they all
drank too much, the women too. Then when a child was born, no
one knew who the father was, but that didn't bother the Primingers, they all tended to look alike anyway, and it was all in the
family. So sometimes Mitzi was in the smokehouse, and sometimes
she was behind the counter and made the meat rolls for the customers, and it was there that Dezsö said to her she should put extra
mustard on his, but to make sure it was Kremser. . . ."

"How do you know that so exactly?"

"Dezsö told me that himself, extra mustard, but Kremser,
those were his first words to her. I can't get the cucumber mustard
in Los Angeles, I would have to have it brought from Vienna, if it
is still available there. Everything has changed, the sausage stand
has disappeared from the Prater junction, they always sold the best
Boor sausage there."

"Didn't it bother him that she was a Christian?"

"Why should that have bothered him? So were the shop girls, and with Mitzi at first it was just a flirtation, and then he slowly got seriously involved with her. But it bothered Jenö, he never liked Mitzi, he always called her the dumb *shiksa* and tried to talk Dezsö out of getting attached to her."

"I don't understand that, Olga. Why should it have bothered Jenö, he was not in the least pious and only made fun of everything!"

"He was not pious, you're right about that," said Olga and looked at her watch. "Don't let me forget, Peterl, I still have to buy veal cutlets for dinner. He was not pious, but he was crazy, that's what my Marti always said. But there was also an incident that made Jenö really angry, he told me so himself. When Dezsö and Mitzi were already lovers, Jenö met her on Ringstrasse and she invited him for coffee. He thought it wasn't proper for her to be inviting him, did she want to take up with him too, but he said yes anyway, and then over coffee she asked him if it's true that the Jews kill a Christian child at Easter and bake bread with its blood, she had heard that from her grandmother and didn't dare to ask Dezsö. Can you imagine how angry Jenö was! He told Dezsö about it right away, Dezsö only laughed, but Jenö never forgave her. But now I've talked the whole time, tell me about your Bobby, he must be a big boy already, and then we have to buy the cutlets before they close. . . ."

So Jenö had agitated against Mitzi, but without success. To be sure, he was the older brother, but Dezsö had started to have doubts about his judgment. Dezsö loved the store on Rotenturmstrasse, not only because it brought in money and he liked to live well, but also because there were dozens of little things there that gave him pleasure. He loved the barely perceptible, but characteristic smell of the fabrics, the shape of a skilfully sewn frill, the miracle that occurred when a woman who looked like a butcher's wife in her red polka dot blouse was transformed by the right dress and suddenly looked like the *Frau Kommerzienrätin* they addressed her as; he loved the negotiations with suppliers, the selection of accessories for the new styles, the weekly arrangement of the shop windows, which he still took care of himself, and he knew that he could do all that well. With Jenö it was different, he was actually more interested in the stock market than in the store. Dezsö thought that was eccentric, but would not have held it against his brother if he had drawn the consequences from it! But Jenö didn't do that, he meddled in the store, bought styles that were too *outré* for Rotenturmstrasse, found fault with the salesladies and made foolish suggestions for the arrangement of the shop windows. But if someone understood nothing about clothes, then he probably also understood nothing about the women who wore the clothes. . . . So the fact that Dezsö did not get engaged to Mitzi before he reported for duty had nothing to do with Jenö. It simply hadn't occurred to him to do so, he had not yet, to quote Olga, got sufficiently involved with her. It was less painful for him to part from Mitzi than to part from Rotenturmstrasse, and he would have perhaps accepted Gisa's suggestion that she arrange for his military service to be deferred after all, if his sister hadn't promised to take care of the store in his absence.

Incidentally, the store prospered while Dezsö was on the battlefield, because the war brought money into circulation, and at the beginning there was a major victory to be celebrated every few weeks. After the Germans had marched into Belgium, they overran Lille and Cambray and occupied Arras, Compiègnes and Montmirail; soon they were – and with that Jenö's prophecies seemed to have been refuted – thirty kilometres from Paris. But then the advance slowed down, the positional warfare began and didn't want to end, and when the mood in Vienna got darker, the government saw to it that from then on the endless trains with the wounded only arrived in the Viennese train stations at night. The first member of my family who arrived on such a train was Dezsö. In the early summer of 1917, on one of those days when it was "all quiet on the western front," he had been buried alive in a trench and dug out again more dead than alive. When my grandmother visited him for the first time in the hospital, he was unconscious, and she and Mitzi sat by his bed in the big ward for many weeks, alternately or together. It was there that the two women got used to each other, Mitzi learned how things were done at Passover, and she told Sidonie how Catholics celebrate a confirmation. . . . Finally, Dezsö's good health won out, and Mitzi, who was a Priminger (though that was not the name on her baptismal certificate) and therefore had access to the sources, made sure he did not depend on the bad hospital food. By mid-summer of 1917, he was ready to leave the hospital, but his vocal chords hadn't recovered, and to the end of his life he spoke in a toneless whisper. That drove me to despair when I was six or eight years old, when he phoned us at Augartenstrasse and I unfortunately picked up the receiver: I couldn't understand him, and the otherwise so good-natured man was sensitive in this regard. His fits of anger on the telephone contributed to my ongoing hatred of the phone, and today, if an hysterical poodle owner talks to me on the telephone in Hebrew, I understand little more of what she says than I understood back then when my uncle was on the other end of the line.

Obviously, Dezsö appreciated the cold roast meat, the Pressburg sausage and the Kremser mustard with which Mitzi provided him when food in Vienna was already quite scarce – we know that the way to a man's heart is through his stomach – but it was probably the devotion with which she had sat by his bed for nights on end that removed his last doubts, and when he had recovered enough to go outside again, it was on one of the first walks he took on Mitzi's arm, between the beds of roses in the Stadtpark, that he finally spoke the word she had waited for so long. He was still in the hospital, though, when my father arrived from the front with grenade splinters in his back. Such injuries were dangerous back then, before the discovery of penicillin, and as it turned out, the wound healed poorly; but that did not prevent them from celebrating a double wedding in October of that year. Mitzi was hurt that Sándor and Elli were married at both the registry office and in the Schiff Schul, while she and Dezsö were only married at the registry office because he could not decide to convert. He did promise her,

173

however, that the children would be baptized, and that explains why, ten years later, when I was running around naked with my cousin Teddy in the big garden of Dezsö's villa in Pressbaum, I saw an uncircumcised penis for the first time in my life. Mitzi's sorrow was lessened by the fact that the double wedding ended with a huge reception, for which Primingers had rented a large hall. Wine and champagne were flowing, and although already at that time a large part of the Viennese population was starving, the tables were groaning under the piles of roasts and cold cuts, cakes and fruits. For that, they had to accept the fact that there were a few men among the guests who looked as comfortable in their tails as the Pope in a bathing suit. Whether the one or the other of those black marketeers was called Mehl, I do not know.

CHAPTER FIVE

Fraternal Feud

1.

WHEN THE FOUR MANDELBAUM BROTHERS, Leo Rosten tells us, founded their export firm in London, they changed their names, and so the firm was called McNeil, McNeil, McNeil & McNeil. One day a client calls up and says: "May I speak to Mr. McNeil?"

"I am sorry, he is taking a holiday," says the man on the phone.

"Then I would like to speak to Mr. McNeil."

"I'm sorry, he is on a business trip."

"Then please connect me with Mr. McNeil!"

"He has just gone out for lunch."

"Well, then," says the client resignedly, "give me Mr. McNeil."

"Speaking," says Mr. McNeil.

If I had to tell the story of the McNeil brothers, I would have difficulties. I would have to report in succession what the first of them did on his holiday in Brighton, what the second experienced in Tangiers on his business trip, how the third got poor service in Lyons Corner House on Oxford Street, and how the fourth spent the day on the telephone; because all narration is linear and consecutive. No narrator can do justice to reality; there is no less correct picture of a real event than that of a train that runs undisturbed on its tracks. Only in a physics textbook is an event an autonomous causal chain, and even the tiniest corner of the world consists not of trillions of autonomous chains, but of trillions of causal chains that are matted, threaded and woven together. Assuming, though, that a narrator decided to tell things simultaneously instead of consecutively, then he would really get into difficulties. Lessing has already shown that the representation of simultaneous events is contrary to the modality of language, and when Saussure in his *Cours de linguistique générale* broke with historical philology à la Grimm and described language as a synchronous system, that was admittedly a step forward, but he couldn't explain how this system had come about. I could try to combine Grimm and Saussure and weave the four linear stories of the McNeil brothers together by mentioning in the story of the first brother the postcard that he received from Paris from the second brother, and by reporting on the phone call from London with which the fourth brother ruined his breakfast for him. But then I would run the risk of creating confusion in the reader's mind; because since the second brother was allegedly in Tangiers on a business trip, why did the postcard come from Paris? So I would be forced, in the middle of my report on McNeil Number One's holiday trip, to explain that McNeil Number Three had a sister-in-law in Paris whom McNeil Number Two was visiting there, and that he could only afford the time to do so because McNeil Number Four was taking care of the London store in the meantime, from where he later phoned McNeil Number One in Tangiers because his sister-in-law, that is, the wife of McNeil Number Three, in Brighton.... I'll have to interrupt that explanation because my readers have probably already forgotten that McNeil Number Three remarried after the death of his first wife – but can I expect my readers to keep the four McNeils separate? I can't do it myself.

As far as the Kahn family is concerned, it was relatively easy for me in my capacity as narrator at the beginning, when my grandparents' five children were still children and had hardly any stories of their own, but I am now reaching the point where I can only cope with the diachrony à la Grimm and the synchrony à la Saussure by making chronological notes in five columns and marking in the connections with red pencil: it is all matted and woven together. For example, not only would I not be bathing poodles today in Haifa if my grandparents had not journeyed from Tapolca to Vienna, but all my grandparents' children with all their connections with each other have contributed to this event. But the joke about the McNeil brothers did not occur to me because of the problem of portraying simultaneous events, but rather because they were in business together, and some of the red pencilled lines on my sheet of notes indicate business partnerships. The partnership of Jenö and Dezsö was followed after the war by two further partnerships. They got along so well when they were celebrating *erev Shabbos* at my grandparents' table; so why not?

In the first winter of peacetime after the war, the table had to be extended to its full length again every Friday evening. Around it sat, counter-clockwise, Josef and Sidonie (the latter, of course, just on the edge of her chair); Jakob, Gisa and Olga, who, however, had to go to bed at ten o'clock in the small room to the right of the dining room that I would later share with my brother and the nanny, where she couldn't fall asleep, nor could I later, because the adults were all talking so loudly; Dezsö and Mitzi; Jenö, who had spent a small fortune to have new English woollen suits made for himself from imported material as soon as the war was over, in spite of the shortages of everything; Klara and Ferenc; and finally, at least once a month, my mother and Sándor from Linz, where he had got his old position back. Therefore, synchronously, since every small family can be considered a unit, there would be not twelve, but no fewer than six narrative strands to follow, a desperate undertaking that I only dare to attempt because not all strands are equally interesting.

My grandfather was by now over sixty, but still looked very handsome with his Kaiser-Franz-Joseph-beard and his upright gait. His connection with Perolin had ended when the war broke out, but he now represented another firm that sold sand for sweeping, and from time to time he still went door to door; but just as the factories with their mass-produced wares were supplanting the shoemakers who made shoes to measure, the vacuum cleaner now began to supplant oiled sand, and Josef's canvassing was soon little more than an excuse for going for long walks. My grandmother sometimes spent an entire day doing the shopping for *erev Shabbos*, because food was even scarcer since the end of the war; she only rarely went to Tuchlauben, where she had sometimes helped out during the war when Gisa was checking on things on Rotenturmstrasse, actually only when she wanted to talk with her daughter undisturbed; but now the narrative strands are beginning to get entangled.

In October of 1917, Jakob Pinsker succeeded in getting a short leave from the front to attend the wedding of his brother- and sister-in-law. In July of 1918, after an interval of fifteen years, Gisa brought a second daughter into the world – my cousin Edith, who today, in spite of her two sons, is very lonely in her old age in Amsterdam. During her pregnancy, Gisa no longer had to check on Rotenturmstrasse, because Dezsö was back again, but she had a lot of work in her own business. There was no shortage of orders, and it took an endless effort to obtain the goods: one day there was no thread, the next day there were no buttons, the materials were loosely woven and expensive, and when a cable or a little wheel broke on one of the sewing machines, they could find neither the replacement part nor a mechanic who knew how to fix it: the old mechanics didn't understand the electric machines, and the young mechanics had died in action. After the birth of her second daughter, Gisa was tired, and as much as she loved Edith, the child put an additional strain on her. There was a nanny who changed the diapers, but the girl was breast-fed (Jenö only kept a cow in Pressbaum after 1919, and milk was scarce), so that Gisa either had to take the child with her to Tuchlauben and to the blouse factory in the suburbs, or she had to keep riding from her work to her apartment and back again. Whether she already had the beginnings of the disease that would lead to her early death, or had simply taken on too much, the vital and energetic woman gradually used up her reserves.

"You look tired," my grandmother said to her a few weeks before the general strike of 1920, when she was visiting on Tuchlauben. "Why don't you take a holiday? Mitzi is going to the Lido, you could go with her."

"I can't go away, Mama. We have to deliver a big batch of skirts, two machines are broken again, and the spring collection has not yet been assembled."

"Martin should look after that," said my grandmother, "that's why you have him!"

Martin. that was my future Uncle (cousin, really) Martin Becker, who plays an important role in this account because he procured the English visas for my brother and me in 1939, without which we would not have survived, and whose remark in Beverly Hills, "Your mother did not support Sándor," took me so by surprise. . . . But unfortunately the narrative strands get twisted there.

In my mother's shoebox there are a dozen group photos that include Martin Becker, with his beardless, oval face, straight, carefully parted black hair and good teeth; and in every picture, if it doesn't show him just wearing a bathing suit on the Lido, he is incontestably the most elegant man: he was known for having his suits made by the most expensive tailor in Vienna. He didn't look like a Kahn, Róth or Kálmann, and in many regards he belonged to a later generation than Jenö or Dezsö. His father had been born in Vienna, and in contrast to my grandfather, he was not a poor shoemaker, but respectably middle-class. In the 19th district, not even five minutes away from the trade school on Rosensteingasse, he owned a large grocery store. His comfortable, spacious apartment was located over the store, and I often ate lunch there when I attended the trade school. He must have been an educated man; in any case, his books in the living room included the Brockhaus edition of Schopenhauer's works, of which I borrowed volumes II

179

and III in 1937, *The World as Will and Representation*. I don't need to feel badly for not having returned the books – they have accompanied me to England, Canada and Israel – because, like the rest of the Schopenhauer edition and all his other things, they would have fallen into the hands of the Nazi who acquired the house and the store for a fraction of its value when Martin's parents succeeded in fleeing at the last moment before the war broke out.

Of Martin's early years, I know only that he already played the violin passionately when he was a little boy. Like so many Jews of the Viennese middle class, he should have studied law or medicine; the fact that he didn't do so, although he wanted to, was because his mother, a nice but primitive woman, held the reins and kept telling her husband "that the boy inherited his skill as a businessman from you, he is wasting his time in school."

Gisa, who had a good eye for people, met the twenty-three-year-old in 1919 in the office of an export firm and brought him to Tuchlauben as a sort of personal assistant; but if she thought hiring him would lighten her load, she had another thought coming. To the end of his days, Martin did not get over his disappointment at not having gone to university. He was ambitious, and he hardly had an overview of the Gisela Kahn firm when he explained to Gisa that since the disintegration of the Austro-Hungarian Empire, Vienna had become too big for the country, the Austrian market was too small, and there was no future for the firm other than to strengthen its contacts with England that had already been established before the war. Soon he was spending half the year in London, Manchester and Leeds, and the commissions came pouring in. That brought in not only a lot of money, but also the advantage that Gisa could import material from England with foreign currency, but instead of half the work, Gisa had twice as much.

"Martin is in London again, Mama," Gisa said resignedly. "He has just closed a deal with Drysdale & Co. and sent me a mile-long telegram, he will get the material from Leeds, but I have to do everything else here myself. I am tired of it, Mama, I am tired of it. . . ."

"The hard work with the store?" said my grandmother, "You can't persuade me that's the problem, I know you. Do you have problems with Jakob?"

"Why with Jakob?"

"You are not so depressed because Drysdale & Co. has ordered blouses, Gisa. I will gladly believe that you work very hard at the business, but it is blossoming. Tell me what's on your mind, my child, then you'll feel better."

"Not here," said Gisa, but when they had coffee in Café Schubert, where the head waiter still treated her as if she were Princess Liechtenstein, she told her mother what was wrong. On the previous day, she had laid two blouses needing alterations on the table, and had then gone to Rotenturmstrasse with a folder of fashion drawings to consult with Dezsö. When she came back to Tuchlauben, the blouses were gone. Gisa looked for them, two of the salesgirls looked for them, and finally little Marie (she was a pretty brunette whom Gisa used as a model) said: "Mr. Pinsker was here, madam."

"And what did you say, Gisa?"

"That has nothing to do with the blouses, I said, Mama, what else should I have said, that would have been all I needed, to let the personnel in on my problems!" Gisa stirred agitatedly in the half-empty cup. "But Marie will have seen that he took them. It is bad enough that he steals from the till, but that he takes the samples to give them away to God knows whom, that is too much!"

"So you had an argument?"

"I have looked the other way and said nothing for twenty years," said Gisa, who was getting worked up, "but there has to be a limit to everything. He naturally pretended he knew nothing about it, what should I do with the blouses, he said, I don't wear blouses. Then I said to him, 'What you are doing is despicable,' and we haven't exchanged a word with each other since."

My grandmother had to bite her tongue to stop herself from saying that she had predicted all that to Gisa and had gone on foot

181

from Vienna to Tapolca to try to make her daughter forget the man. "Throw him out," she said instead. "It will do him good to have to sell carp again. You have ten times as many reasons as you need to get divorced."

"I have reason enough, you can say that again," said Gisa, "but I can't. You know that I love him, God knows why, I can't help myself."

"Then I'll make another suggestion," said my grandmother. "The business brings in a lot more than you need, and you are wearing yourself out. Take Klara and Ferenc into the firm, then you'll have help."

The narrative strands are getting tangled again, but this time in a harmless manner. The engagement of Ferenc and Klara had already been celebrated at Josef's fiftieth birthday party. Now my grandfather was over sixty, and the pair were still just engaged – for no better reason than that Klara had got it into her head that a mere cutter was "unmarriageable" for the sister of Gisela Kahn and of the Kahn Brothers, Rotenturmstrasse. If seen objectively, of course, that was nonsense. Gisa had married a fishmonger, and she, Klara herself, was the daughter of a shoemaker, but objectivity is a rare virtue, it hadn't even helped that Ferenc had returned from the war in a first lieutenant's uniform. . . . But back to Café Schubert.

"What kind of help would that be?" said Gisa and gestured to the waiter to bring fresh coffee. "What should Ferenc, who understands nothing but cutting, do in my store?"

"Look, Gisa, I've been thinking about it for a long time, you know how it is, one good turn deserves another. . . . The children have been engaged now for over ten years, Klara is well over thirty, you can wait until *Jurigelt* before Ferenc amounts to anything if we don't help him. You are right, he isn't very able, but he has an air of authority, that's why he became an officer. You can train Klara, she has had some contact with this kind of business, and you just sit Ferenc down at the till, and when Jakob comes along, there is someone there to say no. . . ."

182

That's how it came about that Ferenc sat at the till on Tuchlauben for fifteen years, where he didn't say "no," but rather, since he preferred to speak Hungarian, "nem." ("Nem" was one of the few Hungarian words that Jakob understood.) Ferenc said it in the deep voice in which only a former first lieutenant can say "nem," and he guarded the blouses.

Why only fifteen years? That can be told quickly. Like thousands of others, Martin Becker (the narrative strands are getting tangled again) married his boss's daughter and thus became my uncle (cousin, actually) (I was already alive then). So after Gisa's untimely death, he became the main owner of the firm Gisela Kahn, and he didn't like the idea of having to drag Klara and Ferenc along on his way up in the world. Besides, the women didn't get along. "You know, Peterl," Olga told me in the Beverly Hills Café, "she was jealous of me, even at that time I knew how to draw and design blouses and dresses, and Klara always found fault with what I was doing. When Marti was there, she didn't have the nerve to say anything, but he was so often out of town, and when he was in England, she played the manager and harassed me." Every time Martin was back in Vienna, he had to listen to a long litany of complaints. Then when the Great Depression began after the New York Stock Exchange crashed in October of 1929, and from week to week the Tuchlauben got fewer contracts, Martin spent his time – according to the rumour that went around in the family – playing the Guarneri violin he had bought in the meantime, instead of making up for the losses through doubled efforts. I am not inclined to believe this rumour. It doesn't fit the image of this thoroughly honest and respectable man that he would intentionally have brought the firm to the brink in order to get rid of his associates. In any case, by 1934 the business no longer brought in enough to provide two families with the comfort to which they were accustomed, and at the end of the year Klara and Ferenc left the firm with a settlement of more than half its value. Since they had never paid a penny into it, you would have to be Jenö to maintain that my cousin cheated them. Be that as it may, Martin's trips to England soon had the desired success again, and he didn't have to sell his Guarneri until 1948 in Los Angeles.

With the settlement, Klara and Ferenc founded a business on Mariahilferstrasse that flourished because Dezső advised them. After the *Anschluss* it was Aryanized – to be exact, stolen – and Ferenc and his family fled to London, where he was forced to return to the lowly occupation that had made him "unmarriageable" for so long. Once again, he earned his living as a cutter. He retained the ability to say "nem" in a tone of utter conviction until the end of his life, but as far as I know, he said "nem" to his wife as seldom as my grandfather did to his.

2.

With that, I have brought you up to date on McNeil Number One and McNeil Number Two. How are things with McNeil Number Three? In the spring of 1918, Jenő had been wounded and discharged. Encouraged by Gisa's example, he rented a few rooms on Fleischmarkt where he had blouses and dresses sewn. Setting up the workshop – buying sewing machines, racks and tables, material, buttons and thread, hiring workers, searching for suitable patterns – took up the time that remained to him after his daily study of the stock market prices, so that for weeks at a time he abandoned the store on Rotenturmstrasse to its fate (more exactly: to Dezső's care). When he then showed his face there again to, as he said, "check on things," an unpleasant surprise awaited him. It wasn't Dezső, but Mitzi who greeted him, and she did so with the words: "How nice, Jenő, that you are visiting us at last!"

"Visiting?" said Jenő, as he shook his sister-in-law's hand. "Why visiting? It's my store!" In spite of the widespread misery in the country caused by the war, Mitzi had not been badly off. After the wedding they had gone on a little trip, on which she had actually been somewhat bored – the beautiful seaside resorts in the south were all in enemy lands, and it also wasn't the right time of year. (Dezsö was never bored on such trips, because he was keenly interested everywhere in what the women wore on their morning walks or for dinner and how the shop windows were arranged. As the story goes, K.P. who headed the men's fashion section in the Grossbard department store, saw the Pope while he was on a trip through Italy. "And what did you think of him?" his brother-in-law asked him after his return. "A robust old gentleman," said K.P. "size 40 short.") When they were back in Vienna and had moved into the small apartment on Strauchgasse, she had to cope with the first Friday evenings in her new family circle – no easy task, since she had to learn a long series of expressions like *chochem, ganef, ponim and gewure in order to follow the conversation*. It went without saying that Dezsö took her into the business, as both the Primingers and the Kahns had their wives working in their stores, and of course the smokehouse was out of the question by now. So she helped serve the customers (she already knew from the smokehouse to address *Frau Kommerzienrat* as Frau Baroness, even though the aristocratic titles – even the genuine ones – had been recently forbidden in the Republic), she learned to sew a bit, and she soon began to help buying the new stock and that sort of thing; after all, she was the boss's wife. Admittedly, it showed that she was a Priminger (or, to be exact, a Mehl). The smokehouse on the Graben was incontestably the finest in Vienna, but its owners were, to use Jenö's phrase, "utterly vulgar," and the taste she had grown up with did not suit Rotenturmstrasse, which was, after all, in the first district. So it cannot be denied that the *niveau* of *Kahn Brothers*, as the sign above the entrance to the store had proclaimed since 1912, declined. Dezsö could have put a stop to that and spent a lot of time initiating Mitzi into the secrets of the business and critically appraising with her what was in the shop windows on Kärntnerstrasse, but he enjoyed seeing how after just a few months she acted as if she had grown up in the business, and it soon turned out that it didn't do any harm to their turnover if they had a somewhat more mixed selection. Things weren't the same as

185

they had been before, the black marketeers now had more money in their pockets than the *Kommerzienräte*; customers to whom Mitzi had previously sold Hungarian salami or smoked meat made in their own smokehouse now came to Kahn Brothers to have her show them a dress, and after all, they did have Frau Marie, who had been waiting on the more elegant customers since 1912 and made sure that a Frau Dr. Breuer was not shown the same clothes as a carpenter's wife. Besides, Dezsö was head over heels in love with his young wife.

But Jenö was *not* in love with Mitzi. He wanted to rise to the top of the business world, and he was annoyed that the store was "only" on Rotenturmstrasse, and at the cheaper end of the street at that. On a day when everything was running well on its own on Fleischmarkt, he would appear around eleven-thirty in the Rotenturmstrasse store to "sniff around," as the sales ladies said behind his back, and it sometimes happened that he stopped in front of one of the dresses hanging in a long row on the side walls of the salesroom, swung it back and forth on the coat hook with his outstretched arm, and said with wide open eyes to Frau Marie: "How did this hideous stuff get into the store?"

"Frau Kahn chose it," said Frau Marie truthfully.

"But it's vulgar," said Jenö, "you can't wear something like that!"

"Just yesterday we sold two very similar dresses," said Frau Marie, to whom it was a matter of complete indifference whether a dress was vulgar or elegant, as long as she could sell it, and who had noticed that Frau Kahn was within earshot.

"Hello, Jenö," said my Aunt Mitzi, beaming with happiness. Although the store only opened at nine o'clock, she had been there since eight; in the smokehouse they had started work at seven at the latest. "Did you enjoy your breakfast?"

"Why do you ask?" said Jenö. "But there's something I wanted to ask you, where does this terrible dress come from?"

"I don't find it terrible. What don't you like about it?"

Jenö swung it again on the coat hook. "Look at the cut of it, it belongs in a cheap suburb, in Brigittenau! And no one is wearing red and black now!"

"I do," said Mitzi with an even broader smile – none of the Primingers was ever at a loss for words. "Have the stock market prices risen?"

Jenö noticed that Frau Marie was having a hard time keeping a straight face, admitted that he was temporarily defeated and hung the dress back up in its place again.

"Those are ugly dresses that are hanging in our store now," he said a little while later to Dezsö in the office, from which they could see the entire salesroom.

"Come on," answered Dezsö in his whisper, "the new dresses that have just arrived are the prettiest in a long time."

"I don't mean the dresses *you* bought. I mean what Mitzi has landed us with, for example, there's a red thing tarted up with black, that belongs in Brigittenau!"

Jenö obviously enjoyed bringing the district into it that took up the north half of the island formed by the Danube and the Danube Canal, and that was inhabited for the most part by workers, and for the lesser part by poor Jews. But Dezsö, after being in the war and in hospital, was enjoying his young marriage to the full and was not quarrelsome by nature, so he didn't let Jenö get under his skin. "Let Mitzi do what she wants," he said contentedly. "We also have customers from Brigittenau."

"That's just it," said Jenö heatedly, "we're going in the wrong direction. Instead of working our way up and competing with Wohlfahrt or La Couture Moderne, we're getting cheaper and displaying clothes for butchers' daughters!"

He should not have said that; Dezsö's good mood suddenly disappeared. "While you're talking about working our way up," he said, "who is actually working in this store, on the way up or down? Mitzi and I are here every morning at eight o'clock while you're still lying in bed, and by the time you've finished reading the newspapers, it's already lunchtime for us. It's easy to criticize, anyone can do that, why don't you do the shop windows!"

187

But Dezsö should not have said that – it was a challenge for Jenö to play a more active role in the store! Not that he would also have appeared in the Rotenturmstrasse store from now on at eight o'clock, where soon after the end of the war Mitzi didn't show her face so early either, because she was in an advanced state of pregnancy. However, he did come now more frequently than Dezsö liked, arriving in the early afternoon and expressing his disapproval of everything that was to be seen or not to be seen in the store. The changing rooms were in the wrong place and should be rebuilt, new mirrors should be installed – at a time when everything in Vienna was scarce and therefore very expensive – the salesgirls should dress better, Frau Marie looked like a cook. . . . But Dezsö was used to the salesroom as it was, and it was his principle not to change anything that was functioning well. Also, he had learned as a sixteen-year-old from Leonhard Bamberger that a saleslady should not be more elegant than the customers she serves, and he knew that *Frau Kommerzienrat* Mendel, who had stood behind the counter of a perfumery twenty years previously, preferred Kahn Brothers to La Couture Moderne precisely because Frau Marie did not intimidate her. . . . So they had an argument, and when Jenö insisted on going to Paris and buying dresses there, they had another argument. The schilling was weak, Jenö wanted the best, so he bought the most expensive things, and when the bills came, Dezsö held his head in his hands and groaned. However, what Jenö had spent in Paris was not the worst thing, the worst thing was what he had got for the money – dresses for which there were no customers on Rotenturmstrasse.

"If you keep on like this," said Dezsö in his whisper, "we'll be ruined in six months."

"Don't talk nonsense, Dezsö! We now have the most interesting collection in the business!"

"It's interesting, you can say that again, I wish it were less interesting. Our customers do not buy such short dresses, they do not go to the opera wearing such plunging necklines, they do not wear venom-yellow!"

"That is not venom-yellow, it's a very beautiful yellow, and if no one buys the dresses, that's because your Mitzi brings the wrong customers into the store. If you support me, instead of speaking of venom-yellow, you will be amazed at who is coming to us in six months instead of to Kärntnerstrasse!"

"If it keeps on like this, we won't be able to pay the bills in six months!"

"Leave that to me, Dezsö. You have to risk something if you want to accomplish something!"

"I have already left too much to you, Jenö. You are over your ears in debt, and now you want to drag me in too!"

"I'm not dragging you in, but up! You have no ambition anymore, since you married that *shiksa.*"

"Whom I married has got damn-all to do with you!"

Dezsö wheezed – when he wanted to raise his voice, he could only wheeze. "But I'll tell you one thing, that was your last trip to Paris, you will make no more purchases!"

"I can buy what I want," said Jenö and stared at his brother with his frightening eyes. "The store belongs as much to me as it does to you!"

"For now! In six months we'll be bankrupt, and then it won't belong to either of us!"

So one word led to another, and it would be boring to write it all down. . . . If Mitzi was enthusiastic about an "impossible" ball gown or a skirt with an "indecent" slit, Dezsö wasn't annoyed, he found it amusing or even touching. If the silk scarves she had bought didn't sell, Dezsö consoled himself with the fact that they hadn't cost much and didn't take up much space, and now and then one of them did sell. Otherwise, he remedied the situation with a stroke of genius. In the fashion business, as in every other business, it was customary to lower the price on items that didn't sell. Dezsö – and for the few who knew about it, he was considered an Einstein in the business – did the opposite, he raised the price, and Frau Marie was stunned again and again when a scarf that no one wanted for thirty kronen found a buyer for sixty. (When he opened a boutique fifteen years later in the most expensive part of Kärntnerstrasse, it became almost a habit for him to have clothes that had been hanging around too long on Rotenturmstrasse altered and sold for twice as much on Kärntnerstrasse. That wasn't dishonest, because the men who bought their girlfriends presents there were not paying just for the dress, but also for the fact that it had come from Dezsö's Boutique.) But if Jenö had bought the wrong thing, it was a thorn in the flesh for Dezsö. Jenö's purchases were expensive, they could not be sold at half price or at twice the price, and from his chair in the office Dezsö needed only to turn his head to see the yellow Parisian dresses that had been hanging on the wall for the past three months. In the end, it was no longer always Jenö who spoke the first angry word.

"Just look at these venom-yellow rags," Dezsö would say, or something to that effect, and, as we know, it wasn't the first time.

That was perhaps not as abusive as it sounds today, because "rags" was a common term for a cheap dress. But it wasn't that word that gave Jenö offence. "Venom-yellow?" he said, "Venom-yellow? You always were colour-blind. This is not venom-yellow, it is butterfly-yellow, this is the great fashionable colour, I know that, you weren't in Paris, there you see nothing but yellow on the boulevards."

"I see red," said Deszö. "If you are waiting for an invasion of butterflies on Rotenturmstrasse, you can wait until *Jurigelt*. In my next shop window display, there will be only black and green, even if it drives you to distraction."

"I can well imagine that, you're doing that intentionally to annoy me, and I know that you tell the girls not to show the Parisian dresses."

"I don't need to instruct them, they laugh at you and your checkered suits behind your back."

With that, the brothers were off again in the wrong direction, and soon there was mention of the "butcher's daughter" and of the *shiksa*, whom Dezsö had only married to hurt Jenö's feelings. . . . Soon things were so bad that Jenö no longer appeared at

Augartenstrasse on Friday evenings, and ultimately, the business suffered too from the constant strife; because the two bosses didn't just argue in the office, but also within earshot of the customers. They had enough fuel for conflict. Was it not, as Jenö maintained, a "fact," that Dezsö had "unlawfully and at too high a salary" brought his wife into their joint enterprise without asking his partner, who had equal rights? And why did Kahn Brothers order dresses and blouses from everywhere in the world except from the firm Johann Kahn on Fleischmarkt?

"Because it's *Pofel*, it's rubbish, what you manufacture there," said Dezsö, using a word that would later play a disastrous role in another context.

"So it is *Pofel*," said Jenö, "but if it is just *Pofel*, why are all our competitors so eager to buy it?"

"If they're eager to buy it," said Dezsö, "then why do you want to sell the stuff to me?"

"To me!" said Jenö, "you keep talking as if it were *your* store! It is ours, and I am the senior partner!"

"Senior? I ran the store while you were still selling sand, and who is running it now?"

My grandmother observed their quarrels with sorrow and concern, especially since Dezsö's health was not the best. Whether being buried alive had damaged his lungs cannot be determined, but from time to time he had an attack of breathlessness, so something had to be done, and my grandmother saw to it that it was done. At the beginning of November, she met Gisa in Ginsberg's Café on Karmelitermarkt, so that she could talk with her undisturbed. She came a few minutes early and sat at one of the little tables "with northern exposure," from which she could look out at the market. Gisa had hardly joined her when the coffee and the obligatory water glasses with the coffee spoon laid diagonally across them arrived. "Have some plum cake, Mama, it is always good here."

"I know, Gisa, but I have no appetite. You can imagine why I wanted to talk with you."

"I can."

"The children are wearing each other down, they are ruining the store, and Dezsö cannot stand the eternal arguing anymore. We have to do something, Gisa."

"A forced march to Tapolca won't help this time," said Gisa and smiled.

"It didn't help then either," said my grandmother dryly. "We have to bring Jenö to his senses."

"Jenö is no child anymore, Mama. What can you tell him?"

"That he should let Dezsö make the decisions. Jenö is the most intelligent of us all, he must see that Dezsö grew up in the business and knows what he is doing. He should concern himself with the Fleischmarkt and leave the Rotenturmstrasse store in peace."

"You will waste your time, Mama," said Gisa. "Jenö is in his mid-thirties, he's not going to change anymore, he has never got along with a business friend, he can't help it." (Jakob can't help it either, she said to herself, you have to get along with people as they are, I can, why can't Dezsö?)

"But we have to do something," said my grandmother, "it can't go on like this. You are a clever woman, Gisa, advise me."

"They have to separate."

"Yes, I think so too, but how do you imagine it happening? Dezsö won't leave the store, it's like his baby, we can't expect that of him, and Jenö won't want to leave either."

Gisa beckoned the waiter and ordered plum cake, even though the conversation was ruining her appetite. "He won't want to, but maybe he'll have to. I think he's under pressure. He has debts, Jellinek told me that he has taken out a third mortgage on the villa, and if Dezsö buys him out, that will get him out of the quandary. It's strange, he is the most intelligent one of us all, and he always does the wrong thing."

"Because he is a *chochem*," said my grandmother, "a smart-aleck. He has always thought he knew everything better, even as a little boy."

"I know. When it says in the stock market report that you should sell, he buys, and when his agent tells him he should buy, then he sells, in order to prove to the world that he knows best. Do you think you should talk with him?"

"I will," said my grandmother, "but first with Dezsö, and you're coming along."

This conversation, too, took place in Ginsberg's Café, and the little group could have been a subject for a painting by Chassériau: my grandmother with her still-black hair, as almost always wearing a simple, black, high-necked dress, on which she had pinned a large brooch in antique style, a gift from Gisa; Gisa, who now looked almost alarmingly like my grandmother, likewise in black, but very elegant, this time with heavy earrings, semi-precious stones in a gold setting; Dezsö in a brown suit of rough wool, with white streaks in his hair that contrasted with his fresh-looking face (his hair had started to go grey right after he was buried alive and was later as white as snow), and in spite of the quarrels, enterprising and cheerful.

"I quite agree," he said, after his mother had given him a little lecture. "I can think of nothing nicer than to be rid of Jenö, but he won't let go!"

"Maybe he'll have to," said Gisa.

He did have to. He met with his mother and his sister in Café Schubert, because the Café on the market wasn't good enough for him. "I won't go into that *Tschoch*," he had said when Gisa had suggested the place to him. "Not that little *Tschoch*. That's bad for my credit." It was early afternoon, and Jenö was in a good mood: he had had lunch with his stockbroker, whom he had entertained with a bottle of old burgundy. He told them about a trip to Italy he was planning, Milan, Venice, Rome, maybe also Naples, because he "had to see something new to get new ideas. . . ." That gave my grandmother an opening. "Maybe it will be good if you get new ideas," she said. "I don't like to interfere, Jenö, but you are no child anymore, you know it can't go on the way it is with you and Dezsö. You don't even join us anymore on *erev Shabbos*, and I don't like it when there's a feud in the family."

"It is not my fault if there's a feud. I can't help it that Dezsö lets Mitzi turn him against me, that doesn't bother me at all, but the fact that he brought her into the business without asking me, I won't put up with that, I am the senior partner!"

And then came a torrent of complaints and accusations. He described the dress with the red frills, talked about the difference between venom-yellow and butterfly-yellow, about the vulgar taste of the *shiksa* whom Dezsö had married just to annoy him, he spoke of how he would long since have made the store the most elegant in Vienna, if Dezsö had only let him have his way. . . . My grandmother let him talk, and when he finally took a break, she said quietly: "Let's assume you are right, but Mitzi is there now, Dezsö won't change, and you won't change either. If you think that Dezsö is standing in your way, then you two have to go separate ways."

"Go separate ways?" asked Jenö. "How do you envisage that?"

"If you can't abide each other, you will have to dissolve the company. You can't keep on fighting forever, you're wearing each other down."

"I don't know how you think that can be done," said Jenö again. "If I buy out Dezsö, he can buy himself a store in Brigittenau for all I care, but he won't want to."

"You can't buy him out," said Gisa, who had been silent until now. "You don't have the money. But if you leave, you can pay off your debts with the settlement, and then you'll have a free hand and can put the Fleischmarkt in order."

"Don't pester me with my debts, Gisa," said Jenö heatedly. "I have no debts, I have the villa on the Lawies, the Kreditbank will lend me any amount!"

The two old ladies at the next table looked over at the man in the checkered suit who was waving his coffee spoon in the air. Jenö put it back on the water glass. "You have always been against

194

me, Gisa, you already took Dezsö's side when he was still a little boy, but I won't be driven out, not by him, and not by you!"

"Don't talk nonsense," said my grandmother. "No one is against you, I have always wanted the best for you, you know that. You have always been the brightest one. You should have the good sense to give in and avoid a fight."

"Of course," said Jenö and emptied the little glass of liqueur that the waiter had put beside his coffee cup in one gulp. "Isn't this just exactly how I always wanted my life to turn out – he married the *shiksa* who has ruined the store, and I am supposed to give in!",

"Because there is no other way," said Gisa, "you must see that."

The discussion ended as expected, without their agreeing on anything, and perhaps I could have spared myself the trouble of writing it down. Jenö wasn't bothered by constant fighting. People say of Bobby Fisher, who won the World Chess Championship in 1972 (is it really so long ago? It frightens me how quickly time passes), that he played best when everything annoyed him – the room he played in, the chessboard, the lighting, the television cameras, the audience: anger seemed to inspire him. It was somewhat like that with Jenö, he had inherited the trait from his grandfather. But whereas old Róth could nurse a grudge for his entire life (it was, as Brecht's Mother Courage said, a long grudge), Jenö, like Bobby Fisher, seemed to need a new provocation every day, and he found it at that time on Rotenturmstrasse. But he really was in a predicament. He had neither the money for the trip to Italy he had blathered on about, nor the credit he had boasted about, and he really was in debt, to an even greater extent than Gisa had suspected. He had not been able to pay for the new roof in Pressbaum, his lawyer was demanding his still unpaid fee for the lawsuit with the furniture company, the shares he had bought on the morning of his conversation with his mother and sister turned out to be a bad speculation, and there wasn't enough demand for the clothes that were manufactured on Fleischmarkt. He had the feeling that he hadn't really made any headway in the last ten years, and he began to suspect that without a substantial infusion of capital not much would come of that enterprise. However, it seemed to him unwise to take the first step toward dissolving the partnership, and since he knew that his mother had also spoken with Dezsö, he decided to wait.

He didn't have to wait long: ten days after the conversation, he received a registered letter that kept him for a while from his otherwise obligatory study of the stock market. Dezsö had consulted again with his sister, but then also with his lawyer, a Dr. Jellinek, who later, after the civil war of 1934, defended the social democratic workers free of charge, and so was among the first to be arrested after the *Anschluss*. Jellinek, who knew how to do things, was of the opinion that they could only reach an agreement with Jenö if the latter considered it a great victory, and so the negotiations they now entered into were not unlike the negotiations that take place when you buy a Persian rug from an Armenian in New York: on the rug there is a tag giving the origin, size and price – let's say: $1,000. So you offer $100. The Armenian is so appalled that his hair stands on end, but he gets a grip on himself, throws a little prayer mat onto the Persian rug as a free gift, consults with his manager and finally declares that he is prepared, since nothing concerns him more than the satisfaction of his customer, to sell the rug at a loss, for $800. With that, you've made a start. An hour later you stop at an offer of $400 with him demanding $600, but by now the Armenian is so exhausted that he has to make coffee – an exceptionally strong coffee that is served in tiny cups and for the likes of us can only be made drinkable with huge quantities of sugar. The buyer forgets how such coffee is made, takes a good swig, gets the coffee grounds stuck in his throat, and only recovers from the coughing fit that causes with the help of a second cup of coffee, which he now sips carefully. Lying on the object of contention now as free gifts are, in addition to the prayer mat, a dozen napkins, a tablecloth, an embroidered scarf and a pair of earrings. Another hour later you agree on a price of $500. That is admittedly more than the rug is worth, but less than you would have paid if you hadn't bought it from an Armenian, and in addition you have the free gifts. You can hang the prayer mat on the wall, give the napkins and tablecloth to Aunt Marga on her next birthday, and for the scarf and earrings hopefully you have a girlfriend. . . .

The letter Jenö received explained with extreme courtesy – Jellinek had seen to that – why it was necessary for them to separate, and suggested as a separation payment the sum of 200,000 kronen. It stated that the store had been purchased for 300,000 kronen (200,000 in cash and 100,000 in instalments), and so Herr Johann Kahn's share amounted to 150,000 kronen. However, Herr Dezsö Kahn was willing (that was what is called a gambit in chess) to take into consideration the diminished value of the currency since then and to add 50,000 kronen – an exceedingly generous suggestion; because it must also be taken into consideration that Herr Dezsö Kahn, at least since the founding of the business on Fleischmarkt, had essentially managed Rotenturmstrasse on his own, while Herr Johann Kahn had only occasionally appeared there, as well as, and above all, the fact that the firm Kahn Brothers under the currently prevailing circumstances in Austria was facing an uncertain future, and after the dissolution of the company Dezsö would have to take the entire risk upon himself. . . .

After Jenö read and re-read the letter, he was, as mentioned, in no mood to study the stock market; he went to his lawyer – Dr. Korn, to whom Jenö still owed the fee for the previous lawsuit, and about whose exceptional brilliance he had told Elli years ago, but who in lawyers' circles was famous primarily for the fact that (like the chess champion Dr. Lasker), he smoked exceptionally strong-smelling cigars whose smoke he blew into his opponent's face. (In that, he had a certain advantage over rug salesmen, who usually don't smoke because of all the rugs piled up on the floor; the customer of course may smoke, and the rug salesmen hope that the glowing ash will burn a hole in a rug, which must then be bought at the original price.) Since the settlement that would be paid to his client offered the lawyer the only chance of ever getting his money for the case against the furniture company, he said he was prepared to serve as Jenö's adviser, but insisted that, before he would tackle the matter, they draw up a contract obliging Jenö, immediately after receipt of his settlement, to pay both legal bills, the old one and the new one. It took a while to draw up this contract, and so Dezsö, in turn, only received a registered letter three days later.

It was a long document that, although Dr. Korn had done his best, was not quite as polite as the one composed by Dezsö and Dr. Jellinek. If, it said, the partnership had to be dissolved, then that was exclusively and entirely the fault of Herr Dezsö Kahn, who had not only, without first obtaining the approval of his partner, brought a third person into the joint business, namely Frau Mitzi Kahn née Priminger (sic), who had no knowledge of the business and was therefore completely unsuited for it, but he had also, in every way imaginable, hindered and prevented his equally entitled co-owner and older brother from ensuring that the management be actualized advantageously in a manner corresponding to the currently existing conditions in the area of ladies' fashions. (The word "actualized" can be attributed to Jenö.) To charge the senior partner with not having been in the store every day and all day was, to put it mildly, eccentric. (The word "eccentric" can be attributed to Dr. Korn, who devoted a highly paid quarter of an hour to talking his client out of using the word "shameless.") The senior partner, far from voluntarily wanting to distance himself from energetically participating in the work of the firm Kahn Brothers, had of necessity and only to preserve the peace reduced the amount of time he spent on Rotenturmstrasse, because only by making this sacrifice had he been able to avoid having Frau Mitzi Kahn née Priminger, who had been unlawfully hired there, hurl insults at him. If the firm Kahn Brothers unlawfully paid Frau Mitzi Kahn née Priminger, who had no knowledge of the business, a salary of 800 kronen that had never been approved by the senior partner – for reasons, incidentally, to do with taxes, which alone sufficed to make them not entirely irreproachable from a moral

198

standpoint – then the sum of at least 2,000 kronen per month should be credited to the senior partner, Herr Johann Kahn, who held his diploma in commerce and was internationally known for his competence, i.e. for his six-years' (aha!) collaboration 2,000 x 96 = 144,000 kronen, which sum, since the value of the krone during that time had fallen to approximately half its worth, would have to be valorized and would therefore amount to at least 200,000 kronen. . . . Furthermore, Leonhard Bamberger had sold the store in 1912 at far below its actual value because he had been in a hurry, but the sum paid at that time had long since, as the adversaries Dr. Jellinek and Dezsö Kahn had admitted in writing, in view of the devaluation of the currency that had taken place since then, ceased to reflect the current situation, and the actual value of the business would have to be calculated entirely differently. The business brought in roughly 180,000 kronen per year (which was of course vastly overestimated), and it was exceptionally accommodating of him, Johann Kahn, to refer to the current return and not the incomparably higher one that could have been realized if the junior partner had not prevented the senior one, among other things by the improper and by him, Johann Kahn, not approved employment of the said Frau Mitzi Kahn, who had no knowledge of the business, from actualizing it in, as mentioned, a manner suitable to the currently prevailing conditions in the area of ladies' fashions. However, even if you merely took into account 180,000 kronen and the likewise very fair assumption that capital held in trust earns 4% interest, then the firm Kahn Brothers, quite apart from the sharply rising real estate prices, was worth 4,500,000 kronen, so that the reasonable sum for the settlement came not to 200,000 kronen, as the adversaries Dr. Jellinek and Dezsö Kahn had astonishingly professed to assert, but to a total of 2,250,000 kronen, in addition to which, though, in view of the fact that he, Johann Kahn, although he was the senior partner, had obligingly declared himself prepared to leave the firm, instead of, as was his right, insisting on buying out the junior partner, which would have given him, Johann Kahn, the opportunity, by means of the, as already mentioned, long overdue updating of the management, to double the turnover, above all, though, the annual profit and, therefore, the real value of the firm within a short time, a compensation of 100,000 kronen was to be paid to him, a ridiculously small sum in view of the circumstances; to which, however, would still be added, as mentioned, the above calculated 200,000 kronen owed him, for a total of 2,550,000 kronen.

To retain the metaphor suggested to me by Dr. Korn's and Dr. Lasker's cigar smoke, that was a Sicilian game (an opening, mind you, that only became popular in tournaments after Dr. Lasker's death): Dr. Jellinek and my Uncle Dezsö began with the aggressive move e2-e4 (in as far as a first move can be aggressive at all), to which Dr. Korn and my Uncle Jenö responded with the aggressive move c2-c4. But it was a correspondence game, and I know from bitter experience how a correspondence game affects you. Let us assume that, after receiving an adversary's move by letter, you have to answer within 24 hours, and that the letter is then 24 hours en route, then the game, even if I generously do not take into account that no mail is delivered on Sundays, only gets as far as the seventh move after four weeks and so is still in the opening phase. Meanwhile, you have already spent 28 days and nights at the chessboard, an entire library of reference works is lying on the table, the telephone isn't answered, the mail is – with the exception of the one immediately opened letter with the next move – not read, the computer equipped with the latest chess program is running 10 hours per day, your wife, if you have one, is threatening divorce. . . . After phenomenal exertions on the part of both lawyers using the correspondence route had narrowed the opening gap in the first two letters of 2,550,000 kronen minus 200,000 kronen = 2,350,000 kronen to 1,500,000 kronen, Dr. Korn, who occasionally played chess in his favourite café while he smoked his cigars, recognized the hopelessness of coming to an agreement by mail and arranged a series of "discussions," to be held alternately in his and in Dr. Jellinek's office.

200

Here, however, new complications arose, unforeseen at least by Dr. Jellinek, among them that every discussion began with an argument about whether the window should be open or shut: Dezsö could not tolerate the cigar smoke, Dr. Korn could not tolerate the draught, Jenö could not tolerate the street noise that came into the office through the opened window, and Dr. Jellinek could not stand the fact that the air polluted by Dr. Korn's cigar was damaging his client's health. Only after this dispute, since no agreement could be reached, had been temporarily shelved, could suggestions and counter-suggestions about the matter itself be presented. Would it not be possible, said Dr. Jellinek for instance, since they could not agree on the settlement sum, to leave Herr Johann Kahn in the firm as a "sleeping partner" and to pay him an appropriate portion of the monthly profit – let's say: 50% minus 15% for the work done by Herr and Frau Dezsö Kahn? "Impossible!" shouted Dr. Korn, who would never have got his fee in this manner; they simply could not expect Herr Johann Kahn to pay, as it were, out of his own pocket a salary for a person he had not wanted in the store and whose presence he found detrimental to the business. Cash or nothing! Fine, said Dr. Jellinek; then an impartial appraiser, for instance the business manager of Couture Moderne, Herr Nathan Politzer, should be called in to determine the value of the firm and, with that, the settlement sum. "Don't make me laugh!" shouted Jenö. Politzer impartial? It was notoriously well-known in the business that Politzer was a business friend of Dezsö's and was a notoriously unreliable fellow who considered everything that wasn't located on Kärnterstrasse to be inferior. By the way, he really could not tolerate the street noise anymore! And he got up and shut the window, while Dr. Korn lit his fifth cigar.

After three stormy meetings, the negotiations about an appraiser who would be acceptable to both sides had to be broken off as hopeless, and I don't know if there ever would have been an agreement if the krone had not started to fall again. That was detrimental to the negotiations because the contested settlement sum now had to be calculated anew from week to week, which exercise, because there was no reliable standard for the currency devaluation, naturally led to new differences of opinion. On the other hand, the Cuban cigars that Dr. Korn smoked were getting more and more expensive, while the fee that Jenö owed him was constantly declining in value. So the lawyer was interested in a rapid settlement, which meant that Jenö almost had an enemy in his own camp, and it could only be attributed to this circumstance that the adversaries finally, in a meeting during which the window was opened and shut again three times, agreed on a lump sum payment of 400,000 kronen – a sum whose value is exceptionally difficult to estimate today. If you ask economists about it, they shrug their shoulders.

At the last minute, Jenö demanded that he still be entitled to take 30,000 kronen worth of commodities from the store. "Don't let yourself in for that, Herr Kahn," said Dr. Jellinek imploringly and put his hand on Dezsö's arm. But not only Dr. Korn was under pressure, Dezsö was under pressure too, since the rise in prices was making it necessary for him to use all the money coming in to buy merchandise as quickly as possible, and he was convinced that he simply could no longer afford to sit around for hours in a lawyer's office. So a contract was drawn up and signed, Jenö travelled to Paris with a suitcase full of hundred kronen bills to be changed into francs, Dr. Korn got his fee, and Dr. Jellinek swore he would never again set foot in Dr. Korn's office. However, Jenö had hardly returned to Vienna when he appeared on Rotenturmstrasse to take his pick of the commodities. Things hadn't gone well for him in Paris, since no one wanted Austrian kronen, and he had had to sell them at a considerable loss. So he was convinced that Dezsö had cheated him (was it not his fate to be defrauded again and again?), and was full of righteous anger; and if there had previously always been an argument when he entered the store, the argument now escalated into a terrible and grotesque event.

Jenö wanted to have the new mirrors, but they were built in and couldn't be taken down without damaging the walls and the fitting rooms. He wanted jointed mannequins, not just any mannequins that were lying about in the storeroom, but rather the long-legged ones in the shop window. He did not want the yellow Parisian dresses that Dezsö handed to him, because they were already six months out of fashion, and anyway, what should he do with dresses, since he had no retail shop? He wanted the sewing machine that Dezsö needed to alter clothes, and the thread that went with it. He didn't want the paper string that had been bought during the war, but the hemp string they still had on hand from 1913. Finally, the brothers argued about packing paper and buttons while the salesgirls looked on, more horrified than amused. It was an argument with unequal weapons, because while Jenö was shouting, Dezsö could only wheeze, and after three hours he fled into his office and turned the key in the lock. Jenö stood outside the locked door nonplussed for a second; then he broke it down with a well aimed kick, and glass shattered noisily on the parquet floor. In the end, Frau Marie fetched a policeman who put his arm around the raging man's shoulder and led him out of the store.

The store looked like a battlefield. Shards of glass, dresses and accessories lay on the floor, balls of string, packing paper, clothes hooks and broken mannequins lay on the tables, Dezsö sat in his devastated office with his face in his hands. . . . But all that could be straightened up, and even the fact that Jenö, who had not succeeded in taking 30,000 kronen worth of things out of the store, initiated proceedings against his brother proved to be no misfortune; because Dr. Jellinek, with the tacit assistance of his colleague Dr. Korn, who had lost interest in the affairs of his client after receiving his fee, successfully employed a delaying tactic. When Jenö died of a heart attack twenty years later, it had still not come to a hearing, and it can be assumed that today the files of the unfinished lawsuit are still in some cupboard of the Viennese District Court waiting to be processed. But Dezsö felt that he was free at last, for the first time he was the sole ruler in his kingdom on Rotenturmstrasse, and a new day dawned. When he negotiated with his bank to borrow the 400,000 kronen that he needed to pay Jenö, he discovered that people in the business world believed in his future and were prepared to give him credit (admittedly at interest rates determined by the inflation, which bordered on insanity). By chance, the jeweller who owned the store next to his had died. Dezsö bought the premises, temporarily closed the store, had the dividing wall removed, renovated, and opened again two months later with a shop window display that caused a sensation in the business. In the following years he acquired two houses in the suburb of Alsergrund and gradually became a rich man.

CHAPTER SIX

Kahn & Engelmann

1.

AFTER A LONG SEARCH, Sándor had found a small apartment on a hill overlooking Linz, the Freienberg. From the dining room window, he could look down over the city, which now lay in the last glow of sunset. The table was set with white linen and the heavy silver cutlery that is enthusiastically collected today by lovers of the past. I find it clumsy; modern stainless steel cutlery suits me better.

There was potato soup and chicken for dinner, and Elli was proud to be able to take such good care of her husband this time. She was highly pregnant, so for the past few weeks she had not gone to the store anymore, where she had been helping since it had been set up. She had spent almost the entire afternoon doing the shopping: in the summer of 1919, over half a year since the end of the war, almost everything was still in short supply.

"I didn't get any vegetables, Sándor," she said, "and I had to throw away half the potatoes. I had good luck with the chicken, though I had to stand in line for half an hour, and it was the last one. But don't you want to make yourself comfortable?"

At Pressburger's, Sándor had learned to dress with care, and since he had become the manager of his own business, he attached even more importance to making an elegant impression. Now he took off the dark jacket and got himself a light woollen one from the bedroom. "I don't know if it's good for you to be on your feet so much," he said as he came back. "You are in the seventh month and should take it easy."

"I don't think," said Elli, as she put a piece of chicken on Sándor's plate, "that the exercise and the fresh air can do me any harm. But sometimes I do get a little impatient. There are line-ups for everything, there is no coal, and the firewood is damp and doesn't burn properly. It's a good thing winter is behind us!"

Sándor didn't say anything, and Elli looked at him with a smile. What an attractive man he was, with his black hair and dark eyes! She was glad she had married him, and not stupid Franz. But she saw from his expression that something was wrong. "You look dejected and tired. Is it something at the store that's troubling you?"

"Of course it is! We unpacked the parcels from Fleisch-markt, and once again half of the contents cannot be used. Jenö has sent me crumpled, dirty shirts again, although I have explained to him a hundred times that there is no good dry cleaner in Linz. A new shirt has to look new, I can't sell my customers junk. And then there are dresses with a plunging décolleté, people don't wear things like that in Linz."

"Maybe it's the latest fashion in Vienna, then we'll be the first to show it here, Sándor. You're fussing too much about the shirts, they can't be dirty, maybe they were just badly packed. But if you can't sell the shirts as they are, send them back to Jenö, he can have them cleaned in Vienna. You will manage to sell the dresses, there's such a shortage of everything here that the women will be happy if they can get anything at all!"

"I don't understand why Jenö produces such rubbish on Fleischmarkt," said Sándor. "He is such a clever man! Sometimes I think he only sends me what he can't sell in Vienna, it's supposed to be good enough for the provinces."

"I can't imagine that," said Elli. "My brother doesn't do that kind of thing. And he would harm himself, it's his store too!"

The problem was that my father and Jenö had become business partners. After their marriage, my parents had spent a few cold, rainy days at Lake Balaton, and then my father had to go back to the front, although his wound was still painful and hadn't healed properly. Finally, it began to fester, and when he was under particularly severe stress – crossing a river while under fire – the wound broke open. By the time he arrived at the field hospital, he had almost bled to death, despite an emergency bandage. This time it was a better surgeon who cleaned the wound and sewed it up. After four weeks, Sándor could leave the field hospital and had the good fortune that he, like Dezsö and later Jenö, was discharged as being "unfit for service." He made his way to Vienna, and the weeks he spent convalescing with Elli at my grandparents' on Augartenstrasse were perhaps – or so it seems to me at least at my desk in Haifa – the happiest of his life. When he could move again without pain, he began to look for a job in Vienna, but in vain: the winter of 1918 was still a good time for the Viennese black marketeers and the people supplying the armed forces; you just had to look at what the refined and unrefined ladies paid for clothes on Kärntnerstrasse or at Dezsö's store on Rotenturmstrasse to know that the war had brought money into circulation. But nine-tenths of the population were starving, and after Corporal Sándor Engelmann was released from the army, there was no work for people with his qualifications or that interested him. As much as he would have liked to stay in Vienna, he had to be glad in the end that Pressburger offered him his old position in Linz again. . . .

There, my father could have enjoyed the happiness of his young marriage, if he had not been tormented by ambition. "I don't like working at Pressburger's anymore," he would say, as he and my mother lay in bed under the warm eiderdown. (They needed the eiderdown; there was no coal.) "Jenö, Dezsö and Gisa have their own businesses, my sister has her own tailor shop, only I am just working for wages."

"Come on, Sándor," said my mother. "You're not just working for wages. You have full signing powers in a respected firm, isn't that enough?"

"For me perhaps," said my father. "But for you it isn't good enough, and in the long run it isn't good enough for me either. I have lost four years at the front, and now I'm almost thirty. . . ."

By the time summer was drawing to a close, it had become obvious that the victories reported every day in the newspapers were nothing but propaganda. Then, at the end of October, the collapse came suddenly: the soldiers had had enough and went home by the thousands, starving and begging. Among those who returned home was Jakob. Only Ferenc stayed in his trench in his first lieutenant's uniform to the bitter end. When the Republic was proclaimed, Sándor was pleased, he saw it as the beginning of a new and perhaps better time; Elli cried, as she had cried when the old Kaiser had died. The widespread hunger caused a bad riot in Linz that the police barely managed to break up, but then life went on as usual again, as if it didn't matter who was in power in Vienna. Two weeks later, when Sándor was on his way home, which took him from Landstrasse through the Promenade, he saw that Siegmund Bell's drapery and knitwear store had closed: the store windows were nailed shut with wooden boards.

My father hadn't even taken his coat off when he began to talk about it. "Just imagine, Elli," he said excitedly, "Siegmund Bell has closed, you know, that's the knitwear store on the Promenade. That is not a bad location, the entire city goes past there, and I happen to know a bit about it. The building belongs to Frau Baumann who has the fur store next door, maybe the store is for rent."

"Really?" said Elli, helping him out of his coat and kissing him.

"I'll have to enquire," said my father, "that may be my big chance."

The next morning, he spoke with Frau Baumann, who showed him the empty and therefore quite dreary-looking space. She was in a hurry and wanted to persuade Sándor to put down a deposit right away, but he couldn't make up his mind that quickly.

"Give me a few days' time," he said, "at the least, I'll have to discuss it with my wife. . . ."

Their discussion did not take place until the evening, since Sándor still had to attend to his duties at Pressburger's. "The store is really available, Elli," he said over their evening meal, which was again better than could have been expected under the circumstances: at Mitzi's request, Primingers' had sent smoked meat. "You've been in the store a few times, Elli, it is more than big enough, almost as big as Dezsö's store, but it is not set up for men's fashions. It would have to be renovated, that will cost a tidy sum, when there isn't even decent firewood for sale."

"So you think you should go for it? The times are so troubled."

"I think it is a unique opportunity. The Promenade is not the best location, I would prefer Landstrasse, but the Promenade is the second best, and God knows when something will become available again anywhere. Nothing has been built in Linz since the war started. I don't know where the money is supposed to come from, I will have to offer the customers something when I open!"

"You should discuss it with Jenö, Sándor. He promised us that he would help us if we started a business!" Sándor got up, fetched a pad of paper and began jotting down numbers as he chewed Primingers' famous smoked meat. "I'll take two days off," he said at last. "Tomorrow morning I'll talk with Frau Baumann again, and then I'll travel to Vienna to sell the etamine."

They had the etamine because Elli's dowry had consisted of a savings account to which Jenö, Dezsö and Gisa had contributed. Since the outcome of the war was uncertain in October of 1917, and since Sándor did not trust the currency, he had used part of the money the day before he returned to active duty to buy a large supply of etamine that happened to be available just then, and stored it at Dezsö's. . . .

The train Sándor took to Vienna was so full of soldiers that he could just manage to squeeze onto an open platform and had to stand the whole way there. There were no cabs at the train station, the streetcar didn't run, and Sándor walked to Rotenturmstrasse, where Dezsö, whose wife was, after all, a Priminger, could offer him real coffee and a meat sandwich. While he was eating, Sándor told his brother-in-law what had brought him to Vienna. Then they went into the storeroom. Dezsö ripped open one of the big bolts, pulled out a handful of the thin, loosely woven cloth and rubbed it between his fingers.

"That's poor material that you bought," he said at last. "Where did you get this *Pofel?*"

Sándor was overly touchy, like all people who lack self-confidence, and his pride as a businessman was hurt. "You remember," he said, "I already had the call-up order in my pocket and had no time to look around for long. The offer came from Preissig – that is a famous firm that can be trusted!"

"Preissig is famous all right," said Dezsö, "but he's also a scoundrel, and you have to keep a close eye on him. You won't get much for the etamine, go to Preissig and see if he'll take it back!"

Dezsö's apprentice fetched a cab from the stand on the Graben, and Sándor asked about the fare. The driver wanted seventy kronen – an outrageous sum for the ride to Wieden. "Do you know what oats cost today?" he said, as Sándor shook his head. "I can't even get decent hay anymore." Sándor shook his head again and got in. A quarter of an hour later, he was at the entrance to the large courtyard, over which the inscription A. Preissig and Son was written in big, ornate lettering. He told the porter that he wanted to talk to the boss, and an apprentice led him into the office. The grey-haired gentleman, whose frock coat was as old-fashioned as the sign over the door, inspected the sample of cloth that Sándor had brought with him and shook his head. "Wartime merchandise," he said at last, while he rubbed the material between his fingers just like Dezsö, "hardly usable."

"But I bought the etamine from you," said my father, "you can't have sold me inferior material!"

"If you don't like the material, Herr Engelmann," said Preissig, "then you should have complained right away. You cannot expect us to take it back from you now, after it has been lying around for eighteen months."

"I already had the call-up order in my pocket, Herr Preissig," said Sándor, "and I relied on your reputation."

"We have the reputation," said Preissig smugly, "and rightly so. But a cloth merchant is like a stock broker, my father always said, he has to know when to buy and when to sell. You are a young man and will learn that." Sándor blushed, but he didn't say anything, and Preissig continued: "We sold you the etamine at the price it was worth at the time. But it is important to us to have satisfied customers. Perhaps I can take the material back from you at the price it is worth today." And then he named a sum that was approximately a quarter of the original price.

Sándor got up, left the office without saying a word and returned to Rotenturmstrasse on foot. It was a long way, but my father felt he could no longer afford a cab, and he needed the exercise to help him calm down. "If you want," said Dezsö, after he had listened to Sándor's story, "I can try to sell the etamine for you, but I'll have to sell it for next to nothing. However, to help you get started, I can lend you 10,000 kronen."

By then it was afternoon, and my father went over to Fleischmarkt. Jenö wasn't there, apparently travelling, and Sándor sat down in the office, where he wrote a long letter to his old friend and brother-in-law. Then he took the unheated and dirty train back to Linz. He was tired and depressed, and told Elli about his failure and about Dezsö's offer.

Three days later, Jenö arrived in Linz, announced by a telegram, dressed in his newest checkered suit, and took a look at the store on Promenade. The ensuing long conversation that took place in the apartment on the Freienberg can be summarized briefly. His business on Fleischmarkt was a lot of work without bringing in much, said Jenö, the times were uncertain, he had to be careful with his money, and he had ongoing expenditures in Pressbaum, where he was feeding the whole family. . . . Of course it was correct that he had at one time promised Sándor that he would help him found a business, but he had also contributed to Elli's dowry, and the misfortune with the etamine – Sándor had told him about it with a red face – was not his fault. Of course he was prepared to help out his friend and brother-in-law, that went without saying, but if he, Jenö, was supposed to help finance the founding of the business on Promenade, then it was absolutely necessary – Jenö corrected himself: totally absolutely necessary – that he have a share in the business. And since Sándor, who hadn't been thinking at all of having a partner in the business, remained awkwardly silent, Jenö continued with a flowing torrent of words. Number 15 Promenade was a good address, everyone in Linz who had money and was respected went past there, they would have lots of space, they should probably think of carrying blouses and dressing gowns in addition to men's fashions, he made blouses on Fleischmarkt, and then the new firm would have credit; as Sándor knew, the women liked to go along when their husbands bought suits, and so they would have them in the store as well and could show them something. . . .

Since Sándor nervously lit his third cigarette, but remained stubbornly silent, the torrent of words continued. To be sure, the times were uncertain, the young Republic was standing on shaky legs, and the fact that there had been hunger riots in Linz again was not exactly encouraging, but it was a time of new beginnings, they had to grab the opportunity. With peace, the economy would flourish again. The store on the Promenade was only the beginning, Linz was the gateway to the provinces, soon they would have branches in Salzburg and Klagenfurt, and why not in Vienna? And while they were on the topic of Vienna: the purchases for the store would of course have to be made in Vienna, it was obvious how the business would be organized. Sándor, who lived in Linz, would manage the store, while he, Jenö, would do the buying in Vienna, he had the space and the personnel for it on Fleischmarkt – and since the bookkeeping for Fleischmarkt was already done there, they could also do the bookkeeping for Kahn & Engelmann there, that would halve the expenses, and after all, Sándor was a beginner at bookkeeping. . . .

Sándor's face darkened. The words "beginner at bookkeeping" upset him, and so did the name of the firm that Jenö had so casually introduced. "Those are entirely new prospects, Jenö," he said rather meekly. "I'll have to think about it."

"Don't think about it too long," said Jenö. "Anyone who works for other people remains a poor devil his whole life, I learned that in London when I was fourteen. Frau Baumann does not depend on us, there will be others who want to have the store. We have to grab it today, by tomorrow it may already be too late!"

The three of them were dining in the most expensive restaurant in Linz, because no other one was good enough for Jenö, and it took considerable effort on Sándor's part to prevent his brother-in-law from celebrating the founding of their joint business as a done deal with a bottle of champagne. "Please, Jenö, we aren't that far yet," he said, as Jenö had already beckoned the waiter, "you have to give me time to think about this!" In the end, Jenö paid the bill and in a rather tipsy state took a taxi to his hotel – instead of the champagne, he had ordered two bottles of Burgundy – while Elli and Sándor walked up the Freienberg.

"I imagined it differently," said my father. "The firm was supposed to be called Alexander Engelmann, I dreamed of such a shop sign all the years I was at the front; and the reason I want to get away from Pressburger is to be my own boss!"

My mother knew about the argument with Dezsö, but Jenö was still her beloved brother. "You will be," she said, "Jenö told you so, you'll manage the store here, and he'll stay in Vienna where he has more than enough to do. And don't forget how much easier that makes everything for us. There will be enough money to get started, Jenö has the Fleischmarkt and has credit everywhere."

"Maybe so, Elli. But why do the purchases have to be made in Vienna? I buy for Pressburger here in Linz, the representatives of the Viennese firms all come to Linz, and every few weeks I have to go to Vienna to see what's new there."

"Jenö will do it for you, Sándor, and when the baby has arrived, you won't want to go away as often. I am so looking forward to the child!"

"I am too, Elli, as you can imagine. But the bookkeeping can't be done in Vienna, because then I'd have no overview. Peier can do it here in Linz, he does the books for Pressburger, and I already had power of attorney for Pressburger before the war, I am not a beginner at bookkeeping!"

"That was just a slip of the tongue," said my mother, "Jenö didn't mean anything by it, you mustn't be so touchy. You will see, in one or two years you two will have the most elegant fashion shop in Linz. I can't imagine anything nicer than having my beloved husband and my brother build up a business together!"

The next morning, Sándor went to the Linz branch of the Länderbank and negotiated for a long time with the loans manager, who finally told him that every large loan needed the approval of the central bank in Vienna, the future was uncertain, he could not give him any great hope, perhaps he should go elsewhere. Then Sándor went to Jenö, who had just finished his breakfast in the hotel and hardly let his brother-in-law get a word in edgewise. Twice humiliated – like Preissig, the loans manager had treated him like a supplicant – he let himself be bullied: he insisted that the bookkeeping be done in Linz, but agreed slavishly to everything else. From the hotel, it wasn't far to Frau Baumann's. She was very pleased with the decision of Herr Kahn and Herr Engelmann, but wanted to have the lease drawn up by her lawyer; Bell still had certain rights, so the matter was not that simple. Nevertheless, she did accept a deposit from the brothers-in-law – or rather from Jenö, who wrote a cheque – and gave them the keys. Sándor and Jenö spent the rest of the day discussing how they would have the space renovated, first just the two of them, then with advice from a carpenter. Two days later, they went to see Frau Baumann's lawyer, who explained that his client wanted the rent paid in advance to the end of the year. While Jenö negotiated with the lawyer and Frau Baumann, my father went – as he remembered later, at Jenö's suggestion – to the carpenter to remind him to build in shelves and a locker under the large counter, and when he got back, the contract had been signed.

I am not sure where they got the money for the renovations and the merchandise. As we already know, Dezsö lent them 10,000 kronen at a low rate of interest, and then there was the remainder of the dowry. Some of the men's fashions could be taken on commission, and blouses and dressing gowns came from Jenö's production on Fleischmarkt. According to a document presented to the tax authorities in the spring of 1920, Sándor paid 48,000 kronen and Jenö 44,000 kronen into the public company Kahn & Engelmann; Jenö later maintained that those amounts were fictitious, simply made up to satisfy the authorities. On the first of February, 1919, they celebrated the opening of the store, an event that had been announced a week earlier in a dozen newspapers in Linz and in the Alpine provinces. Three days later, the store was looted during the last and largest hunger riot in Linz, and it seemed to Sándor that he was lucky to have his brother-in-law as his partner: the damage had to be repaired, the looted inventory replaced, the insurance company came through only after months of delays, and in contrast to his brother-in-law, Jenö had credit. Soon, though, long-term problems arose for which there was no insurance.

At Pressburger's, Sándor had done the purchasing without anyone's interference; he was accustomed to buying only first class merchandise, and he knew from long experience what "went" in Linz and what didn't. For Kahn & Engelmann, Jenö did the purchasing, and what he bought from other firms didn't seem all that bad; but he also sent things from his own company – he had reserved the right to do so from the start – and as we already know, Sándor had cause to complain about the goods from that source. There must have been correspondence – long since lost – dating from the spring of 1919 between Sándor and Jenö that contained primarily business information, but was not always very pleasant. In the late summer, probably during one of my father's visits to Vienna, there must have been a heated quarrel between the partners, and it pains me to think of such a quarrel: Jenö in his checkered suit, loud, articulate, self-confident, boastful, his wide open eyes fixed on the person he was talking to; my father nervous, chain-smoking, but precisely because he didn't have Jenö's self-confidence, stubborn and unyielding even when it wouldn't have mattered, as that would have hurt his pride. . . .

The correspondence that was kept starts in September 1919. My brother found it in 1965 when he was winding up our mother's estate in London. In addition to the shoebox of photographs that I have mentioned so often, there was also a thick pile of papers in brown wrapping paper. A brief inspection revealed that they were old business letters; he wasn't particularly interested in the family history, but he kept the package. A few weeks ago, he sent it to me at my request. Aside from several other documents of various kinds, it contained my father's correspondence with Jenö from September 1919 until the end of 1926, with Jenö's letters in the original, but only drafts, copies or carbon copies of my father's letters.

I have to admit that after I started to read it, I could hardly put it down. From dinner time until late into the night, I sat over the letters, fascinated and nauseated, and more than once I thought I should destroy the whole package. I can't copy out all five hundred pages, so I have to select excerpts, although that is actually a falsification: it is relevant that there are so many letters and that they are so long, and it is relevant that Jenö dictated his letters quickly and perhaps not always completely sober to a secretary, while my father, who knew that his German was not completely flawless and didn't want to reveal his ignorance, turned every word over three times, as it were, before he wrote it down. . . . Obviously, some letters got lost or were destroyed; but you can guess what preceded the first letter that was kept.

Jenö to Sándor, 16 typed pages, double-spaced.

Vienna, September 17, 1919

Dear Sándor!

Confirming receipt of your letters of the 13th and 16th of this month, in particular, receipt of the enclosures.

I will have textiles made up by Kampf & Pick and have already repeatedly invited the gentlemen to come to me to discuss the job. [...]

Reorganization of our bookkeeping, but especially in the organization of my deliveries, in the matter of expenses and calculation has taken many hours of my time in the past few days. [...] I try with every means at my disposal to look for, find and send you the various little items, that not only takes my own personal time, but also that of my employees, who work on every shipment that goes out by mail or by train, and we use forms, take the risk of all damage in transport, pay the insurance premiums, assume the costs of packaging and the very expensive costs of transporting the packages to the train station, etc. We have already discussed this matter in person the last time I was in Linz, and I indicated to you that as part of our production costs we also have to charge you a fee for management done by the parent company in Vienna. At the current level of the insurance premiums, these management costs amount to

1. at least 1% of the value,

2. for the administration and handling of the merchandise we have bought, and for having it packed by my personnel, at least 1%, and further

3. my net cash expenditures on the shipping costs for a purchase, for its packaging, freight or postage, are also almost 1%, so taken together, the real expenses can be estimated at 3%. Since these costs cannot be exactly determined in advance, I suggest that the 3% expense to the Viennese parent company that I really have for deliveries out of the city be rounded up to 5%, whereby of course the additional 2% possible cost on top of the real cost of 3%

217

would be rounded up to our mutual benefit, i.e., I intend to share this 2% with you. [...]

If you are in agreement with this suggestion, then I want to bill Linz retroactively for about K 2,000 for the time until now, but at the same time I am in agreement with your drawing the agreed monthly sum of K 1,500 for the work of your wife, without having to settle these monthly withdrawals with me retroactively, and of all deliveries from other sources that go through my firm in Vienna to Linz, 1%. [...]

Sándor to Jenö, 6 pages written by hand.

Linz, September 24, 1919

Dear Jenö!

The September 23rd profit and loss statement is enclosed, and now I want to answer you in detail about the reorganization. So now you want to reorganize, but what? There is nothing to be reorganized in Linz, after everything was so well organized by you, and we will stick to that.

There is no reason to reorganize the bookkeeping, everything is running fine here. The adjustments cause me no difficulty and are not a lot of work, but I want to remind you of your nonconservative style of bookkeeping: at first, you absolutely wanted to have the books done in Vienna, and I reluctantly consented to that. A few weeks later, you indicated to me that Fräulein Konrad will not be able to keep on doing our books, because she would get behind with your bookkeeping. So you insisted that we engage a bookkeeper for the Linz store, you were satisfied with the person I chose, and so I do not see why I should send you the invoices in order that Fräulein Konrad can check them and you can regulate them. [...] Linz is an independent body and needs no external control, the firm Johann Kahn is simply a supplier for the firm Kahn & Engelmann, that is what we agreed on, but it is not a parent company and not a central office! Consequently, as a matter of principle, I will not let any invoices out of my hands. They will be available for you to peruse here at any time, but no one else has permission to examine the books of our Linz store. If you find any sort of error when you are next in Linz, I will gladly accept that with gratitude, because I like to learn, but if you want to start having everything delivered to Johann Kahn and everything paid for by Johann Kahn, then I am the drudge until your business gets off the ground, and then you will be completely occupied with your firm and will say to me, dear brother-in-law, I have no time for you, and you will chuck the whole business.

As far as the deliveries from the manufacturers are concerned, I must ask you to have every manufacturer deliver directly to Linz. These people do a big business with us, and it should be their worry how to pack the merchandise for shipment. [...] But I also do not want to lose contact with the manufacturers, and want to order the men's clothing myself and take delivery of it myself. If you accept something in Vienna, and I for some reason have to complain about it, the manufacturers will say, but Herr Kahn accepted it and found it in order, etc. That will create friction between us, and I want to avoid that at all costs. [...]

Cretonne shirts. I have read your letter in which you informed me that you would send them, but I was not prepared for the fact that these shirts were delivered dirty. I can sell shirts that have not been dry-cleaned, but not shirts that are dirty and crumpled. [...]
Happy New Year!
Sándor

Jenö to Sándor, 13 pages typed, double-spaced.

Vienna, September 26, 1919
Profit and loss statement received with your letter of the 24th of this month, but your letter is not in the same spirit as my letter, is not an answer to my suggestions, and has no connection whatsoever

with the reorganization, which I simply suggested in connection with production costs. Perhaps it was the key word "reorganization" that caused your confusion and I should have chosen "production costs" as the key word in order to make myself better understood. But I will gladly turn onto the side street you are on in your answer and go for a walk with you, because as is well known, the end justifies the means.

It is quite correct that Linz is an independent body and the firm Johann Kahn is just a supplier, but you should draw the right conclusions from this fact, rather than making it into a question of prestige, as the firm Kahn & Engelmann in Linz has only enjoyed credit, trust and a good reputation from the start because it is supported by Johann Kahn in Vienna; consequently, it can only be of future benefit to that reputation if we, for reasons of prestige, formally acknowledge that Vienna is the parent company. However, I am not so ambitious and I can content myself with the practical side of this question, so I agree with you that Linz is an independent body, for which the independent Viennese firm Johann Kahn cannot make a single pen-stroke or flick of the wrist without calculating the cost. That gets us back again to the question of expenses, which is actually the matter at hand, and to which I will return. First, though, I would like to deal with your quite superfluous offer to let me see all the Linz invoices, receipts and books the next time I am in town. [...] In this regard, as well, you are throwing stones at an open door, because I am already satisfied with the way the Linz bookkeeping is organized because it was set up in accordance with my wishes. So that is not what all this is about.

Getting deliveries from other suppliers ready for mailing takes a great deal of my time, and occasionally my entire staff works a whole day just getting deliveries from other suppliers ready for mailing to Linz – but all I meant by referring to that was that the addition of a 5% production costs surcharge would only be justified if these deliveries from other suppliers really were prepared for mailing by Johann Kahn, and that has really been the case with the knitwear that I buy, with ties, etc. The only new thing would be to have the men's fashions shipped without exception by Johann Kahn, but that is also not what all this is about.

Delivery delays occur frequently now that the streetcars are no longer running, because no store employee goes on foot to the train station. Therefore, the firms in Vienna want to ensure the packages at our expense for 1.5% premium and send them through the ordinary mail. I happened to run into Herr Leo Frank, who told me that he would send the merchandise to Linz by mail and insured at a cost of 2%, which we would have to pay; instead of that, I suggested that the merchandise be delivered to me, because I can arrange for the shipping at a much lower rate, and because of that I acquire a legal right to charge the independent body in Linz 5% production costs – and that is what all this is about!

Acceptance of the merchandise naturally takes place only in Linz, and it has never occurred to me to interfere with you, even though, as your business partner, I am not only entitled, but also obliged to take an interest in the appearance of the merchandise that we purchase jointly. [...] So if I inspect the merchandise in Vienna, I am not doing so to forestall your specialized knowledge, and it is most certainly incorrect of you to maintain that the suppliers could then simply say, Johann Kahn in Vienna had accepted the merchandise. We don't live in the woods, and you know as well as I do that deliveries to Kahn & Engelmann are finally accepted only in Linz and not in Vienna.

Now I also want to say to you that for a third party business I would not carry out any shipping activities even for 10%. However, since it involves our own store, in which I am a partner, and to which I have lent my entire capital and my good credit and my good reputation, but particularly because I am interested in it and would like to see every item, I have suggested that I take on the enormous amount of work, because if I hadn't, I would not be justified in making an additional production charge, and this additional production charge is what all this is about! [...]

I only wanted to take a cursory glance at the books here until you have acquired more experience in bookkeeping, but I am also completely satisfied if you tell me that everything is in order. [...] We are business partners by agreement and of our own free will, and as long as there are company enterprises, there will also be differences of opinion, but with good will and love of peace, all questions must be settled peacefully. In this spirit, I beg you not to go your solitary way, because we are now, as God and Providence have decreed, brothers-in-law and business associates, and both of us are therefore obliged to get along with each other, and that is what all this is about. [...]

With kind regards to you all,

Jenö

The powerful rhetoric of this letter would have impressed me more if it had contained fewer logical blunders; I console myself, though, with the thought that powerful rhetoric is rarely without logical errors. I can only guess at my father's reaction, since only one page of his reply has been preserved, and it deals with tobogganing outfits to be ordered for the coming season. If all the letters exchanged between Sándor and Jenö had only dealt with tobogganing outfits, he might have lived to a ripe old age – provided that the Nazis had not killed him – and since all events are interconnected, I would not be sitting at my desk in Haifa, but at another desk somewhere else. . . .

In addition to the fragmentary letter just mentioned, sixteen complete letters have been preserved from the period before April of 1920. They obviously represent only a portion of the original correspondence. They aren't worth copying out, but it does emerge from them that at the latest in early 1920 a further discussion must have taken place between the brothers-in-law, and it must have been in Vienna, where my father had travelled by boat, since there was no coal and the trains had stopped running. It is obvious that Sándor must have decided to give in, as in return for concessions that can no longer be determined, he agreed to the five percent production costs charge. With that, it had come to a reconciliation between the brothers-in-law, or at least to a peace agreement, which led to an amazing result at the end of the following summer. But before I get to that summer, I have to go back a bit.

At the end of March, the just recently installed telephone rang in Jenö's office on Fleischmarkt, and the person at the other end was none other than Sidney Lionel. He had, he said, recently been appointed a director of the internationally famous firm Barnum (the firm really did have the same name as the much more famous circus). Barnum was in the process of founding a branch in Vienna that would be responsible not only for Austria, but also for all countries along the Danube, and he wanted to seek the advice of his old friend who was so well acquainted with the circumstances in the whole of the former Austro-Hungarian Empire. He was staying at Hotel Sacher; could Jenö perhaps drop by?

I know little more about Barnum than what I can deduce from the letterhead of the Viennese branch of the firm, which looked like this in March of the following year:

BARNUM'S EXPORT LTD
Head Office: London, E.C.2
67-69 Aldermanbury

Branch Offices: New York, Paris, Milan

Exclusive Agency for Austria,
Czechoslovakia,
Yugoslavia and Hungary
33 Wipplingerstrasse, Vienna I

GENERAL PURCHASING HOUSE for
Barnum's Oriental Stores, Ltd., Cairo
Barnum Brothers Ltd., South Africa
Trieste-Turin: Guido Zernotti
Vienna: Johann Kahn
Linz on the Danube: Kahn & Engelmann

What Barnum traded in cannot be deduced from this letterhead, but the firm apparently bought and sold everything it could get its hands on – locomotives and buttons, pocket knives and ploughs, but above all textiles, in the manner that Sidney Lionel explained to his friend: the tremendous strength of their capital let them buy enormous quantities of merchandise at a ten or twenty percent discount and pass them on for a small premium to the smaller enterprises they looked after. Judging by the impression Lionel made on an impartial observer, that seemed to be a lucrative business: he had thoroughly changed since the time when he was Jenö's London mentor and bosom friend. He was now a plump man in his forties, wore a dark, custom-made suit, had a trimmed moustache and greying hair, and you could tell at a glance that he was prosperous and contented. "Two weeks ago I visited our storeroom in Cairo," he said, as the two, at Jenö's suggestion, walked from Sacher to Café Schubert. "Ten thousand square metres, the largest storeroom in all of Africa."

The thing was that he needed Jenö to gain access for him to Viennese firms. Jenö, who discovered with pleasure that he had not forgotten his English in the twenty years since his return from London, and who sensed that this was his big chance, declared without further ado that he was prepared "to place all his energy, his many years of experience as a merchant and a manufacturer, his knowledge of the Austrian and Hungarian market, as well as his knowledge in the export business at the disposal of" Barnum; through his brother-in-law, who came from there, he incidentally also had connections with Yugoslavia. He was, of course, only too happy to help Barnum in the search for a suitable location for the branch that was to be founded, and Lionel could count on him in every respect. Could he first show his guest Vienna?

He showed him Vienna – the Opera, the Burgtheater, St. Stephen's Cathedral, the Belvedere, the view from the Kahlenberg; and as they sipped cognac after a lavish evening meal, he returned for the second time to the topic of his experience. Didn't it follow, he suggested at last, that he, Jenö, was the right man to be in charge of Barnum's Viennese branch? Another man with his business experience and his connections who could speak English, German and Hungarian would be hard to find.

A General Director for Vienna, Lionel said, was already provisionally planned, but the final decision would have to be postponed for a little while yet. . . . At first, Jenö didn't need to hear any more, and his letter to my father of the 22nd of April, which I am only quoting in part, demonstrates the determination with which he made the concerns of the English firm his own.

Dear Sándor!

The international firm Barnum, about which I have already told you, is opening its Head Office for the Republic of Austria, for Czechoslovakia, and for the kingdoms of Yugoslavia and Hungary on the 1st of May at 33 Wipplingerstrasse in Vienna. I.V. Mautner has let us have the larger half of his space on the mezzanine floor and also half of his space in the basement for 5 years, and the two stores will be separated by a wall. [...]

Mautner has given Barnum certain buying privileges and has entered into a contract that will have all his foreign purchasing done and delivered by Barnum, because the buying power of the firm Barnum is so immense that all competition is underbid from the start. Entirely for this reason I have also insisted that everything required for Kahn & Engelmann be bought and delivered by Barnum, and signed a contract, a copy of which is enclosed. For Kahn & Engelmann, as you can see from the enclosed inventory, I have also delivered on behalf of Barnum an order for more than K 148,000 of men's and boys' clothing to Egypt. [...]

For Barnum, I have now also bought more than three million kronen worth of men's clothing from Palmer, I.V.M., Kassowitz, and others, and have seen that with such buying power the prices can be forced down by at least 12%. Linz will also profit from this great advantage. [...]

I have bought shares in Barnum for K 20,000 and urgently advise you to do the same. [...]

The firm Johann Kahn will have its own section in the space owned by Barnum at 33 Wipplingerstrasse, and I will move my administration, bookkeeping, buying and selling there. That means that after May 1st only my technical operation will remain on Fleischmarkt. I have also made a very significant delivery of blouses to Egypt, and have likewise handed over all the buying and selling for my firm to Barnum. [...]

Kind regards and kisses,

Jenö

When you read about three million kronen in this letter, you must keep in mind when this was written. In one sense of the word, the Austrian krone had not existed for the past two years (unless it was the crown still embroidered on Baron Polack's shirts); and in another sense, it was weak. While a streetcar ticket in Vienna had cost 40 kreuzers in 1918, you now paid three kronen, and that was just the beginning. In January of 1922, the ticket cost 60 kronen, in 1923 1,500 kronen, and while you could buy goulash with a bun for one krone in 1918, at the end of 1924 you had to put 40,000 kronen on the table. Nevertheless, in April of 1920 three million was still a considerable sum, although one was well advised, even if one did not speculate like Jenö in foreign currency, to spend it as quickly as possible. Of course it was all the more tempting to work together with a firm whose "parent company" (as you see, my Uncle Jenö has contributed considerably to my vocabulary) was in London; and Jenö looked after Barnum's business with zeal – with such zeal that in a few weeks he succeeded in making the man designated by the London directors as the general director of the Viennese branch unpopular with Lionel, with the result that at the beginning of August, after he had travelled to London twice to make himself known there, he moved in triumph into the Barnum office next to his own. (If God had not wanted us to use our elbows, said Jenö, he wouldn't have equipped us with them.) From his appointment as general director, though, it followed with the most compelling inevitability (I notice again that my style is improving hourly under Jenö's influence) that he no longer had any time for his own business on Fleischmarkt, and so it came about that the next letter in my stack contains astonishing things.

Vienna, August 20, 1920

Dear Brother-in-Law!

During my short visit in Linz I suggested that you move your place of residence to Vienna and take over the management of the firm Johann Kahn. I think this suggestion is feasible if we organize our Linz business as follows: bookkeeping in Vienna, inspection of merchandise in Vienna, definitive determination of the retail prices in Vienna. [...]

The management of our store in Linz will be taken over by our brother-in-law and friend Heinrich Herzog, who will act in keeping with directions and instructions that the two of us together will send him from Vienna. [...]

In Vienna, I would like to entrust you with power of attorney and, according to commercial law, the management of my business, and to give you one third of the net profit. Once you assume this job, your salary in Linz, which is hardly worth mentioning, will be discontinued. In addition to this one third of the net profit, I guarantee you at the very least K 120,000, and you will be entitled to take this guaranteed minimum in monthly instalments at 10,000 K from the expense account of the firm Johann Kahn. So you are guaranteed a long-term minimum salary of K 10,000 per month and can look forward to the future with complete assurance. If things turn out as I hope, your share of the net profit will be at the very least 3 to 5 times as much as the guaranteed minimum, so that you will be splendidly taken care of and will of course also still enjoy your share of the Linz business. You will therefore have the power in your hands to run the Linz store from Vienna as you see fit.

227

I put this suggestion in writing so that everything is clearly laid out. We don't need a special agreement, because if you are the right man, both you and I will benefit, and if our hopes and expectations should not be fulfilled, we will still be good friends and brothers-in-law and can seek and find a change or a better solution at any time by mutual agreement. [...]

With kind regards, I remain,

Your

Jenö

When I read this letter, I feel almost like my Aunt Olga in Beverly Hills with her memories: I know the facts, but I don't understand them. Had Jenö not quarrelled bitterly with Sándor, and could he really find no other man for Fleischmarkt? He must – in view of the later events I would like to stress this emphatically – have been convinced of my father's diligence and reliability in spite (or because?) of all their quarrels. What is even more astounding than Jenö's offer, though, is that my father accepted it. Had he – this respectable, by nature rather timid person – been robbed of all common sense by the promised riches, which actually were only riches if the association with Barnum gave the Fleischmarkt a massive new impetus? Did he not at least see that a promised minimum wage of K 120,000 at a time when the krone was rapidly losing value didn't offer him the slightest security? He obviously didn't see it, because in September he moved to Vienna, to my grandparents' apartment, because at that time it was next to impossible to find suitable lodgings there. That is how – as my mother was pregnant again at the time of the move – I came to be born at 21 Untere Augartenstrasse at midnight on the 15th of October, 1921. I know the time, because Dr. Grübel, who was supervising the midwife, noted this event with a thick indelible pencil on the left doorpost of the double door leading from the dining room to the study. (After my mother's departure in June of 1939, the pure-blooded Aryan who took over the apartment from her probably had the doorpost painted over.

During my two later visits to Vienna, I couldn't make up my mind to take a look.)

With my father's move to Vienna, the correspondence between the brothers-in-law stopped of course, only to resume when they had to take recourse to written communication because they were no longer on speaking terms. From the interim, though, my stack contains letters from the Linz lawyer of the firm Kahn & Engelmann, bills, hastily handwritten notes from Jenö on his travels to someone I don't know, etc., almost a hundred pages in all, from which it emerges that for the year 1922 three events in particular should be noted – one of them joyous, and two of them more comparable to an exploding bomb.

I will begin with the joyous event. In May of 1922, Jenö had gone on a business trip to Budapest and decided to add three days in Balatonfüred. Although he was urgently needed in Vienna, the three days turned into three weeks, because on the terrace of the most expensive hotel in this resort – like Lionel, Jenö owed it to the reputation of Barnum's to stay in the most expensive hotel – he met Herr and Frau Horvát and their three daughters. Horvát owned a large estate in the vicinity of Balatonfüred, and the youngest of the three daughters was an astonishingly pretty blonde. Her name was Maritza, and although I have heard many stories about her, I have only one clear memory of her, probably from the early 1930s. For some reason that I cannot remember, I was visiting at her place, her son Felix was not at home, and Maritza – Aunt Maritza – was sitting, as I recall, on a sofa in an elegantly furnished room and blowing smoke rings.

In order to develop any skill to the point where you can give great performances, three things are necessary: first, the native ability that we call genius, to disguise the fact that we do not understand this phenomenon; second, the strength of will that makes it possible, for example, for a budding virtuoso pianist to practise at least six hours a day; third, though, the genius, even if he is a genius, has to make the decision very early on to devote his life to the development of his talent; because (for example) you don't become a chess master if you play a Spanish Game for the first time when you are twenty. In Maritza's case, all three conditions must have been met, because she was a Capablanca, a Menuhin – what can I say? – an Einstein in the art of blowing of smoke rings. Back then, as a ten- or twelve-year-old, I watched with delight as she first of all, as an overture, blew three concentric smoke rings, followed by three rings that were intertwined like the links in a chain, and how she then, since her performance was for a child, blew two eyes and a mouth, and sent a straight nose and eyebrows after them, until finally a grey smoke ghost hovered through the afternoon sunlight in the room. . . . Maritza could have earned her living in a cabaret with her smoke rings, which she never needed to do: for her whole life, even after 1938 in New York, she was an affluent woman.

Until then, and thus well beyond the usual age for getting married, Jenö had made do with prostitutes, at least when he could not sublimate his libido by taking people to court. He didn't want a wife who would have been good enough for any Tom, Dick or Harry, and waited for someone special. He recognized this special person at first sight when he saw Maritza, and he rushed to win her. Horváts soon knew that Jenö was the chairman of the Vienna branch of an international firm and would undoubtedly in a short time also have a position in the London head office of this enterprise. Jenö arranged an evening boat trip for the three girls and had champagne served while Gypsy musicians were playing for them. Horvát, who didn't want to be outdone, organized a rabbit hunt, whereupon Jenö talked the hotel director into having a ball for the Horváts and their friends. (It worked to Jenö's advantage that through Barnum he had access to English pounds, because that sort of thing could no longer be paid for in Hungary with kronen.) Horvát gave a big dinner party, and Jenö invited the family to Budapest for a weekend. In this manner, one festivity followed on another. Maritza, who had been bored in Balatonfüred and in her parents' home before Jenö appeared on the scene, was in seventh heaven. Horvát made enquiries through an acquaintance who worked in the credit bureau, and when the day came that Jenö had to return to Vienna, the engagement was arranged, if not yet celebrated. Since Maritza was the youngest of the three daughters, and the oldest was cross-eyed, the dowry they had agreed on was not as great as he had expected, but a chairman of a Barnum branch could not appear to be a penny-pincher.

The engagement was celebrated, of course, in the Horváts' imitation castle. The wedding was just a few days off when the second noteworthy event of the year 1922 occurred.

Shortly after Jenö's engagement, Frau Baumann, the owner of the building at 15 Promenade in Linz, got into temporary financial difficulties. The lease with Kahn & Engelmann ran until December 15, 1922, but Frau Baumann knew the store wasn't doing badly and tried to get out of her predicament by suggesting to my father that they pay K 100,000 to extend the lease for another five years. The Linz lawyer my father consulted advised him to come to Linz for a meeting and to bring the lease from 1918 with him.

My father received Dr. Pramer's letter in the new office on Wipplingerstrasse, from where he directed the business on Fleischmarkt. He went to the safe, and after a short search found a sealed envelope on which was written "Lease, Linz." He tore it open, took out the document he had been looking for, and read:

Linz, December 15, 1918
We herewith transfer the lease signed by Herr S. Bell in Vienna on
December 4, 1917 for the retail space at 15 Promenade, Linz, to Herr
Johann Kahn, with the following amendment . . . .

Sándor could not believe his eyes, he read the sentence a second time, walked quickly over to Barnum's next door, barged into Jenö's office without knocking and silently put the lease on the tabletop in front of Jenö, who looked up in surprise.

231

"What's wrong, Sándor?" asked Jenö. "You look so upset."

"Read this," said my father and tapped on the document with his finger. "Read it, and tell me what it says."

"That is the lease with Frau Baumann," said Jenö, "the lease is entirely in order, no one can cause us trouble."

"The lease is made out to you," said my father, who was outraged by his brother-in-law's calmness. "Linz is *our* business, and you had the lease drawn up in your name only."

"That doesn't make any difference, Sándor," said my uncle. "We are partners with equal rights, it doesn't matter whether both names are on the lease or only one."

"It does matter, very much! I remember exactly what happened! You sent me to the carpenter's, and then behind my back you had the lease made out in your name!"

"Stop shouting, and don't talk nonsense, Sándor," said Jenö, and stared at my father with wide-opened eyes. "You absolutely wanted to go to the carpenter's, instead of helping me with the negotiations."

"That's not true," said my father, and now he was really shouting. "You sent me to the carpenter's like an errand boy, so that you could suppress my name! Now I know why you locked the lease away immediately, now I know how it is with the parent company and the branch, you did it like that so that you can throw me out when it suits you, but you did that to the wrong person! Do you know what I'm going to do now? I have always got along well with Baumann, I'm going to Linz now to have the new lease made out in my name, and then I can throw you out."

"Aha," said Jenö, "so that's what you've been aiming at! I taught you how to stand and walk, you have become an affluent man through me, and now I get the thanks, you kick me out. The Moor has done his duty, the Moor can go. That is my wedding present from my old friend and brother-in-law. But it shouldn't surprise me, I should have known better right away, instead of getting involved with you. There is truth to the Hungarian saying (and he said it in Hungarian), "If you give a Slovak your hand, he'll steal one of your fingers."

That was too much for my father. He clenched his fists and was about to hit his old friend and brother-in-law in the face. However, he controlled himself and left the office without saying a word.

The third event of the year 1922 that should be recorded took place in September 1922, two weeks after Jenö's magnificently celebrated wedding (and if it had taken place a few weeks earlier, Horvát would have called off the wedding). The internationally famous firm Barnum Export Ltd. could not pay its bills. The matter was simple. Barnum (London) had founded the branch in New York with borrowed money, Barnum (New York) had taken out a loan to set up a branch in Paris, Barnum (Paris) had financed the founding of the branch in Milan with borrowed money, Barnum (Milan) had raised the money to put Barnum Brothers (South Africa) on its feet – and so it had gone around in a circle until one day the bank to which Barnum (London) still owed the original loan got suspicious and demanded repayment. Three weeks later the house of cards had collapsed.

Barnum's creditors in the countries along the Danube expected compensation for their losses from the Austrian chairman of the firm. The latter travelled to London and Paris, negotiated for nights on end with lawyers and valuators and saved what he could. He owed the fact that he still had the villa in Pressbaum, the business on Fleischmarkt and his share in Kahn & Engelmann after the liquidation to Maritza's dowry, of which not much remained. The shares that he had bought in Barnum proved to be worthless; he knew, however, "from the most reliable sources," as he put it, that Sidney Lionel had sold his shares at the right time, but out of pure malice had not warned him. So from now on, as far as Jenö was concerned, the old friend was called neither Sidney Lionel nor, as previously in London, Sammy Löwenzahn, but tersely, the perfumed Polack.

2.

Old stories about people who have long since died a terrible death – Jenö of a heart attack brought on by excessive use of alcohol, my father in the waters of the Danube, Dezsö of intestinal cancer, which was rampant on the Róth side of the family; Gisa and my grandmother also died of cancer. But it is a truism that the death sentence is spoken over each of us at the hour of our birth, and I can understand that Byron therefore had his Cain refuse to serve the Lord. The alternative would admittedly be incomparably worse, and even a Byron would not have been able to imagine a world without death. To be Peter Engelmann for eighty years could be endured if necessary, but eight hundred would be too much of a good thing, and to be Peter Engelmann for all eternity would be unbearable.

As a veterinarian, of course, I have the means in the cupboard to give myself a gentle end, but I'm in no hurry to do so. I may be called bourgeois, but for the time being I love my daily routine: the hot shower after I get up, the breakfast with toast, ham and jam, morning rounds to check on the dogs and cats in their cages, the "office hours" from ten to one, the walk along the beach in the afternoon, if I don't have to do any operations, the evening at my desk and at the chessboard, if my son doesn't visit me, which I far prefer over all else, then the eleven o'clock news and a little music before going to bed. . . .

To be sure, the news is usually not pleasant. Yesterday morning in the *Jerusalem Post* there was a report about an officer who had brutally beaten an Arab teenager for throwing a stone at a civilian vehicle. In the evening, I spoke with my son about it, who phoned from Tel Aviv to invite me and Joschi, as my assistant is called, to dinner, and then really did turn up at the door in a dark suit and white shirt at six-thirty.

"Of course it is appalling," said Bob, "but – "

"There's no but about it," I interrupted him, while the waiter put the hors d'oeuvre on the table.

"Yes there is, Peter," said Bob. "First, the man will stand trial, and where else does that happen? If someone in Syria kills a Jew, he isn't prosecuted, he is celebrated as a hero. Second, you know as well as I do that there's a double standard. If the Turks kill five hundred Kurds, no one cares, but if an Arab is shot in Galilee, that appears on the first page of all the newspapers in the world: *we* have to be perfect. But the question is, how does the world see this perfection? When we didn't hit back, we were cowardly. Now we defend ourselves, and we are murderers and oppressors. The UN has sent observers to Israel again, but when thousands are murdered in Africa, people look the other way."

"Don't grumble," said Joschi, "tell us something instead about the Moroccan girl you were sitting with last week in the bar at Berkowitz's. I must say, you have taste! Actually, how old is the girl?"

"Seventeen," said Bob, "and Orthodox, or rather, her parents are Orthodox. By the way, she has only been in the country for six months and already speaks better Hebrew than my Papa."

"Thank you for the compliment," I said. "Seventeen! That is the right age for learning something new. I was seventeen when I sneaked across the border into Belgium. At that age, everything is an adventure, and you don't have enough imagination to be afraid." And then, over the burgundy we had ordered, I began to talk about the six weeks I spent in Brussels. . . . But perhaps it would be better to write about that. I need a rest before I can tackle the correspondence of my father and Jenö again.

It isn't pleasant, even for a seventeen-year-old, to arrive in a foreign city without a penny in your pocket and to have to find your way around when you can barely speak the language. Nevertheless, we had the address of the Jewish Aid Committee and were able to ask our way there. It was a spacious old house with dozens of men and women standing around in it. We were shown into an office where our personal information was entered in a book, and we were told three things (in German): we were not allowed to work, we would get 49 francs a week from the Aid Committee (that was a dollar, I think, in the currency of the time), and we had to register immediately at the police station. Then each of us received the first 49 francs, we were given a free meal in the cafeteria on the second floor and we went to the police station, where they took our fingerprints and impressed on us once again (this time in French) that we could not do any work: Belgium already had enough unemployed people. Then we (Heinz Polatschek and I; we had got rid of Meixner) found ourselves a small room for forty francs a week. It had only a double bed, but there was one of those pot-bellied stoves on which we could boil water for tea or cook a stew. With that, we had taken care of the essentials, and we learned quickly how to live cheaply. We drank our tea black, because milk was surprisingly expensive, now and then we went to the Aid Committee cafeteria for a free lunch, and for our evening meal we usually ate bread and cold cuts that didn't taste bad, but were so cheap that I was convinced they were made of horse meat; otherwise, we lived almost exclusively on spaghetti boiled in salt water and seared with a tiny drop of olive oil. . . . If we fasted for a day, we could even afford a standing place at the opera, and aside from that the Aid Committee provided us with entertainment: the waiting room in the old house served as a sort of club room or café for the refugees, albeit without coffee or adequate seating, and I found a chess partner there.

Toward the end of January, my cousin Edith arrived from Amsterdam and brought money, preserves, cake and a big jar of delicious strawberry jam that is no less precious to me in memory than the quince from Yugoslavia: Heinz and I had not enjoyed such luxury since we had left Vienna. There is nothing else worth mentioning about the remainder of my stay in Brussels, and I told Bob and Joschi less about myself than about the strange fates I heard about in the "club." For example, there was a former banker from Nuremberg who, like Heinz and me, had got off the train in a village in the vicinity of the border, but didn't have a compass, and so was standing around in the evening twilight not knowing what to do. "Suddenly," he told us, "a car stopped beside me, the driver

236

jumped out, pushed me hastily onto the back seat and drove off, drove (why he could do that, I do not know) over the border without stopping, stopped in a suburb of Brussels, pulled me out of the car and roared off, without having exchanged a word with me during the whole four hours. The gods alone know what became of the man who really should have been smuggled across the border in this way, and who probably had paid a small fortune for it."

The stories told by a bearded man from Düsseldorf were amusing and terrible at the same time. He was a photographer by profession, always carried a big black camera with him and took photographs whenever he could find somebody who paid for it. Since he couldn't keep that a secret, sooner or later the police arrived in his room, where he had set up a little dark room for himself, and deported him, not back to Germany, the Belgians were humane, but rather to France. From the clearing in the woods near the border where they dropped him off, he could probably have made his way through to Paris; but since he had no desire to start all over again from the beginning in a foreign city, he stood around patiently until the French border patrol discovered him and surreptitiously brought him back to Belgium. He had come through this adventure three times, he told me. "It isn't so bad," he said, "I always wear good warm shoes anyway, and the trip back to Brussels isn't very expensive." The reason this is not just amusing, but also terrible, is that he probably did not survive the German occupation of Belgium.

The way I left Belgium was just as amusing. In mid-February 1939, Zwillinger's efforts in London had finally born fruit, and my mother had made sure that the English visa was sent to me in Brussels. Edith sent me the money from Amsterdam for the train and ship tickets. For some reason, I arrived late in Ostende and was among the last who wanted to get on the ship. The customs officer examined my passport with the big J on the first page, leafed through it twice, and then said, in French of course: "You have no entry stamp!"

"That's right," I said, "I don't have an entry stamp."

"If you haven't entered the country," said the officer, with compelling logic that would have done even my Uncle Jenö proud, "then you cannot leave it either."

"Actually, I did enter Belgium," I said in my miserable French. "I just don't have a stamp to prove it."

The officer called over a second man in uniform and consulted with him in Flemish, so I couldn't understand what they were saying. "That's bad," he said at last. "I have to put the exit stamp on the same page as the entry stamp, those are the regulations, but how am I supposed to do that if you don't have the stamp?"

Meanwhile, a third officer had processed the other travellers and the sailors were starting to remove the gangplank, while my two officers continued their discussion in Flemish. In my distress, I hit upon the right idea. "*Je ne vois pas de problème*," I stammered, while the effort it was costing me made the sweat break out on my brow. "If you don't stamp the passport at all, so that there is neither an entry nor an exit stamp in my passport, then everything will be all right again – *les lois de la symétrie seront observées*." The man could see that, and when the gangplank was hanging by the last rope, I was allowed to board the ship.

After arriving in London, I once again had to get used to a foreign city and a foreign language. Although I had learned a little English in Vienna, I didn't understand a word of the Cockney spoken by, for example, the conductor on the bus. As in Brussels, though, I had the advantage of not being alone: my brother had arrived in London at almost the same time. The first thing I did, as I had in Brussels, was to go to the Jewish Aid Committee, where I was temporarily employed as a sort of errand boy until something else could be found for me. It was my job to bring files to a Miss Findley, a vivacious blonde – dozens of files, whose fate determined the life and death of dozens of families. My working for Miss Findley proved to be a stroke of good luck; I was able to persuade her to apply for a visa for my mother that arrived in Vienna at the end of July.

Meanwhile, the people of the Aid Committee had found me a job as an apprentice in a company that installed electric wiring in new buildings. The affluent English Jews who financed the Committee – I have reason to be grateful to them – knew that it provoked anti-Semitism that so many Jews owned stores and factories or were active in the learned professions. That didn't prevent them from taking their own children into their business or having them study at the university; but the refugee children were supposed to learn a trade. Although I didn't learn a trade at M. Samuels & Co., I learned something else: since then, I have understood why, as West Germany experienced miraculous economic growth in the post-war years, England almost went bankrupt. The electricians worked as little as possible, not because they were inherently lazy, but rather for ideological reasons: the employer was the enemy, and if you worked more than four hours in the course of an eight-hour day, you were putting another electrician out of work. The apprentices were of the same mind, at least in the head office of Samuels & Co., where I worked washing the linoleum, cleaning the toilets, and delivering the telephone wire or the fuses that the electricians had forgotten to take with them to the various construction sites in London. The apprentice who supervised this activity – a thoroughly decent chap – had, over time, acquired a detailed knowledge of the London public transportation system and knew two routes to many construction sites, a more expensive route and a cheaper one. The apprentices – there were four in all – took the cheaper route, Danny billed the company for the more expensive one and shared the profit. It was only pennies he was embezzling, but Danny was more concerned with the principle of it than with the money: the boss was the enemy and had to be exploited.

It didn't bother me that I wasn't learning anything at Samuels & Co., as I was convinced that I was born to be a writer, would soon earn my living with my pen and become a great poet. I really did write a poem now and then, but my actual passion was not writing, but reading. I had happened across Yeats's *Oxford*

Book of Modern Verse, I read Hemingway and Henry James, and an acquaintance, a young man by the name of Jeremy Paulsen, lent me James Joyce's *Ulysses*, which for many years was virtually my Bible, even though at first I had to look up twenty words a page in the dictionary. Even today, there are dozens of English words that I know only because of *Ulysses*. Although I spent much time reading, I spent more time with Conchita.

Back in the eighteenth and nineteenth centuries, Lessing and Goethe described the difficulties of writing. Lessing saw the problem in the unavoidable sequential nature of verbal communication, which makes it impossible to cope with the simultaneity of the events you wish to describe. Goethe complained about the deficient vocabulary. To this comes the particular difficulty of describing what is beautiful. A useful "wanted" poster mentions only the ugly deviations from the norm – the scar, the birthmark, the hooked nose, the club foot. What is beautiful in humans is, as Winckelmann wrote, what is normal: a beautiful nose is neither too long nor too short, in a beautiful face the eyes are set the average distance apart. The fatal flaw in this theory is that the beautiful would then inevitably have to be boring, but we can learn from Winckelmann that it is especially the beautiful that cannot be described. I must content myself with stating that Conchita had a Portuguese father and an Indian mother. She had the black hair, the slightly brownish skin colour and the big dark eyes of this mixture – but that isn't saying much. What mattered was her sex appeal. When we went for walks on Saturdays or Sundays in Hyde Park, we often first had tea and strawberry cake in the Lyon's Corner House on the edge of the park. When we entered the big dining room and walked toward an empty table, all the men turned their heads to look at her, and I was as proud as a peacock.

Conchita's parents in Bombay must have been well-to-do – we never spoke about that. She shared a charming little apartment in London with an English girl who worked as a secretary, and while I was an errand boy in dirty overalls during the day, in the evening, bathed and with a change of clothes, I was an intellectual, a future great poet. But it is not this double existence that interests me today about the Peter Engelmann back then. . . . What fills me with consternation when I look back is the autism of this person who is a total stranger to me, the autism that was already characteristic of him as a ten-year-old. Conchita's friend, Runia, had a boyfriend, a short, plump young man about ten years older than I was, who was always in a good mood. He wrote a popular radio series for the BBC, and I didn't even go to the trouble of listening to one of those broadcasts. Conchita was in London to study piano, and she played Liszt and Chopin fast and poorly: all the notes were there, but without any phrasing. It never even occurred to me to be concerned that she was preparing herself for a career for which she had no talent; and it also never occurred to me that you cannot become a good writer if you go blindly through the world and are not really interested in your fellow human beings.

In at least one respect, however, the whole circle that gathered at Conchita's was autistic: none of us ever spoke about the political events that should have attracted our attention. Percy Simon had nothing in his head other than his radio series, good wine and sex. When he had gone back to his desk one Sunday morning after breakfast, Runia told us at great length and with all anatomical details how her boyfriend had once again tried in vain to give her an orgasm. Jeremy Paulsen, through whom I had met Conchita, earned a meagre income by working, among other things, for a monthly publication in small format, which at that time was the first to publish (one in every issue) coloured photographs of nudes; it was Jeremy's task to select the "girl of the month" from a pile of photographs and to make up a suitable caption. But he busied himself mainly by working on a strange prose text that he refused to call a novel. Conchita reproached us "writers" by saying that literature was condemned to make statements about the outer world, and so, in contrast to music, was not a pure art – an attack against which Jeremy defended himself with the argument that he just used the real world in his text as a musician uses notes or a painter uses colours: the fragments of reality, in and of themselves, are merely unimportant signs, what matters is their configuration. "The nurse with the red face trundled a barrow," he read aloud from his manuscript. "Black birds sat winnowing on the commode. In the dawn, the brown trees marched into the sunset." I, at that time, read Clive Bell with enthusiasm (who today still knows who Clive Bell was?) and liked to read fragments of his aesthetic philosophy aloud: the only thing of real value was good states of consciousness, everything else was just the means to an end. The direct, privileged way to good states of mind, however, was art, and that was therefore the only thing that a reasonable person could take seriously – as a creative artist and as connoisseur. If that were the case, though, then it followed that there must be a class of people who had the time to develop good taste and to seek out the best from the jumble of art being offered, and the vitality of a civilization rested, therefore, on the existence of a class of drones. . . . "Wrong, completely wrong," said Percy; because, to begin with, there was yet another, entirely different, no less effective direct route to good states of consciousness, for example, roast meat with onions; and secondly, it was unfortunately the case that the drones, at least in England, occupied themselves much less with art that with horse races and fox hunts. . . .

While we sat on the pretty, green-covered chairs in Conchita's apartment, chatted about such matters and drank coffee, world history was being made outside the window, and – as I said – we ignored it. In September of 1939, the Germans marched into Poland, and there was war. That was *mea res*, that concerned me as a Jew and a refugee in England, which was waging war. It was no war like any other one, but a war that would decide the fate of mankind for decades to come, a war in which my own life was at stake, but I didn't understand that, I didn't turn the radio on, I hardly ever read a newspaper; I read Thomas Mann's *The Magic Mountain* and didn't understand that I myself was living on a magic mountain.

Then world history suddenly overtook me. In spring, 1940, the Germans occupied Denmark and Norway, they overran Belgium, the Netherlands and half of France while I read Clive Bell. At the end of June, Conchita and I noticed when we went for a walk that a trench was being dug in the middle of Hyde Park. England stood alone, and things looked bad for the free world. But now there were about 60,000 German and Austrian refugees in England, in France there had been a large "fifth column," and it was by no means certain that the 60,000 enemy aliens in England were really all refugees. . . . This thought had already occurred to some clever man in the War Office and the English had already attempted to sort out the enemy aliens soon after the beginning of the war. I should have told Bob and Joschi how that was done, it would have amused them. Everywhere in Great Britain, committees were set up to interview the "hostile foreigners." They consisted of bank directors, college principals and similar dignitaries who had obviously not given their task a moment's thought. In my interview, a friendly old lady asked me: "Why did you leave Austria?"

"Because I am a Jew," I said.

"What do you think of Hitler?"

"I think he is an evil and dangerous man."

So it continued for a while, and I don't think a German spy would have answered these questions any differently. The result was that a few hundred people were already interned at that time – people who could be charged with something obvious, homosexuals, a female acquaintance of mine whose uncle was the brother-in-law of a German general, perhaps a few real spies – and the others remained at large.

Then in June of 1940 the English government discovered that the committees hadn't done their job very well, and as a result, all male enemy aliens between the ages of 18 and 65 were to be interned – only the males, because the minister in charge was apparently convinced that there was no such thing as a female spy. I should also have told Bob and Joschi about internment proceedings, because they were both amusing (especially for those who were not affected by them) and also touching – and more than that: you can laugh about it, but you should also understand that it proved that the English were the most civilized nation in the world. One morning, an English policeman came to the small apartment that I shared with my mother and my brother, one of those "bobbies" who at that time really were as nice, friendly and fatherly as they are still reputed to be today. He informed us that we unfortunately had to be interned, we should please pack our suitcases, we would be picked up the next morning. . . .

So Hans and I packed our suitcases, which wasn't the smartest thing to do. Erich Fried, the poet with whom I had a nodding acquaintance at the time, took the train to Brighton, waited there until the roundup was over and was left in peace after his return to London. I spent the evening with Conchita and said a sad goodbye to her. When I stepped out the front door of the building late at night, she called after me that I had forgotten something and threw Jeremy's copy of *Ulysses* out the window. The book smacked down flat on the sidewalk and has accompanied me to Australia, back to England, to Canada and finally to Haifa; for sentimental reasons, I still prefer it to the revised edition of the novel that I bought in 1986 as soon as it appeared.

The next morning we were picked up and transported to a racecourse in Lingfield, in the south of England, that had been turned into a temporary camp. We slept in the stables, but that wasn't uncomfortable, since racehorses are expensive and delicate. From Lingfield, we were supposed to be taken to an internment camp on the Isle of Man, but in Liverpool everything was in chaos, and as the result of an administrative error, two thousand internees, including my brother and me, were put on a troop ship, the HMS *Dunera*, that was supposed to take prisoners of war to Australia. We were almost three months en route, and the journey on the overcrowded ship was unpleasant. As the *Dunera* has since become quite famous and there is more literature about the trip than it warrants, I will content myself with a personal observation. All of us suffered from diarrhoea during the crossing, and after we

244

had landed in Sydney, everyone else was cured of the troublesome complaint in a few days, but not I. I suffered from recurring attacks for many years and could only get over them by living on tea and toast for days on end; today I know enough about such things to suspect that the stubbornness of that complaint had psychosomatic causes.

There are also publications about our life as internees in Australia, which are, however, to the extent that I am familiar with them, quite superficial. A sociological study of the life in the camp would be worth doing, but I am not the right man for that, because I was a poor observer. Of course it was significant that most of us were German and Austrian Jews, and so of the two thousand men in the two camps in which we were held, at least fifteen hundred were intellectuals. So almost as soon as the ship had taken off, there were lectures on all kinds of topics, from astronomy right down through the alphabet to zoology. Since there was a shortage of paper to write on, my brother came up with the idea of removing the labels from the empty soup and vegetable cans in the ship's kitchen and using their white reverse side to write on. He still has the notes he made about advanced algebra and differential calculus on those labels. Then, in the internment camp in Hay, on the edge of the desert, there was a real little university in the camp. The International Student Service and the Quakers sent us books, and we were allowed not only to register as correspondence students with the University of Melbourne, but also to take the examinations, which were invigilated by a few professors from Melbourne who made the long trip to Hay for that purpose. We were not badly off in the midst of that terrible war, and I made use of the opportunities it provided me. I improved my Latin, and in the large dining hall where a dozen lectures took place simultaneously, I took courses in mathematics, organic chemistry and English poetry, read whatever I could get my hands on and became a fairly educated person. If there should ever be a third world war, I would like to spend it in an Australian internment camp. But the life behind barbed wire intensified my

245

isolation and is indisputably responsible for my making the wrong decision at that time, a decision that contributed perhaps more than anything else to my living now in Haifa and not, for instance, in Beverly Hills.

The internment of all "enemy aliens" was a result of the panic in June 1940, and when the panic was past, the authorities in London and in Canberra were advised by various parties that it was absurd, at a time when England was desperately short of people for the war industry and the army, to be feeding hundreds of Jews who were foreigners, but not enemies, huge quantities of legs of lamb and preserved peaches at the expense of the taxpayer (albeit the Australian) while they learned Latin or played bridge. So in the summer of 1942, a major in the English military showed up in our camp and gave a short speech inviting the men between eighteen and thirty to enlist as volunteers in the English army. I didn't sign up, and when the major spoke with me personally, I refused.

It has taken me many years to understand that I failed at the decisive moment. In Joseph Conrad's Lord Jim, a young ship's officer saves himself from a leaking ship and leaves the passengers who were entrusted to his care to their fate. The awareness of his failure destroys his life. It wasn't that dramatic with me, especially since, as mentioned, it took me years to realize that I had made the wrong decision; but I must confess that once I understood how badly I had failed, I never forgave myself, and I still blush with shame when I talk with someone who served in the Second World War on the side of the Allies. Of course there are excuses ("There are always excuses," my Latin teacher, Herr Epstein, at the Sperl Gymnasium used to say when someone came to class unprepared.) First, I was sick, and if I had volunteered, I might not have been accepted. Second, we couldn't enlist in the regular military, but only as pioneers, and that was not romantic. Third, there were older men in my camp – a mathematics professor, a musicologist – who had as little understanding of the situation as I did, and who explained to their protégés that the main duty of a gifted young man during wartime was to stay alive. That appealed to me, because I was so sure that I would become a great poet. Fourth, the major didn't go about it in the most effective manner: he could have made it clear to me in five minutes that this was not a war like any other, that it had a special relevance to me as a Jew, and that my staying alive would be worth damn-all if the Germans won. Fifth – but as I said, there are always excuses.

In the autumn, the internees who hadn't joined the sapper corps were transported back to England, and in January of 1943 I was free again and in London, where my slow ascent began from scrubbing toilets to bathing poodles. I had arrived in time to experience the last few months of air raids on London, and the fact that I didn't take much notice of the bombs falling on the city had nothing to do with courage; it was just one more symptom of my autism. I didn't spend a single night in an air raid shelter. I also developed another symptom: in addition to my usual stomach complaint, I now had a duodenal ulcer that was quite painful but did not prevent me from leading a normal life.

I now earned my living in a laboratory where they were working on a method of synthesizing vitamin D, but I regarded that merely as temporary employment. At first, I spent most of my spare time with girlfriends, but without finding a proper replacement for Conchita; in Australia, I hadn't seen a woman for over two years, so I had considerable catching up to do. (Incidentally, I did see Conchita one more time – on a spring afternoon in 1945, while I was going for a walk in Regent's Park. She had married an officer from the Polish air force, was pushing a baby carriage and looked somewhat faded.) I also spent a lot of time writing poems – dozens of them, which I entered in notebooks, including the date they were written, but I also made typed copies and collected them in a folder. In Australia I had discovered the Parnassians, especially Hérédia, and had started work on a cycle of sonnets on themes from the mythology of the ancient world. In addition to the French influence, there was the influence of Rilke. Here are some examples:

The Centaurs

Since the first stallion carried the royal princess
across the river – his ribs to her were just
a saddle – the lips of all the stallions lust
and long for human hair and human kisses.

In vain, the wind blows blossoms on the manes
of mares whose mating call unanswered goes.
Alone, they dimly sense they have new foes
beyond the bounds of what their woods contains.

With that sweet poison slowly they are finished:
Cursing the god whose games with light and earth
had forced disparate bodies to be one.

A memory has made them all succumb.
The stallions since that day feel only dearth.
The band of contradictions is diminished.

Or:

Aurea virga

There where the shades assemble at the shore,
a coin beneath each tongue to pay for crossing,
Aeneas strides to where the boat is tossing,
attempting what no man has done before.

The ferryman, who cannot be ignored,
spies among the reeds in a concavity
the proud guest haling from the realm of gravity,
betrayed by his famous guide and shining sword,

by the prints of his heavy footsteps in the mud,
and refuses the living an entrance to the night.
But before the Trojan's hand can smite him down

the sibyl speaks, prevents the shed of blood,
proves as she reaches into the folds of her gown
with gleaming gold the gods' superior might.

After my return to England, this cycle grew to a considerable length, and soon my notebooks also contained English poems,
in free verse, between the German sonnets and exercises. Even so,
I must have suspected that I would never be able to make a living
with my poetry; in any case, since chemistry bored me, I decided I
had to come up with an alternative. A few months after my return
from Australia, I wrote the entrance examination for the University of London, enrolled as an extension student and applied to the
senate of the university for permission to take the Intermediate
Examination right away. Since those were years when I could suck
up knowledge like a sponge, I could write the final examinations
for the B.A. as early as 1946, and I finished well enough to get a
scholarship and quit my job as a chemist. The senate allowed me to
skip the M.A., and two years later, having written my dissertation
on Ludwig Tieck, I had my doctorate. Five years from the entrance
exam to the doctorate – that was a speed record that still makes
me proud, all the more so because I had to earn my living for three
of those five years. . . .

In the spring of 1948, when my dissertation was almost finished, I was offered a position at Bedford College London for the
coming fall, and it occurred to me that I would now have to lecture
there, but that I had no idea how one did that; I had never
attended a lecture in my life. So I went to hear Professor W., an
exceptionally intelligent and elegant woman who could boast of
being the first woman to be offered a chair at University College
London. She spoke interestingly about Schiller's aesthetics and
their connection with Kant's "Purposiveness without Purpose,"
but a glance at the faces of her listeners was enough to convince
me that they didn't understand a word of it. The second lecture I
attended was held by the same professor who later found a position
for me in Canada. He lectured and derided Baroque lyric poetry.

That was bombastic stuff, he complained, full of far-fetched images, and if it wasn't bombastic, then it was fantastic. For example, if you wrote about a fir tree, then you set up the poem so that the typography resembled a fir tree. That annoyed me, because I loved Gryphius, and the anthropologist and poet Franz Baermann Steiner, with whom I was acquainted and whom I greatly admired, had pointed out to me that I could learn a lot from Lohenstein's rhythmic variety. But then came a sentence that completely took my breath away. The poets of the Second Silesian School, the professor explained, hadn't even known that a poem is for the ear and not for the eye – there were even brackets in their poems, and you can't hear a bracket! A bracket, I said to myself, can be heard as well as a period or a comma. What about, for example, the extra half-line in Rilke's sonnet "The Egyptian Maria," "(and so the two of them dug)"?

The two lectures gave me confidence; I would be able to do just as well, I thought. But these lectures also ushered in a process of disillusionment. Until then, because I had been thrown out of school at the age of seventeen, I had imagined a university to be an inexhaustibly fascinating concert of brilliance, intellect, wit and erudition. . . . But I also gradually began to lose another illusion, and that was even more painful.

My poetry notebooks show that I gradually began to tire of traditional forms after 1945. I now inclined increasingly to free verse, learned a trick or two from T.S. Eliot, and after Erich Fried had shown me poems with *ablaut* rhymes, I experimented from the beginning of 1947 with a new rhyme form. "The first man who rhymed love with dove was a genius," Arno Holz had said, "but the thousandth is an idiot." Erich Fried didn't just rhyme love with dove, but also with live:

At the Brother Abel's Inn
There was a pretty barmaid
Who had turned against the men
Where Abel had the beer made.

I thought it would be a little too easy just to imitate his *ablaut* rhymes; but weren't alliterating rhymes also possible like dove – door or rain – rail? They didn't sound like rhymes, because we didn't have the ear for it. But rhyme isn't something innate, instinctive; it's something learned (the Greeks didn't hear end rhymes), and so we could learn to hear the rhyme rain – rail just as well as the rhyme rain – pain or rain – rune. I wrote a long poem in which I used all three kinds of rhyme, and of which I was very proud at that time. I still have a copy of it, but I cannot objectively judge its quality: the fact that I have known it by heart for over forty years made it dear to me. It certainly has a tone of its own. But that is of no consequence: from 1948 on, although the poetry I wrote improved somewhat, my production steadily decreased.

In the winter of 1949, a few months after I had taken up my position at Bedford College, I began to work on a cycle of poems that was supposed to evoke, in encoded form, a release from a neurosis, a sort of psychoanalysis through writing poetry, but after the first few stanzas the manuscript lost its direction in a thicket of crossed-out lines, corrections and individual verses out of context. I was convinced that I had to write this poem to find my way as a poet, didn't want to take on any other project before it was finished, and so returned stubbornly again and again to the increasingly messy manuscript, but it didn't work, and I finally gave up.

3.

After the altercation with Jenö about the lease, my father had not gone back to his office, but went home, where the women tried to calm him. "It is not possible that my son wanted to cheat you, it was an oversight," said my grandmother. "It is not possible that my brother wanted to cheat you, it was an oversight," said my mother. That was not what my father wanted to hear, but it seems to me that the women were right: I cannot believe that Jenö deliberately wanted to deceive his brother-in-law back then. Anyway, Sándor let himself be persuaded to go first to Linz. There, he negotiated with Frau Baumann, who was prepared to prolong the lease in return for an advance payment. Then he spoke with Dr. Pramer, who at his request sent an express letter to Jenö, and Jenö, without making any objections, made out a declaration in which he explained that he "quite obviously, when drawing up the lease with Frau Therese Baumann, had the joint enterprise Kahn & Engelmann in mind and since then and henceforth would regard and recognize the rent laws for the Linz store as always applying to myself and S. Engelmann together." He also undertook to clarify the legal position in a letter to Frau Baumann.

With that, this matter was resolved on the factual level, but not on the personal level; distrust and resentment had lodged in Sándor's soul just as the shrapnel had lodged in his back, but there was no operation that could heal this wound. Immediately after his return to Vienna he wrote Jenö a letter that has not been preserved, in which he resigned his position as director of the firm Johann Kahn as of 31.12.1922. He didn't want to return to Linz, where Heinrich Herzog was managing the store, and after long consultations with my mother, Dezsö and Martin Becker, with whom he had become friends, he rented premises on Neutorgasse in the first district of Vienna, founded his own firm and now had the sign over the door that he had wanted for so long, with only his own name on it:

ALEXANDER ENGELMANN

Blouses, Dresses and Dressing-Gowns

Wholesale　　　Export

But the founding of the firm fanned the flames of the discord that already existed between the partners who were linked by the Linz store. Jenö was annoyed that he now had a new competitor who had acquired his expertise in the manufacture of fashions in his firm and had gained access to his clients; and while Sándor, who as manager of Johann Kahn on Fleischmarkt had bought the goods for the Linz store, now thought it was obvious that he would continue to make these purchases, only now from Neutorgasse, Jenö was of the opposite opinion; if Sándor had his way, instead of Jenö's firm getting the production costs surcharge, it would go to the firm Alexander Engelmann! After they had agreed that no more could be bought for the Linz store by Sándor's firm than by Jenö's, Jenö relented.

But the peace was short-lived. For them to be able to calculate Sándor's share of the profit that was owed him for the time he had worked at Fleischmarkt, the brothers-in-law had to agree on the value of the warehouse there. The fact that that wasn't easy is shown by the next letter I have to quote here.

Jenö to Sándor, nine typed pages single-spaced

March 3, 1923

Dear Sándor!
As I told you recently, I have been threatened with an income tax of over 32 million for last year on account of Barnum, and in order to defend myself I am spending my Saturdays and Sundays putting Barnum's completely confused bookkeeping in order. [...] In addition to that catastrophe, I am also at odds with the Merkurbank about Barnum: the bank is threatening to sue me on account of an erroneous entry into an account, and this just two weeks after I was only able to avoid a lawsuit with a Swiss supplier by a payment of many millions [...], not to mention the lawsuit

with Marx & Dorfinger about the pants pockets. [...] On top of that, I have suffered heavy losses because a travelling salesman cheated me, and so you will understand that even with the best of intentions I simply have not had, and will not in the near future have the time or the peace of mind to be able to calculate a final and accurate compensation payment due to you for your share of the profit from Fleischmarkt. [...]

Anything in the world for peace and harmony, that's my motto, and that's what I see as the basis for a tolerable future; therefore, this evening after closing time I am going to the trouble of making a proposal to you. [...]

Your claims to a third of the net profit of the firm Johann Kahn are limited to the time from 1.1.1921 to 31.12.1922. The profit in 1921 is so insignificant that only one thing is worth mentioning, and that is, that I made the firm Johann Kahn viable and got the warehouse stocked with Swiss supplies. [...] In the first half of the year 1922 we continued buying busily and sold ridiculously little, because the total annual turnover for 1922 amounts to K 494,000,000. [...] So it is necessary to determine that your assistance, the terrible amount of work you did, that caused you to compare your job to that of an Italian labourer, can be proved by our books to have yielded only a total turnover of 494 million in the year 1922. Check with Gisela Kahn's sometime, or make comparisons with Dezső's store on Rotenturmstrasse, and then pass judgment about the concrete result of your business efforts. The net profit, as I have explained to you, must amount to less than 10% of the turnover, that is, less than K 50,000,000 for the year 1922. So for your assistance with the running of the firm Johann Kahn, we would be looking at a third of about 50 million, say: K 17 million. [...]

But the situation is somewhat different now because the increase in value of the goods as a result of the depreciation of the krone results in a profit. But this would have accrued even if we hadn't done any business at all, but had simply bought goods, and if you hadn't lifted a finger for the firm Johann Kahn. But according to you, the profit from the increase in value of the stored goods should benefit you as well, and that's how the land lies. [...] I'm sitting here now looking at the goods inventory, and along with normal goods I see the worst kind of junk. [...] If I calculate the approximate worth of the etamines, gabardines [...] on 31.12. 1922, then I don't come anywhere near a profit, but rather a loss of about K 50,000,000. [...] To arrive at an exact figure, of course, we would have to laboriously assess the goods inventory, individual collars, coloured etamine remnants, buttons and embroidery ends, etc. that were on hand on 31.12.1922. Just the thought of all that work makes me feel sick, and as I explained to you at the beginning of this letter, I have neither the time nor the peace of mind that would be necessary to do it now. [...] Therefore, I'm going to settle the account as follows:

Your purchases and monthly
withdrawals amounted to . . . .   K 8,000,000.-
As a result of a withdrawal of
CK 20,000 you owe me CK 4,000, i.e. . . . .   K 8,000,000.-
For your share of the expenses in
Pressbaum you owe me approximately . . . .   K 3,000,000.-
For unusual withdrawals you owe
the firm Johann Kahn ca. . . . .   K 3,000,000.-
As part payment of net profit I gave
you an advance of . . . .   K 20,000,000.-
So you are in possession of advance payments of . . .   K 42,000,000.-

I have now arrived at the point where I can formulate my proposal to you in a palatable manner. You have, as I have proven to you, debts to me and to the firm Johann Kahn amounting to roughly K 42,000,000.

If I now, for the sake of keeping the peace, suggest a figure that is too high by an incredible amount, i.e., if instead of the K 17,000,000 to which you are entitled, I suggest K 50,000,000, then you will still be entitled to another 8 million, and then at last there will be order and clarity, and everything will be straightened out between us, so that we shouldn't waste any time thinking about whether one of the two of us has received a few million too much or too little.

There's an old saying: "He who defends himself, condemns himself." In spite of knowing this saying, and without fear, I am going to speak in my defence and use this opportunity to settle a moral account with you. I solemnly declare, to the best of my knowledge and in good faith, that I, more than any of our relatives, have always stood by you in a brotherly way, and even before your marriage and the beginning of our relationship as brothers-in-law I have always led you along with honest, brotherly and well-meaning intent on the paths that we have taken together.

You have every reason to be content with your fate since, from the time of our setting ourselves up together, in good times and in bad, in economic upturns and downturns, in boom times and times of stagnation, you have always had an honest, sincere and upright brother in yours truly, who has firmly and loyally stood by you, has honestly shared joy and sorrow with you, and on several occasions, with all his might, has thrown his entire fortune, with all his experience and connections, into the treadmill of our joint enterprise.

Settle all things quickly and peaceably, that's my motto, with which I send you kindest regards as
Your
friend and brother-in-law,
Jenö

After my father had read the letter the next evening, he said dryly: "Jenö wants to cheat me of payment for two-and-a-half years' work by giving me a tip. That's just like him." Then he spent the night drafting an answer that was so bitter that my mother persuaded him not to send it. He couldn't bring himself to write a calmer response until a month later.

Sándor to Jenö, ten pages typed single-spaced, with no salutation.

Vienna, April 4, 1923

Writing long-winded letters is not my specialty. But in view of the fact that you took so much time in your letter of March 3rd to outline the balance sheet and to offer me a settlement quota of K 8,000,000, I will have to give you a detailed answer. The reasons you cite: income tax, Merkurbank, lawsuits, being cheated by a travelling salesman, etc., would in the past have made a deep impression on me. However, the fact that the good old friendship has cooled considerably since then as a result of your behaviour toward me, as well as the fact that your outline of the balance sheets is pure invention, forces me to require from you a settlement such as is common practice among business people.

Based on the balance sheets, without taking the warehouse into consideration, you draw up a deficit balance of K 295,000,000 and offer me, despite my allegedly having already withdrawn K 42,000,000, which I do not accept because it has no basis in fact, a further K 8,000,000 to restore the good, loyal friendship and our relationship as brothers-in-law. So this friendship would cost you fifty million, and I don't want that. A business with a deficit of K 150,000,000 must not incur superfluous expenses and has no reason to make such a large sacrifice for a bookkeeper who has frittered away the business, and I am therefore of the opinion that it is better to settle in a purely businesslike manner, as if you were dealing with a stranger. [...]

You pretend that you are so tremendously stressed out from dawn to dusk that even with the best of intentions you do not have the time to settle with me in the near future. You have never been at a loss for excuses, this time it is the travelling salesman or the Merkurbank, and on Sundays you are busy dealing with the tax catastrophe and the inextricably complicated bookkeeping of Barnum! As far as I know, you have had two bookkeepers for months now. Where is the great theoretician who has mastered even the smallest details of bookkeeping? If that had happened to me, it would be no surprise, after all, I am the illiterate in book-keeping, but you???

I already wanted to settle with you a year ago, and you always said then there was no big hurry, my share of the profit, etc., was invested to my advantage in your business. So in 1920 ca. K 50,000 production costs remained there, in 1921 over K 700,000, in 1922 over 15 million, and the money was paid out to me when it had lost almost all its value. The share of the profit, if you valorized it, as you have done with the old goods, would already in 1921 be ten times more than what you are offering me for my entire two-and-a-half years' work. [...]

No matter how ridiculously little the business yielded in 1921 in your eyes, I am still laying claim to what is owed me. When I started with you, the store was as empty and desolate as a graveyard, then we were always without working capital on Fleischmarkt, and when I told you that we had to stock up on goods, you always waited for the crash in the price of goods that never came. Then, in mid-season, we had to make up our collection from material that had in the meantime become much more expensive. [...]

You reproach me with the fact that the business, under my wise management, had a turnover in the ridiculous amount of K 494 million last year, and that I slaved away at it like an Italian labourer. You have deliberately forgotten that I also procured goods for the Linz store, all on my own and without your help, and that had a turnover of 1.2 billion. In brief, you describe my accomplishments and my ability as a businessman as ridiculous, brand me as an idiot and even spread the rumour in the family that I, as your associate, have ruined you.

You are as reliant on all the tricks of which you accuse me again and again in your letters as another person is reliant on air to breathe. I believed the perpetual great lie that I had a brave brother in yours truly until I discovered that you wanted to take me for a ride right from the start with the lease, and that's how it is too with your throwing your entire fortune, with all your experience and connections, into the treadmill of our joint enterprise. I, and I alone, have worked in Linz and in Vienna, and if you have thrown yourself anywhere with all your might, it's been into bed or onto the ottoman. [...]

Before I close, I also want to say to you that your assertion that I owe you K 8 million because of the CK 20,000 withdrawal is incorrect; on the contrary, I demand CK 6,368 from you because at the exchange rate on 9.6.1922, at 303.40, I am owed CK 26,368 for the K 8 million. [...] When you speculated with foreign currency, you always put the profit in your own pocket if the stocks rose in value, but if they fell, Kahn & Engelmann paid, and I have only said nothing about that for the sake of peace. [...]

Yours,

Sándor

I will skip over the letters exchanged between my father and my uncle during the next six weeks, in which the adversaries strayed again and again from the actual matter under discussion in order to hurl insults at each other, and will content myself with the observation that, with the help of an expert bookkeeper, a settlement was finally reached in mid-May, and consequently Sándor was paid not eight, but fifty million kronen. Of course this settlement did not erase the past; there was no real peace between the business partners, only a sort of ceasefire, and the war could break out again at any time. However, not many letters were exchanged during the next eight months, and they were, even if you read between the lines, not very nasty. As previously, Sándor made the purchases from "outside" firms for the Linz store, while for the sake of preserving the peace it was left to Heinrich Herzog to place the orders from the firms Johann Kahn and Alexander Engelmann, and so there are letters from Jenö to Herzog reminding him of the agreement that no less should be bought from Fleischmarkt than from Neutorgasse, but even these letters are relatively peaceful.

So there was a kind of break for my father, and it should be emphasized that he was not continually preoccupied with the quarrels with Jenö or with the ongoing annoyance that he alone did the work for the Linz store, but had to share the profit with Jenö. There were other things he had to do. He was trying hard to build up his new business, and my mother was a loyal help to him in that. He took beginner's lessons in English from a Russian emigrant by the name of Schaljapin, who was a French teacher by profession (and you can imagine the English accent that he learned from a Russian French teacher). He took care of the "outside orders" for Linz, and when the personnel there was overworked at peak periods like December and the beginning of spring, he and Elli went there at Herzog's request, and both my parents helped unpack the goods coming from Vienna and served the customers. That was a lot of work, but there was still time for pleasure, and I like to imagine how he went to the opera with my mother or lay on his back on their double bed before falling asleep – that was my earliest memory of him – and sang a ballad by Löwe or an aria from La Bohème or Tosca. . . . There are also numerous photographs from the summer of 1923, taken on the bathing beach in Italy, most of the pictures admittedly without him, since he only seldom granted himself a short holiday. But when he came, he seems to have been treated like a guest of honour; at least, there is a photograph that must have taken a long time to set up: more than three dozen swimmers are lying on the sand in concentric semicircles, among them my mother, Mitzi and Dezsö, the grown-ups in very chaste bathing suits, the little boys (Hans and I, Teddy, and a few others I cannot identify) naked, and in the middle, lying on his stomach with his head propped up, my father.

The summer of 1923 also brought the birth of Jenö's and Maritza's only son, Felix, which was abundantly celebrated on Augartenstrasse; my grandmother had even been able to persuade Dezsö to accept the invitation. But that was the last celebration at which the entire family came together. There was only anger and distrust between the brothers-in-law; a tolerable harmony could not be re-established.

I have two of Jenö's letters of March 10, 1924, in front of me, which he had an errand boy deliver to Neutorgasse: one letter to the accounts desk at Kahn & Engelmann, and a second under separate cover to my father. In the letter to the accounts desk, Jenö requests immediate information about the exact amount of the "private withdrawals from the joint Linz account of *Messrs.* Kahn and Engelmann in 1923 and 1924," the "value of the total shipments from the firm Alexander Engelmann to Linz in 1923" and the "value of the total outside shipments to Linz in 1923." Obviously, Jenö wanted to have these figures to be able to verify whether Sándor had taken more from the Linz store than he himself had, and whether the firms on Fleischmarkt and on Neutorgasse had really supplied the Linz store equally, as agreed. In the second letter, Jenö writes that Sándor should from now on make sure that he, Jenö, will be paid a monthly share of at least 15 to 20 million kronen from the profit of the Linz store, "because my Viennese store unfortunately does not make it possible for me to support my family"; also, he was "stressed by excessive demands" and needed an advance of 20 million "immediately."

Two days later, he received the answer. My father wrote that Jenö should inspect "our joint accounts" on Neutorgasse, where he could look up the desired figures for himself. By doing so, he could also convince himself that the Christmas turnover in Linz had been moderate and business since then had been bad; monthly payments in the amount of K 15,000,000 were, therefore, not possible, let alone the wished-for advance. Incidentally, he, Sándor, would like to avail himself of the opportunity to expedite the delivery of the two dozen etamine blouses that the firm Kahn & Engelmann had ordered on the 2nd of February and that had still not arrived, in spite of the two reminders by telephone. . . .

With that, the fat was in the fire again. Payouts, Jenö answered by return mail, were an "irrefutable necessity, because our joint enterprise exists for the sole purpose of providing us with a living." As far as the blouses were concerned, he would like to allow himself the observation that Sándor sent "finished goods from storage" to Linz, whereas he, Jenö, in each case received orders that first had to be manufactured, and that Sándor was just using the delayed delivery as a means of insinuating that "the firm J. Kahn, due to tardy deliveries, was to blame for the fact that the firm A. Engelmann was making deliveries in disregard of the principle of parity and was arranging everything to its advantage, but my disadvantage." Then came the worst: as long as he, Jenö, still considered peaceful communications to be possible, he would limit himself to making objections and complaints; but he reserved the right, if necessary, to take other measures to which he was legally entitled.

Sándor answered that Herr Herzog, on his last two trips to Vienna, had been shown nothing on Fleischmarkt but "the old clothes from last year's collection" – and so it could have gone on for weeks, if my grandmother had not intervened. At her instigation, a discussion took place between the brothers-in-law in the presence of my mother, in which they found a temporary solution for the question of parity, and I gather from a conciliatory letter of my father's at the end of the month that he, in the name of the Linz firm, was prepared to make a considerable payout to Jenö.

No letters have been preserved from April to September 1924, and probably none were exchanged. Jenö commuted between the apartment in the first district that he had acquired before his marriage by means of a considerable transfer fee, his villa in Pressbaum and the house in the vicinity of Lake Balaton, and this with the help of a car; since Dezsö had bought one in 1923, his older brother couldn't very well do without one. He would have done better making fewer trips to the country and spending his time preparing the fall collection. My father took care of Neutorgasse, and since Herzog, although decent and reliable, was inclined to be unimaginative and somewhat lethargic, my father travelled repeatedly to Linz to check on things and accompanied Martin Becker on a short business trip to England. Becker enjoyed Sándor's company and took pleasure in familiarizing him with the English lifestyle, going to concerts with him and showing clients his friend's collection as well as his own. Since the krone was worth so little, the trip to England was expensive, but for the same reason it was easy to sell Austrian goods across the English Channel, and the firm Gisela Kahn flourished. It was in this summer that Martin bought his Guarneri violin, and in the following autumn he realized an old dream: he purchased a villa in Döbling, in the vicinity of the Türkenschanz Park, a district that according to a strange Viennese usage we called the "Cottage." My father got just enough orders to cover the travel expenses, but things were off to a good start.

But Sándor wasn't even back a week when the quarrelling started again. It was about two dresses, an allegedly poorly sewn serge dress and a crepe de Chine dress, "façon Mimi," that the Linz store had complained was "totally stained" and sent back to the firm Johann Kahn with the request that such goods in future be removed before shipping. You would think that Jenö and Sándor, who each had his own business and were joint owners of a second, couldn't possibly let such petty things get in the way, but they sufficed to initiate an extensive correspondence. "In principle," writes Jenö, for example, "we are always grateful to you and like to see, indeed see with admiration, that shipments for our jointly-owned store in Linz undergo such a thorough, exact and attentive inspection on your part, and we ask that you, if possible, in future exert even more care and notify us of every flaw, be it ever so tiny. However, we do not like to see you accusing us of inattentiveness." As for the serge dress, it was obvious that not every dress sewn for a wage of 30,000 kronen could be completely perfect, and if the firm K. & E. wanted to buy things cheaply, then it must be prepared to bear the consequences. In the "façon Mimi" dress, on close examination, he could find only two small stains in the folds of the pleats.

In the answer to these explanations it says that the ironic and uncalled-for remarks about the "thorough examination" were inappropriate, because the stains on the crepe de Chine dress had caught their eye immediately when it was unpacked; the serge dress, however, was not only poorly sewn, but completely unusable, it had a neckline like a horse collar; also, it was obvious that no saleable dresses could be manufactured for a wage of K 30,000, you had to pay at least K 50,000 and put up with a more modest profit, that is what our dear competition does, "which the firm Alexander Engelmann has adopted as its model." To which Jenö responded that even the professional dry cleaner where he had sent the crepe de Chine dress could find the stains only after arduous searching; the goods delivered from the firm J. Kahn to other firms had all been accepted without difficulty and without complaint, so that he couldn't help thinking that the lectures and complaints he had been given by K. & E. served the sole purpose of fabricating a reason for having A. Engelmann, in defiance of all their agreements, still deliver twice as much to K. & E. as did Johann Kahn.

There could be no talk of fabrication, read the answer; Herr Kahn would remember, for example, that in April of 1924 he had delivered completely unusable, "worn and sweaty" pongee blouses to Linz, that not even a washerwoman could have been expected to buy. These blouses, Jenö replied, that Sándor had found unusable and therefore worthless last April, were the same ones that he had evaluated at K 40,000 each when he calculated the value of the stored goods on Fleischmarkt for his share of the profit. But at least it hadn't done Sándor any harm that, in the course of these altercations, he had read so many well-written letters. He, Jenö, had observed with pleasure that Sándor had recently made considerable progress in the writing of business letters in German; it was just a pity that the lack of objectivity of these letters considerably reduced his delight in the good style. Indeed, if one surveyed the long list of suspicions with which he had bothered his brother-in-law and business partner over the years, one could almost get the impression that he suffered from a persecution mania. . . .

That was bad enough. But the following spring the correspondence became even more hostile. There was not just the *threat* of legal measures, there were lawyer's letters, and one has the impression that everything was heading for a lawsuit.

Herr
Johann Kahn
33 Fleischmarkt, Vienna I.

April 2, 1925

On the occasion of the consultation that took place with you in May of 1922 about the premises of our joint business in Linz, you confirmed that the store at 15 Promenade in Linz had been rented for the firm Kahn & Engelmann. The lease should, therefore, not be in the name of Johann Kahn, as you had it recorded in the lease without my knowledge and consent, but in the name of the firm Kahn & Engelmann, which is registered in the commercial court in Linz. You confirmed this to me at my request in a notarized letter and at the same time undertook to send a letter with the same content to our landlady Frau Anna Baumann. However, to this day, contrary to your promise, no such letter has been sent, and on the advice of your lawyer, for reasons unknown to me, you have refused to carry out your promise. Since it is legally inadmissible to enter into such one-sided contracts, I hereby respectfully request that you send a notarized letter to Frau Baumann within three days.

If I am not in possession of the notarized confirmation within three days, then I will be forced to hand this matter over to my lawyer for legal action.

Alexander Engelmann

This was followed by the intervention of a lawyer who was friends with both parties, Dr. Sonderling, in whose presence a meeting took place that was a success insofar as it did not lead to legal action. But more letters followed, among them a very long one dated May 8, 1925, in which Jenö returned to the question of the lease. Herr Engelmann, it says there, had repeatedly found cause for hateful suspicions in this matter; the thought that Herr Kahn had acted "with dishonest intentions" back then was nothing but a "malicious fantasy, filled with hate," that revealed nothing more than "Herr Engelmann's unrefined way of thinking," because you

265

are treated as you treat others. It was different, though, with the threat Herr Engelmann had uttered in May of 1922, that by virtue of his good relationship to Frau Baumann he would drive his partner out of the Linz business – a threat that deeply horrified and angered Herr Kahn; if Herr Engelmann was still "riding his old hobby horse of the lease," that suggested that he "was perhaps still, in the sense of his threat of May 1922, developing further the idea he had given voice to at that time. . . ."

My father consulted with Dezső and then, working long hours at night, composed a letter in which he rehashed in minute detail everything he had against his brother-in-law. I must at least summarize this document, as it leaves no doubt that he was on the verge of a breakdown. He repeats yet again the whole story about the lease and mentions again that Jenő sent him to the carpenter's at the critical moment. He complains about untruths expressed by Jenő in the course of their discussion at Dr. Sonderling's and reproaches him for "not having done a stroke of work" for the Linz store in the past four years while nevertheless enjoying half the profit. He gives voice to his "outrage" about the fact "that you impertinently harmed my reputation by boasting to my relatives and acquaintances that you had offered up a cornucopia full of gold for me and yet still had not succeeded in making me a real *mensch*." He reports on a bad speculation with Czech flannel that was exclusively Jenő's initiative, who afterwards, though, told his father-in-law "with tears in his eyes" that he, Sándor, had thereby "ruined" him. (Obviously Maritza occupied herself not only with blowing smoke rings, but also with spreading stories in the family about what went on between Jenő and her father.) He reproaches Jenő for having taken foreign currency worth K 70,000,000 from the cash box of the firm K. & E. in 1924 to pay down the debts of the firm Johann Kahn and then having miscalculated the value of the foreign currency so that it amounted to a loss of K 9,000,000 for the firm K. & E. He repeats in great detail the story about the Czech korunas that were bought for K 8,000,000. He proves with a detailed list that when Jenö looked after the insurance premiums – "the only work you have done for K. & E. in years" – he also paid the bills for the firm Johann Kahn from the Linz account, and then at last he comes to the conclusion:

"As a consequence of the incidents described here and your breach of contract, I hereby, in accordance with Article 124 of the Code of Commercial Law, terminate the business relationship existing between us as of the end of December 1925. Should you object to this termination and, in arrangement with me, not want to carry out the liquidation of the company by mutual agreement, I reserve the right to demand the dissolution of the company, in accordance with Article 125 of the Code of Commercial Law."

After this letter had been typed, Sándor showed it to my mother, who sought my grandmother's advice – and now the women made a big mistake.

My grandmother was no longer the imposing woman she had been, who could deal with any difficulty. While my grandfather continued going door to door with his sand that no one wanted anymore, in order to return home with huge bouquets of flowers, watermelons and large paper bags of apples, when they were in season, and had even found a café where he could talk with other elderly gentlemen over a Hungarian kümmel, my grandmother lacked a sphere of activity. Miriam Horowitz, whom she had enjoyed visiting so much, was no longer alive. There was a cook at work in the kitchen, although my grandmother helped her and insisted on cooking herself when there were guests. The grandchildren were taken care of by a nanny. I do not know whether there is a connection between her inactivity and the fact that she had been ailing since the summer of 1924 – even today, physicians know only a very little about such things. She suffered from attacks of dizziness and had difficulty breathing, complained about feeling tired and about her increasing deafness, and Dr. Grübel was at a loss. Now she picked herself up and attempted for the last time to make sure things were in order in her family. Together with my mother, she convinced my father "not to go to extremes" and to try one more time to get along with her son (as if she hadn't known him enough!). The letter that would probably have saved my father's life was not sent.

So everything remained as it was, the firm was not dissolved, and the quarrel continued. Jenö sent Sándor a list according to which – in the meantime the schilling had been introduced in Austria – the firm A. Engelmann, in the years 1923 to 1925, had delivered goods amounting to S 74,796 to Linz, but the firm J. Kahn had only delivered goods for S 33,343, he demanded compensation for "being thus disadvantaged in contravention of our agreement," and received an answer in which, among other things, it was asserted that in the summer of 1925 there had been "neither a finished dress nor usable materials" on Fleischmarkt and that the entire personnel had sat around unoccupied. Jenö insisted on receiving an exact statement of expenses every week from the bookkeeping "of our joint firm." He suddenly remembered that in 1922 he had attempted to get his brother-in-law a highly paid position with Barnum's, where they had rejected his proposal with the remark, Herr Engelmann was "quite inept as a businessman." He returned to the K 24,000,000 plus K 8,000,000 which had been "withdrawn without the approval of his partner, and therefore illegally," which amounted to fraud. He discovered or invented a new Hungarian saying: "If you let a Slovak into the front hall, he'll drive you out of your house," and the "Slovak" didn't fail to respond. In August, Jenö happened to enter a compartment in the train to Pressbaum in which my grandparents and my parents were sitting. He greeted them affably, but my father stuck his head into the newspaper and didn't return the greeting, which gave Jenö cause for long written instructions on how a well-mannered man had to behave, if not generally and as a matter of principle, then at least out of consideration for their parents. . . . My father's answer – I find this appalling – exists in three drafts and a carbon copy of a final version.

By the summer of 1926, things had got to the point where, frankly, my father feared the arrival of the mail and would delay opening the letters for as long as possible, because if a letter from Jenö had arrived, that meant another sleepless night. And these letters came and had to be answered. . . . I'm going to pass over them, but have to report that my father made a second trip to England with Martin in mid-November. Decades later, my cousin Olga told me about that trip in Beverly Hills.

"In principle, I am not at all opposed to suicide," I had said; we were having coffee in her living room and had started talking about my father. "Everyone has the right to chuck the whole business if he's fed up with it – but not if he has to take care of a wife and two small children!"

"You must know," said Olga, "that Sándor was not himself anymore, he was already a sick person. He used to laugh so heartily, almost like Dezsö, I still remember when we visited him and your mother on Freienberg and went dancing. But in the last year of his life he was always nervous and agitated, he smoked as much as Maritza, he even argued with my Marti on their last trip!"

And then she told me what her Martin had told her after their return from England. The trip had started not badly. Sándor and Martin had first spent a weekend in London going for walks and sightseeing, and then travelled on to Edinburgh overnight in the sleeping car: Martin hoped to find new customers in Scotland for both firms, A. Engelmann and Gisela Kahn. They had quite a long stay in Glasgow, then canvassed Leeds, Manchester and Birmingham and were well received everywhere. It was only natural that Martin got more orders than Sándor. "Gisela Kahn," said Olga, "was a well-known firm, people everywhere knew Martin and trusted him, and most of them just gave Sándor small orders to try him out. It is always difficult at the beginning, Marti and I also had to work very hard later on when we had to start from scratch again in Los Angeles and Marti had to travel across the entire country as far as New York." It was the beginning of December when they returned to London. But now the weather changed, the city was stuck in the infamous, sooty London fog that at that time was fed by thousands of chimneys and factory smokestacks, and Sándor's mood took a turn for the worse. He couldn't tolerate the bad air, he suffered from shortness of breath and headaches, and while for almost four weeks up until that point he had been a cheerful and enterprising companion for Martin, now he recounted all the awful things night after night. He complained about the weather, about the bad coffee they made in England, about the "bad habit" of the English of not opening their mouths when they spoke, so that you couldn't understand a word, and over breakfast and over high tea in the big drawing room of the Cumberland Hotel he talked heatedly about all the ways Jenö had wronged him, about the lease, about the difficulties with the account, about the insulting letters Jenö had written him and the fact that they were composed so that Jenö could present them to confirm his slanderous remarks in a coming lawsuit, about the accusations Jenö was constantly hurling at him, about the way he had swindled him years ago with foreign currency. . . . Martin forced himself to be patient; but since Sándor mentioned again and again that he was afraid Jenö could use his absence to hatch some new plot against him, that he actually should be in Vienna to be able to defend himself, Martin finally said that if Sándor really thought it was necessary for him to be in Vienna, then he should go back – he, Martin, would then present both collections to the customers he had yet to visit. . . .

"He meant that well," said Olga, "Marti was always generous like that. But Sándor didn't take it as it was meant, he said angrily: 'You want to get rid of me, you are against me too, you are all against me' and went out into the fog."

The next morning Sándor apologized and went with Martin to visit the customers. On the 16th of December they arrived back in Vienna, where two letters were waiting for Sándor.

Since I knew what had happened the following day, I expected when reading through the collection of letters the first time, the closer I got to the end, that there would be an unexpected turn, something suddenly worse that led to the catastrophe; but it was not a drama that I was reading. The correspondence ended with nothing worse than what I had already read in earlier letters, but Sándor was so exhausted from years of quarrelling that he couldn't go on anymore. In the first of the two letters that awaited him on his return from England, Jenö demanded prompt payment for the deliveries he had made in the fall, commented once again ironically on the incident on the train to Pressbaum that was already five months in the past and dragged up old conflicts. In the second letter, Dr. Pramer, who as the lawyer for the Linz firm had both partners as his clients, writes that he had had a consultation with Herr Johann Kahn about a "legal issue." It was – and this throws an interesting light on the social conditions in Austria at that time – a petition from the Linz tailors' co-operative to the local chamber of commerce to prohibit the firm Kahn & Engelmann from making custom-made suits, and Pramer thought he could clear up the matter without much difficulty. At the same time, though, he continues, Herr Kahn had informed him that he had already repeatedly requested that his partner "return the bookkeeping and financial management, i.e., the entire business concerning the firm Kahn & Engelmann to the jurisdiction of the commercial court in Linz" and was determined, if this request had not been met "by January 1, 1927," to take legal measures to have it done. Herr Kahn's wish was, in view of the deplorable relationship between the two partners, quite understandable, but it also had a basis in law, and he, Pramer, was therefore taking the liberty of advising my father to give his assent to the reorganization, since he could not expect a favourable outcome from a lawsuit in this matter. . . .

Prejudiced though I am, I have to admit that Jenö's request this time was not unreasonable. It could not be denied that he could not exercise his "rights of supervision and participation," as Dr. Pramer expressed it, if the bookkeeping was carried out in rooms he could not enter without having to fear an embarrassing scene with my father. The latter, though, feared something entirely

271

different. If he turned down Jenö's request, he placed himself in the wrong. But if he agreed to it, he was handing all the firm's documents over to Jenö, who would then be able to sit in all comfort in an office in Linz to glean from the firm's long tale of woe what he needed for the lawsuit that had been in the offing for a long time, and would be able to organize it to his advantage. . . . He was distracted when he answered my mother's questions about the trip to England before they went to sleep, and in the early morning hours she woke up and discovered that he had got up and was pacing back and forth in the dining room.

He spent the morning on Neutorgasse, ate in a little restaurant at noon and then went to Rotenturmstrasse once more to consult with Dezsö. There is no record of the discussion that took place there; it must have been painful for Dezsö to talk about it. According to family legend, though, Dezsö is said to have made the remark that was perhaps the last straw: "You'll never shake the scoundrel off."

When my father returned, only the cook was in the apartment: my mother had gone to Neutorgasse, my grandfather was going door to door, and my grandmother had gone with the children and their nanny to visit Klara on Landstrasse. My father – it is all documented, I couldn't have invented it – took off the good suit he had put on after breakfast, hung it up in the closet and took out an old jacket and an old pair of pants. Having changed his clothes, he went into the dining room and wrote neatly on a small piece of paper:

December 17, 1926
Dear Elli!
Forgive me, but I had no choice! I am tired of fighting, and I am afraid of having a lawsuit with Jenö. I forgive him and do not want to take any resentment with me, but I must ask Jenö to at least be kinder to you. I meant well, and if it had to end like this, it must have been someone's fault – perhaps mine? It grieves me greatly that I have to leave you and the two boys unprovided-for, but my

brother-in-law, friend and worthy business partner has robbed me of my peace of mind, and the years of discord have used up my power of resistance. So the despicable Slovak and swindler is going and leaving it to Jenö, maybe he'll share it with you? Please forgive me!

Your Sándor

My father weighted the paper down with his pocket watch – I own it, it is a very beautiful watch with an astonishingly modern face – and went out into the street, where a thin, dirty rain was falling. In the vicinity of the Reichsbrücke he spent, as the police later determined, half an hour with a cup of coffee at a cheap public house where people noticed him because even in his old suit he was too well dressed for that place. Then he went on the bridge, waited until there were neither vehicles nor passers-by, and jumped into the water. His corpse washed up three days later on the other side of the Hungarian border.

Gisa undertook the task of informing Jenö. She wrote him an astonishingly primitive letter in which she swore at him and solemnly cursed him, but also phoned him immediately, before the letter arrived. When he put down the receiver after a short conversation, Maritza, who had just lit a cigarette and was blowing the smoke through her nose, asked: "What's wrong with you, Jenö? You are as white as a sheet."

"Sándor has taken his life," said Jenö in a flat voice.

Maritza blew four congruent smoke rings that wafted equidistantly through the room and watched until the first of them hit the ceiling and dispersed. "You're wrong, Jenö," she said at last. "Sándor didn't kill himself. You killed him."

CHAPTER SEVEN

Children

1.

I CAN NO LONGER RECALL how I spent the day my father committed suicide. But I clearly remember an apartment full of weeping women, with me standing frightened among them. My mother was crying, my grandmother was crying, my nanny was crying, the maid was sobbing hysterically. Finally, my grandmother ran her hand over my hair and led me to the children's room. Later on I was told that my father had fallen out of the train on the trip to Linz. I only learned the truth six years later.

My father was buried in the Zentralfriedhof, which was actually not centrally located, but far out in a suburb. I don't remember the burial, but can describe his headstone. It was a rectangular block of granite almost as tall as a man, and my father's name, birth and death dates and the usual Hebrew inscription were engraved on its polished front side. In its simple elegance, the gravestone may have reflected my father's taste.

At the time his gravestone was erected, the "Israelite" section of the cemetery had been an immense, carefully tended garden. (It was called "Israelite" because many non-Jews in Vienna considered "Jewish" a swearword; for the same reason, in Germany after 1945, instead of saying "Jew" people often said "Jewish person" – a dreadful description that sounds as if the Germans had just discovered that Jews are persons, and are still a little surprised by it.) In the early fifties I was back in Vienna again for the first time since 1938, visited the cemetery and was shaken by what I saw. The funeral chapel had been set on fire on Kristallnacht and the two walls that were still standing had swastikas painted on them. In front of the Third Gate, the entrance to the Jewish section of this city of the dead, a dozen policemen were standing on guard: the living had not been protected, but now they protected the dead.

I went in, and an old man in a caftan spoke to me, offering to help me find the grave, for a small fee, and to recite the prayer for the dead with me. The place behind the gate was bare and clean, with six or seven opulent gravestones placed at irregular distances. Immediately behind them, there was a wilderness: ivy run wild, ornamental bushes that hadn't been trimmed in years, weeds, and roses everywhere, wild roses or roses that had gone wild. If the Jewish community had not paid a gardener to keep the paths clear between the rows of graves, you would have been caught in the branches after the first few steps. Some of the gravestones had been pushed over, some were damaged. If you bent down to read what was on the toppled stones near the entrance, or stopped to read the upright ones, you could see that the Jewish upper class around the turn of the century had found their eternal rest here: Professor Dr. X, Dr. Dr. h.c. Y, Consul Z, judges, lawyers, business people, bankers, publishers, surgeons. . . . The granite block on my father's grave was not damaged; the inscription was almost completely covered by wild branches, the roses were blooming. The man in the caftan said the prayer while I remained silent: I didn't know it and felt ashamed. Then he led me out again. On the way back it occurred to me that the City of Vienna should actually pay for the care of the cemetery, since the tiny, aged and impoverished Jewish community that once again existed there could not pay for the upkeep, but I abandoned that idea again immediately: the wilderness with its blooming roses was probably the right memorial to that lost world, and it seemed to me that even the swastikas still belonged on the walls. They bore witness to the way that world was lost.

If my father had hoped, as he had written in his farewell letter, that Jenö would be "kinder" to Elli after his death, that is, that he would care for her financially, he had based that hope on false assumptions. News of his suicide spread like wildfire in the business world, and every supplier who was owed something by the stores in Linz and on Neutorgasse pressed for payment. Since my mother was at her wit's end, Dezsö undertook to liquidate the business in Vienna. Jenö fought desperately for the Linz store, but he was not in good shape. He had lived with the conviction that he had always done the right thing and had only defended himself in the long line of quarrels, because "the others," the English furniture company, Dezsö, Sidney Lionel, my father, had wanted to take advantage of him. Now he recognized his guilt, at least in this last case; but because he couldn't live with this insight, he started trying to put a different construction on things, and since he could succeed in doing that only when he was drinking, he drank. He spent the morning dictating business letters, negotiating with creditors and consulting with his latest lawyer, and the bottle of wine on the table at lunch was the first of three or four. In March, Kahn & Engelmann went bankrupt. It didn't suit Maritza's spoiled tastes to blow her smoke rings in the company of a bankrupt alcoholic, and they separated in early summer.

The divorce court acted on the principle that a child up to the age of fourteen primarily needs a mother, but a boy from that age on above all needs a father: it must have escaped the experts who were responsible for this regulation that the children of solid middle-class parents at that time were brought up by neither their father nor their mother, but by their nannies, and so custody should have been awarded to the parent who had greater skill in choosing household personnel. (I lost all faith in Sigmund Freud once it occurred to me that he is always talking about fathers and mothers, but never about housekeepers; because it was obvious that for every boy from a good family who wanted to sleep with his

277

mother, there were at least ten thousand who wanted a more intimate relationship with a housemaid, but whose advances were mostly thwarted.) Be that as it may: the court awarded custody of Jenö's and Maritza's son Felix to his mother, but decided at the same time that when he was fourteen, if his father was then in a position to care for him, he should be put in his father's care. . . . At first, after Maritza and the boy had moved back in with her parents, all that remained for Jenö was the empty apartment, the struggling business on Fleischmarkt and the villa in Pressbaum that had three mortgages on it, but with which he was not prepared to part.

If I include Felix, whom we didn't set eyes on for a long time, Hans and I had three male cousins and three female cousins on the Kahn side of the family; but I had to draw a family tree to be able to check: it is confusing that I always called my cousin Olga Aunt Olga right up until her death, while I regarded Edith (her sister) and Rita (her daughter) as cousins.

So although my maternal grandparents had five children, they had only eight grandchildren.

Among the eight children, I stood out to a certain extent because I was fat, short-sighted and a loner. If I remember rightly, I already mentioned that I shot up during puberty and have been rather too thin ever since. At that time, my vision also improved significantly, which is rare for short-sighted people. By saying I was a loner I don't mean that I had no friends in school, for example, or that I didn't talk to anyone. Quite the opposite, I was even the class spokesman for many years, but in my spare time I liked to be alone, found my own amusements and after I discovered the world of books – at a young age – I read as if my life depended on it. For entire afternoons, I lay on the carpet in the dining room, propped up on my elbows, completely absorbed in reading whatever I could get my hands on: Karl May, later Stefan Zweig, Werfel's *Forty Days of Musa Dagh*, Mirko Jelusich's *Caesar* (without understanding that it was fascist propaganda), all of Jakob Wassermann's novels. . . . That could lead to difficulties. For example, I had arranged that I should meet my schoolmates at three o'clock in the Prater to play football, and I had promised to bring the ball. I got out of school at one, got a book for myself after lunch, lay down flat on the carpet, read and forgot the rest of the world. . . . Then at three o'clock my friends stood around on the meadow and waited for me: no Peter Engelmann, no ball. At a quarter past three, my friend and admirer Bornstein was sent to Augartenstrasse to get me. When he came in, I looked up from my book in confusion: an arrangement to meet them? In the Prater? Almost three-thirty already? So we ran with the ball to the park, where my friends were happier to see the ball than to see me: I was a terribly bad football player. With unfailing instinct, I was always where the ball wasn't. Now and then a bigger boy watched for a while and then asked if he could play with us. We didn't dare to say no, because he could have taken the ball away from us, but we insisted that he play barefoot. But since he ran faster and shot the ball more forcibly than we did, he ruined the game anyway.

My absent-mindedness did not diminish as I got older. On the *Dunera*, for example – the ship that brought me to Australia – we ate at large tables that sat sixteen. Every eight days, two of us were responsible for washing up. We washed the dishes in a big bowl and then poured the dishwater into a funnel, from which it flowed into the sea. When I had wash-up duty for the third time, I fished the plates and cups out of the bowl, but I was thinking about a chess problem and poured the water with the cutlery into the sea. . . . There was no replacement cutlery on board, but my brother brought us wood from the crates in the kitchen and we carved that into spoons and knives. The makeshift wooden cutlery was a poor substitute (of course we couldn't carve proper forks out of wood), but it had the advantage of floating at the top of the dishwater, so that I didn't pour it into the sea as well.

As is very often the case with advancing age, my absent-mindedness has become even worse in the past few years. When I go from my study to the kitchen to make coffee, I no longer know when I get there what I wanted. At work, though, I always had my mind on the job and still do, whether I'm at my desk or in the operating room – with the exception that although I know all the dogs and cats I look after by name, I am often unable to learn the names of their owners. But I've strayed from the topic again, I wanted to write about the children.

At the time of my earliest memories, Hans and I knew Rhonda and Teddy best. In the winter, we didn't see each other very often, but I remember that when I was seven or eight I saw a real Christmas tree for the first time, aside from the ones in store windows, in Dezsö's apartment – a tall fir tree decorated with garlands, the usual Christmas decorations and many candles. In the summer, until Siegfried Liptauer entered my life, we were usually guests for weeks at my Uncle Dezsö's estate in Pressbaum, where my Annie, who later married my dentist, quickly became friends with Rhonda's and Teddy's nanny, Hansi.

If I (may the Lord protect me!) lived in Vienna and could afford a villa, I wouldn't exactly choose to live in Pressbaum. What do you get from the most beautiful villa if there is neither water nor mountains? But Pressbaum had the advantage that you could get there quickly and comfortably by train or by car, and I remember how exciting it was when Dezsö's chauffeur drove us there in the big Daimler: on straight stretches we roared along at a hundred kilometres per hour! In my memory of the villa, sounds and smells play a big role – the slightly foul-smelling geraniums blooming in all the wooden window boxes, the grossly foul-smelling polar bear skins lying around, and the almost endless clattering, squealing and rattling of the freight trains from the valley below that could be heard particularly clearly in the lavatory I used. The sound of the trains produced in me a pleasant longing for distance that I hadn't known otherwise, and I spent a lot of time daydreaming in the lavatory.

The two nannies didn't always have an easy time with us, because when the four of us were together, we could go wild. When the weather was fine we had tea outside, sitting at a round table with a big, colourful sunshade above it, and for reasons that made no sense to an adult, we went off into fits of laughter that made the tea, that we drank with sugar and lemon juice, spill and run in streams across the tablecloth. My brother loved to tease me until I had a tantrum, threw myself bawling on the ground and kicked anyone who came near me. Rhonda fought with Teddy, of course, as it seems to be inevitable that girls fight with their younger brothers. But it was mainly Teddy who made sure we weren't bored.

At Teddy's instigation we played hide-and-seek on the big, flat plot of land that we called the Big Meadow; it was part of Dezsö's property, and was overgrown with grass and groups of hedge roses. For this purpose, he rounded up children from the neighbouring villas, and here too my absent-mindedness prevailed: I would hide, which was part of the game of course, between the hedge roses, for example, but then promptly lose myself in some daydream and only reappear three games later. Teddy called himself Rinaldini Rinaldó (accented on the last syllable), as a result of our grandfather's stories, who was convinced that at the time of his childhood a band of thieves had been up to mischief along the shores of Lake Balaton, and their captain had gone by that name. But Teddy was not only a notorious thief, but also a famous surgeon who performed the most astonishing operations in his operating room high up in the tall beech tree in front of the villa, where no one could watch him: he had to protect his professional secrets. If he climbed up too high, Hansi shrieked with horror and called the gardener, but his ladder couldn't reach up to where Teddy was. . . . When he had climbed down again unharmed and without using the ladder, he told us how he had just saved the king of England's life by giving him a brain transplant. "A sheep's brain?" asked Rhonda spitefully. "A brain that I built myself," said Teddy, picked up a soda water bottle from the table (I haven't seen one like that in a long time, they probably don't exist anymore), splashed soda water down the neck of his shirt and announced: "I have to wet my hero's chest with water from the Holy Grail."

281

Teddy particularly loved to play charades, but it wore us down playing with him. While the rest of us contented ourselves with real proverbs that could be guessed, Teddy changed them and invented new ones. The early bird gets the coffee, He who laughs last has not understood the joke, There are two sides to every bur-ger, A bird in the hand is worth a peck or two, The squeaky wheel gets replaced, You can't see the forest for the mist. But he also had a passion for inventing "unnecessary occupations" – eggbeater, clothes hanger, candleholder, saltshaker, bulldozer, flicker, type-writer, stapler, toaster, reamer, pencil sharpener, panhandler. He liked to announce his latest discoveries over tea. "Screwdriver," he would suddenly call out, or "skyscraper." We would just about choke with laughter, the tea spilled all over the clean tablecloth, and the nannies didn't understand what was actually so funny about a skyscraper.

Rhonda's hair was as black as Gisa's, Teddy's was flaxen blond, even lighter than my mother's. Aunt Mitzi idolized him and spoiled him in every way imaginable: he was allowed to do almost anything, and it can only be put down to his healthy disposition that he harmed no one but himself with his extravagances. In later years – the years before the *Anschluss* – his flamboyance made him almost a Viennese celebrity. On principle, heaven knows why, he wore only white linen suits and ran around the city followed by a half dozen fans and admirers whom he treated to cake and dough-nuts in Hotel Sacher. He played tennis badly (Dezsö had had a tennis court built soon after he bought the villa, even though he himself did not play any sports), but he had a large collection of tennis rackets and bought a new one every few weeks. "If I find the right racket," he said, "I'll win at Wimbledon some time soon." When he was sixteen, he discovered sailing. The small sailboat he liked to rent at the Old Danube was built for regattas, so it had too much sail for Teddy, who weighed less than 60 kilos, and it tipped over in the first strong gust of wind. He knew what was to be done in such a situation, so he climbed on the centreboard, grabbed hold of the edge of the boat and leaned back, but he was not heavy enough to right the boat, and the man who rented out the boats had to send two lads after him in a dinghy to pull him out of the water. Despite that, the owner and his helpers liked to see Teddy come, because he didn't scrimp with his tips.

It was, of course, Uncle Jenö who came up with the biting expression to describe the way Teddy carried on. "Teddy!" he exclaimed, when, in 1937, he associated with us again after a ten-year hiatus. "He should actually be called Teddy von Hapsburg, he's acting as if he were the uncrowned king of Vienna." The fact that I was in contact with my Uncle Jenö at the time, but not with Teddy, is because of my stepfather Siegfried Liptauer; but for you to properly appreciate his entrance into my life, I have to go back to the year 1927.

2.

My mother was brave. In the beginning, Sándor had been mainly her brother's friend; but there's no doubt that she very quickly forgot stupid Franz, and she loved Sándor as if there had never been another man in her life. When she read his farewell letter and his corpse was fished out of the Danube, she was just as much in despair as she had been seventeen years earlier when she had jumped out the window. But she had the children to care for, and life must go on. To be sure: she delayed going to bed as long as possible, and it was weeks before she could lie down in the empty bed without being shaken with sobs. She clung to Hans, her eight-year-old, and so it was a doubly difficult time for him. In March, though, my mother was ready to start thinking about the future, and there was another family consultation. It was clear that my mother needed something to keep her busy, and Dezsö had succeeded, through a lawyer (Dezsö no longer spoke to his brother and never even greeted him on the street again), in getting 40,000 schillings out of Jenö. The upshot of the consultation was the founding of a further, if more modest business, to which Gisa and

Dezsö contributed additional capital: a small store for fashionable novelties, Elisabeth Engelmann, Dresses, Blouses and Dressing Gowns. The store never brought in very much, although Mitzi got models for her sister-in-law; but it helped to take my mother's mind off her grief, and most of the household expenses were paid anyway with the help of my grandmother's brown envelopes: admittedly, there was no envelope from the bankrupt Jenö, but to make up for that (in addition to the ones from Dezsö and Gisa) there was one from Klara.

Strangely enough, I cannot remember my mother's store, but there is an even more astonishing gap in my memory: I do not remember my grief about my father's death. But I do remember that my grandfather taught me a short Hebrew prayer at that time, that I said for many years before going to sleep, without thinking much about it. I like to think of the simple man with the blond Kaiser-beard and the happy twinkle to his eyes, even though he played only a small role in my life. As before, he went door to door without success. Perhaps because he had hardly been able to afford an apple as a child, he like to buy fruit – grapes, plums, greengages, muskmelons and, since I didn't like muskmelons, watermelons just for me, and it hurt his feelings if I couldn't eat up a whole huge watermelon. He complained about the poor shoes that were made nowadays, smoked his Virginias, drank his caraway brandy in the evenings and regarded it as his right to have the children he had brought into the world do everything for him.

The Vienna we lived in no longer exists, and it will never exist again. During the First World War, more than 50,000 Jews had fled before the Russian troops to Vienna, many of them Hasidic Jews from Galicia. The majority of those who remained there – about half – settled, of course, in the second district, the Leopoldstadt. There were temples and synagogues there, kosher butchers and cholent bakers, a *cheder* for the boys and perhaps even neighbours with whom you could speak Yiddish. From the end of the war until the Shoah, about 60,000 Jews lived in Leopoldstadt – Orthodox, Reform and assimilated, like us. The Christians, who still made up over half the Leopoldstadt population, must have been surprised at the number of old men standing around the Karmelitermarkt who had full beards, *peyes*, and wore broad-brimmed hats, and at how many women now spoke Yiddish when they did their shopping. . . .

There was nothing unusual about that to me, because I had grown up with it, but of course I only saw it from the outside. For example, I knew that the devout Jews did not cook on Saturday and arranged to have warm food by making their cholent on Friday, taking it in a bowl to the cholent baker and picking it up on Saturday; but I didn't eat this bean dish myself until I was in Haifa. From our hallway window that looked out on the inner courtyard, I could see a young man in the opposite apartment who put on his phylactery and spent at least a quarter of an hour with that ritual every morning. Then, because he wanted to be a cantor, he did voice exercises that still ring in my ears – two octaves up and down again. During *Sukkos*, the courtyard was full of tabernacles. I am sorry today that we – my brother and I – did not take part in the religious life around us. Even though I cannot understand how a sensible person manages to believe in a god who watched from his golden throne on high and saw what was going on in Treblinka without lifting a finger, the old rituals have a great appeal for me, and I always accept with gratitude when a devout neighbour invites me to the Seder. I too have fasted again regularly on Yom Kippur for over ten years now, albeit not for religious reasons, but as a small and helpless gesture toward the millions who were gassed, starved and shot. After all, we also fasted on the Day of Atonement when we were children and up until 1938, while we took next to no notice of the other Jewish feast days, and that was out of consideration for my grandfather. The fact that we, Hans and I, made a farce of this day, the holiest in the Jewish religious year, was without any ill intent, out of pure thoughtlessness. It had become our custom to meet with friends and acquaintances in the Stadtpark, where we walked back and forth in our best suits, holding our right gloves in our gloved left hands, telling each other how

285

terribly hungry we were, and then, to show off our willpower, went into the Inner City and with growling stomachs looked at the magnificent cakes displayed in the pastry shop windows. . . . By the way, we didn't eat any pork on Augartenstrasse, not because my grandmother tried to keep a kosher kitchen, but because it simply wasn't common practice in Jewish households. While I have completely forgotten so many important events that had far-reaching consequences for my life, I still know exactly when I first ate pork. In the guest house in Kamegg in Upper Austria, where we spent a few weeks one summer, there was a pork dish with parsnips and herbs for lunch, and I still have its piquant taste on my tongue when I think back on it.

It almost goes without saying that at school I had hardly any more contact with Orthodox Jews than with Christians, although there was one exception. Among my schoolmates I enjoyed talking with during the breaks was a boy by the name of Tauber who displayed his orthodoxy by wearing the *yarmulke*. I must have been twelve or thirteen when I found out that the earth was millions of years old, which meant that the story of creation wasn't right, and I told him triumphantly what I had discovered. He listened to me patiently and said at last: "The Lord created the tree in full blossom." That impressed me, but I didn't understand it until many years later.

It was also at that time that I spent a rainy afternoon, when I could think of nothing better to do, rummaging through the safe in the back room that looked out on the courtyard and was now occupied by my grandparents. There was old writing paper there with the letterheads *Kahn & Engelmann* (Linz) and *Alexander Engelmann* (Neutorgasse), and there were cardboard boxes full of inflation money, coloured bills with long chains of zeros. There was a big pile of old letters that I didn't look at closely (probably my father's correspondence with Jenö, which is now in my study in Haifa), but on the top of it lay a small, folded piece of paper: my father's farewell letter.

When my brother came home, I asked him about it, and he told me what little he knew. In that same year, Gisa died, and a few weeks after her burial, my grandmother was brought to the Rothschild Hospital with an incurable cancer. My grandfather would perhaps have been able to maintain the tradition of Friday evenings, but he was satisfied to spend the evening with his youngest daughter and her children when he didn't go to Pressbaum for the weekend. The family was starting to fall apart. Elli, after losing her husband, had now also lost her mother, in whose arms she had always been able to have a good cry, and she had always needed support. . . . In her late thirties she was still an attractive woman, she owned a store that possessed a certain cachet, and so it was not surprising that from time to time there was a widower or bachelor who courted her. I can only remember one, from the summer when we spent three weeks in Kamegg. The guest house we were staying in was on the river Kamm, and there was a major with two children the same age as Hans and I. He was a nice man and liked to see the children making friends, and he spent a lot of time with us. Since all of us liked to play cards, he gave us bridge lessons, and we played chess. I owe him my knowledge of the openings in which a bishop is fianchettoed, but he wasn't interested in my mother. In comparison, there was another man who occasionally sat with us for dinner, and one day he got into the little rowboat with her that belonged to the guest house. I had spent many hours in that boat, knew my way around, watched with interest as the man rowed, and was horrified when, deep in conversation with my mother, he let the boat drift too near to the weir that stretched from shore to shore about a hundred metres downstream. When he recognized the danger and turned the boat around, it was too late – the current was too strong. Although my mother was wearing a dress and high heels, she jumped resolutely into the water, which was less than fifty centimetres deep there, pulled the boat ashore and by doing so demonstrated that she had more of my grandmother's blood in her veins than one might have assumed at first glance. I was not unhappy when the man disappeared from the scene shortly after. But there were also other men who were interested in my mother, whom I never saw, and it is, to say the least, difficult for me to understand, why she chose Siegfried Liptauer of all people.

I need no help in remembering my stepfather, but for the sake of remaining objective I prefer to use a photograph. It shows him standing in front of the house on Augartenstrasse, his pointed shoes toeing in slightly, and wearing – seriously, I didn't invent this – knee breeches, not real knickerbockers, but a sort of riding-breeches that were supposed to look sporty: Siegfried Liptauer was a motorcycle enthusiast, although he no longer had a bike. The shoes (I have to add this from memory, as of course I'm not looking at a colour photo, but a brownish monochrome) are light brown, the knee socks and pants a faded-looking beige, above them a woollen vest of the same colour, buttoned only half way up, under it a blue striped shirt (I hated those striped shirts!) and a very nar-row tie with a small knot. The face oval, no distinguishing features, clean-shaven, cheeks slightly chubby and all of it crowned with a huge bald spot. . . . So he wasn't attractive, no one would have married him for his looks, but he could be – as it seemed to me – rather charming in his own clumsy way. I even saw him dancing a few times, and that was bad. (In spite of the photograph, my description has not turned out to be objective, but I don't want to report on things objectively, but from the perspective of a rebel-lious, defiant twelve-year-old.)

My mother had met him on the patio of Dezsö's villa. Liptauer had ridden out there on a big motorcycle – a Harley-Davidson – that an acquaintance had lent him for the day. When it turned out a few weeks later that Liptauer had serious intentions about my mother, Dezsö made enquiries and found out that the man was deeply in debt. Dezsö spoke with my mother and tried to wield some authority as her older brother, but to no avail, perhaps because my mother thought that Hans and I needed a father.

It can't be denied that Liptauer tried to establish a fatherly relationship with me and my brother, but I didn't give him a chance. I was convinced that my mother should have remained faithful to my father: I had just read Hebbel's *Nibelungen Trilogy*, and so I knew something about unshakeable loyalty. But there was something else about her betrayal of my father. Did my mother absolutely have to – thus asked the twelve-year-old – marry a man called Siegfried Liptauer? You could be called Kahn or Engelmann, Pollak or even Finkelstein, but Liptauer? That was a cheese spread! And if you were called Liptauer, which in and of itself bordered on the unbearable, why *Siegfried* Liptauer? And vice versa, if your name was Siegfried, which, if you hadn't slain a dragon, was an inexcusable example of bad taste, then you should at least have the decency not to be called Liptauer. . . . Even worse than the name, though, was the fact that Siegfried Liptauer owned a girdle store on Spiegelgasse, not far from the Grillparzer House. If a man owned a girdle store, then it was understandable, it was almost to be expected that he'd be called Siegfried Liptauer. The store had been founded by Liptauer's father, the son of Moravian Jews who had moved to Vienna in the middle of the last century. The old Liptauers had brought three children into the world, at first two girls, and then the boy they called Siegfried. Instead of slaying dragons, Siegfried studied technology, but broke off his studies prematurely when Liptauer senior died and he took over the store, something from which he apparently derived little pleasure; we already know with what success. Then, when he moved into Untere Augartenstrasse, he sold my mother's store and with the proceeds from that he paid off the debts on his own store, where my mother now worked with him, and she eventually ran it all by herself, but without much enjoyment; because with their constant shortage of money, they had an inadequate assortment of merchandise, and my mother later told me that sometimes, when a customer wanted to buy something that they didn't have on hand, she would sneak out the back door and run through half of the Inner City to get the article. Dezsö had predicted all the hardship my mother would have, and was very angry about it. In the end, he invited us to Pressbaum only rarely, probably because he didn't want to run the risk of having to introduce Liptauer to his guests as his brother-in-law. Nevertheless, he did come to my mother's assistance from time to time, but without much success, because Siegfried Liptauer was one of those unfortunate people who can't keep any money in their pockets. If Jenö had speculated in foreign currencies, my stepfather speculated in inventions, and when Dezsö had diverted a few hundred schilling notes to us from the Rotenturmstrasse store, Liptauer invested them in two-stroke engines that used less gasoline but didn't start, in high performance pumps that burst apart when first used, and in a hail-proof plastic coating for greenhouses that couldn't withstand sunlight. If Dezsö called him a *ganef*, but only in his own home, because he didn't want to hurt my mother's feelings, that shows that over the years at Mitzi's side he had lost his feeling for the precise use of Yiddish expressions, because Siegfried Liptauer was not a *ganef*, but a *shlimazl*. (Leo Rosten defines the word in three sentences: if a *shlimazl* winds up a clock, it stops; if he buys himself an umbrella, there's good weather; if he makes coffins, people stop dying.)

As a veterinarian who at times has also dealt with breeding problems, I incline to the belief or superstition that our character is largely determined by our genetic makeup. A sheepdog doesn't need to learn how to deal with a herd of sheep or a dozen young steers, that is pre-programmed in his brain, and a pedigreed retriever can retrieve and does retrieve passionately as soon as he can run; but the human being is not a pea, and with us there is no relying on genetics. Racine didn't father a poet, Tycho Brahe didn't father a mathematician. My stepfather played chess with me now and then, and even as a thirteen-year-old I could beat him effortlessly. In the evenings, he liked to go with my mother to a cheap café to play the stupidest of all games there, rummy, for which you didn't need a brain at all, and yet he had two intelligent and educated sisters. The older one, my Aunt Grete, as I called her, had studied English language and literature at the University of Vienna at a time when that wasn't easy for a Jewess; because she had been unhappy in love when she was young, she remained single, and since she was a brilliant teacher, she earned a comfortable living giving private lessons. The younger one, Roswitha, originally a nurse by profession, had married a young bank employee shortly before the outbreak of the war. He reported for military duty in 1914, was taken a prisoner of war by the Russians in 1917 and only returned to Vienna in 1924 after an adventuresome walk through Siberia: that was my Uncle Paul. During his ten-year absence, Roswitha had managed, in the little spare time that her job as a nurse afforded her, to study medicine. I was only seldom in her doctor's office, but I liked to go to the childless couple's apartment on Liechtenstein Street, where I sometimes helped Uncle Paul with his cataloguing. As I have already mentioned, he collected first editions, and their apartment has often reappeared in my dreams. Along the walls in the large, bright rooms, there were varnished shelves with Paul's books and a large cupboard for musical scores that housed an exquisite Beethoven collection. In my dreams there were big glass cupboards in the middle of the room, each of which held a gigantic incunabulum, and Uncle Paul took the thick volumes out and let me leaf through a Gutenberg Bible.

When I had these dreams, Uncle Paul was no longer alive: after the *Anschluss*, this intelligent, sensitive man did not want to believe the game that was being played; and even when the Länderbank, where he had a top position, dismissed him without notice, he still thought the Nazi rule was a transitory aberration, and he would survive the few years until the horrific episode had passed again by living modestly and selling a first edition now and then: Uncle Paul could not imagine that this madness would last any length of time in the land of Goethe and Beethoven. Roswitha sized up their situation more realistically, but could not change his mind, and so they remained in Vienna. For a while, things really did go almost as Uncle Paul had imagined. Roswitha continued to care for her Jewish patients long after the war had broken out, visiting them in their apartments and eventually in their hiding places. Paul hardly left the house, regretted that the three friends with whom he had played chamber music twice a week for many years were now far away, made notes for the monograph on Beethoven he had always wanted to write and waited for the horrific "episode" to pass. Three years before that really happened, they were arrested and transported to Theresienstadt, where he very quickly lost his illusions. He turned his face to the wall and died of a kidney infection that presented itself as soon as he finally lost his belief in the land of Goethe and Beethoven. Roswitha, who as a physician did not get put on the transport lists, or was crossed off them again at the last moment, survived, and I visited her in the fifties in Vienna.

Suddenly, without actually having intended to do so, I've arrived at the year 1938 and a little beyond that, and I'm content to leave it that way. Not that there would not still be things to tell from my school years that would not be unworthy of being told, but I do not want to, it does not interest me anymore – it's no coincidence that the word "not" has already occurred five times in this sentence. The years before the great jubilation in Heldenplatz lie for me today, at my desk in Haifa, in the shadow of the end. You can see everything as a "dyskolos" or a "eukolos" (those are terms I learned from Jakob Wassermann when I was sixteen). I have to admit that my grandmother made a tough decision over a hundred years ago, when she moved with her husband and children to Vienna, where the other man with a Kaiser-beard, Kaiser Franz-Joseph, held his hand protectively over the Jews, and God knows whether her great-grandchildren, who now eat their dinner in the Yale Club or own a potter's studio in San Francisco, would have been born if my grandmother had not made that decision; but the great-grandchildren, with the exception of my son, hardly know anymore that they are Jews, and the grave of my grandmother is as untended today as that of my father. But there are still some things to tell from the year 1938, although not about myself. I'll begin with Jenö.

He must have been very lonely after Maritza went back to Hungary, taking little Felix with her. I vaguely remember – almost as if it had just been a dream, but my brother has confirmed it – that a short while before Liptauer entered our lives, a gardener spoke to us in the park in front of Dezsö's villa and asked us to go for a walk with him; Jenö must have bribed him. The lad led us up to the top of the Lawies hill and through an overgrown garden into a house where a man was sitting who looked familiar to me, and who stared at us without saying a word. After a while, he offered us candies, tucked a chocolate bar each in our pockets and let us go again. Jenö was still drinking then. He knew, however, that he would only get Felix back if he could care for him, and so one day – it must have been in 1936 – he threw the wine and beer bottles, the spirits and whiskey out of the apartment, drank only soda water and made a fresh start. As he had thirty years before, he found an English firm to represent. Soon after that, by coincidence, he made the acquaintance of my stepfather in a café, who invited him to our place. I don't know how my mother managed to make peace with Jenö, but you probably forgive a brother what you wouldn't forgive a stranger. At that time I didn't know what role he had played in my father's life, and I liked the eloquent man who visited us from time to time. But Jenö didn't reach his goal. He had drunk too long and too much and died in February of 1938 of a heart attack, before getting Felix back.

At just that time – have I already mentioned it? – my grandfather died too. He died peacefully and painlessly of old age, in his own bed, and he died at the right time, because we would not have been able to explain to him what happened next. My stepfather – to bring this story to an end as well – bought himself a forged visa to Shanghai a few weeks before my mother received her British visa, but was able to leave the ship in Singapore because a former pupil of his sister's had connections there. It didn't seem to worry him what became of my mother. On one of my visits to Vienna, Roswitha told me how he had fared later, but that is a boring story that is not worth the effort of telling.

My Uncle Martin had gotten visas to England for Klara and her family, just as he had for me and my brother, and Ferenc had to go back to the basics there and find work as a cutter. After his death, Klara and my mother shared the apartment and enjoyed their twilight years listening to the radio and watching television.

The children – Klara's son Kurti, Hans and I – were able to provide well for them. Martin, although he had so many business ties to England, emigrated with his family to Argentina. That surprised me, and Aunt Olga explained it to me in the Beverly Hills café long after his death. "Marti," she said, "started arranging our departure for England right after the *Anschluss*, but he did it slowly and carefully on account of the foreign exchange control regulations, and because his mother was still alive and the business on Tuchlauben had to be wound up and the house was there in Döbling and his father's house with the grocery store. I told him he should just walk away from it all, but he wanted to conclude everything in an orderly fashion, and then suddenly we had the SS in the office."

Olga told me what happened next in great detail. One morning the end of June, 1938, a man by the name of Josef Wondratschek showed up on Tuchlauben wanting to speak to Herr Martin Becker. A man in a black SS uniform came with him, and the two of them were asked into Martin's office, where they sat down across from him without having been offered a seat.

"It is known to me that you no longer like it in Vienna, Herr Becker," said Wondratschek, "and since we are almost neighbours, you know my store is on Bognergasse, I would like to be of assistance to you."

"Really?" said Martin and looked nervously at the man in the uniform. "Actually, I don't need any help."

"Maybe you do," said Wondratschek, lighting a cigarette for himself. "I have thought for a long time that I need more space and a better location. I'm offering you sixty thousand schillings in cash for Gisela Kahn, and then you will no longer have any worries about your business."

"I am not thinking of selling," said Martin. "By the way, the firm is worth at least ten times your offer."

"That depends on the circumstances," said Wondratschek. "For me, Gisela Kahn is worth sixty thousand schillings. For you, the firm will be worth nothing at all anymore in a few weeks."

"I don't know what you mean, Herr Wondratschek," said my cousin.

"Herr Wondratschek means," said the man in uniform and pointed out the window, through which they could see a clear blue sky, "that it will be a very hot summer, and I don't think you can tolerate the heat."

"I don't understand what that has to do with it," said Martin. "I don't even know your name."

"I am here in an advisory capacity," said the SS man. "Herr Wondratschek is a party member, and it is right and proper for us to stand by our members. Incidentally, you should consider yourself fortunate that you are still living in your house in Döbling. You will have noticed that most of the houses out there that were occupied by Jews have been confiscated. But I am advising not only Herr Wondratschek, you will permit me to advise you as well. As I said, a very hot summer lies ahead of us."

"So you brought your friend along," said Martin to Wondratschek, "to blackmail me?"

"That is an ugly word you're using, Herr Becker," said Wondratschek, without losing his self-control. "It is not my fault that you no longer feel comfortable in Vienna, and I have no other wish than to be of help to you. But I'm not in a hurry, you can take time to think about my suggestion, perhaps you also want to talk with your wife. In any case, I'll send my lawyer to you, that can't do any harm."

"That's how it was," said Olga, "Martin recounted it to me word for word, and the next day the lawyer really did come, with the party badge in his buttonhole, and said, if it were found out that we had money in England, then Marti would wind up in Dachau, and then Marti signed everything. But Wondratschek was afraid that we would compete with him in England, and so Marti also had to sign that we would not go there."

"That contract was signed under duress," I said, "you didn't have to comply with it."

"That's what I told Marti too, but you know how he was, he

was always so proper, under duress or not, and he said, I have signed it, and as a gentleman I will act accordingly."

"And how did you then get to Argentina?"

"That wasn't so difficult, Peterl, but it cost money. Order another piece of strawberry cake for yourself, it is so good here. Do you still remember Schaljapin? All of us took French lessons from him, and Sándor, I think, took English from him too. He had been a rich man in Russia before the revolution, Marti thought he was a count."

"And so he had a Saint Bernard complex?" I asked, as I spooned whipped cream onto the cake.

"A Saint Bernard complex?"

"You must know the joke, Olga. There's a dachshund in Beverly Hills, he comes from Vienna and is upset because he's only a dachshund, and then another dog says to him, why are you upset, you're a very attractive dachshund. I know, says the dachshund, but where I come from I was a Saint Bernard."

Olga laughed. "No, Schaljapin didn't have a Saint Bernard complex, he went from house to house and gave his lessons, but he never spoke about Russia, that was finished for him. But after the *Anschluss*, his time had come."

"He collaborated with the Nazis?"

"No, not that, but he also gave lessons in the embassies, the Argentinian and the Brazilian ones, and now he was Mr. Fix-it. People stood in line-ups for days in front of the Argentinian embassy, but he let us in through the back door. That cost ten thousand schillings because he had to bribe the people in the embassy, but it was worth it, money could get you everything there. It was the same way in Buenos Aires, Dezsö had an Argentinian who arranged the bribes for him. Things didn't go badly for us in Buenos Aires, the firm Gisela Kahn was known everywhere, and we managed a big department store for a Jew from Berlin, without knowing a word of Spanish, you can imagine what a nuisance that was. Marti wanted to stay there, but you know, Rita" – did I forget to mention that their daughter was called Rita? – "had lung problems, she couldn't tolerate the climate."

"And then you went to Los Angeles, and Martin sold his Guarneri violin."

"Yes, Peterl, he sold the Guarneri, he hated to part with it. But he was such a kind man, he always said to me, if I have you, I don't need a Guarneri. With the money from it, we bought the premises here and the sewing machines, we had to start again on a very small scale, Rita helped a lot, she is such a good fashion designer. Now she is only in Los Angeles because of me, she would actually prefer to be with her children in San Francisco, but she doesn't want to leave me alone. By the way, Schaljapin also procured the Argentinian visa for Dezsö, but they had an easier time of it, Mitzi was a *shiksa*, and right after the *Anschluss* Dezsö put everything in her name, the two stores and the apartment and the villa in Pressbaum. Then, when Dezsö and the children were already gone, she smuggled out everything she could, the Persian carpets from the apartment in Vienna and from the villa, all the silverware and so on, actually, she didn't smuggle it herself, the Priminger boy did it for her, you knew him didn't you?"

"I remember him vaguely," I said, "but tell me more exactly."

"He was Mitzi's half-brother, actually his name was Poldi, but we always just called him the Priminger boy, God knows why. A nice boy, always willing to help, but a big Nazi, an illegal one from 1934 on, and then when the Germans came, he was a big shot right away, uniform with oak leaves or something like that, and he made sure the crates got out of the country. He also tried to get Teddy out, but he wasn't able to save him."

"Rhonda told me that," I said, "but I didn't quite understand it. What exactly did happen with Teddy?"

"I would rather tell you that at home, over a whiskey," said Olga, and so we walked to her apartment. It wasn't far, but it took us a while to get there because she was almost ninety and was having trouble with her knees.

"I only know about it from Rhonda too," she said, after we had made ourselves comfortable. "When the crates arrived in Buenos Aires, Dezsö sold everything, Mitzi sold her jewellery, and he opened a store right away. He and my mother were always the most efficient people, and he was making good money again right away, but it wasn't as easy as in Vienna, they worked day and night, he and Mitzi and Rhonda, Teddy was the only one who couldn't or didn't want to, Mitzi always spoiled him so."

"Jenö said that Teddy went around as if he were the uncrowned king of Vienna," I interjected.

"Jenö always spoke ill of people, God rest his soul, but he may not have been entirely wrong there. Teddy was always a little extravagant. In Vienna, Dezsö put up with everything, he never made a fuss about a few hundred schillings, but in Argentina he felt insecure, none of us knew Spanish, and because Teddy liked to sleep in until noon, they quarrelled, and then the boy ran away and worked in a wire factory, that was the beginning of the tragedy."

"Rhonda told me that there was a Communist group among the workers there, Olga."

"Yes, Peterl, and they thought the time had come to assassinate Hitler, and Teddy was supposed to throw the bomb."

"Do you really believe that? It sounds like something from a bad detective novel."

"I don't know what I should believe," said Olga. "I was there then and always met Mitzi and Dezsö for coffee, they believed everything and were terribly worried about the boy, but he wanted to show his Papa that he was a grown-up and what he could do, maybe he just made up the story about the bomb. But it is correct that someone got a forged passport for him, and then he sold his Leica camera to be able to pay for the trip and went to Athens, and from there he wrote home that his friends had reconsidered, it wasn't the right time for an assassination, that would just make a martyr of Hitler. But he stayed with a friend of Dezsö's in Athens, he was well looked after there, he could easily have stayed."

"That wouldn't have done any good, Olga, all the Jews in Greece were murdered too."

"No one could have known that then, Peterl, but of course Mitzi sent him the money for the trip back and begged him to come, and instead, the boy went back to Vienna."

I know the rest of the story from Rhonda, who visited Vienna after the war was over and spoke with the Primingers. "Teddy had a girlfriend in Vienna," Rhonda told me (I had flown to New York for a conference and met her for lunch). "A pretty girl, as blonde as Teddy, pure Aryan, her father had a furniture factory in Mödling, she was sixteen, he was seventeen, and the two of them thought they had found the love of their life. I can imagine how Teddy impressed the girl with his craziness, in comparison with him the other boys were boring, but then the Nazis came, and Resi wasn't so stupid that she still wanted to have anything to do with a Jew. Teddy insisted that she run away and come to him in Buenos Aires or Athens, he sent her one letter after another, and Resi didn't dare to answer. Then when he got the money from Mitzi, he went to Vienna to persuade her. The Primingers wanted to hide him in the cellar under the smokehouse, but he didn't want that, he wanted to wait for Resi on her way to the Gymnasium, but people noticed him, after all, he was known everywhere in Vienna, he was almost a sort of local celebrity, and the Gestapo grabbed him right away. The Priminger boy showed courage, he asked around, soon knew where Teddy was being held, and he went to the Gestapo in his SS uniform. At first they laughed, but because he absolutely wanted to have Teddy and didn't let up, they finally said, if you absolutely want to have the Jew boy, then we'll give him to you, and then they dragged him in. He was unconscious, Poldi told me, and had bled from the mouth and nose. He took him to the hospital right away, but it was too late."

When the uncrowned king of Vienna was laid to rest in the Zentralfriedhof, Poldi Priminger was the only mourner.

CHAPTER EIGHT

The Way to Haifa

1.

BOB IS COURTING in earnest, and Joschi is right – my son's taste isn't bad! The little Moroccan girl, who by the way isn't so little, just so young that she could be my granddaughter, is really very pretty, and her somewhat darker complexion that she has in common with so many North African Jews reminds me of Conchita. Her name is Leah Blum, and her family came to Morocco via France. She tells charming stories about her childhood in Marseilles, and if I were forty years younger, I could fall in love with her. Since Bob knows how happy this makes me, the three of us sometimes dine in the evening at Berkowitz's, enjoy the fillet of beef that they make so well there, and then sit for a long time over coffee and the cognac Bob likes to have at the end of a meal. If only I weren't so tired! It has already happened to me twice that I fell asleep in the middle of our conversation and Bob had to wake me up when it was time to go. When I was younger, I could work effortlessly for twelve hours at a stretch, and now I am completely exhausted after a quite ordinary day without any kind of excitement. So it's just as well that I have almost finished this account. I have to pick up the thread again where I was writing about my position at Bedford College. What I had to do there was stimulating and not nearly as difficult as I had expected. It wasn't difficult for

301

me because I only taught five hours a week, four of which were conversation classes for which no preparation was necessary. It was stimulating, because among my students there were some very pretty girls I got to talk to for an hour a week about German lyric poetry of the 20th century, which was my favourite topic. I spent part of my spare time with a girlfriend who now, much to my regret, lives in Australia; I would love to have a chat with her again. . . . In the college library, whose tall windows let in a lot of light, I worked on a book about Tieck, and at home, since I no longer wrote poetry, I tormented myself with a novel, rewrote the first chapter four times and got nowhere with it. No matter how hard I struggled – after a few quite original sentences, I would start imitating Thomas Mann, and finally I had to admit to myself that I was not only no great poet, but also no great novelist. At the college, though, I just had one of those beginners' posts that were usual then at English universities, where you were automatically let go after three years, if a foreign language assistant from the department didn't happen to be called to another university just then, so that you could move up into his place. So my future was uncertain.

In March of 1950 – during my second year at the College – a professor from Liverpool gave a lecture at the Institute of Germanic Studies of the University of London, which I don't remember, and an hour beforehand sherry was served in a conference room with a big table. On the way from there to the lecture hall, my thesis supervisor told me that there was a vacant position as Assistant Professor in Canada, they had made inquiries of him, was I interested? The three glasses of sherry I had drunk must have made me adventurous. After a short conversation, I said yes, and six months later I was an Assistant Professor at King's University in Queenstown on the north shore of Lake Ontario. I could now insert a long chapter with the heading, "Memoirs of a Former Germanist," and maybe sometime, if I live long enough, I really will write something about it, but that doesn't belong in this account. Here I have to be brief.

At that time, Canada had already been an independent country for a long time, but in Queenstown you sometimes still got the impression you were living in a British colony. It was typical that the university had not looked for a Canadian or brought in someone from Germany or the United States for the position in the German Department, but had made inquiries in England, and in 1951, for the first time in its long history, the university had a president who was born in Canada. In other ways, too, if you disregard its pretty location on the lake, Queenstown was a not atypical small Ontario town. Since I had previously lived only in Vienna and in London, I found the small town stifling at first, but Toronto was easily accessible by train, even New York was not out of reach, and I spent the summer months in England. Then I discovered that you need a car in Canada, and like many of my colleagues, I bought an English one that didn't start in cold weather. (Volkswagen modified the Beetles they shipped to Canada to suit the Canadian climate.) Fortunately, I had interesting colleagues, with whom I could discuss the latest philosophical trends and English lyric poetry. I shared a nice little apartment with an English professor who was an excellent cook, I had a Latvian girlfriend for a long time who was studying psychology and had a post-doctoral research assignment, and although I had to teach four courses (twelve hours a week), I had enough time for research; in short, I led a bachelor's life that, as it seems to me now, left hardly anything to be desired. But as the German proverb has it, when a donkey is too well off, he goes dancing on ice. I got married.

I dine once a week at Berkowitz's or in a fish restaurant on the harbour with Dr. P., the sociologist. A few weeks ago, when I told her about my marriage, she said, "All men are stupid when it comes to women." Then she explained to me at length that many immigrants in a foreign country, for example Jewish refugees in England, suffered from a "refugee neurosis," the desperate need to fit in, to belong, not to be regarded as "different" or as a "foreigner."

That led, not infrequently, to their marrying the wrong woman. . . . I don't know whether this theory holds; but I married Mary Lynn Primrose and to this day do not understand why.

Mary Lynn! She is the mother of my son, and so I have good reason to remember her justly; but does one always have to do the reasonable thing? I must admit, though, that she was both intelligent and pretty and that she had good taste. She always wore the right clothes, and my Uncle Jenö, if he were alive still, would reduce the entire history of my marriage to the formula that I married a fur coat. I had met Mary – she was seventeen years my junior – at the home of a colleague whose student she was, and then everything went very fast, too fast. After spending the first few nights with Mary Engelmann, as she was now called, I began to suspect that I had made a mistake. ("You were really stupid," said Dr. P., when I told her about it a quarter of a century later. "You should have tried it out before you went to the registry office.") So it is perhaps forgivable that I occasionally went back repentantly to the Latvian, especially since I was convinced that Mary knew nothing about it, so it didn't bother her. What did bother her was that our first year of marriage coincided with her last year at university, that living with me took a lot of her time, that she had to clean and cook and that I occasionally liked to have guests in the house, while her main concern was to get good marks in her courses. But it also bothered her that I didn't spend as much time with her as she had expected, that there weren't any "pleasant evenings by the fireside" that she had apparently dreamed of. We didn't have a fireplace, and I was accustomed to spending two or three hours at my desk after dinner while Mary wrote essays for her courses and was glad to be able to do that undisturbed, while at the same time feeling annoyed that I was neglecting her. What bothered me more than that – what hurt my feelings – was not just that things weren't working out too well in bed. Mary was proud of having married a professor, but very quickly lost all interest, indeed all respect for my professional activity. She would never have admitted that – not even to herself

– but it could lead to embarrassing incidents. For example, we had to take Bob to the doctor for some reason a few months after he was born. When we were still sitting in the waiting room fifteen minutes after the time of the appointment and I made the disgruntled remark that I had to be more punctual in my profession, she said – and these are her exact words – "That's different; he saves lives" – a remark that would have wounded me less if it hadn't hit a sore point: sometimes I asked myself if it really made any difference to mankind that I edited Tieck's manuscripts.

Dr. P. was the first person to point out to me the possibility that Mary may have known about my occasional infidelity and that such incidents were, therefore, acts of revenge. At the time, I asked myself why Mary, whose subject was also nothing that could save lives, philosophy, had so little respect for the humanities in the depths of her soul – and the answer to that was comparatively easy. In the fifties, in the course of the delayed reception of existentialism in North America, it had become fashionable to talk about "authentic" and "inauthentic" lifestyles, and I owe my understanding of this terminology to Mary. She didn't engage in any of her activities for their own sake, but for the opinion of others whom she accepted as authorities, so she was the inauthentic person *par excellence*. Thus, for many years, she practised the piano for two or three hours a day in order to earn praise from her teacher. She read Plato and Kant attentively, as long as that resulted in her getting good marks, but she never opened Bertrand Russell's fascinating autobiography that I bought for her to celebrate the completion of her degree. Granted, Dr. P. tells me that all men talk this way about their divorced wives, that I was unforgiving far beyond what is acceptable, and that Mary would probably have much worse things to say about me than I about her. She may be right about that. But for Bobby's sake we were determined to put up with our disagreements, although we weren't always quiet about them. The fact that we separated after all was not my fault: Bob wasn't even a year old when someone new arrived who was soon the talk of the town. He was called Wilfrid

MacDougal, and in him Mary found the authority she had always been seeking.

The little that I know about MacDougal is what he told me himself. He had grown up in Winnipeg, but had studied at the Theological Seminary in Houston, where one day he had a flash of inspiration. It occurred to him during a lecture about the theophanies of the church fathers. It had occurred to him – so he told us over tea, to which I had invited him at Mary's request – that the Jews in the time of David had neither castigated themselves nor strewn ashes on their heads, but had danced; and so the way to God was not repentance, penitence, abstinence and castigation, as his grouchy, senile professors claimed, but joy. This inspiration, so he told me, as he spread butter and honey on a piece of cake, had overwhelmed him in the middle of the lecture, it had gripped him and shaken him like a grizzly bear, and it had changed his life at one blow. He had stood up from his seat in the packed lecture hall and left, never to return there, because many other things followed from this inspiration.

It followed, above all, that the famous theologians, whose supposed knowledge of God brought them huge salaries, understood nothing about the matter – at least not nearly as much as he, Wilfrid MacDougal, who was now obliged to share with his fellow men the radiance that filled him from within. In the light of this radiance he recognized that the suffering Christ on the cross could not be the right model for the worship of God; and while he paused for a moment, because he had his mouth full of cake, it became clear to me that he didn't think much of the Saviour at all. Did he, who as it were had a direct line to God, need a mediator? And as for his disciples, he claimed they had him and so didn't need a mediator, either.

I'm paraphrasing, but think I have correctly conveyed the gist of what MacDougal said. I thought about it for a minute, while I too spread butter and honey on a piece of cake, and then I said, to Mary's horror, as well as I could in English: "So you are, strictly speaking, not a Christian at all, but a goyish Hasid?" He didn't seem to know what a Hasid was, but insisted that he was not only a Christian, but maybe even the only real one. . . .

With this conviction he would indisputably have become a millionaire if he had set up shop as a guru in California. Instead of that, he went to Cambridge, Massaschusetts, where he began to convert Harvard students to his teaching, and in fact, as he maintained (Mary had already heard it all at least three times, but was nevertheless listening as if the archangel Michael were speaking), with considerable success. What had gone wrong, then, with his temple in Cambridge, so that he now had to proclaim the new Gospel in Queenstown, he didn't say. In any case, MacDougal was here now seeking converts. He found enough to be able after a few months to afford the low price for a small church that had been standing empty because the roof leaked. There, his disciples didn't dance, as in the time of David, in front of the Ark of the Covenant, but in front of a pseudo-Gothic altar, and Mary played the organ: if you can play the piano, and if God helps, MacDougal had explained to her, then you can play the organ too, and Mary played that instrument, as I was told, quite well. She practised again, too – organ, not piano; and she practised with surprising diligence, because what was the praise of a professor or an elderly piano teacher in comparison with the praise of an immediate tool of God, as MacDougal incontestably was? She of course regretted that she could not play the organ and dance in front of the altar at the same time, but in spite of his direct line to the Almighty, MacDougal could not bring about the miracle of simultaneity: the Supreme Being does not want everything at the same time. Mac-Dougal could console her, however, by pointing out that everything you didn't get here you got a thousandfold above the clouds. . . .

O golden source from a sacred chalice! MacDougal preached about God's unfathomable love and omnipotence, the disciples danced before the altar, Mary played the organ, and as the snow melted, the water splashed down through the leaky roof. When spring came and the laburnum and lilacs were in bloom,

307

they set up camp on the shore of one of the small lakes to the north of Queenstown, the disciples danced in the open, and instead of organ music there was choral singing. While Mary now danced and sang, so that the miracle of simultaneity was granted her after all, I was ever more desperately trying to think of a way out – and then I too was granted a miracle. All of MacDougal's disciples paid a tithe, but since most of them were students and therefore mostly out of cash, it didn't cover the costs of the banquets associated with the worship services. By the time the trees beneath which they had danced while singing lost their leaves, MacDougal had to take out a second mortgage on the church, and when the first snow fell, he had, as he made it known, received a sign from on high that Queenstown was too small a sphere of activity for him. Three weeks later he left town with a half dozen disciples, among them Mary. The fact that he had decided to take her with him may prove that the Lord in his unfathomable love was no less concerned with my well-being than with MacDougal's. The fact that she went with him proves God's unfathomable omnipotence.

But now it is high time to explain why I changed my profession, even though I very much enjoyed reading Rilke or Kafka with my students. For this purpose I have to go back a long way and first mention that my autism, as I have called it in this account so far with coquettish exaggeration, did not always hinder me from taking notice of the outside world. For example, to start with something important, I had spent the 29th of November 1947, like every other weekday back then, in the Reading Room of the British Museum, and when I heard the news on the radio that evening about the vote in the United Nations, I forgot myself, my bad poetry, my dissertation and the girls I slept with, and was ecstatic. I hadn't had any contact with devout Jews for so long that I didn't even take notice of Yom Kippur, but it did affect me that there was now to be a Jewish state, and when the British mandate ended the following May, and Syria, Iraq, Egypt, Lebanon and Transjordan with the Arab League that had been trained by Sir John Bagot Glubb attacked Israel, and Egyptian airplanes bombed Tel Aviv, it affected me. It was fifty million Arabs against one million Jews. I bought newspapers, sat by the radio for hours, and it distressed me that there was nothing I could do to help (I had never in my life held a weapon in my hand). So I looked out through a tiny hole from the cocoon I was wrapped up in. I don't really know what I should call the development that began then. *The Way into the Open* is the title of a novel by Schnitzler; that would be a possibility. Another would be an expression I found in Heimito von Doderer, "becoming a *mensch*," at least, when you think of the significance that a *mensch* has in Yiddish: you are a *mensch* in this sense if you know that there are other people who are just as important as you yourself, and if you act accordingly; and I had taken the first step on this path. A further step was perhaps the move to Canada. From the moment I went ashore in Montreal to take the train to Queenstown, the stomach aches and the diarrhoea that had plagued me for so many years disappeared, thus proving that they had been psychosomatic. It is quite likely, though, that I was not completely cured, that a good part of what I had experienced and suppressed, the death of my father, Liptauer, the *Anschluss*, life as a refugee, the internment, was still festering within me, otherwise I would not have married Mary Primrose. It may also have helped that my appointment at King's University gave me financial security, although that cannot have played a big role, or else I would not have decided to put an end to my career as a Germanist. What was good for me, though, was the wide expanse that surrounded me when I drove out of Queenstown. During my first few Canadian years I had spent every summer in England, and I can still distinctly recall the feeling of freedom that overcame me every time the ship on the return trip sailed up the St. Lawrence, and I looked out from the deck on the endless expanse to the north, on the long fields and little villages with their church steeples glistening in the sun. Here in Israel there is no such space, we're stuck on top of each other in this tiny land (and I wish the politicians in the Knesset and worldwide who are constantly pressuring us to give back the Golan Heights understood how tiny this land is). But here, instead of that wide expanse, there is something else that makes me feel good, the warmth of the stable: in my part of Haifa there are almost only Jews. . . .

I'm shaking my head as I read over this last paragraph, first of all because the great expanses in Canada surely contributed much less to my development than my simply getting older, the natural way to maturity that would have followed the same course anywhere else. Second, because the warmth of the stable in Israel isn't all it's made out to be. Israel is a land with a large minority that hate us. All the more reason for me to feel comfortable in my quarter of Haifa where I am surrounded almost exclusively by Jews – but why? I don't even know what that actually is, a Jew. It's obvious that it has nothing to do with race, we are all half-breeds. Just look at my blonde and blue-eyed mother and compare her with my black-haired father or the dark-skinned Jews from Ethiopia or the Yemeni Jews who look like Arabs. That it also has nothing to do with religion is adequately demonstrated by my own case. I once took part in a panel discussion on this topic in which we ultimately agreed that a Jew is whoever feels he is a Jew.

I passionately felt I was a Jew in 1948 when the young state of Israel had to fend off forces ten times its own. I also passionately felt I was a Jew when the Suez crisis broke out. From the fall of 1955, the Soviet Union had been indirectly providing the Egyptian army with airplanes and tanks by sending them through Czechoslovakia. The Israelis were convinced that it would come to a war, and that it was better to wage it before the Egyptians had learned how to use their new weapons. Gamal Abdel Nasser was agitating not only against Israel, but also against the "imperialist forces," France and England, and at the end of September, 1956, he expropriated the Suez Canal Company. Now there were secret negotiations between London, Paris and Jerusalem, and on the 29th of October Israeli paratroops landed in the Sinai. The poorly prepared and misinformed Egyptians were quickly driven back, and on the 6th of November British and French troops landed in the canal zone "to separate the warring armies." But what had begun with a military victory ended with a diplomatic defeat. The Soviet Union threatened to intervene, President Eisenhower exerted pressure in Jerusalem, London and Paris, and on the 7th of November the United Nations, with 67 votes, called for the "immediate withdrawal" of the Israeli troops from the Sinai. The next day the commotion was over: the diplomatically isolated government in Jerusalem promised through its representative in New York to obey the United Nations' resolution. We know today that Israel was not in serious danger during the Suez crisis, but back then it didn't always look like that. As long as the fighting went on, I sat as if spellbound by the radio or in front of the television, and it tormented me, as it had in 1948, that I was unable to help. I never forgot this torment.

The ten years after the Suez crisis were a time of relative peace in Israel, but not in my life. These years contain the comedy of my marriage, which was not helped by the fact that I was working then with dogged diligence on short scholarly articles and on my second book. Certainly, what drove me on was ambition, but the greater reward for me was my delight in the work itself, the triumph when I succeeded in deciphering an almost illegible sentence in one of Tieck's drafts, the pleasure provided by an elegant turn of phrase, or the pride when I believed I had come up with a new and in my eyes better interpretation of a famous novella; but it was certainly also the fact that the work at my desk was part of the cocoon in which I was still enclosed. But if I had too little time for Mary – for Bob I always had time, I was always prepared to get up from my desk to change the baby's diapers and spread talcum powder on his bottom. I loved giving him his bottle, to the annoyance of Mary, who saw that as an intrusion into her world – not entirely incorrectly: when you have a sucking child in your arms, you really are assuming the mother's role. But she didn't disapprove nearly as much when the baby had gas and it was I who got up in the early morning hours and carried him around the room until he fell asleep again. For the first time in my life, there was something that was more important to me than myself, and with that I was already halfway to freedom. Then, when the knight in shining armour came and took Mary with him into the wide blue yonder, Bob distracted me completely from myself: it wasn't easy to practise my profession and to take care of the child. Then I met Herbert Snyder, who without wanting to or even knowing he was doing it, threw my life off course.

Snyder was an American from Philadelphia, and had written important books about Berkeley and John Stuart Mill. He had landed at King's University, which didn't have a doctoral program in his subject back then, because he had spoiled his career with his insuppressible talent for catty remarks. For many months after his arrival in Queenstown we knew each other only by sight, although I had heard about his legendary erudition from colleagues. Our first longer conversation took place in New York when we were both giving papers at the annual conference of the Modern Language Association, he about Hume, I about Thomas Mann's *Death in Venice*. Two Germanists who taught at Yale and Harvard had published articles that had to do with my topic, and I acknowledged them briefly at the beginning of my paper. When the session was over, Snyder came up to me with a grin, shook my hand (he had been in Germany for a long time) and said: "I know you would like to get a job at Yale or Harvard, but your kowtowing to Weigand and Hatfield won't do you any good!" I was shocked, but also amused, since I knew about his sharp tongue. At that time, for example, there was a female English professor (women professors of high standing were still quite rare in the sixties) who was famous for her brilliant papers delivered with exceptional élan and skill as a performer, but Herbert Snyder's jokes about her were circulating busily behind her back. Since she – an imposing figure – liked to wear jeans and had red hair, he referred to her as the "red devil with the tight pants" – a turn of phrase my Uncle Jenö would have envied him. I explained to Snyder that I had had to refer to Hatfield and Weigand for purely professional reasons, but instead of contenting himself with that, he asked me if I really considered it meaningful to add a twenty-first interpretation to the twenty interpretations of Thomas Mann's novella that had appeared in the past few years. That annoyed me, and I resorted to a counterattack: "If you think like that, what about your paper on Hume?"

"I am ten years older than you," he said, "and I write my papers only out of despair."

A conversation ensued that we continued in the bar of the Hilton Hotel, after I had phoned the friends in Queenstown who were taking care of Bob during my absence. Snyder told me that after the early deaths of his parents he had been brought up by Dominican monks and educated for the priesthood. Shortly after his ordination, though, he had converted to Lutheranism "out of anger about the Pope's theological stupidity." Then, with borrowed money, he had studied with Bultmann, chewed his way through the entire "God is dead theology," and when he finally had lost all belief, he returned to his birthplace, Philadelphia.

In good German, he quoted the beginning of the first monologue in Goethe's *Faust*: "Alas, I studied Philosophy . . ." and then said bitterly that he, unlike Faust, hadn't tried magic or made a pact with the devil, although he would only too gladly have done so, if he could believe in the devil. His problem was that he couldn't believe in anything, but neither could he wipe out the fact of his baptism. He had sat down between two chairs. If you looked at the basics, you saw only comedy and misery, and the only thing that still made it bearable was the fun in formulating a malicious phrase.

After our return to Queenstown, we often met for a chat, a game of chess or a conversation about a new book; but I wouldn't have had to mention him in this account if, six months after our talk in the Hilton, he had not made a remark that threw me off course. Without knocking, he had come into my office with a wide grin on his face and said: "Are you hard at work teaching the German alphabet too?"

"The German alphabet?"

"You know, Peter," said Snyder, "the Greek alphabet: alpha, beta, gamma, delta; the Hebrew alphabet: aleph, beth, gimel, daleth; the Latin alphabet: a, b, c, d; the German alphabet: Auschwitz, Belsen, Chelmno, Dachau." That was all, but it was as if I had been hit by a bolt from the blue, or as if the roof had caved in. It wasn't clear to me at all what Snyder had in mind with his remark. He had probably just burst into my office so abruptly out of pure delight in the cutting comment that had just occurred to him, but I had the feeling that an avalanche had been started. (I'm piling on the metaphors because that's the best way I can describe what was happening to me.) So I did what I had to do – I taught a German class, spoke with a small group of students about the first act of *Ifigenia*, read the incoming mail, answered a few letters and then walked through the streets of the town like a sleepwalker, without seeing what went on around me. I had suddenly become fully conscious of the fact that I had spoken with my students about Goethe and Hölderlin, about Keller and Storm, about Kafka, Thomas Mann and Brecht, but never about the Holocaust. It disturbed me that I knew so little about Auschwitz, Belsen and Dachau and had never even heard of Chelmno. I went to the library, took down half a dozen books and began to read. Then I read for days, for whole nights, indiscriminately, whatever I could find in the library in Queenstown or get from Toronto (a book list today would look different): the Auschwitz documentation by Kraus and Kulka, Eisenbach's book about the Holocaust in Poland, Reitlinger's *Final Solution*, the two volumes by Braham about the extermination of the Jews in Hungary, Grossman's report on Treblinka, Primo Levi's book about Auschwitz, Mary Berg's *Diary from the Warsaw Ghetto*, Crankshaw on the Gestapo, the report of the Polish-Soviet Commission on Maidanek, the autobiography of the Auschwitz commander Höss, Miklós Nyiszlis's appalling eyewitness account about Auschwitz with the uncomprehending foreword by Bruno Bettelheim, Elie Cohen on human behaviour in the camps – read until I had to stop because my stomach aches started again (my doctor diagnosed a duodenal ulcer) and because the images of horror pursued me into my sleep, until I hardly dared to go to bed anymore.

But the fact that I stopped reading didn't help me much, because now nothing distracted me from the awareness that I had done nothing while those dreadful events were taking place, I had thought of nothing but myself. While the machinery of murder was put into action in Chelmno, I had learned Latin and read Catullus. While the deportation trains ran to Belsen and Treblinka, I had been in bed with a girlfriend. While the chimneys flamed in Auschwitz, I had written poetry. The world – my world – had been destroyed, and I had done nothing. That could no longer be mended, I was branded with it, but did I now, in Queenstown, have to celebrate the literature of the murderers with my students? Was that what Herbert Snyder had wanted to tell me? I shook off the thought; Goethe's *Ifigenia* had not been made less splendid because one hundred and fifty years later a Hitler had come to power. But the fact that *Ifigenia* had not prevented this takeover – did that not prove its futility? Goethe's house on the Frauenplan in Weimar wasn't an hour away from the Ettersberg, where the Buchenwald concentration camp stood, and yet it might as well have been on another planet: the one, the concentration camp, was reality, the other, German Classicism, was the dreams of effete intellectuals. You could not see the Ettersberg from Goethe's house. Schiller's essay on "Aesthetic Education"? There were SS officers who relaxed from their duty in the extermination camps by listening to Beethoven string quartets.

Of course these thoughts about the powerlessness of the mind were nothing new to me, I had been tossing them about for a long time. But now it was different. From the powerlessness of the mind, a theorist like Gottfried Benn could draw the comfortable conclusion that intellectuals enjoyed the freedom to do as they pleased; since I had learned the German alphabet I could no longer afford to grant myself that freedom. I had, as best as I could, to pay a debt, and if this debt could not be paid – it could not be paid – then I at least had to learn to live with it. While the chimneys flamed in Auschwitz, I had written poetry, and with that, I had gambled away the right to spend my life with Trakl and Hölderlin. While the Arabs attacked Israel, I had sat in comfort at the radio – "I know nothing better on Sundays and holidays / Than a conversation about war and war-cries" (townsman in Goethe's *Faust I*). But if that was the case, then I would at least have to show now – show *myself* – that I had at last understood that other people also existed and that I owed them something. . . . But how should I show that to myself? I had to do penance, but how did one do penance? I had to go to Israel.

That was absurd. Looking back, I can of course see that it was absurd, but it was still the right thing to do; without making such a desperate decision, I would not have been able to go on living, and I do not regret the decision: I am happy here. But what should I do in Israel? Give lectures on Schiller's aesthetics in the shadow of The Wailing Wall? I walked up and down Princess Street for hours, to the end of the city and back again, without being able to think of anything but the old refrain: while the machinery of murder was operating in Chelmno, I had read Catullus. While the trains rolled to Belsen, I had visited my girl-friends. Then I had a vision, completely concrete, as if I were seeing it in technicolour, of how Peter Engelmann, an entirely new and completely changed Peter Engelmann, drove from one kibbutz to another in a little old Peugeot and looked after the cows. That was also absurd (in Israel there are more veterinarians than cows), but it consoled me. A few weeks before the end of the semester, I took a few days off, got in the car and drove to Guelph, where there is a famous faculty of veterinary medicine. The Dean of the faculty, with whom I had an appointment – his name was Gary Peterson, and he deserves to be on the honour roll in the history of my life – listened to me with disbelief. Did I really think it was meaningful, he asked, because of an *idée fixe*, a quirk, to jump track at my age and start all over again? Moreover, I didn't have the necessary prerequisites and could not be admitted to study in the faculty. Fortunately, he was a patient man and listened to me attentively, and when he had convinced himself that I was serious about my decision, he promised to help. In Queenstown, I took the prerequisite biology and chemistry courses, and in 1962 I moved to Guelph. I can't claim that my student years were a pleasure. My brain could no longer soak up information like a sponge, as it had twenty years previously, and I had financial worries. The fact that it was manageable at all was due to the IBM and Alcan shares I had bought years before that now increased enormously in value, and to helpful people. Now and then I was able to work in the German Department, Peterson provided me with a scholarship, and the energetic widow of a successful lawyer who had four children of her own took Bob in when I could not take care of him. Bob still sends her a postcard every few months.

Five years after my move to Guelph, I could sit the final exams. For me – for my "healing," if you will, but I don't like those big words – it was just the right time, it could not have been better. On the 10th of May, 1967, after I had sold the last stocks and the little furniture I possessed, Bob and I flew to Tel Aviv. The Israeli government provided well for the "educated" immigrants from the West (and, I am ashamed to admit, not nearly as well for the "primitive" immigrants from the Islamic countries). There was an intensive Hebrew course for me and, as a provisional measure, a children's home for Bob. On the evening of the 15th of May, 1967, I heard on the radio that Nasser had ordered the total mobilization of the Egyptian army. On the 17th, three Egyptian divisions marched into the Sinai, and on the 18th, the sparse United Nations troops who were supposed to have kept the peace withdrew. On the 22nd, the Egyptians closed off the Gulf of Akaba to Israeli ships; that was a *casus belli*. On the 25th, Nasser announced to the Egyptian parliament that the task of the Arab nations was the complete annihilation of Israel. With that, the *hamtana* began, the waiting period, for the Israelis the most nerve-racking time since 1948. I was somewhat distracted from it by cramming Hebrew vocabulary twelve hours a day. Then Mosche Dayan was named Minister of Defence, and on the 5th of June,

317

the Israelis destroyed the Egyptian air force. In the meantime, I had gone to the military authorities in Tel Aviv and had offered my help: if you can sew up a cat again after an operation, you can also take care of wounded humans. So I was there when our soldiers freed the old part of Jerusalem and conquered the Golan Heights. . . . By the way, I also helped in the Yom Kippur War, and so I could send Mary, whose surname has not been Engelmann for a long time now, but has married for a second time, a card with the four words: "I have saved lives." But I am too old for such foolishness.

In a field hospital on the Golan Heights, I met a veterinarian from Frankfurt who offered me a position as assistant in his clinic in Haifa, and for many years, even after I had acquired the clinic, I drove out two or three times a week to various kibbutzes in the vicinity. . . . I know that I cannot ever make up for what I failed to do during the World War, but I have learned to live with my past.

2.

"I have a problem," Bob had said to me a few weeks ago over dinner. "Leah's parents want an Orthodox wedding, but their rabbi refuses. He says I am not a proper Jew. . . ."

"And *you* are not refusing? You have always been such an atheist!"

"I got my atheism from you, Peter, so you don't need to make fun of me. But for Leah's sake I probably have to swallow the bitter pill, if it can be done."

"You will have to grow a beard, and I will buy you a caftan," I said, but then I did promise to help. I visited Leah's parents, and with their approval I found a liberal rabbi who was prepared to turn a blind eye, but who adhered to the beautiful old rite that is hardly any different today in Haifa than it was a hundred years ago in Tapolca, when my grandmother married her Josef.

The ceremony took place on a Tuesday, because on a Tuesday and only on that day, the Lord had said twice while creating the world that it was good. While the guests partook of the cold buffet that consisted mainly of Moroccan delicacies, Bob and Leah, who, as was customary, were fasting, admired the golden illuminations on the *ketubah*, the marriage contract. After the contract had been signed by two witnesses, Bob pulled the veil Leah was wearing down over her face, because Rebecca had been wearing a veil when she saw Isaac for the first time, and the rabbi spoke the blessing that the sons of Bethuel had spoken over Rebecca: "You, our sister, grow to many thousand times a thousand."

In front of the *baldachin* that was standing outside, Bob put on the white coat that devout Jews wear on Yom Kippur, and Leah, who looked so delightful in her wedding dress that it brought tears to my eyes, walked solemnly around him seven times, because it says seven times in the Torah: "and when a man takes a wife." The rabbi spoke the blessing over the bride and groom, they sipped wine from a silver cup, Bob put the ring on Leah's finger and repeated the old wording after the rabbi: "*Harei at m'kudäschät*" (with this ring, be sacred to me according to the law of Moses and Israel). Then the rabbi read the text of the *ketubah*, and the seven guests of honour on whom Jakob Blum and I had agreed said the *sheva berachos*. Finally – that was the end of the ceremony – the cantor placed a glass wrapped in a napkin on the floor under the *baldachin*, and Bob crushed it underfoot; because just as he now crushed the glass, so the temple had been destroyed. . . .

It goes without saying that now there was a banquet and toasts to the bride and groom, but I had become pensive and was glad when, long after midnight, I could sit alone at my desk and didn't have to talk anymore. "This year here, next year in Jerusalem," my ancestors had said for two thousand years at the end of the Seder, but Haifa was just as good, and I would have descendants in this land. It would not be easy for them, but it has seldom been easy for the descendants of Abraham. What did it say about

319

him? "Then he gave up the ghost, and died in a good old age, an old man, and full of years; and was gathered to his people." That's how I wish my end to be – if possible (in contrast to Abraham) with a cigarette between my lips.

Coda

1.

MARRIAGE AND CHILDREN! There is no better ending for a novel. But this account cannot end that way; I still have a duty to fulfill.

My family was lucky. I know of parents who lost three sons in the First World War, but Jenö, Dezsö, Sándor, Ferenc and Jakob all came home again. After the *Anschluss* we knew that we had to leave. From March of 1938 until the outbreak of the war, the Austrian Jews had a year and a half to emigrate, and two-thirds of us, about 120,000, succeeded. Of the remaining 60,000, only a few survived. So there were two clear turning-points, the *Anschluss* and the outbreak of the war. The fate of the Hungarian Jews depended on very confused domestic, diplomatic and military developments, with which I am not very familiar, since I don't know Hungarian, and there is not very much about it in the libraries here. The decades around the turn of the century were, despite such events as drove my grandparents out of the country, not a bad time for the Hungarian Jews. They lived in a state where the feudal social structure had survived much longer than in the European West. There was almost no middle class, and the Jews filled the gap. They founded the factories, directed the banks, bought and sold the cattle and studied at the universities. In 1914, almost every second lawyer and almost every second physician in Budapest was a Jew. But if it was the Jews who helped Hungary become a modern country, you could thank them for it or not thank them for it; for you could also think that it was the Jews who profited the most from the modernization. The anti-Semitic propaganda had not let up again since the trial of Tiszaeszlár. The justice system was "Jewified," the hospitals were "Jewified," the university was "Jewified," the press was "Jewified," and it probably goes without saying that the banking system was "Jewified." This you could read for thirty, forty, fifty years in the press that wasn't Jewified but existed in spite of it all, while the priests preached anti-Semitism from the pulpit. During the White Terror there were pogroms; it's true that the *numerus clausus* that was introduced shortly afterwards was soon abolished again, but after 1918 it was the first anti-Semitic legislation in Europe.

After the dissolution of the Hapsburg Empire, Hungary had lost about two-thirds of its territory, so that there were now three million Hungarians living outside its borders. That provided the right-wing parties with a second program in addition to their rabble-rousing propaganda against the Jews, it gave them chauvinism. More than half a century after I saw it, I still clearly remember the huge flower bed in Balatonfüred, the picturesque resort on Lake Balaton that we visited in 1933 with Ruben Kálman and his family; it showed a map of the former Hungary, on which the areas lost since the Treaty of Trianon were planted with red geraniums. Beneath it, written with red flowers, the caption: NEM NEM SOHA – "No, no never," as my mother explained to me. Hungary's foreign policy, until it was dictated from the Kremlin, revolved around nothing but the revision of the Treaty of Trianon. The fascist right flourished, and the pressure on the Jews increased steadily. But the Hungarian Jews believed in their country and loved it. Nothing illustrates this better than the fact that Aaron Kálman, the schoolteacher, was annoyed that he did not have a "proper" Hungarian first name, and he had chosen Hungarian as his main teaching subject. His happiest hours were when he recited Petöfi in a musty classroom with a tile stove in the corner. . . .

When he read a particularly poisonous editorial in one of the newspapers lying about in the teachers' room in the school, he said – with a common word that we repeated without thinking – like a thousand other Hungarian Jews, *megússzuk* – we can put up with it, we'll survive.

As for his brother, the rabbi, he was, like his father, a moderate reformer, who wore a small trimmed beard instead of a full beard, a small cap on his head instead of a wide-brimmed felt hat, and so when he walked from his house to the temple he hardly looked any different from a Protestant minister. He preached in Hungarian, but understood better than anybody else how to offend neither the "progressive" members of his community nor the orthodox ones. The community in which my grandfather had earned his living with such difficulty as a shoemaker had become prosperous, and Ruben could afford an assistant rabbi who conducted the service when he was visiting in Papá or Veszprem or was on holiday in Abrahamhegy – a holiday that no one begrudged him: he was not only a good diplomat, but also a scholar, and it was known that he didn't get up early in Abrahamhegy to catch carp, like his brother, but spent the morning hours with his books and with academic correspondence. Incidentally, like his brother he associated almost exclusively with Jews.

That was true of the children as well, who in this regard hardly grew up any differently than I did in Vienna. There was nothing intentional about it on either side; it just happened all by itself, it simply did not occur to a Christian to invite a Jew to go for a walk with him, and vice versa. But that means that the children, Ruben's Arpád and Aaron's two boys, at least initially, as ten- or twelve-year-olds, were not under pressure, that they, metaphorically speaking, did not feel the noose that was already around their necks.

It was not a bad life. Rachel Kálman suffered from asthma, so things were quite quiet in the rabbi's house, but Aaron loved company and liked it when the children brought friends home with them. They had a piano, a frequent guest played the violin, they made short trips to Budapest two or three times a year that included a visit to the opera, they spent the summers in Abrahamhegy, and Árpád had grown up to be an unusually handsome lad who was spoiled by the girls. . . . But it could not be denied that things were getting darker in the world around them. Everywhere, in Tapolca too, there were more and more Nyilas, the Hungarian national socialists, who marched through the streets in their uniforms and whose vicious songs could be heard in the house even when you shut the windows, and it didn't look as if the world were willing to put a stop to Hitler's game. In March of 1938 the Germans marched into Austria, and at the end of May, the parliament in Budapest with a large majority passed a law that would limit the admission of Jews to the professions. A few days later, the first of a series of conversations took place in which the Kálman brothers discussed the future. "The government passed the law to take the wind out of the Nazis' sails," said Aaron.

"I know," said Ruben. "What will it do next for that reason?"

"Hungary is the land of Petöfi," said Aaron.

"Germany was once the land of Goethe," said Ruben. "Look at it now."

"Don't be so pessimistic. In Hungary, only a little more than five percent of the population is Jewish. In the course of the years, the law is supposed to limit the participation of Jews in the professions to twenty percent. Is that really such a terrible injustice?"

"It takes away our equal rights. If there are so many Jewish physicians, it's because we work hard, because we study, because we make an effort. No one has given us anything."

"Megússzuk," said Aaron. "This too will pass."

"Maybe, maybe not. From day to day I see more Nyilas, and who knows how long the government will last."

And then the rabbi said, and with that he belonged to the minority of Hungarian Jews who did not just say megússzuk: "Think of the children. Do me the favour, Aaron, travel to Budapest and let yourself be put on the American waiting list. That can't do any harm, it doesn't obligate you to anything, and who knows what the future will bring. János in Brooklyn can provide you with an affidavit."

"Why me and not you? And what should I live on in America? Hungarian teachers are not needed there."

"Rachel can't travel any great distance with her asthma," said Ruben, "and I can't leave my community in the lurch, especially not now. Now, they need comfort. All of you are healthy, and you are not yet fifty. It won't be easy for you, but you can retrain."

"That's all nonsense," said Aaron. "The White Terror has passed, and the terrible episode of the Nazis will pass as well."

But Aaron himself didn't quite believe what he was saying, and after another conversation with Ruben, in which his wife also took part, he travelled to Budapest and went to the American consulate. A year later, he had reason to be grateful to his brother for his advice. In September, Munich had sold out, and in May 1939, the Hungarian parliament passed the Second Jewish Law, which mandated the exclusion of Jews from the civil service and the business world. There was no longer any talk of twenty percent, and in the next four years, all Jewish teachers would be dismissed. Aaron wrote the long overdue letter to his cousin in Brooklyn. In September, the war began, and everything seemed to be running as Hitler had planned. The Germans occupied half of Poland, they occupied Denmark and Norway, they overran the Netherlands and Belgium, and in June of 1940 they were in Paris. Who doesn't like to be on the winners' side? In November, after hesitating for a long time, Hungary became a member of the Axis. Since the American quota for Hungarian citizens was far more generous than for Austrians, the American visa for Aaron and his family arrived while it was still possible to leave the country. There was a sad goodbye. The women cried. Aaron promised to have Arpád come after them, but Arpád didn't want that. "Only if Papa and Mama come too," he said morosely. "Maybe they'll need me."

In June of 1941, the Germany army invaded the Soviet Union, and the Germans seemed at first to succeed in the East as well as they had succeeded the previous year in the West. Hungarian troops were marching with them.

At the beginning of August, the Third Jewish Law, which corresponded roughly to the Nuremberg Laws, was passed in Budapest. The community in and around Tapolca became as poor again as it had been a hundred years before. Ruben, who had to make such decisions on his own, reduced his own salary to a third of what it had been and sold the house in Abrahamhegy. Then the tables seemed to turn again. On December 7, 1941, the Japanese bombed Pearl Harbour, and four days later, in an act of total megalomania, Hitler declared war on the United States. Stalingrad did not fall, and in March of 1942, when Rachel Kálman baked the Haman-doughnuts for the Purim festival with a few eggs and a handful of flour that she had somehow managed to get, Arpád, who took the risk of listening to the British radio stations, said: "Hitler will fare like Haman, and so will his friends in Hungary."

In July of 1943, Mussolini was overthrown, and in the East the initiative passed to the Soviet Union. The Hungarian Jews were starving, but hopeful – and then the catastrophe came suddenly and unexpectedly. At the beginning of March, 1944, it was clear to everyone who could hear genuine news that the Germans had lost the war. The government in Budapest was negotiating with the Allies, Hitler ordered the occupation of the country, and on the night of the 18th of March German troops crossed the Hungarian border. On the 19th a special action unit from Mauthausen reached Budapest, and two days after that Adolf Eichmann arrived to organize the "Final Solution" for Hungary. On the 23rd of March a long proclamation dictated by Eichmann appeared in *A Magyar Zsidók Lapja*, the only Jewish newspaper that still existed in Hungary. There was no reason for panic, no one would be arrested "on account of his Jewishness," the "Jewish religious, cultural and social life" would continue to exist. On the 5th of April the Jewish star was introduced, on the 22nd the rations for Jews were reduced to the minimum to sustain life, on the 28th the first transport to

Auschwitz left from Kistarcsa, and on the 15th of May the fully deployed Hungarian police began the mass transports.

Eichmann's plan was simple: he wanted to kill as many Jews as possible before the Russians occupied the country. So he divided Hungary into zones, and the deportations began in the East, in the areas that had been annexed by Hungary since 1938; then followed north Hungary, south Hungary east of the Danube and Transdanube, and finally, Budapest was still supposed to follow; but it didn't come to that, so that more than 140,000 Jews in the capital city survived. On the 7th of July, 1944 (really as late as the 7th of July, 1944?), the Regent, Nicholas Horthy, discovered where and for what purpose the Jews were being deported, and ordered it to stop; but for about 450,000 of the Jews in "Greater Hungary" it was too late. On the morning the 3rd of July – four days before Horthy stopped the deportations – the notorious rusty bus stinking of diesel oil had stopped in front of the Kálmans' house, followed by a Volkswagen with two policemen and an SS man. The policeman who knocked on the door with his rifle butt said, using the familiar rather than the formal form of address: "You have two minutes to pack." In the bus, from which the seats had been removed, there were about twenty Jews standing up, men, women and children; Ruben knew them all. The bus made the rounds, and when it drove out of Tapolca three hours later, it was packed full.

Ruben knew the village that the bus reached two hours later: Zalaegerszeg, where there was a small Jewish community and a temple. The bus drove through a gate in a wooden fence into the old Gypsy quarter and stopped, the SS man roared: "Get out." The alleyway was full of people lying on the ground, alone or in small piles, sleeping or dead – you couldn't tell. It stank of rotting carcasses. In a corner near the fence that blocked off the street, a policeman with a club was beating a man who was lying on the ground. An SS man with a cigarette in the corner of his mouth was watching. They stood around until it got dark, and the Kálmans spent the night pressed close to each other on the cobblestones. In the morning an SS officer made a short speech, a man in civilian clothes translated into Hungarian: they were supposed to line up in rows of five and be ready to march. The frightened people ran around in confusion, and the policemen – there were a dozen or more of them – hit out at them with clubs and rifle butts until the gate in the fence opened and the column that had been formed began to move.

At the railway platform, a long row of cattle cars was waiting with "G.A. Resettlers" written on them. The SS officer roared "undress," and the man in civilian clothes translated. The people in the column didn't understand; they were supposed to take their clothes off here, on the platform, in the open? Then the policemen started hitting out again at the helpless people standing there, and Arpád saw naked women for the first time in his life. The policemen and a few helpers in civilian clothes searched through the clothing and the small amount of luggage for valuables and tore up the documents. Then the SS officer roared: "Get dressed and get on," and the clubs went into action again. There were too many people. When the sliding doors were shut by the policemen, there was hardly enough room to stand.

In each car there was one pail with water and one pail for excrement, but anyone not standing directly beside it could not reach it in the over-crowded car. After a while – for the people locked inside it seemed to be hours – the train started to move, no one knew where it was going. It was a long trip, it seemed endless. It stank of excrement and cold sweat; people were suffering from thirst. On the second day of the journey, Rachel, whose husband and son were holding her upright with an effort, began to wheeze. When she stopped wheezing, Ruben closed her eyes and let her slip down to the floor. Fragments of the Haggadah were going through Arpád's confused mind: "And the evening and the morning came. This year here, next year in Israel. This year servitude, next year freedom."

"You should know, Abraham, that your descendants will lead an unsettled life in lands that do not belong to them, where they will be made slaves and will be oppressed for four hundred years. But I also judge the people who will oppress them."

"Have mercy, Eternal God, on your people: You led us out of Egypt with a strong hand and with an outstretched arm, and for that we give thanks and praise and glorify your name. Have mercy, Eternal God. . . . It is not the dead who praise the Lord."

Loaded with the living and the dead, the train rolled into Auschwitz on the fourth day of the journey. The sliding doors opened, and the cars spewed out the survivors. It was more than a metre from the floor of the cattle car down to the hard clay soil. Those who fell did not get up again. The smell of burning flesh and hair hung in the misty air, in the background they could see huge, square chimneys with flames shooting out the tops. A man in an officer's uniform made a speech that was translated by a man in striped overalls: they were to go immediately to the dressing rooms – the officer pointed to ten descending cement steps – to get ready for a shower and disinfection; so they should get undressed, tie their clothes and shoes together and hang them on the wall, note the number on the hook so that they could find their clothes again after the shower; then there would be hot coffee. There were benches and coat hooks in the huge room. Arpád helped his father, who could hardly stand anymore.

After a few minutes, an SS man opened an oak door that led directly to a second huge room: cement floor, glaring light, perforated metal columns that led from the floor to the low ceiling. Hitting them with their rifle butts, SS men drove more and more naked bodies into the room, until it was as full as the cattle cars. Men in striped overalls with a green patch sewn on them pushed the door shut and bolted it. Then the light went out.

A well-polished car with the insignia of the Red Cross stopped outside the entrance, an SS officer at the wheel. A man wearing the uniform of the medical corps got out and took a basket with four big cans from the back of the car. They were pretty cans, yellow, with a red rim around the top and bottom. On the upper rim it said in capital letters: POISON GAS!, on the lower rim in capital letters, but without the exclamation mark: ZYKLON B. The private put on a gas mask, climbed up on the flat roof and poured the contents of the cans into four openings. Then he carefully stowed the empty cans away, went back to the car, took the gas mask off and got in again.

2.

In the year 1972, the architects of Auschwitz-Birkenau, Walter Dejaco and Fritz Karl Ertl, were arrested in Vienna and tried by jury. They solemnly declared that they had not known for what purpose the camp was intended, and were acquitted.

3.

The Rabbi of Radsin decided in the autumn of 1942 to flee to Warsaw. He didn't know that extermination awaited him there too.

In the vicinity of Wlodawa, where he was walking along the railway embankment, the rabbi saw a cattle car standing on a siding. The doors were open, he looked inside, his blood ran cold, and he went to the nearest village. There, with the money he had intended to use to buy his train ticket to Warsaw, he bribed a few farmers to take the corpses out of the car and bury them.

When the corpses had been taken out, the rabbi still heard a sound in the car. He climbed in and looked: God was cowering in a corner of the car and crying. The rabbi refused to comfort him.

Afterword

WITH THIS BOOK, I wanted to commemorate the Viennese Jews who were driven out of the country or murdered after the *Anschluss*. It quickly became clear to me on my first attempt that a documentary such as I could have written was completely unsuited for that purpose, and finally a novel emerged, in which there is little that didn't actually happen, but also little that happened as it is reported here. For example, there was a real model for Jakob Pinsker, but the man's name wasn't Pinsker, and the woman he married had neither been engaged to the owner of a café nor did she ever have a store on Tuchlauben. It's like that with the other people and events in the novel, and so they are all to be regarded as fictitious.

I owe the story about the Rabbi of Radsin, with which the novel ends, to a poem written in the Warsaw ghetto that I read many years ago. Although I made numerous attempts to discover the source, I could not find it.

Glossary

almenor: the raised rostrum from which the Torah is read out

am-haaretz: "man from the country," i.e. an ignorant person

Anschluss: the annexation of Austria by Germany in 1938

baal-shem-tov: the founder of Hasidism, Israel Baal Shem Tov, also Besht

bar mitzvah: the celebration of the 13th birthday, on which a Jewish boy assumes all religious duties

bocher: (bo´kher): apprentice rabbi

borsht: beet soup

broche: blessing

chammer: a mean and stupid person

Chanukah: the festival of lights

cheder: a private Talmud school

chochem: a very bright person or a smartass

cholent: an Ashkenazi Sabbath dish of meat and vegetables

chutzpah: shameless audacity

erev Shabbos: Friday evening (the eve of the Sabbath)

ganef: a crook

gewure: skill, know-how

ghetto: a forced residential area for Jews

goy, pl. goyim: gentile

goyim naches: a deprecatory phrase

meaning "in the manner of the non-Jews" or "for the delight of the goyim"

Gymnasium: a school that prepares pupils for university entrance

Haggadah: narration of the Exodus from Egypt, recited at the Seder

Hasid, pl. Hasidim: an adherent of a Jewish mystical religious movement founded by Israel Baal Shem Tov

Judengasse: a Jewish neighbourhood

Jurigelt: the end of time, doomsday

kanehore: "knock on wood"

kehila: community

ketubah: marriage contract

Kommerzienräte: those who had earned the title "distinguished businessmen"

kosher: prepared and stored according to Jewish dietary laws

kreuzer: a small copper Austrian coin

Kristallnacht: the night of November 9-10, 1938 when the Nazis destroyed Jewish property and burned almost all of the synagogues

krone, K: a silver Austrian coin

mazel: luck

menorah: the candelabrum used on Chanukah

mensch: in Yiddish, a decent, humane person, a good human being

meshuga: crazy

333

mezuzah: parchment scroll with quotations from the Talmud, placed in a small case and attached to the doorpost of a devout Jewish household

mikve: ritual bath for women

minyan: the minimum of ten male adult Jews required to form a congregation

mishpoche: family

mitzvah: a good deed

mohel: the individual who performs a circumcision

naches: pleasure, delight, satisfaction

nebbish: a poor devil

Orthodox: Jews who adhere to rabbinical law and tradition

Pesach: Passover

peyes: sidecurls or sidelocks worn by many Orthodox Jews

Pofel: something worthless, trash

ponim: face

Purim: festival commemorating the defeat of Haman's planned massacre of the Jews

rabbi or **Rabbi:** any Jewish cleric; a title and form of address

Rosh Hashanah: the Jewish New Year festival

Seder: the celebration of the Exodus from Egypt

Shabbos: the Ashkenazi Hebrew name of the Sabbath

shammes: caretaker of a synagogue; extra candle used to light the Chanukah candles

Shavuos: Feast of Weeks

Shekinah: the living presence of God

sheva berachos: the seven blessings recited during a wedding ceremony

shiksa: a disparaging term for a non-Jewish girl

shlemiel: simpleton, bungler, fool

shlimazl: a mess

shtetl: a town with many Jewish inhabitants

Sukkos: Festival of Tabernacles

tallis, pl. talleisim: prayer shawl

Talmud: the body of Jewish law and tradition

Talmud Torah: a Talmud school

Tepp: a fool

Torah: the entire body of Jewish learning and tradition

Tschoch: dump

tzaddik: an exceptionally wise and righteous man

yarmulke: skullcap worn by religious males

yeshiva: an Orthodox school devoted to Talmudic studies

Yom Kippur: Day of Atonement

Acknowledgements

The author: I am greatly indebted to Prof. Jean Snook, who produced a wonderful translation of my novel and with great patience and forbearance put up with my petty suggestions for changes here and there in the text. I would like to thank Stephen Henighan for taking such good care of the page proofs and Prof. Hartwig Mayer for countless favours big and small; and I would like to thank last but by no means least my wife, Prof. Kari Grimstad, whose linguistic skills in four languages are so far superior to mine.

The translator: I thank Hans Eichner for his close collaboration, including revising some sections of the original.

The editor: I thank Hans Eichner for his tireless collaboration, and Kari Grimstad, Hartwig Mayer, Ruediger Mueller and Paola Mayer for assistance in completing this project.

About the Author

 Hans Eichner was born in Vienna in 1921 and, being Jewish, escaped to England after the annexation of Austria by Hitler's Germany. He enrolled at the University of London as an extension student in 1943, got a Ph.D. in 1949 and taught German language and literature at Bedford College in London, Queen's University in Kingston, Ontario, and the University of Toronto from 1948 to 1988. He published books on Thomas Mann and Friedrich Schlegel. His novel *Kahn & Engelmann* was first published in German in 2000 and was reprinted in 2002.

About the Translator

Jean M. Snook is an Associate Professor of German at Memorial University of Newfoundland. She has translated Else Lasker-Schüler's *Concert*, Luise Rinser's *Abelard's Love*, Evelyn Grill's *Winter Quarters*, and Gert Jonke's *Homage to Czerny: Studies in Virtuoso Technique*.